SECOND FIDDLE

Susan —
I hope you
enjoy reading Second Fiddle

A Novel by
Carol Reigh

Carol Reigh

authorHOUSE®

AuthorHouse™
1663 Liberty Drive, Suite 200
Bloomington, IN 47403
www.authorhouse.com
Phone: 1-800-839-8640

First published by AuthorHouse 8/18/2008

ISBN: 978-1-4343-7370-0 (sc)

Library of Congress Control Number: 2008902370

Printed in the United States of America
Bloomington, Indiana

This book is printed on acid-free paper.

I dedicate this book to myself.

I <u>knew</u> I could do It!
And to my family
for their unconditional love, support and encouragement.

PROLOGUE

David played the violin. No. It was more than that. It was a love affair. A love affair so torrid, scorching and searing that when his fingers brushed across the black leather case to unlatch it, when he lifted the shapely form from the plush amber lining, when he drew her near and rested his chin upon her, when the pungent smell of rosin filled the air, when he drew his bow across her yielding body - his eyes glazed over and he was consumed with passion. A passion few men will ever know.

And as they gently swayed together to the sweet notes that filled the air, he was oblivious to his surroundings. In the whole world, there were just the two of them - David and his violin. So it was. And Cydney knew - from the moment she realized that she loved David, from the moment she accepted his marriage proposal - she knew - that if she chose to spend her life with David- she would always be playing *Second Fiddle*.

CHAPTER ONE – FEBRUARY, 2000

The airport doors opened automatically and Cydney DuPrey was engulfed in the hot afternoon air. She stopped and looked back for the porter who had just a few minutes ago been so eager to help with her bags but was now nowhere in sight.

Ahead were the busses, rows and rows of them. All numbered and color-coded, their smelly diesel fumes polluting the brilliant, blue winter sky.

The tourists were making their exodus toward the busses now. Families, couples, lovers, all eager to find the bus that would take them to their hotel and a fabulous Cancun vacation. Cydney remembered a happier time when she and David had been among them. A lump formed in her throat and tears welled up in her eyes but she turned away, trying to blot out the memory and hailed a taxi.

Just a few months ago, David told her, "Cyd, you need to lose a few pounds, and I wish you would color your hair, it looks so drab." She was so angry with him.

Now, she stood alone on the platform, the epitome of fashion. Her dark brown eyes still sparkled from the abated tears and were framed with long brown lashes. Her brows, a perfect arch. Her slender 5'5" frame was enhanced by a pale yellow dress from Dior. The soft brown hair usually hung free, but today it was tucked up under a straw-hat with a matching yellow band, perched atop her head at a sassy slant. A few wayward wisps fluttered slightly in the gentle wind. Her handbag and espadrilles were the same natural color as the hat and around her neck was a Gucci scarf, ablaze with color. Her jewelry was expensive but not ornate and her skin had acquired a healthy glow thanks to the spa. She looked soft and lovely. How ironic! Twenty pounds lighter – well actually twenty-one and a half - but not on David's terms, which surely would have irritated him.

Although the tears were checked, her nose was running and she rummaged in her bag for a tissue but couldn't find one. "If this wasn't so pathetic, it would be funny," she thought, "nothing to wipe my nose with but this damn Gucci scarf." She discreetly blotted her upper lip with the tail of the scarf. David would not have found it amusing.

The taxi and porter arrived at the same time and as David had taught her, she stood by the trunk of the taxi until all her bags were loaded. "Never give one of these guys the chance to walk away with some of your luggage," he had warned her time after time. She gave the porter a generous tip and sank into the back seat of the taxi while the driver held the door.

He settled into the driver's seat and asked, "¿Adónde va, Señora." *"Where are you going, Madam?"*

Ah, Spanish! One of the romance languages. How she loved the sound of it. The melodic crescendos, the trill of the "R's", the nasal "N's". Cydney loved to speak it, too. She had studied Spanish in both high school and college and over the years had become more fluent.

When she and David honeymooned here, she liked communicating with the natives in their own language and she continued to do so during the other times she visited.

Cydney easily lapsed into dialogue, "Avenida de las Lagunas ocho ciento cuarenta y cuatro, por favor." *"Eight forty four Avenue of Lagoons, please."* The driver started the meter and eased into traffic. Cydney knew he was watching her in the rear view mirror so she kept her gaze diverted.

Avenue of Lagoons was located in the northwest part of the city. The shortest route to the condo would be Avenue Tulum but Cydney always enjoyed the drive through the strip, and she asked the driver to go that route now knowing the ride would be much longer. She hoped that she would not have to engage in conversation with him during the trip.

Finally, he spoke again, "La Señora es muy triste." *"The lady is very sad."* It was a statement, not a question. Cydney's eyes met his momentarily.

Her reply was curt, "Si Señor, muy triste." *"Yes Sir, very sad."* He did not speak to her again and she was sorry that she had been so short with him.

When at last the condo came into view, her heart skipped a beat. The beige tone stucco was capped with a bright, red tile roof. The landscaping was meticulous. Royal palms, with their smooth trunks, towered high over the building. Queen palms dotted the front walkway, their sweet fruit already beginning to drop. The fronds branched out like a thatched roof, shading the sidewalk and the entryway. The hibiscus were plentiful and in full bloom. Their orange and fuchsia blossoms in brilliant contrast to the colorless stucco. The crotons were heavy with bright colored flowers and the philodendron lush and green. Cydney remembered her grandfather trying unsuccessfully to grow some of these same plants and here they grew like wild flowers in a country meadow. The orchids were also in bloom and Cydney drank in this view like a thirsty traveler at a desert oasis.

When the taxi stopped in front of the building and the driver unloaded her luggage, Cydney made a special effort to smile and wish him a good day. The generous tip she gave him erased her guilt feelings.

Favio was waiting by the building for the taxi and began jumping up and down and shouting when it pulled to the curb. Cydney couldn't help but laugh at this vivacious nine year old, who was awaiting her arrival. His mere presence would warrant a dolar americana, *"an American dollar",* and he knew it.

Favio was the grandson of Juan and Hermi. They had sort of come with the condo and Cydney was so grateful for their loyalty and hard work. Juan was responsible for the beautiful landscaping and did outside maintenance. Hermi kept the inside spotless. This rotund woman was full of enthusiasm for whatever she was doing. She chattered constantly about nothing and to no one in particular but she always knew exactly what Cydney wanted and when she wanted it, without being told. Juan was more reserved and quiet. A once handsome *hombre,* he was now starting to show signs of age, but never complained about the hard work he did for many members of the condo association, several of whom were Americans.

Whenever Cydney planned to visit Cancun, she simply called Hermi, who immediately began cleaning and cooking and Cydney knew that this time would be no exception.

Favio hurried toward the taxi to help Cydney with her luggage. Juan heard Favio's rhetoric and also came to help. He nodded to Cydney and quietly said, "Lo siento mucho, Señora DuPrey." *"I am very sorry, Mrs. DuPrey."* She could see the sadness in his eyes and she knew he was thinking about his good friend, *Señor* David.

Favio led the procession, whooping and hollering through the hall. When Hermi heard the noise and finally opened the door, he shouted, "Abuela, Abuela, Señora DuPrey esta aqui, esta sola – esta sola!" *"Grandma, Grandma, Mrs. DuPrey is here, she is alone – she is alone."*

Hermi buried her face in her hands and began sobbing uncontrollably. Favio fell silent and clung to her apron, Juan set the bags down. He too was silent. Cydney stepped into the room and looked around. Everything was the same. Well, almost everything. Like Favio said, she was alone, and that was different.

To ease the tension, she once again dug into her handbag. She pulled out a crisp dollar bill for Favio and a five for Juan. The money brought sheer joy to Favio's face and he raced through the door brandishing his dollar and shouting for his friends. Juan shook his head and pushed her hand aside, reluctant to accept the money. "Por favor," *"Please,"* she said. "Por favor, acepta." *"Please, accept it."* He nodded, took the money and left. She stood there face to face with the sobbing Hermi, who was becoming quite annoying.

Cydney set her handbag down and walked to the balcony. She took off her hat and shook free her thick mane now highlighted with caramel colored tones. The air was crisp and clean, she breathed in deeply, mustering up some courage, then turned back. "Para, Hermi, para!" *"Stop, Hermi, stop it!"*

Her sobs muffled, Hermi dabbed her eyes with her apron. They stood in silence for just a moment, looking at each other. Then Hermi advanced, wrapped her arms around Cydney and drew her near. Now it was Cydney's turn to cry. And she did and Hermi held her close until there were no tears left inside.

Physically and emotionally exhausted, Cydney sank into the recliner, the most functional piece of furniture in the condo. Pablo, the decorator, had been very unhappy that they chose to keep it but there was no question in David's mind. The recliner was staying! She was happy now that David had won the argument. She leaned back ever so slightly and closed her eyes. "Just for a moment," she told Hermi.

When she awoke the sun was low in the sky and Hermi had obviously slipped out through the kitchen. Cydney was glad to be alone. She just sat there a few minutes contemplating what to do next and decided that she was famished. Hermi, God bless her, had left a pasta salad, Cydney's favorite, and a bottle of sangria in the refrigerator. Right now the sangria seemed the most appealing. She poured herself a large glassful and wandered out onto the balcony to once again breathe in the wonderful Caribbean air.

There is nothing like a Caribbean evening. The water is so clean and clear, the air so fresh, the stars so brilliant. If she decided to sell this place and couldn't come here anymore it would hurt her heart. Cydney sipped the wine and watched the beachcombers.

She refilled her glass a few times, finally bringing the decanter out to the balcony. There was so much to think about: David, Max, the condo, the farm, Brock, and Sarah. Especially Sarah and she would have a lot of time to think about her while she was here.

Cydney took stock of her life. She had been an unwanted baby, a lonely child, a timid teenage. Then somehow, someway things changed. She found self-worth and self-confidence. She found strength. These attributes, along with her stunning good looks, helped her become the woman she was today; a woman who expected so little from others but gave wholly of herself. Perhaps that's why her marriage to David lasted as long as it did.

Perhaps she _could_ survive without David but she needed God to help her with the heavy burden she now shouldered. And there on her balcony overlooking the beautiful sea and breathing in the fresh, clean night air, she knew He would help her overcome it. It would certainly take time, but she had lots of time, and she had the resources, too! She could do exactly what she wanted. She would stay here a few weeks to ponder her future and take stock of her wealth. Her wealth! Now what would Sarah think about that? She refilled her wine glass and smiled to herself.

CHAPTER TWO – JUNE, 1932

Caleb Brown sat on a wooden chair propped against the wall at the old Grange Hall. He shuffled his feet around trying not to look and feel so conspicuous. To add to his discomfort, it was hot and stuffy.

Women! He'd never understand them. Constance had invited him to this stupid Sadie Hawkins dance and then she went and left with that fella from Iron County. Caleb was sure everyone there had seen the two of them leave together and he was feeling pretty low. The guy was handsome looking, certainly older than Constance but hey, if she wanted to leave with him, Caleb couldn't stop her.

He looked around the room and saw Gwendolyn Peters fumbling around the punch bowl. She probably was more embarrassed than he was since she had invited the other guy to the dance. Caleb got up, his lanky frame reaching six feet plus. He was sun tanned and healthy looking. His eyes were bright blue and his hair, the color of an August oat field, was damp with sweat around his collar. He strolled her way.

"Hi," he mumbled. "Looks like you and I are in the same boat." He smiled a crooked little smile, and Gwendolyn turned bright red.

"Yes, I guess we are," she said, trying to smile back in spite of her burning face. She diverted her pale blue eyes from his. Her blond hair was pulled back into a ponytail held by a pretty pink ribbon that matched her skirt. She was at least five inches shorter than Caleb and bean-pole skinny.

"I'm sorry," Caleb said, "Constance was flirting with him all evening."

"It's not your fault," Gwendolyn said. "Besides, Gabe and I are just friends. Our parents know each other. It's not like we're sweet on each other or anything like that. It's just embarrassing to be left behind."

"Do you want to dance?" Caleb asked.

Gwendolyn didn't hesitate. "Yes." Caleb steered her into the crowd and she immediately felt more comfortable. "I'm Gwendolyn Peters," she said.

"I know, I remember seeing you at school last term. You live west of Balsam Hills near the Whitman place right? I'm Caleb Brown." He was feeling more comfortable, too. "I live about twenty miles from you, near County Line Road. Our place is called Oakwood Acres. You must've liked Gabe or you wouldn't have invited him to the dance," he said.

Gwendolyn laughed, "You sure talk a lot." She ignored the statement about liking Gabe. "I know about you, too. You just graduated, didn't you?"

"Yup, and now I work on the farm with my Pa. I love it there. You'll have to come around and see it some time."

Gwendolyn was pleased when Caleb suggested that he take her home. He reminded her that she should come around and see the farm. She promised that she would.

Named for the lofty pines that dot the terrain, Balsam Hills was located in Ashland County in the northern part of Wisconsin. Summers there were spectacular. The fields were a patchwork of green: lush, dark hunter and bright emerald. The blue green spruces were coupled with clean fresh air and wide-open spaces. The people were kind and friendly, always willing to help each other out. Caleb was one of those kinds of people. True country folk, preferred the farm to the city and appreciated every sunrise, every sunset, every change of season. Caleb found joy in spring planting, in watching the crops grow and the fall harvest. At seventeen, he was wise beyond his years. Material things didn't matter much. Family and friends did.

It was no surprise to Caleb when Gwendolyn came calling one hot August afternoon. He expected that she would. After all, he had invited her. She said she just happened to be in the vicinity but Caleb didn't buy that! After all, she was twenty miles from home and there was nothing much around. Caleb knew she was interested in him. That's why she stopped by and he was very pleased. Soon they began dating on Saturday nights.

News travels fast in small communities and before long, Balsam Hills and the surrounding area were abuzz with the news of a courtship between Caleb Brown and Gwendolyn Peters. Caleb was already out of high school and Gwendolyn would be a senior in September. Rumor had it that this was the real thing and that Gwendolyn was already starting a hope chest and Caleb was repairing the old cottage behind the main house at Oakwood Acres.

CHAPTER THREE

Gwendolyn graduated from high school on Saturday, May 28th, 1933 and just two weeks later, on Saturday, June 11th, in the Balsam Hills First Presbyterian Church, before God and half the people of Ashland County, she married Caleb Brown.

The Grange Hall was just as hot and stuffy as it had been at the Sadie Hawkins dance where they met a year ago. The doors and shutters stood open, letting only a wisp of air in every now and then. But the heat and humidity didn't bother the newlyweds as they greeted their guests and danced on the sawdust-covered floor.

Later, since Caleb didn't have a car, they just loaded Gwendolyn's hope chest on the back of an old farm wagon and set off for the newly whitewashed and renovated cottage behind the main house at Oakwood Acres. It was haying time, so a honeymoon was out of the question. Besides, there just wasn't much money for that right now. But someday. Someday they'd have the money to go away for a real honeymoon.

Gwendolyn knew that Caleb had put his heart and soul into fixing up this lovely cottage just for her and she vowed that she would be the best wife in the world. All the books and magazines Gwendolyn read said being in love was wonderful but being in love with Caleb Brown was beyond her wildest dreams. In the first few weeks of their marriage, he taught her all the things a woman needs to know to please her man.

"He must have had some experiences with other women," Gwendolyn thought, because he certainly knew how to please her. But she was too embarrassed to ask questions about an issue as taboo as sex. Even though it was 1933, there were some things a girl just couldn't discuss with her mother. She also learned to clean, cook and sew and she would do all of those things, along with what Caleb taught her in the bedroom, to make him happy. This was bliss! Mrs. Caleb Brown, it sounded so beautiful.

By the end of the summer, Caleb and Gwendolyn had become accustomed to life together and it seemed like they had never been apart. He worked the land with his father and brother while Gwendolyn canned vegetables she raised in the garden. The happiness they shared was bested one frosty November morning when Gwendolyn announced at breakfast that she was pregnant. Caleb jumped up and down and strutted around the kitchen like a cock sure rooster and then suddenly turned serious, "Are you sure, Gweny? How do you know for sure and how do you feel?"

"Oh, Caleb," she chuckled at his dancing, "yes, I know for sure. I went to see Alva Morningbreeze and I'm just fine. She said we'll have a healthy baby in July."

Alva Morningbreeze was a Chippewa Indian. She lived on the Bad River Indian Reservation just north of Balsam Hills, where she practiced midwifery. Alva's looks could scare a young child but in spite of her leathery, wrinkled skin and near toothless smile, she had a reputation as the best midwife in a tri-county area. If Alva Morningbreeze was your midwife and you went into labor in the middle of a Wisconsin blizzard, you could rest easy knowing that some how, some way, she would find her way to your bedside. She was kind and gentle. She would teach you proper breathing techniques and muscle control and before you knew it, that baby would just slide right out. Oh yes, Alva Morningbreeze knew her midwifery! Alva Morningbreeze was the best!

So for Caleb and Gwendolyn, life just got better with each passing day. When winter settled in, so did Gwendolyn. Alva made regular visits to Gwendolyn, who stayed close by the cottage, sewing and knitting and preparing to start the family she and Caleb had dreamed about.

When spring finally came, Caleb's Pa suggested that they swap living quarters. The main house was too big for him since Caleb's Ma had passed several years before and brother Chet had his own place a mile or two up the road. The main house would give Caleb and Gwendolyn more room for their growing family. Pa said just to leave the furniture as it was and take only their personal belongings, so the week prior to spring planting, Caleb, Chet and Pa began moving things to the main house. Pa had lived alone for a few years and his house keeping left something to be desired, so in addition to planting her garden, Gwendolyn had plenty of work to do before the baby arrived.

When Caleb and Gwendolyn moved into the main house, Gwendolyn took great pains to decorate it to her liking. She was so excited. Only recently had electricity come to their area, and somehow Pa had managed to pay to have it run into the house from some money he had stashed away and it was his gift to them.

The house was a large two story with a railed porch wrapped half way around it. There were white wicker chairs, an old porch swing, and pots of geraniums gracing the main entrance, which led into the dining room. Tall windows flanked the doorway. The room had a large oak table and high backed caned chairs, a china cabinet built by Caleb's Pa for his bride, a rocking chair, and several built in bookshelves.

To the north was the living room, with two large windows that faced Apple Road and two smaller ones that faced the driveway. It too was large, with lots of comfortable furniture and a player piano, which would bring Gwendolyn much joy on cold winter nights. A huge fieldstone fireplace filled most of the west wall of the living room. The windows were adorned with curtains that Gwendolyn made from some lace she found in Caleb's Ma's cedar chest. In addition to making baby clothes, she spent hours knitting afghans and making throw pillows for the furniture.

On the other side of the dining room was the kitchen. The back door faced the south and the windows, which adjoined the entryway, let in plenty of sunlight. Another row of windows banked the east so anyone coming up the driveway could be seen from the kitchen. Gwendolyn made blue and white gingham curtains and painted the cupboards white, which gave the room a most cheerful atmosphere.

In the center of the kitchen was another table and chairs. Caleb had painted them a soft blue, which was almost a perfect match with the crisp curtains. There was a big cook stove fueled by wood and an icebox, which required a pan underneath to prevent the water from running onto the kitchen floor as the ice melted. The iceman delivered big blocks of ice every other day in the summer but in the winter, it didn't matter if he got there or not, since they could always keep things cold outside. The sink on the west side of the kitchen didn't have running water yet. But someday there would be an electric refrigerator and water from the spigot.

Just off the kitchen was a bathroom with a big claw foot bathtub, a sink and toilet. The plumbing wasn't in place there yet, either, but the tub and sink could be filled from the new well that Caleb drilled to replace the sand point. The toilet facilities were still a few steps from the house but Caleb was working on that, too. He didn't want to have his family going out to the "privy" in the cold and he remembered the awful smelling chamber pots from his childhood so he was determined to provide his family with yet another modern convenience.

On the northwest side of the dining room, next to the living room was the master bedroom which, like the living room, opened right off the dining room. A big four-poster bed, chests and armoires filled the room along with Gwendolyn's hope chest. A rocking chair was in the corner next to where the cradle stood. A comfortable, quiet place to make their babies and then lull them off to sleep.

On the west side of the dining room, a grand archway gave way to an open staircase, which led to the second floor. There were about ten steps, a landing and then more steps to the left. At the top of the stairs was a sitting room of sorts with four adjacent bedrooms. A settee, two rocking chairs and a chest were in the sitting room and the bedrooms were all filled with oversized beds and chests, most of which had been made by Caleb's granddaddy and handed down through the years. Caleb planned to put a bathroom on this floor when he had the money to run the plumbing into the house.

The out buildings included a barn, corn crib, shed, milk house, garage and the outhouse and were located to the south west of the main house. They were screened from view of the main house by a row of towering pine trees. The cottage stood directly west of the main house next to a pond that attracted all sorts of wild life. This was, Gwendolyn thought, the perfect place to raise a family.

On July 17th, 1934, with the help of Alva Morningbreeze, Luke Anthony Brown came slipping, sliding and squawking into this world. Gwendolyn thought her heart would burst as she peered into the face of her beautiful, baby boy. Wisps of golden hair and eyes like his Pa, she now knew the meaning of unconditional love. His cries must have been heard throughout Ashland County because for days a steady stream of neighbors stopped by to drop off a "dish" and a little something for the new arrival. After only seven days of bed rest and pampering, Gwendolyn declared herself healed and got up to take over the duties of motherhood, which had been delegated to Alva Morningbreeze's granddaughter Lucy, while Gwendolyn was recovering.

On October 26th, 1935, Caleb summoned Alva Morningbreeze to Oakwood Acres a second time. This time, despite the muscle control, proper breathing and pushing, it took an entire 24 hours for Aaron Joseph to make his appearance and Gwendolyn was not up and about in a week.

Alva came again on September 1, 1937 when Sarah Elizabeth joined the family.

So it was that the main house at Oakwood Acres was once again alive with the sweet sounds of children. In spite of the Great Depression that was overtaking the country, Gwendolyn never imagined that she could be so happy. She had a lovely, comfortable home; there was plenty of food; a loving husband; a beautiful family, many relatives and friends to make her life full and complete. She was a strong believer in God and knew in her heart that all of her earthly possessions, including her wonderful family, were a gift from Him.

As the years went by, Caleb and Gwendolyn enjoyed their life very much. As their family grew, so did their love and commitment to each other.

Someone had taken a photograph of them at a church social and posted it on the bulletin board at church. The whole family was dressed in their Sunday finery and smiling broadly. Below it was written, "The perfect family. Three beautiful children, all with biblical names. Truly a gift from God." It was summer, 1939.

CHAPTER FOUR

The toddlers became youngsters and before long they were teenagers. Games of tag, and hide and seek gave way to high school, homework, girlfriends and boyfriends. They attended church every Sunday as a family and found church and the activities associated with it to be a great place to socialize with other teenagers.

Like their parents, the Brown children found life to be fun and exciting. They were happy teenagers, who adored their parents and each other. Just let some guy pick on Sarah and Luke and Aaron would be right there to blacken his eye. There was an incident when Aaron and Luke were fourteen and fifteen, respectively. They got in a fight over some trivial thing neither of them could remember later, but when Luke saw blood running from Aaron's nose and when Aaron saw the big bruise on Luke's cheek, they stopped fighting and each was more concerned about his brother than about himself.

In spite of her many duties as wife and mother, Gwendolyn found time to volunteer at church, at the community center and at school. She loved being such an integral part of her children's lives.

Some of their happiest memories were around the big blue table in the kitchen after dinner. Everyone told about their day and they talked about their plans for the future.

Sarah was the one who had her life in order. At the age of twelve, she announced that someday she planned to go to a big city and become a fashion designer for famous people and maybe become famous herself.

She wasn't going to get married and settle down here in Balsam Hills. She was going to travel and be famous. Luke had big plans to travel, too. He didn't know where yet, but someday after graduation, he'd travel the world. Aaron was more reserved. He never said too much about leaving home. Gwendolyn felt a twinge of jealousy when they had these discussions. Somehow she hadn't thought much about her children growing up and leaving home. They surely would get big enough and smart enough but their lives here were so perfect, it just never occurred to her that they might want to leave.

Another topic of discussion each evening was world events. They had survived the Great Depression unscathed. Poorer now than before, but otherwise – unscathed. The United States had emerged from World War II as a super power and post war America was prospering. There were unlimited opportunities for the younger generation and more specifically for the returning soldiers.

In 1950, news of a war in Korea came to everyone's attention. They talked about it all over the county, at church and at sewing circles. Wasn't this really a civil war between the two Koreas? Why would the United States want to get involved in another war? Would this war be as bad as before? How many young men from this area would be called to serve?

Gwendolyn knew that way back in October of 1940, President Roosevelt had ordered that all male US citizens, over the age of 18 must register for the first ever peace time draft. It was still in effect, but she was not concerned. Luke was only sixteen and Aaron, fifteen. Surely, this war, like the big one, would be over soon and it would not affect them.

Now, in June of 1950, President Harry Truman ordered air and naval forces in the Far East to give armed aid to South Korean forces. More news came on June 30, 1950, when the President ordered ground troops into action and on July 5th, US troops were involved in their first battle in Korea. Still, Gwendolyn was not troubled.

The boys were older now and every night at dinner, they talked incessantly about the war. Gwendolyn told Caleb not to encourage the conversation, but he always joined in when they discussed the most recent news about the growing conflict.

It was June of 1952 when the reality of the war hit Gwendolyn smack in the face. School was out and Luke had graduated. There was no pomp and circumstance, just a simple graduation ceremony for the families. Luke spent a couple of days helping bale hay and then one day, he asked Caleb if he could borrow the car to go to town. He burst in the door, just as everyone was sitting down to dinner and quickly took his place at the table. Luke's golden hair was messed and his blue eyes sparkled. Like Caleb he was tall, lean and handsome and tanned from working the fields. No one spoke until after Caleb said grace.

"We thought you left home, Luke," Caleb said jokingly, "you usually don't miss dinner."

"I didn't miss it, Pa. I'm just a little late."

"Where were you, son?" Gwendolyn asked.

Luke's face colored slightly but he didn't answer right away. He kept shoveling his dinner into his mouth as fast as he could. Gwendolyn just stared at him, her usual method of getting their attention. Slowly, he put his fork down across his plate.

"I enlisted today," he said in a voice that trembled every so slightly. "I leave for basic training on July 18th."

"Hey," Sarah said, "that's the day after your birthday!"

"Yeah, I know," said Luke, "you have to be 18 years old, that's why I can't go now. I have to wait."

Caleb glanced at Gwendolyn and saw the color drain from her face. He actually felt a surge of pride that his son wanted to serve his country, but he thought better of making a big deal of it now. Instead he just reached over and patted Luke on the back. "You'll make a fine soldier, son," he said.

Gwendolyn gasped and her bottom lip quivered. "Well, tomorrow you just go down there and unenlist," she said with as much conviction as she could muster up.

"I can't do that, Ma," he said. "It's official, as of July 18th, I'm a soldier in the United States Army."

Aaron and Sarah clapped and cheered. Caleb smiled ever so slightly. Gwendolyn didn't say anything else. She slowly got up and left the table. They all heard the bedroom door slam - hard.

The days that followed were very difficult for Gwendolyn. She was so angry with Luke. How could he have done such a thing without discussing it with Caleb and her? How would she ever get along without him?

On Tuesday, July 18th, 1952, Caleb took Luke to the Greyhound Bus Station in Balsam Hills. Sarah and Aaron rode along but Gwendolyn refused to go. She couldn't control her tears as she bid Luke a solemn good-bye. He promised he would write and call. He promised he'd be back soon. She said she would miss him terribly, she said she would pray for him. She watched the car go up the driveway and turn right onto Apple Road. Then she flung herself across her bed and cried uncontrollably.

Gwendolyn followed the war very closely now. When she learned that the armistice talks had resumed after a two-year delay she was very encouraged. She felt less afraid as Luke's calls and letters started to arrive. But when he came home on leave after basic training and he brought his orders with him, a new panic overtook her. He would be shipping out in a week. He was bound for South Korea.

CHAPTER FIVE

It was a beautiful day and the April sun had warmed the air enough that Gwendolyn opened some windows. Like Luke, she had always loved the fresh smell of spring. She sat at the kitchen table, inhaling the fresh air and thinking about what Luke would be doing if he were home. She would write to him now and tell him about this wonderful spring day. She felt very connected to him through his letters which arrived on a regular basis. They were long and full of details and she read them over and over again. It was like having a conversation with her beloved Luke, whom she missed terribly.

She had become a supporter of the war and followed the news closely. When the children were younger, Gwendolyn always sang. Hymns like ***What A Friend We Have In Jesus*** and ***Amazing Grace*** filled the house as she moved from room to room. Now there was no music. The radio was always tuned to a station that had all the news and latest updates regarding the conflict. Korea was labeled as a "police action", never as a war.

She knew that General MacArthur had suffered many setbacks two years before Luke enlisted. She knew that Seoul had fallen to the North in June of 1950 and the South Koreans and their allies continued to fight hard and heavy to retake it. The armistice talks stalled in October of 1952, which dampened her spirits. She listened to news of heavy fighting along the Han River and Pusan, a port on the southeast tip of

Korea. At Inchon, a port city south west of Seoul, a marine division hit the peninsula followed by a division of the army. The UN launched attacks on the North and ground and air fighting intensified, but not without heavy casualties.

Gwendolyn looked up to see a car she didn't recognize coming slowly up the driveway. It was a new car, she could tell that by the shiny black finish, but she didn't know what kind it was. She walked out onto the porch and watched as a very tall, thin man unfolded himself from the driver's seat. In spite of the pleasant early afternoon sun, he wore a long dark overcoat and hat. When he saw her, he touched his hand to the brim of his hat but did not remove it. He moved toward her silently with long strides. In his hand was a large, white envelope, which he extended toward her. Neither of them spoke as she reluctantly accepted the envelope. He doffed his hat once again and turned back toward the car. Just before he got back into the car, he gave her a solemn look, "On behalf on the President of the United States and the United States Army, please accept our sincere sympathy." Having said that, he was gone.

Gwendolyn stood riveted to the porch, a confused look on her face. Finally, she looked down at the letter and the large gold seal on the flap. She clawed at the envelope and wrenched the letter from it, eyes wide, nostrils flaring, she scanned the page........ "The US military, Division of the Army, regrets to inform you --- Private First Class, Luke A. Brown was killed ---in --- service to his country ---- the Republic of South Korea---- April 3, 1953 ----heavy casualties -----overtook------ many lives lost-----President --- extends deepest ---- sympathy ---- to ---- families of those ----".

Gwendolyn grasped the porch post to support herself. She was trembling, she couldn't stand. Still holding onto the post, she slid down to the step, clutching the letter, rocking back and forth. From somewhere deep inside a piercing scream emerged. Sobs wracked her body. Not Luke. Not Luke. Luke, her life, her breath, her reason for living. Not Luke, dear God, not Luke! Darkness engulfed her. Her sobs were uncontrollable. Her breathing was labored. She lurched and spewed vomit next to the steps. Still she sat, not moving, not bothering to wipe her mouth. This was a mistake! It had to be wrong, why look

- there was Luke now, just a little boy, swinging on the tire swing tied to the big oak on the other side of the driveway. Swinging high, so high. "Be careful Luke," she called out, "be careful, we don't want any casualties. No --- heavy --- casualties."

The afternoon was waning and still she sat sobbing, gulping down big breaths of air to calm herself. Again and again she vomited, no longer bothering to lean over or turn her head. The letter lay on the ground now, spattered with puke, the late afternoon dampness already curling the edges of the big gold seal. Caleb and Aaron found her there when they came down from the barn. Caleb felt a stabbing pain in his heart as he picked up the letter and wiped it off with his red handkerchief. He read the words and handed it to Aaron. Caleb knelt before Gwendolyn; he wiped her face and mouth. He lifted her up and pried her hands from the porch railing. He led her into the house and to the bedroom that would become her sanctuary.

The dark days of mourning dragged on. It was weeks before Luke's flag draped casket was delivered by army transport plane to Duluth, Minnesota and then brought to Balsam Hills by a local hearse. Aaron and Sarah handled the steady stream of phone calls and Caleb greeted well-wishers who had come to pay their respects. Gwendolyn seldom left her room.

When at last the funeral took place and Luke was laid to rest in the cemetery next to the First Presbyterian Church, it seemed liked the entire county was there. The choir sang ***Battle Hymn of the Republic***. An honor guard led the procession and a bugler blew taps. A fitting farewell for this young soldier, naïve enough to think that war was an adventure.

Caleb found solace in the spring days, the crops and the quiet time he spent on the land. Often, as he glanced up from the tractor, across the fields, the first sprouts of corn peeking through the soil, he thought he saw Luke, standing at the other end of the field waving to him.

Aaron and Sarah found comfort in each other and spent more time together. Gwendolyn withdrew from their lives. She built a wall around herself. A wall so thick, so dark, none of them could penetrate it. Sarah took over many of the household chores and when Aaron wasn't helping Caleb, he too, helped in the house.

Together, Caleb, Sarah and Aaron tried desperately to bring normalcy back to their home and to draw Gwendolyn back to life but she was not to be comforted. There were days when she would not bathe or comb her hair; she would just sit in her chair, slowly rocking back and forth, a steady low moan emitting from her throat. Other days, she would sit at the player piano in the living room pressing the foot pedals to turn the rolls that produced music filling the house with hymns. Some evenings she came to the dinner table, but most of the time she did not. Caleb, because he loved her still so very much, continued to hope that in time she would find inner peace and return from the brink of despair. Aaron and Sarah felt they had not only lost their brother, but also their mother and Sarah, especially, was terribly lonely.

Autumn had returned to the north woods of Wisconsin but the beauty of it did nothing to improve Sarah's disposition. She was feeling not only lonely but also neglected. It was a new school year and she had lots of things to tell her mother. Caleb and Aaron spent a lot of time together, working the land, hunting, talking guy talk, but whenever Sarah tried to talk to her mother about school or her social life, Gwendolyn didn't have time to listen. She grieved constantly over Luke. Still listening to newscasts or a presidential address about the country's future, most days she just sat in her rocking chair staring out into space. Gwendolyn was oblivious to the needs of her sixteen-year old daughter.

Sarah got a job at the Five and Dime store in Balsam Hills. She didn't ask her parents' permission, she just went ahead and did it. She worked Tuesday and Wednesday afternoons from three o'clock until the store closed at six. She also worked most Saturdays. There was a soda fountain, a cosmetic department, a linen section that sold flour sack dishtowels and dishcloths along with potholders, aprons and hand towels. They were kitchen utensils, fabrics, small hardware items and even a small clothing section. But Sarah wanted to work in the cosmetic department and she was very pleased when the store manager agreed.

Many of the women who came into the Five and Dime inquired after Gwendolyn. They all knew how devastated she was when Luke died. Sarah got to know some of the locals real well. She helped them select just the right shade of lipstick or rogue; just the right texture and color of face powder; the most appealing fragrances. Sarah read a lot of fashion magazines, so she was a natural for this position. She would tell the women about a famous movie star, who wore this color nail polish in a certain film or a celebrity who used this fragrance on a regular basis.

"That's the perfect shade of lipstick for you, Mrs. Anderson," she would say, "it looks wonderful with your complexion." Or, "You have very nice skin, Mrs. Jones, and this cream will help keep it that way." The cosmetic counter at the Five and Dime was a busy place, thanks to Sarah. She loved the work and even though she was sometimes filled with despair and loneliness, she always looked so perky and happy and she was so polite. She was petite, blonde and blue eyed like Gwendolyn but outgoing and enthusiastic like Caleb. She was also very pretty and very smart.

"Oh, that Sarah Brown," the ladies would say, "she's such a nice young lady, she's so smart, she's got so much potential."

Sarah was happy to have Monday, Thursday and Friday for school activities. She joined clubs and got involved in school activities, while maintaining very good grades. Contrary to her upbringing, Sarah began making plans without first asking her parents. It didn't matter, Gwendolyn didn't seem to notice when she was gone.

It was late October and it was homecoming, one of the most exciting times of the school year. Sarah was chosen by her peers to be on the homecoming court as a representative of the junior class. She was thrilled. One of the football players, Billy Hathaway asked her to the dance, which would be at the school following the football game against rival Sanborn High School. Gwendolyn didn't seem interested in Sarah's news about homecoming, but Caleb was happy for her and so was Aaron. Even though he had graduated, he knew what an honor it was to be chosen for the homecoming court. Caleb always had money stashed away some place and he gave Sarah some to buy a new outfit to wear. So in spite of the ache in her heart, Sarah put on her new outfit and a big smile and went off to homecoming.

Billy was a big, strappin' young man who played defensive end on the football team. Sarah had liked him since her freshman year. Billy was a junior this year too, and Sarah was pretty sure he also liked her a lot. She sat with her friends at the football game, huddled under a blanket to keep warm. She had a good view of the field so she could watch Billy as he made tackle after tackle. Balsam Hills won the game and everyone was in a state of euphoria.

Billy and Sarah stayed at the dance until the homecoming court was introduced and the king and queen were selected. They danced a few dances and reveled in the victory with other football players and their dates. Then some headed out to the soda fountain and some to Cricket Lane, a popular spot for young people to park.

Sarah hadn't been on many real dates before and she didn't recognize Billy's motives when he suggested that they too, go to Cricket Lane. She was just so happy to have someone pay attention to her so she readily agreed. There was a cul-de-sac at the end of Cricket Lane and the cars parked around in a semi-circle. Billy had borrowed his father's car and he eased it into place behind the last one in the circle. The windows were all steamed up in the cars already parked so Sarah didn't know who else was there. They talked for just a few minutes and it didn't take Billy long to start making his move. He kissed her a few times and then put his hand on her breast. She pulled back slightly but Billy just pressed harder. She tried to push away from his kiss but again, he hung on. She relaxed a little, thinking Billy would let her go after the kiss, but he kept trying to stick his slimy tongue into her mouth and it didn't seem likely he would release his hold on her anytime soon. She pushed at his chest and tried to say something. Finally, he released her. "What's wrong, Sarah?" he asked, "I thought you liked me?"

"I do like you, Billy," she said, "but don't be so rough with me."

Billy realized immediately that if he wanted to score with Sarah, he would have to be patient and do it her way. So they talked a little more and he kissed her a few times, much more gently now then before. He told Sarah how he thought she was really pretty and smart and that she was the kind of girl he would want to marry some day. His compliments spewed forth like gushing oil and poor Sarah, starved for attention and eager to please, hung on every word. More sweet talk, more compliments and soon they were necking heavily. This time when Billy felt of her breast, she didn't pull way. If Billy said he wanted to marry her, then surely he must love her.

And there on Cricket Lane in Mr. Hathaway's 1950 Chevrolet Coupe, under a full moon, hanging low in the October sky, Sarah Brown, the perky, polite girl with so much potential became the talk of the town.

CHAPTER SIX

A tearful Sarah found Caleb in the barn and relayed the news to him first. He stared stone-faced at the ground while she explained what happened and how. She said she was so lonesome. Not only did she miss Luke but her Mother had no time for her. No mother-daughter talks, no shopping, no time together, nothing! Aaron had Caleb and of course, Caleb and Aaron were both there for Sarah, but it's different for a girl. Sarah wanted – no – Sarah needed her mother.

And Billy, well, he told Sarah that he wanted to marry her someday but when she told him about the baby, he just said it was her tough luck. He could never think of getting married. He had to finish high school and then go to college. No, he wouldn't be around these parts, married with a kid. Sarah knew now what a fool she had been. She realized that Billy had said those things to her just to get her to do what he wanted. She was wrong, yes. But she wasn't a bad person. If only, she could have talked about this with her mother. If only Gwendolyn cared. Caleb listened and did not pass judgment on his daughter. He somehow understood her feelings, because Gwendolyn was lost to him as well. He told Sarah he would be the one to tell her mother. He told Sarah not to worry. They were a family. They would stick together and help each other.

As they walked together toward the house, with his arm around her shoulder, he simply said, "You'll be a good mother, Sarah." Caleb was only thirty-nine but he felt like a very old man.

Gwendolyn sat in her rocking chair trying hard to sort out her thoughts. The armistice had been signed on July 27, 1953 after three years and 32 days of fighting. Three years and 32 days and Luke. She was zapped of all her energy. She had already lost so much and now this ugly thing to distract her more. What shame this would bring to their family! Gwendolyn had worked so hard to teach her children good morals and proper behavior. And now this! Oh, God, how could Sarah have done this? And to make matters worse, she was foolish enough to believe that this boy loved her; that he wanted to marry her someday. Well, she was wrong about that! While she's walking the floor at night with this baby, Billy Hathaway would be off to college, probably getting some other girl pregnant. Gwendolyn wondered why Sarah didn't come to her to talk things over. She was always here, sitting in her chair, just waiting for Luke to come home.

When the rumor hit Balsam High School that Sarah was pregnant and only sixteen years old, she was immediately summoned to the principal's office. He explained that because of her condition she would not be allowed to attend school. She was a bad person and would certainly be a bad influence on other young ladies, whose morals were obviously higher than Sarah's. The principal said if she passed her exams, maybe – just maybe – the school board would allow her to return for her senior year, but of course there was no guarantee. This was a very grave situation. The school board would need time to think this over and make a decision.

Aaron turned out to be not only a caring brother but a true friend. Aaron was soft spoken. He was shorter than Luke by a few inches and not as muscular. He didn't share Caleb and Luke's love for the land. He preferred drawing and sketching. His brown hair and dark brown eyes were a constant source of family teasing. As a young boy he had learned to say, "recessive genes," when asked where he got his dark hair and eyes. Aaron helped Sarah study at home and they developed a close relationship. Since Sarah was not allowed to attend school, she had more time for household chores. Of course, she lost her job at the Five and Dime store. Certainly a young, unmarried, pregnant girl, no matter how pretty or how smart, would not attract customers to the store.

One evening, while cleaning up after dinner, Aaron told Sarah he was going to leave home. He had not told Caleb yet, but his plans were made. He was going to Minneapolis. He would get a job and attend college. He wanted to become an architect.

Just a few evenings later, Gwendolyn surprised all of them by coming to the dinner table. She looked good. Her hair was combed and her dress was clean. It was unusual for her to join them for dinner. Even though it was a year now since they had lost Luke, she could not, would not, accept it. Although, it was a cool spring evening, the kitchen was warm from the large wood cook stove. The warmth put a soft glow in Gwendolyn's cheeks and it was, for Caleb, almost like looking at the Gwendolyn of old. There was very little conversation during the meal.

Suddenly, Gwendolyn looked at Aaron and with a note of sarcasm in her voice, said, "Well, Aaron, I suppose you'll be leaving home soon, too." Aaron, thinking Sarah had betrayed his confidence, shot an evil look in her direction. Sarah shrugged her shoulders and shook her head no. "Don't look to your sister for help," snapped Gwendolyn. "I've seen the magazines you sent for. I saw the letter from the school." She slammed her fist on the table making the dishes and silverware jump.

Aaron was livid. His mother had been snooping through his things. He tried to stay calm, his voice not betraying his feelings. "I can't live here forever, Mother. I'm eighteen years old. I need to make a life for myself."

Caleb looked puzzled. "What's this all about?" he questioned.

"Mother's right, Pa," Aaron said, "I sent for some literature from a school in Minneapolis. I am interested in architecture and I've made up my mind that that's what I want to do. If you're interested, I will show you the stuff later."

Caleb nodded and smiled his everything will be alright smile. He reached over and patted Aaron on the back. "You'll make a fine architect, son." Gwendolyn pushed her chair back and stood up. She tried to speak but was too overcome with emotion to do so. She walked quickly to her room and slammed the door.

Sarah couldn't get to sleep because of the loud voices coming from her parents' bedroom. She had never heard them shouting at each other before. Later, when things clamed down, Sarah heard her father come up the stairs. His footsteps were slow and heavy. He walked to Aaron's room and tapped lightly on the door. They stood there face to face, not speaking but each knowing the other's thoughts. Caleb hugged his son, pressed five hundred dollars into his hand, turned and silently went downstairs.

In the morning, Aaron was gone.

CHAPTER SEVEN

Aaron's departure presented a great opportunity for Sarah and Gwendolyn to rekindle their dying relationship. But Sarah, deeply wounded by Gwendolyn's rejection and overwhelmed by the uncertainty of her future; and Gwendolyn, blinded still by grief for Luke, enraged by Aaron and shamed by Sarah, each found it difficult to forgive the other. Thus, the gulf between them widened.

A few months earlier, Caleb had driven Sarah up to the Bad River Indian Reservation to see Alva Morningbreeze. Alva told Caleb she was too old to help Sarah. Alva had given up her midwifery practice. The spirits had been passed on to Lucy. But Lucy was still inexperienced and Sarah was so young and so small. Alva thought it best, that Sarah seek out a doctor and have her baby in a hospital where help would be available if that baby decided to put up a fight. Sarah was terrified. She tried, in vain, to ask her mother for advice, but Gwendolyn said she didn't want to talk about a baby, least ways not this baby.

Sarah knew now that she could never ever forgive her mother. They lived in the same house but their paths seldom crossed and when they did, they didn't speak. Gwendolyn stayed in her room most of the time. She spoke to Caleb now and then, but the loving relationship they nurtured in their early years of marriage was gone. There was no communication, no touching, no hugging. Caleb realized that Gwendolyn had indeed, died with Luke.

Aaron began writing letters to Sarah. He was settled in Minneapolis. He had a job and enrolled in school. He would start in September. He also wrote to Gwendolyn. Sarah relished the letters and the newspaper articles he sometimes sent along about high society people in the big city. Sarah read and re-read the letters. Gwendolyn stacked hers, unopened, neatly on her nightstand.

Sarah's belly was huge. She waddled around the house in misery because of the summer heat. She started side stepping her household chores and spent a lot of time reading fashion magazines and she read all about childbirth in ***True Story***. She was prepared for the worst.

Caleb had given her some money to buy some baby things, which they did when they made their now regular trips into the doctor's office. Sarah took to praying again. She prayed that she would live through this terrible ordeal which lay ahead. She prayed for a healthy baby and that she would be able to take care of the baby properly. She didn't pray for her mother. She tried once or twice, but it was difficult to find the right words. The words she did find seemed so inadequate so she gave up. But she did pray for Caleb, because in truth, he was the only parent she had left.

Sarah loved writing to Aaron and he promised her he would come home to see the baby. He thought it would work out well because the baby was due at the end of July and school didn't start until right after Labor Day. He would try to get a few days off work and thumb a ride home.

Aaron sent a newspaper article about the top ten choices of names for new babies. Oddly enough, Sarah had dwelled so much on what the birth would be like, that she never considered a name. Funny. A name – a baby with a name. How real it seemed, now. How soon it would happen. Sarah started poring over movie and fashion magazines in an effort to find a name suitable for this baby, who, like Sarah would be famous someday. She finally decided that if the baby was a boy, she would name him Luke. Actually, Lucas Aaron. She kept telling herself that it wasn't to please her mother but to please herself and to honor both Luke and Aaron.

Sarah was thumbing through a movie magazine one day and came across an interesting article about an actress and dancer born in

Amarillo, Texas. She made her film debut in 1943 but didn't really become famous then. Her birth name was Tula Ellice, but she took the name of Lily Norwood in the early days of her career, which was going nowhere. Then she signed a contract with MGM, "*the*" big studio and she was renamed Cyd Charisse. In 1952 she played opposite Gene Kelly on Broadway in ***Singing in the Rain*** and she became an overnight sensation.

She was known as the gal with the gorgeous legs that just went on forever. Sarah was intrigued. This woman was beautiful, she had numerous musicals to her credit, she played opposite many handsome, famous stars and this all happened after she became known as Cyd Charisse. Cyd, or Cydney, now there was an inspiring name. Surely someone with a name like Cydney, would make the world sit up and take notice. That was it! If the baby was a girl, she would be named Cydney Ellice.

Caleb sought psychiatric help for Gwendolyn. The doctor recommended institutionalizing her. There were advances in the field of mental illness every year. Most recently, there was news on shock treatments administered to patients like Gwendolyn, who were no longer in touch with reality. These treatments were administered at mental hospitals and were literally a series of electric shocks to the patient's system. The psychiatrist believed this treatment might be able to bring Gwendolyn back from the debilitating state she had sunken into. Caleb told the doctor he would give it some thought but he knew in his heart, he could never put her in an institution.

When he left the doctor's office he drove straight to the Bad River Indian Reservation to talk with Alva Morningbreeze. Alva said there was no help for Gwendolyn. Plain and simple, she had a broken heart and it would not heal. The best Caleb could do for Gwendolyn was find someone who could take good care of her at home. Alva recommended her granddaughter, Leta.

Leta had lost her husband and expressed no interest in finding another one. She was beautiful and well into her twenties. Her black hair was long and sleek. Her skin, olive. Although Leta was average in height and weight she was quite strong because she worked so hard. Lucy Morningbreeze had taken over Alva's midwifery practice but Leta didn't want to deliver babies, she wanted to help sick people. She was kind and caring and Alva knew that Leta would be perfect. Caleb didn't hesitate. He agreed that Leta should come to live at Oakwood Acres. She would be paid a proper wage and she would take care of Gwendolyn and help Sarah once the baby arrived.

The next day Leta showed up at Oakwood Acres with all her worldly possessions. She settled into one of the upstairs rooms and immediately went about her business of caring for Gwendolyn.

Gwendolyn's condition had worsened. Her lack of physical and mental activity had weakened both her body and her mind. Even getting out of bed was a difficult task. She needed help with the most basic personal care but she balked at Leta's presence in her house.

Leta was gentle and patient and after several days of Gwendolyn shouting obscenities at her and throwing various items from her nightstand, she collapsed on the bed sobbing uncontrollably. From that day forward, Leta had the upper hand.

On July 30, 1954, Cydney Ellice was born. She didn't put up much of a struggle, but Sarah, who had anticipated the worst, was exhausted after the ordeal. Cydney was a beautiful little girl, 6 pounds and 4 ounces and 19 inches long. Her wisps of hair were the color of sand and her eyes big and brown like chocolate drops. Sarah was in awe of this small creature but reluctant to hold her for fear she would break. And worse yet, Sarah did not feel the surge of love or the tug of heartstrings that she had read about in all her magazines. She just gazed at her baby, not quite sure how she felt but knowing it wasn't how she was supposed to feel. Even Leta, who had never had a child, told her that when she first saw her baby, she would be overcome with emotion, full of love and reluctant to let go of her. But, oh God, it wasn't happening. What if she was like Gwendolyn after all?

Sarah's immediate goal was to get out of the hospital as soon as possible. She had taken her final exams from her junior year early in the summer and had passed them all. If the school board agreed, she could go back to school for her senior year or she could try to get a job. Either way, she would leave Cydney in Leta's care. After all, how would Sarah know how to love this little creature when she had no one to love her?

Caleb came to visit her in the hospital and he brought Leta along. Gwendolyn chose not to go. In fact, when Caleb told her about the baby, she ignored him and withdrew into a trance-like state, which she always did now when she didn't want to hear the truth about something.

Leta held the baby and rocked her and snuggled her as if she were her own and Sarah knew there would not be a problem getting Leta to agree to take care of the baby. Anyone could see it was Leta who was tender and loving and reluctant to put Cydney back in her bassinet.

There were two letters waiting for Sarah when she arrived back at Oakwood Acres. One was from the school board saying she would be allowed to attend school for her senior year but she would not be allowed to participate in any extracurricular activities. The other was from Aaron. He had managed to get a few days off work and would be home about the middle of August.

Cydney was such a good baby and Leta tended to most of her needs. Sarah loafed around the house and always had an excuse why she couldn't do the chores that Leta assigned to her. She was too weak, too tired, was having after pains or was just not in the mood. Leta was running low on patience with Sarah but did not complain. After all, she was being paid to take care of both Gwendolyn and Cydney.

One day while Leta was tending to Gwendolyn she asked her if she would like to see Cydney. Gwendolyn shook her head no, but Leta noticed a little tear running slowing down Gwendolyn's cheek. Later, Leta brought Cydney into the room. At first, Gwendolyn stared straight ahead and wouldn't look at Cydney. Leta sat patiently on the side of the bed, slowing rocking Cydney back and forth, not speaking to either the child or the woman. Then Gwendolyn turned her head, ever so slightly and gazed down at her granddaughter. Slowly, very slowly a smile crossed her face and yet another tear rippled down her cheek. She reached out and touched the baby's hand, rubbing it ever so gently with her thumb and forefinger. After a few minutes, she laid her head back on the pillow and closed her eyes. Leta still did not speak, she just took Cydney and left the room. Once in the dining room, Leta felt like shouting. Hope surged through her veins. It was a break through! This tiny baby touched something deep within Gwendolyn that no one else had been able to do for a long, long time.

At dinner that night, Leta relayed the story to Caleb and Sarah. Sarah was angry. "Don't ever do that again," she warned Leta, "I don't trust my mother. She might hurt my baby." Leta argued that Cydney might be the key to bringing Gwendolyn back to reality but Sarah remained firm. Leta was not to take Cydney to Gwendolyn's room again, ever!

Once a week, Leta gave Caleb a verbal report on Gwendolyn's condition. She continued her quest for permission to take Cydney to visit her grandmother, but Caleb thought it best that they honor Sarah's wishes. He trusted Gwendolyn, of course, and was angered and hurt to find out that Sarah didn't, but he felt that his hands were tied. He was so pleased with Leta and her work and everything she was doing for both Gwendolyn and Sarah, but he felt that Sarah had the right to refuse to let her mother see Cydney.

As promised, Aaron came home about the third week in August. He spent some time helping Caleb combine oats but spent most of his time with Sarah and Cydney. He loved that little girl the very first time he held her and was dismayed to see that Sarah did not. He also noticed what a great job Leta did caring for both his mother and Cydney. Aaron was crushed when Gwendolyn refused to see him or talk to him. He had so much he wanted to share with her. Instead he babbled on to Sarah and Caleb and even to Leta, who had already found a place in the family. He told them about his jobs. The first, as a gopher for a local architect, who might want to take on an apprentice in the near future. The other, washing dishes in the evening, in an elite restaurant in downtown Minneapolis where many rich people came to eat and he was lucky enough to be able to share in the generous tips they left. He was doing well and making good money and would be starting a two-year architectural program at technical school in September. And, oh yes, there was Patrice. A beautiful, wonderful young lady, who lived in the same apartment house that Aaron did. They found they had a lot in common. They spent many hours together, talking and walking and getting to know each other. Patrice – she was the love of his life and he couldn't wait to get back to her. Only a few days passed and Aaron left. Once again, the house seemed empty.

In September, Sarah returned to school for her senior year. After only two days she came home in the middle of the day and told Caleb she quit. The lewd comments from the other students and the way some of the male teachers ogled her really got to her and she was not going to put up with it. Tomorrow she would go to town and look for a job. Caleb said nothing, for he knew in his heart that Sarah, his little Sarah, despite having just turned seventeen years old, had crossed the line into womanhood. The sweet innocence was gone. She had become cold and calloused and he knew she would not stay in Balsam Hills much longer.

Leta continued to tend to both Cydney and Gwendolyn. She also continued to take Cydney into Gwendolyn's room when neither Caleb nor Sarah were at home. Gwendolyn started to look forward to seeing Cydney and once or twice Leta even let Gwendolyn hold her for a short period of time. Gwendolyn was still very weak both physically and mentally, but Leta noticed that Cydney's visits really perked her up. Since Sarah had forbidden her to take Cydney to Gwendolyn and Caleb had agreed that it was probably not a good idea, Leta could not report this progress to Caleb.

Caleb was surprised when Sarah took a job at the mill. She didn't have to do much there, just collect money when the farmers brought in grain for grinding or pay them when they had some to sell. It wasn't exactly a clean place to work, very dusty and dirty and somehow Caleb couldn't picture Sarah in that environment. She was always talking about fashion and modeling and things like that, so the mill seemed far removed from her interests. And it was. But Sarah was growing lazy and discontent and working at the mill gave her the chance to read magazines and foster a plan of escape from this miserable small town that had branded her a scarlet woman. When she had saved up enough money she would go to Minneapolis. She'd get a job there doing something worthwhile instead of pandering to these nitwit farmers, who also made lascivious comments to her.

There was no question about it, Leta loved Cydney like her own child and she was also now extremely fond of Gwendolyn, who no longer resisted the pampering and gentle care lavished upon her. Sarah was disinterested in Cydney's daily activities. It was Leta who shrieked with excitement and ran to tell Caleb when Cydney uttered her first words and took her first steps.

One day, when Cydney was three years old, Sarah came home unexpectedly and found Leta and Cydney playing in Gwendolyn's room. She was livid, she shouted and cursed at Leta and yanked Cydney by the arm out into the dining room. She threatened to tell Caleb and have Leta dismissed. "How long has this been going on?" Sarah shouted. "I don't want Gwendolyn to be involved in Cydney's life. Can't you understand that?"

Cydney was crying, "I want to play with Grandma," she sobbed.

"I'm sorry," Leta said, "I thought it would be good for both of them."

"How dare you!" Sarah shouted, "How dare you decide what's good for my child!"

"Someone has to," Leta shot back, "you certainly aren't interested in her!"

Sarah fell silent. Her face grew pale and her temples throbbed. She left the room in a furor. Leta was right. She didn't care about Gwendolyn, and she didn't care about Cydney. She just wanted to escape. Sarah ran up the steps to her room and slammed the door. "Oh my God," she thought, "I have rejected my child just like my mother rejected me!" She threw herself on the bed and cried.

When she woke up it was dark outside and she heard the muffled voices of Caleb and Leta downstairs. She slept again and when she woke up it was very late. The house was quiet now. She was still very angry and she was also ashamed of herself. She tiptoed down the hall to Cydney's room and peaked in. The child's even breathing told Sarah she was asleep. She peered into the beautiful little face and kissed the damp forehead.

Then, like Aaron, Sarah was gone in the morning.

CHAPTER EIGHT

Sarah was uncomfortable and fidgeted in the pew next to Caleb. She kept her eyes diverted from Gwendolyn's casket. She didn't want to come home for the funeral but Caleb had pleaded with her. He sat stone faced on Sarah's left, his eyes dry. On her right sat Aaron and Patrice. Next to Patrice sat six-year old Cydney. Leta sat behind them and Sarah could hear her muffled sobs. She looked over at Cydney once or twice and saw Patrice wipe away the tears that cascaded down Cydney's rosy cheeks. "Great," thought Sarah sarcastically, "the kid cared about Gwendolyn and now she's dead and the hurting will start all over again."

Sarah had not been home since she left that night after the confrontation with Leta. She knew she was a bad mother and thought Cydney would be better off without her. Sarah wrote to Caleb and told him her whereabouts. She was living in Minneapolis not too far from Aaron and Patrice. Sarah had gone to cosmetology school and became a hairdresser. She still harbored dreams of becoming a rich and famous fashion designer. She just had to meet the right guy and get the big break and then WHAM! She would show them all. The smart-ass kids from Balsam High, the dirty old men at the mill and Gwendolyn. Most of all, she'd show Gwendolyn that she could be somebody. But leave it to Gwendolyn to up and die before Sarah had a chance to prove she could make it big.

"She had to have her revenge one more time," Sarah told herself, "and as soon as she's in the ground, I'm outta here."

The service ended and the group of mourners made their way to the cemetery next to the church. The bells tolled and Gwendolyn at age 45 was laid to rest beside her beloved Luke. "At last," the minister said in a loud voice, "at last, she has joined her Savior, who holds her loved ones, especially Luke, in His arms. They are today, reunited in the Lord."

"Amen." The group chanted, "Amen."

Three years prior, after Sarah left home and it was evident she would not return, Caleb told Leta she could take Cydney into Gwendolyn's room again as long as it wasn't too taxing for Gwendolyn or disturbing to Cydney. The two developed a relationship, though Gwendolyn remained aloof. Some days Gwendolyn read to Cydney or they played Old Maid. Some days they sat quietly, not speaking at all, just enjoying each other's company. Sometimes they even laughed, which filled Leta with great pride and joy. Gwendolyn seemed so much better and Leta was surprised when she suddenly fell ill. The doctor said it was pneumonia and because of her lack of physical activity, her lungs were not strong enough to resist. Slowly, slowly, she slipped away, while Caleb, Leta and Cydney kept a vigil.

Back at the farm, neighbors had gathered for a funeral supper prepared mostly by Leta but as was customary in rural areas during family crisis, many of the neighbors brought in a dish to share. Sarah kept to herself, not wanting to mingle with the neighbors or relatives. She had had enough of this place and was anxious to get back to the city. Aaron, on the other hand was not in such a hurry. He chatted with all visitors, accepting their sympathy and introducing Patrice, his new bride. He boasted about his new career and how well things were going for them. He credited Patrice for helping him achieve his goals and encouraging him to set bigger and better ones. What a handsome young couple! Too bad things didn't work out so good for his sister, Sarah.

Caleb talked Aaron into spending the night at the farm rather than stopping at a motel along the way. Since he was driving, Sarah didn't have much choice but she wasn't going to take the walk down memory lane like Caleb and Aaron were doing as they sat at the big table in the kitchen, drinking coffee. Patrice, Leta and Cydney cleaned up, while Sarah sulked around. It was Patrice who kept the conversation alive, asking questions about Gwendolyn and Luke and Aaron's childhood. It was plain to see how much she loved him. Patrice was as tall as Aaron. Her auburn hair was cropped short and her nose was sprinkled with freckles. Her eyes were bright blue. She looked young and fresh and was very vivacious. Caleb was proud to have her in the family.

Caleb was solemn but honest with them. He said he lost Gwendolyn when Luke died. He had cried all his tears then and none came now. He had been without her for seven years. Her body finally caught up with her heart. He looked forward to getting on with his life. He would have to think about his future, too, and what he was going to do with the farm. He would take his time and not make any hasty decisions. He was happy they had come. He understood they were anxious to get back. He hoped they would come again soon.

The conversation lightened and even Sarah got involved. Then Cydney asked her a question and called her mama.

"Don't call me mama, ever!" Sarah snapped. "My name is Sarah and that's what I want you to call me." She went upstairs and slammed her door, leaving the child confused and in tears. As usual, it was Leta who comforted her and hugged her and reassured her that everything would be all right.

The next morning when Sarah, Aaron and Patrice were leaving, Cydney did not speak to Sarah, but clung to both Aaron and Patrice. Aaron was torn, he loved his sister but he knew what great pain she caused both Caleb and Cydney. Well, he would give her a tongue lashing on the way back to the City! Caleb and Cydney had suffered enough, she could at least show some respect, some love and some kindness! Aaron knew that being in love was a great thing. Patrice had taught him that. She brought back all the things Gwendolyn had taught him as a child: respect, kindness, love of self and fellow man and he could see that Sarah lacked all of these things.

They left with promises of a return visit very soon and as they made that right turn onto Apple Road, Caleb felt a lump form in his throat. Family — it meant so much to him but things didn't turn out quite the way he and Gwendolyn had planned so many years ago.

"But that's life," he told himself, "none of us knows what lies beyond the bend." Caleb put his arms around Leta and Cydney and led them back to the house.

By noontime Caleb had taken to the fields, where once again he found solace. This time when he looked across the field toward the horizon, it was not Luke or Gwendolyn he saw there, but Leta. His mind now in sync with his heart, he spent the rest of the afternoon organizing his thoughts and planning ahead.

Later, when Cydney was tucked into bed, Caleb summoned Leta to the kitchen. They drank coffee and talked far into the night. The next morning, Leta moved her things from the upstairs room to the big bedroom just off the dining room. The room that Caleb and Gwendolyn had shared. She noticed that the room was devoid of all of Gwendolyn's belongings.

CHAPTER NINE

School started just after Labor Day and Caleb and Leta drove Cydney there the first day. She seemed shy and apprehensive, but once she recognized some of the children from last session, she was happy and at ease. They left her there feeling confident she would adapt and headed straight for the Bad River Indian Reservation. Leta had not been back for a long time because Oakwood Acres was her home now. But this trip was to find someone to help Caleb on the farm and Leta had someone in mind; someone whom she knew would be just perfect.

First they visited Leta's grandmother, Alva, who was now very old and feeble. Leta told her of their plans and Alva agreed that Leta had chosen the right person.

Brock Roberts had come to live on the reservation eight years ago. His mother, like Leta, was a Chippewa Indian. She had left the reservation many years before to marry Arthur Roberts, a white man. They had been very happy living on a small farm not far from her tribe. Sadly, she died along with her infant daughter in childbirth. Brock's father had done a fine job raising him. Then, tragically, one warm spring day, he was gored by a bull and bled to death in the field before help could arrive. Brock, being half Indian, didn't fare well alone in the white world so his mother's relatives brought him to live on the reservation. He was now 14 years old and a handsome young man with jet-black hair and olive skin like his Chippewa mother. He was agile and strong and would be a big help to Caleb.

Brock was summoned to Alva's quarters and asked if he would like to go with Leta and Caleb to live at Oakwood Acres. He would have to attend school and work hard, but he would be treated well, fed well and paid a small wage. He would have a family again. When Leta and Caleb left the reservation, Brock went with them.

Cydney was immediately infatuated with Brock. She followed him around the farm and wanted to go everywhere he went. Frankly, Brock found her quite annoying. There was no way he, this big strong teenager, was going to have an eight year old tagging after him. After all, she wasn't his sister.

Brock proved to be everything Leta had promised. He respected Caleb and obeyed him. He worked hard and felt comfortable in the family.

As the years passed, Brock learned to accept or ignore Cydney, whatever his mood dictated that particular day. Cydney loved being with Brock and just when he thought he was alone, when he longed for some solitude, there she was again, asking her annoying questions and chattering incessantly. Leta always said Cydney was stuck like glue to Brock. Cydney never denied or tried to hide her feelings for Brock. Sometimes when Brock had finished his work he would go down to the pond behind the house and sit on the banks. Cydney, always underfoot, found him there many times and some of her best memories were made there. Those were times when Brock didn't shoo her away. Times when they talked quietly on the sand or waded barefoot into the pond or just sat and watched the geese set their wings and land amid a banter of honking.

Aaron and Patrice continued to visit and call and write letters and Cydney grew to love them both so very much. Sarah had long ago stopped calling or writing and it was Aaron who on one visit, gently told her that Sarah was gone. She had left without telling them where she was headed. Cydney didn't mind. After all, she had Caleb and Leta, she had Aaron and Patrice and she had Brock. This was the family she knew and loved as she grew toward womanhood.

CHAPTER TEN

Cydney rose early. She was so excited. It was graduation day. Uncle Aaron and Aunt Patrice had come to the farm last night and they also had some exciting news. They were expecting a baby! They had never done anything to prevent a baby, but since Patrice never got pregnant, they just assumed they wouldn't have children. Now, at age 36 Aaron was anticipating fatherhood.

Leta was a wonderful cook and she had prepared a big breakfast for them. They were all gathered around the big dining room table chatting and reminiscing.

"Where's Brock?" Cydney asked as she slid into her place at the table.

"Not here, Cyd," Caleb answered, "he went over to Bad River to visit his uncle. He'll be back later today."

"But he'll miss my graduation!"

"Can't be helped, Cydney. His uncle is very ill and Brock wanted to see him before it was too late." Leta's voice was soft and gentle as usual. She knew how much it meant to Cydney to have Brock there. "He said to give you his best and you can tell him all about it when you get back."

Cydney pouted. Brock always did things to upset her and then teased her and made her laugh afterwards. "Why do I care about him?" she asked herself over and over.

Later, at the high school athletic field, when ***Pomp and Circumstance*** started to play, Caleb got a little misty eyed. He was very proud of Cydney. She had received excellent grades and she was going off to college in fall. His thoughts raced back to the past, to both Luke and Aaron's graduations. Sarah of course, didn't graduate. He found his mind wandering and quickly chastised himself. He squeezed Leta's hand. "Don't dwell on the past," he told himself. "Just because you're 56 years old doesn't mean you have to lay down and die. You're still young and you have a new grand baby to look forward to."

Cydney talked the whole way home. She shrieked when she saw Brock's truck parked by the shed. It was a beautiful spring day and she knew exactly where to find him.

"Brock, Brock," she called as she ran toward the pond waving her diploma in her hand. He waved to her. She hesitated just long enough to wave back, then ran full force into his arms. He picked her up, spun her around and kissed her. She flung her arms around him and he nuzzled his face into her neck. Something stirred deep within her and she knew she would always love Brock.

It was a wonderful summer. Brock was gone a lot but whenever he was around, Cydney was his shadow. Sometimes he was happy to have her there. Other times he was sullen and ignored her. She didn't care. She loved Brock and she wanted to be with him as much as possible this summer because she would be leaving for college in August. College! She never thought it was possible. But Caleb had seen to that.

Truth of the matter was that many years ago, Caleb paid a visit to the Hathaways. He told them about his sick wife and his departed son, about his daughter with no future, no husband and a little baby. But Billy had to attend college they argued and Mr. and Mrs. Hathaway, well they were prominent citizens in the community. They certainly didn't want a scandal! After much heated discussion, Mr. Hathaway agreed to make a generous donation to a trust fund set up for Sarah Brown's little girl provided there was no publicity, no paternity suits and no future harassment. Mr. Hathaway called it blackmail. Caleb called it taking care of business.

Cydney wanted to become a journalist and finding the right school had taken a lot of time. With Caleb and Leta's help, they pored over brochures and pamphlets, sent out applications and letters. Finally, the answer came. She was accepted at the University of Illinois at Champaign. The school was located about 130 miles south of Chicago and boasted high academic standards. The school was noted for many areas of study including communications.

Cydney wanted to share the news with Brock. As usual, she turned to Leta, "Where's Brock?"

"Don't know, Cyd. I do know that he's not with Caleb. I saw his truck drive in a little while ago, so he's around here someplace."

Cydney set out in search of Brock. She checked the barn and the shed, then headed toward the pond. It was a very warm day, so that's where she thought he would be. She half walked, half ran, calling his name.

Suddenly, he was there, standing on the hill. "What's up, Cyd?" God he was gorgeous! His black hair was tousled, he was bare-chested and his muscles flexed as he jammed his hands into the pockets of his shorts. He was barefoot, too and he looked a little sheepish.

"Hi! I just wanted to show you my acceptance letter."

"Can't it wait?" He sounded annoyed and Cydney stopped short. She looked beyond him and there sitting in the sand by the pond was Linda Radtke. Linda! The girl with the bad reputation, sitting with Brock by Cydney's pond, looking so sexy, so coy. Cydney wanted to scream. Linda's bleached blond hair was half pinned up and half falling down. Her make-up was subtle. She had a deep suntan and wore short shorts cut close to her crotch. Her long, sleek legs stretched out before her. Her feet were partially buried in the sand exposing toes that sparkled with ruby red droplets at the end of each one. Obviously, she wasn't wearing a bra and her nipples strained against the flimsy fabric of her white tank top. She looked directly at Cydney and grinned. Cydney turned and ran toward the house, tears stinging her eyes. What did she expect? She was going away and Brock was here. She was 17 and Brock was 23. He was the target of all the available girls in the area. Why oh why, did she ever think he cared for her? But how it hurt to see him with someone else!

The wound festered and for days she could not look him in the eyes. She avoided the house when she knew he was there. When he wasn't there, she hung around the kitchen complaining to Leta. It was Leta in fact, who put everything into perspective for her. Dear sweet Leta who had given her unconditional love since the day she was born. Someone who rejoiced in her accomplishments and helped her overcome her disappointments. Someone who loved her like a daughter. Leta, who always kept her words soft and gentle.

"What do you expect from him, Cydney? You made it clear that you wanted to go away to college. You made it clear that you wanted to be journalist and live in a big city where there's lots of excitement and newsworthy events. Brock is a country boy. He grew up here, he loves it here and he wants to stay here. He's probably never been out of Wisconsin. Brock couldn't survive in a big city. Trust me, Cydney. I understand Brock. We had very similar upbringings. You made a choice and from Brock's viewpoint, it doesn't include him."

Leta was right and Cydney knew it but she continued to pout and ignore Brock. After all, he had kissed her and it wasn't just a peck on the cheek. His mouth had covered hers completely and she could taste a delicious dampness when his lips parted ever so slightly. He nuzzled her neck and his sweet aroma made her heady. She felt his muscles flex when he lifted her off the ground. Wasn't that some sort of signal? Didn't that mean he cared?

The thought of what he might be doing with Linda enraged her and she decided to continue to ignore him until she left for college.

CHAPTER ELEVEN

The bus was hot and stuffy. The road was bumpy and the ride would prove to be very long. Cydney didn't notice. She was miserable before she got on the bus. She leaned back against the headrest and an errant tear slid down her face.

The morning started off pretty well. Uncle Aaron and Aunt Patrice called to wish her well and told her a package would be waiting for her at her dormitory. Caleb had carved a small wooden box for her. It was about nine inches square and on the top was a pair of geese, their wings set, coming in for a landing. Inside was a gold pendant that had belonged to Gwendolyn. Cydney's eyes filled with tears, "Thank you Grandfather, it's beautiful. I will always treasure it." Caleb was so pleased. He knew how much Cydney liked to watch the geese and he saw the twinkle in her eyes as she admired both the chest and the pendant.

Next, Leta presented her with a soft flannel bathrobe, which she made. "It'll keep you warm when you have to run down the hall to the john," she said and they all laughed, knowing that was one of Cydney's biggest fears - having to share a bathroom with strangers. Leta knew Cydney was looking around for Brock, "We don't have to leave just yet, Cydney, why not get some fresh air, you'll be on the bus a long time."

Cydney just nodded and headed out the door. She walked up to the barn and went in. The cool, pungent smell always made her feel good. She walked slowly among the now empty stanchions. She stuck her fist, with her thumb extended, into one of the calf pens and laughed out loud at the slimy nose that nuzzled against her hand while the little Holstein sucked in vain. She climbed the ladder to the haymow and breathed in the sweet smell of hay. She even stopped in the dusty chicken coop. At last she headed for the pond desperately hoping to find Brock there. She had to say good-bye to him even though she was mad at him. She lingered there alone, wondering where he was when she heard Caleb calling.

From the upstairs middle bedroom on the east side of the house, Brock watched Cydney strolling around the yard. When he saw her head around the side of the house and she was no longer in sight, he knew she had gone to the pond. He wanted to run down there and beg her not to leave but he would only make a fool of himself. She had long ago said over and over again that she couldn't wait to go to college; to some day live and work in a big city. No, she certainly wouldn't stay just because he asked her to.

Brock had come to Oakwood Acres with mixed emotions. He had lived on the reservation for eight years and had been treated very well by his mother's relatives. He seemed a bit aloof to many, but in reality he had built a barrier between himself and the outside world. He remembered his mother a little. Her sweet smell and the wonderful smells in the house. He remembered feeling very sad when his father said she had died. He knew what death was and it frightened him some because he didn't want to be alone. Unfortunately, Brock was also the one who found his father, mired in a pool of blood in the pasture, the murderous bull grazing indifferently a few yards beyond. After that, Brock realized that he was alone. So he put on a façade and pretended that it didn't matter. In truth, he wanted so desperately to have a family. Then Caleb and Leta came to Bad River and he found himself with a home and family again. At first he treated Cydney like the little sister he never had. Later, as she grew up and the gangly legs and arms took shape, the flat chest blossomed and her freckled smattered face became a peaches and cream complexion, he knew that the attraction he had for her was not brotherly. Then there was that day – her graduation day – when he was caught off guard and he kissed her, really kissed her, and he buried his face in her neck and the smell of her skin and her hair intoxicated him. Then there was that other day – when he was trying to make sense of his feelings for her and trying to find a diversion – and she found him at the pond with Linda. He was embarrassed and he wasn't sure how she felt but he knew something had come between them. Now she was leaving and he once again felt a sense of loss.

Nevertheless, he knew he couldn't let her go without saying goodbye so he too headed for the yard when he heard Caleb calling her name. She was half running, half skipping up to the car and stopped short when she saw him. His arms hung at his sides, fists clenched. He would surely have to restrain himself from taking her in his arms. "Cydney," he said with a raspy voice, "I'll miss you." He extended his hand.

"Brock, you jerk, do you think I'm leaving here without a hug?" She laughed but it sounded as fake as it was. Finally they embraced and once again a rush of emotion filled her. There was no doubt in her mind or heart. She loved Brock. He said nothing else but helped Caleb finish loading the car. Cydney got in the back seat and cranked the window down. Caleb turned the car around and inched forward as Brock walked beside the car. Suddenly, he remembered something they often said to each other as children. He bent forward so she could see him. He stuck his tongue out at her and said, "Love you, Cyd."

Remembering too, she stuck her tongue out at him, "Love you back," she called as Caleb accelerated.

He watched the car go up the driveway and turn right onto Apple Road. Then he headed for his truck. He was going to town for a beer.

CHAPTER TWELVE

It was eight o'clock in the evening when the bus pulled into the Greyhound Station in Champaign/Urbana, twin cities in east central Illinois. Cydney was physically exhausted from the long, hot and smelly ride. She was emotionally drained, too, having spent most of the day wondering how she was ever going to get over Brock. Now her first year of college loomed large before her.

She was able to get a taxi and once they reached the dorm, the driver was nice enough to carry her luggage as far as the entrance. Rules prohibited him from entering he explained, so he had to leave her suitcases on the doorstep. She wasn't quite sure if that was true or if he just didn't want to carry them up the steps. With the naivety of the country girl she was, she left some of her bags there while she began hauling the others up to the second floor. After just a few trips up and down, she heard a voice hollering that she should not leave her bags unattended. A good-looking young man, who had spotted her from the dorm across the street, was offering to help her. His name was Allen and he was an electronics major and he suggested they go for coffee as soon as her suitcases were safely in her room. Wow! Her first half hour on campus and this great looking guy was already asking her out. College life might prove to be pretty exciting after all.

But Cydney was too tired to go any place except to bed. She told Allen she'd take a rain check. He offered to take her over to registration. She said she would wait until tomorrow to check in. For now, she just wanted to get a shower and get to bed. In spite of his apparent disappointment, he carried all Cydney's bags upstairs and even introduced her to Carmen, her roommate.

Carmen was a knock out, although she said the same about Cydney. She was tall and slim, with a thick mane of blond hair that hung half way down her back. Her eyes were sapphire blue and she had an ivory complexion. A southern belle from Jackson, Mississippi, her family was in the newspaper business and it was apparent that Carmen's family had abundant wealth.

Cydney worried about their compatibility. The farm girl from northern Wisconsin and the newspaper heiress from Mississippi. But, it didn't take long before they became great friends and they spent many nights talking until the early morning hours. They shared experiences from their childhood and their families and Carmen told Cydney about all her boyfriends. Cydney only had Brock to tell about, and she realized it was a short story.

CHAPTER THIRTEEN

College was the catalyst that Cydney used to free her mind and her heart of Brock. She fell into the routine of classes and late night studies. She became best friends with Carmen and refused romantic involvement with Allen, but they did become good friends. Cydney loved the challenge and hard work her course of studies demanded. Carmen was pledging a sorority and pressed Cydney to do the same, but she declined, preferring not to get involved with a group of gossiping sorority sisters.

Time flew by and soon it was Thanksgiving break. Cyndey cut classes on the Wednesday before the holiday. Thanksgiving was Cydney's favorite holiday and she had purchased her bus ticket several days in advance in anticipation of going home. She left Champaign early on Wednesday and this time she didn't mind the long ride. Again, it afforded her time to think, a luxury she had not reveled in for some time and this time the bus would be cool instead of hot and stuffy. She was so eager to see her grandfather and Leta, and of course Brock. Uncle Aaron and Aunt Patrice would be there too. She chuckled to herself thinking how Patrice would look being eight months pregnant. They had already said they would not be coming to the farm for Christmas since the baby was due on December 20th.

Cydney mulled over her plans for the weekend and paid particular attention to how she would deal with Brock. If he was cool and aloof, she would be the same. If he was friendly and attentive, she would reciprocate. She desperately wanted to spend some time with him but also had so much to share with the rest of her family. She dozed off with a smile on her face, remembering the warm sights and smells of Oakwood Acres, her precious home.

Cydney jolted upright as the bus pulled into the station at Balsam Hills. She must have slept soundly because the trip seemed so short. Much to her surprise, Brock was there alone to pick her up. He stood on the platform, his hands, as usual, were jammed into his jean pockets. His leather jacket zipped high and the collar turned up against the cold November wind. His handsome face lit up when he saw her and he reached out his hand to help her down the last steep step of the bus. He put his arm around her shoulder and kissed her on the forehead. She felt a lump form in her throat.

"Cyd," he said, his voice deep, "we've missed you." She smiled and felt her eyes melt to tears.

"It's good to be home Brock, I missed you, too." He claimed her suitcase and led her to his pickup. They chatted lightly on the way to the farm. He told her about all the things that needed fixing on the farm and how Caleb was trying to find odd jobs for him. He told her he got a second job tending bar to keep him busy, at least until spring planting. She told him about school and Carmen. She also told him about Allen, spicing up the story a little bit in an attempt to make him jealous. He didn't seem to notice.

At the farm, she shared hugs and kisses with everyone and ate the late meal that Leta had prepared for her. Afterward, they sat around the big table in the kitchen drinking coffee, soda and beer and she told them all about college life. Uncle Aaron and Aunt Patrice talked with excitement about the baby. They were still trying to agree on a name. They were still trying to agree on whether or not Patrice would return to work. Caleb talked about his plans for the farm. He was looking into selling the livestock and concentrating on cash cropping. He would surely need Brock, with his skill and know how and he truly needed Leta, who had stood by him through good times and bad.

Cydney's eyes darted around the table. Her family. How she loved them! She had so much to be thankful for. She would say some special prayers tonight. A special prayer that her family would always be this happy and this close. Thanksgiving was, indeed, a wonderful time.

As usual, Leta outdid herself with Thanksgiving dinner. The turkey was picture perfect. Bronze and crisp on the outside, juicy and tender on the inside. Caleb carried it to the huge dining room table and began carving it amidst cheers from the hungry. All the trimmings followed: mashed potatoes and gravy, stuffing, cranberry salad, carrots and cauliflower, banana bread and of course, pie, actually three of them, for dessert. Cydney had forgotten how wonderful they all were and she felt a little sad knowing that soon she would be leaving again.

On Friday morning, when Cydney awoke, she lingered in bed reveling in the clean smell of the sheets, the aroma of coffee drifting up the steps and the familiar muffled voices in the kitchen. She was so happy to be home and she was determined to make the rest of the weekend as ideal as yesterday had been.

She was elated when Brock asked her to go for a ride with him on Friday evening. The first few miles they rode in silence. He glanced her way every so often and she just wasn't sure what would happen next.

Finally, Brock broke the ice, "Cyd," he said, "I have something to tell you. I wasn't sure where to start but since you've told me about Allen, well, it's easier now." She knew. She knew before he said another word, what was coming. "I've met someone," he continued, "and I'm really crazy about her. I wanted you to be the first to know." Her face drained of color and she felt like someone had punched her in the gut. She blinked several times trying desperately not to cry. "Well say something," he said, sounding so damn happy, she wanted to scream, "aren't you happy for me?"

"Yes, yes of course I am, Brock. I'm just a little surprised. I thought you and Linda – well, you know."

"Nah, Linda and me - that was nothing. Don't you want to hear about her?" He was so ecstatic that she really and truly tried to be happy for him, but her heart was filled with pain.

"Of course I do, Brock, tell me all about her." She tried to sound sincere and Brock was so excited that he failed to hear the misery in her voice.

He just started rambling on, "Well, you know I've been tending bar at the Bad River Saloon and she came in one night with a guy. No one knew who he was, so we all figured he wasn't from around here. He got pretty drunk and he started a fight with Ezra Blackhoof. Well, I don't know if you know Ezra but he's a pretty tough guy and he just beat the shit out of this guy. Knocked him cold and there she sat all alone. So I offered to take her home but told her she would have to wait until after hours. Her name is Ellen Anderson and oh gosh, Cydney, she's so pretty. Her hair is a little lighter than yours and her eyes are bright blue. She's not as tall as you are but she is real shapely, like you. She lives near Copper Falls and when I drove her home we talked for hours and then we had a couple of dates. I'm going to see her again tomorrow night. I want you to meet her Cyd, I know you'll just love her."

"So what happened to the guy she came into the bar with?" Cydney asked.

Brock laughed, "I think he knows enough not to come around Ezra's stompin' grounds anymore. So what do you think, Cyd?"

Although her heart was breaking, she said the words she knew Brock wanted to hear, "I'm so happy for you, Brock."

She was deflated and the rest of the weekend was not as pleasant as she had hoped it would be. Saturday evening she saw Brock come down the steps all dressed up for his date. As usual, he was dazzling. He wore a plaid shirt and tight jeans. His black hair was shiny and wisps of it hung down on his forehead. He smelled of musk and she saw green thinking of him holding Ellen Anderson in his arms. She hoped she wouldn't have to see him again before she left.

In fact, she looked forward to getting on the bus Sunday morning and heading back to school. In some strange and unexplainable way, she *was* happy for Brock. Oakwood Acres would always be her home and she loved it here, but she knew the future would lead her away. Away from Brock, and away from the rest of her family.

CHAPTER FOURTEEN

Cydney regularly wrote letters to Aaron and Patrice and also to Caleb and Leta. She remembered that Aaron and Patrice would be spending Christmas in Minneapolis because of the baby and Leta hinted that she and Caleb might be going up to Bad River for the holidays. No one mentioned Brock and Cydney didn't ask. Instead, she asked Aaron and Patrice if she could spend the Christmas holiday with them. If the baby arrived before Christmas she would be able to help Patrice out and if not, she could prepare the Christmas meals and let Patrice rest. It sounded perfect and the plans were made.

The college operated on a semester basis so Cydney actually had off until the third week of January, but she didn't mention that to anyone. If she didn't stay in Minneapolis, she could always plan to spend at least one week at the farm.

As it turned out, she was desperately needed in Minneapolis. Patrice went into labor on December 21st and the *babies* were born on December 22nd. Twins! What a surprise. The doctor was totally unaware but he said that happens sometimes if the heartbeats are simultaneous and the babies are not real big. Evan and Elizabeth came home a few days after Christmas so it certainly wasn't a traditional Christmas, but Cydney thought it was one of the best she had ever had. Aaron was overjoyed with his new family and Cydney couldn't help but share in the excitement.

Cydney worked extremely hard and Patrice was so happy to have the help. The hard work was therapeutic for Cydney because she needed to erase the image of Brock and Ellen from her mind.

After a few weeks, things settled down. Aaron hired a nanny to help out on a permanent basis. This gave Cydney the opportunity to visit the farm for a few days before she headed back to Champaign. Caleb and Leta drove over to visit the babies and pick up Cydney. Caleb was so proud of his new grandchildren and Leta, well Leta was their grandmother, plain and simple and she immediately loved them as if it were so.

On the way back to the farm they had a lot to talk about and of course, the conversation finally got around to Brock. Leta said he wasn't around much anymore. He sometimes didn't come home for days at a time, but she didn't worry about him. He was, after all, a grown man. A grown man in love. He was there, however, when Caleb needed him and Caleb needed him more than ever these days. At 57 he just didn't have as much energy as he used to.

Coming home was exciting as usual. She gasped as Caleb plugged in the lights of the Christmas tree as she walked into the living room. The tree brushed the ceiling and was adorned with white lights and all the ornaments Cydney remembered from her childhood. The house was filled with the smells of Christmas and Cydney basked in the happy memories of years gone by.

Leta was right. Brock wasn't around much during the days she spent at the farm. She knew that he knew she was there because one morning she found a small package outside her bedroom door. The note was brief, "Cyd," it said, "Merry Christmas, I miss you. Love, Brock." Her heart pounded as she tore it open. Inside was a brilliant, silver plated bracelet with a pair of geese, wings extended, dangling freely as if in flight. Her fingers trembled as she put it on.

"Brock, oh Brock, I love you, too," she said out loud.

Cydney returned to school once again determined to rid her heart and mind of Brock. She needed to be involved in more activities, she needed to immerse herself into campus life and leave behind the farm and the life she had as a child, no matter how difficult it might be.

She continued to correspond with both Patrice and Leta and as the semester drew to a close she wrote to both of them that she decided to stay in Champaign for the summer. Partly because there would be nothing to keep her occupied at the farm for three months and partly because she wanted to get a job and save up some money. But mostly she was staying away because Leta had written to her that Brock and Ellen were engaged. She had come to terms with her relationship with Brock. Her love for him was one sided. He thought of her as a sister. She needed to move on and find purpose in her life. She needed to concentrate on her career.

She must really have been obsessed with Brock. Well no more, she was going to get down to business.

CHAPTER FIFTEEN

For the summer, Cydney got a job at the News-Gazette in Champaign. She started out as a gopher which most young hires do, but her hard work did not go unnoticed and before long she was given a few small assignments. They were just local events that appeared on the society page, like engagements and weddings and celebrities, who sometimes came down from Chicago to perform at the theatre on campus. She loved reporting and seeing her byline in the paper.

Then she got a real assignment. Her supervisor, Evelyn Turner, was supposed to cover a Labor Day concert featuring David DuPrey, an up and coming musician, who had done graduate work at UIC.

Evelyn called about two hours before the concert was to begin. "Listen Cydney," she said hurriedly, "my husband's in Chicago on business and he was in an accident. I need to get to Chicago ASAP. Do you have a sexy black dress that you can wear to an interview?"

"Oh, Evelyn, I'm so sorry. Was he hurt?"

"Not seriously, but I want to be there. Can you handle this? If we miss it or screw up, Sam will really be pissed off." Referring to the city editor.

"Of course I can do it. I'm a journalist, right?" Evelyn laughed, confident that Cydney could indeed handle the assignment. David DuPrey would probably be more receptive to Cydney anyway. After all she was young and beautiful and didn't have the reputation for trying to dig up dirt, like Evelyn did.

"The concert starts at 8:00; be there at 7:00 and try to get him before he goes on stage. Do you have a press pass so you can get back stage?"

"No, I don't! Now what?"

Evelyn thought for just a second. "Call Larry, he should be at the office. Have him deliver one to you while you get dressed, okay?"

"Great idea. Good luck Evelyn and give my best to your husband." Cydney dialed up Larry McIntyre, another gopher who always hung around the office waiting to catch a break. She hoped he wouldn't be unhappy that she had this opportunity. He wasn't. Larry was such a nice guy, he said he was happy for her and he could be there in 20 minutes with her pass.

"Now, what to wear!" she said, taking a deep breath.

Carmen came to the rescue. She was taller than Cydney so the dress she suggested, which was very short on her, was perfect on Cydney. It wasn't a sexy black thing. In fact, it wasn't sexy at all but rather demure in a soft shade of peach. The skirt was fitted, the bodice plain. The sleeves were three quarter length and the scooped neckline featured a modest plunge. No cleavage showing here. Together they dressed it up with pearls and a small broach. Cydney dug some old patent leather shoes out of her closet and wiped them clean. She pulled her hair back into a French twist and applied just the right amount of makeup. Carmen let out a low whistle as she stepped back to assess Cydney's looks.

"Cyd, you look fantastic."

"Thanks to you," Cydney said. She tucked her press pass into her bag and hurried out the door, across campus to the theatre and the interview that would change her life.

She had been in the theatre many times before so she knew her way around. She ignored the lines in the lobby and headed for the side passage that would take her backstage. The area was small and there were only three dressing rooms. Cydney found Mr. DuPrey's name plaque on room number three and knocked softly.

"Yes," he called out, "who is it?"

Cydney cleared her throat, "Press," she said, trying to sound assertive.

"Not now." He sounded annoyed.

"Please, Mr. DuPrey, I'll be brief." She needed to get this interview to prove herself!

He yanked open the door, obviously aggravated but his expression softened when he saw her.

"I don't give interviews before I go on stage," he said in a more mellow tone, "will you be in the audience?"

"Yes, of course." She mustered up a most appealing smile. "Hi! My name is Cydney Brown. I work for the News-Gazette and I'm a journalism major. I've done a little research on your background. Seems like you were an Illini yourself."

He raised an eyebrow and suppressed a smile, obviously pleased with her approach. "As I said, I don't give interviews prior to a performance. Not even to young and beautiful Illini. But if you would care to come back after the concert, I would be happy to talk with you." She smiled and so did he, displaying perfectly straight, brilliantly white teeth. His chestnut brown hair was meticulous. His dark brown eyes, intense. She extended her hand and he shook it. She couldn't help but notice the long, slender fingers and perfectly shaped nails, obviously professionally manicured. Cydney knew that David DuPrey was 28 years old. He only stood about 5'9" but somehow he seemed like a giant of a man.

"Well then, I look forward to the end of the concert," she blushed a little, thinking he may have misinterpreted what she said, "What I mean is, I will look forward to meeting you after your performance, which I'm sure once I hear you play, I will never want it to end." He laughed lightly. Still blushing she went on, "I'm sorry, I just better quit while I'm ahead. Thank you so much, and I'll see you after your performance." He closed the door still wearing that smile.

"God, Cydney, you idiot!" she told herself as she walked back to the lobby, "You rambled on like a stupid school girl." She flashed her press card to get into the concert. Good thing, because she didn't have any money to buy a ticket. She sat down still chastising herself for displaying such incredible stupidity to someone like David DuPrey. She took a pen and small note pad from her handbag and jotted down a few questions that she would ask so as not to be a babbling fool once she actually got to interview him.

Then the lights dimmed and the theatre fell silent. The huge curtain parted and music from the orchestra filled the theatre. Amid loud applause, David DuPrey strode gracefully to center stage, his violin in hand. He wore a tuxedo, which enhanced his handsome features. He bowed slightly, first to the right, then to the left and finally back to center. He gracefully raised his violin and rested his chin upon it. It was evident that the violin had become part of him. The music from the orchestra became soft and low. David raised his bow and drew it deftly across the strings. His body moved ever so gently with the sweet notes that filled the air. Cydney didn't know much about music, especially David's kind of music, but she found herself mesmerized, transformed, carried off to some far away place. Never had she heard such sweet sounds. Cydney was totally captivated as David played, blending one song with another. She felt a twinge of disappointment when the concert ended in what seemed like only minutes. The audience was as rapt as she was. The applause went on and on until finally David appeared for an encore. For one more song, she was again enchanted. Then David bowed once, turned and abruptly left the stage. Once again thunderous applause but this time to no avail. He did not return to the stage. Finally the hall emptied out but Cydney remained seated trying to contrive the proper words to address David DuPrey, who was obviously a professional musician.

Her throat was dry and her heart was pounding when she again knocked lightly on the dressing room door. He answered almost immediately, still wearing the tux but he had removed his jacket. "Miss Brown, come in. It is miss isn't it?"

"Thank you. Yes, it is miss." He offered her a seat by simply extending his hand toward a chair and she tried to calm her nerves as she made herself comfortable.

He smiled and his eyes met hers. "Did you like it?" he asked.

"Like it? Mr. DuPrey, it was the most beautiful music I have ever heard! When I said earlier that I had researched your background, I only looked at the time you spent here at UIC doing graduate work. I had no idea that you were a professional. I apologize for under estimating you." He laughed loudly displaying those perfect teeth.

"All my friends call me David," he said matter-of-factly.

"Then please, call me Cydney."

"Cydney, now that's an unusual name. Unusual but very striking."

Cydney colored slightly, "It's a fairy tale name," she said with just a twinge of bitterness in her voice. "My mother picked it out from some Hollywood gossip magazine before I was born. I guess she wanted me......", she stopped talking. "I came here to interview you," she said, again unhappy with her lack of professionalism.

The questions she had written and rehearsed prior to the concert went unasked. Instead they chatted easily and she became very comfortable. She found out that David DuPrey had been born and raised in New York City, the only child of wealthy parents, both of whom had a special affection for the arts. His mother wrote poetry. His father sculpted for years. Unfortunately, neither of them made it big. As a child, David showed interest in music and from that time forward, his fate was sealed. There was no question that he would become a performer. When a sailing accident on Cape Cod claimed the lives of his parents, David's uncle, Harland Jefferson became his father figure, his mentor, his agent. Harland and David still lived together in New York where Harland was constantly striving to further David's career.

They left the theatre and went down the street to a campus coffee house where despite the students congregated there, they were able to continue their conversation in private at a small table in the back of the shop.

Cydney liked David a lot and she found him easy to talk to. She was confident that she could write a feature story about him that would be acceptable to both Evelyn and Sam. But more importantly she wanted to impress David with it. Maybe if she could write a really good article, it would make up for all the foolish, girlish rhetoric she had exhibited earlier in the evening when they first met.

CHAPTER SIXTEEN

Sam Ezpazito was a veteran journalist and a very good one in spite of his presumptuousness. He had been the managing editor of the Champaign/Urbana News-Gazette for 17 years. Evelyn Turner had been his best reporter for the last 14 of those years. She was also a very good friend. Consequently, Sam found it extremely difficult to read her the riot act regarding the DuPrey interview. He understood that there was an emergency. He understood that she wanted to be with her husband, whose injuries turned out to be superficial. But no way in hell should she have decided to give this story to Cydney Brown without consulting him. She had overstepped her boundaries once again and he was pissed.

The University had hired David DuPrey to perform and according to Harland Jefferson, David would gladly make an appearance if, in addition to his fee, he could get some good ink. The Chancellor told Jefferson that would not be a problem. It was all politics. The Chancellor leaned on the publisher, who in turn specifically told Sam he'd better put his best reporter on this because rumor had it that Jefferson was very demanding and sometimes didn't honor contracts if things didn't go just like he wanted them to. The University was pumping money into a faltering graduate program and rumor also had it that an alumnus was considering a large contribution to the program. Thus, they definitely wanted David DuPrey to perform. It would do wonders for the program. After all, he had done graduate work at UIC and was now on his way to becoming a household name.

Sam and Evelyn had even discussed her rather hardnosed approach to doing interviews and she had agreed to tone it down a bit. Then she gives the story to this novice, whose inexperience may have done irreparable damage. If Jefferson wasn't happy with the story, someone's ass would be in a jam. Sam admitted it would probably be his.

Evelyn sat quietly while Sam ranted and raved. She knew Sam and she knew that he probably had not read the article but assumed it was no good because Cydney was a greenhorn. She also knew he was a true journalist and in the end all that would matter was a good story. Sam paced the room. He told her she had overstepped her boundaries one too many times; he told her she was jeopardizing his position as well as her own. He told her she had violated his trust in her. He told her she was much too aggressive to suit him. When he paused and sat down on the edge of his desk, she stood up, got right in his face and with a voice dripping with sarcasm asked, "Have you read the article, Sam?" She stalked out of his office and slammed the door, feigning anger.

Sam sat quietly perched on the edge of his desk, already regretting some of the harsh comments he made to Evelyn. He hated it when she was right. He should not have flown off the handle until he read the piece. Sam paged Larry McIntyre and asked for a copy of the feature article on David DuPrey. It was delivered almost immediately to his office since everyone on the floor knew Sam was in a rage. He read the article, then reread it. This only made him feel worse. It was good. It was so damn good!

He threw the copy down on his desk. Tomorrow first thing he would have to apologize to Evelyn. In fact, he'd probably have to apologize to most of his staff since he hollered and complained about Evelyn to them all day. And then of course, Evelyn would suggest he call Cydney Brown and tell her what a great job she had done on this important story. Hopefully, Evelyn would accept his apology. She could be pretty bull headed at times. Sam took a deep breath and sat back in his chair. One thing he knew for sure, she wouldn't let him forget this for a while and he'd be doing some serious ass kissing for a long, long time.

Harland Jefferson was sorting through the morning mail when the letter from UIC caught his eye. The university had promised him a copy of the article the local paper had done on David and he was anxious to read it. He scanned the article and threw it down on the desk, obviously perturbed, just as David came into the study with a mug of coffee, scanning the New York Times for a review on last night's performance at the Met.

"Good Morning," David said without looking up.

"Good Morning." David knew Harland well and recognized the annoyance in his voice.

"What's up?"

"Well, UIC sent a copy of the article your little coed wrote. Seems she's smitten with you. Concentrated more on your character and charm then on your talent and …"

"Is that bad?" David interrupted.

"No, no of course not, but Carnegie Hall is going to be more interested in your talent than in your character and good looks."

"Don't worry, Harland," David laughed, "when I play Carnegie, I'll find another reporter to charm with my good looks. Where's the piece?"

"That's exactly why we need to emphasize how talented you are, not how good looking you are." Harland handed David the article and continued his mail duty.

"Don't you think concert audiences want all three things in a performer?" David asked.

"You know what I mean, David. You're being facetious because you like her and you know how much she liked you." David smiled and shrugged and turned his attention toward the feature article Cydney had written about him. He was smiling more when he finished reading it. She had really flattered him but he thought Harland was exaggerating. The article had perfect balance. David knew Cydney was a novice but she had recognizable journalistic skills. David sat silently sipping his coffee obviously deep in thought.

"Har," he said, "when do we go to Chicago and do I have anything else going on in the Midwest in the next couple of months?"

"Why?" was the curt reply.

"Why? Because I'd like to see Miss Brown again that's why."

"Chicago's not until early December." Harland said without having to consult a calendar. "There's nothing else on the schedule for that area."

"Then call UIC. Ask if my concert sparked the interest they had hoped for. Tell them I would be willing to come down and do another concert. Actually, tell them that regardless of the outcome of the first one. I know they usually have an alumni weekend in October. We could go then."

"Are you serious?" Harland was aggravated.

"Dead serious. You always tell me I should be looking for a wife. That being married would improve my image. Now I'm interested in someone and you're getting pissed off."

"You know I hate it when you say that. I am *not* getting pissed off. You're right, a wife might improve your image but, David, she's a farm girl!"

"I don't care where she came from. It's where she's going that matters."

"Not always. Those farm families usually have deep roots. You know what they say about taking boys off the farm. Maybe that applies to girls, too."

"Give it a rest, Har." It was David's turn to get annoyed. "Just make the call, please. I want to have dinner with Cydney Brown and soon."

They finished their morning coffee and newspaper in strained silence and when David left for his morning run, he again reminded Harland to make the call.

CHAPTER SEVENTEEN

Cydney, wearing only her bra and a pair of shorts, sat "Indian style" on the narrow bed in her dorm room trying to concentrate on her studies. Brock had taught her how to sit comfortably this way. If you fold your legs in front of you and sit way back on your butt, and don't tuck your legs under your body, they won't go numb or tingle and Cydney found this position very relaxing especially for studying. Although it was late September it was warm and the room's lone window was open wide garnering as much fresh air as was possible. The book open on her lap was ignored.

Surprisingly, she wasn't thinking about Brock, but rather about David DuPrey. The article she had written about him was a success, that she knew for sure. Sam Ezpazito had called and asked her to come in to see him. Evelyn had called and echoed Sam's praises. Her Creative Writing professor had singled her out in front of her classmates and other students now noticed her and congratulated her on a job well done. Carmen said she was green with envy and that Cydney would probably end up in her family's newspaper regime. Cydney had called her grandfather and Leta, also Uncle Aaron and Aunt Patrice and told them about her brief claim to fame and they had reveled in her accomplishment.

The only people who seemed unhappy about her success were the ones who had to answer the phone down at the end of the hall. It rang often these days and it usually rang about ten times before someone came out of a room to grab it. Then they would holler her name several times and it would rebound down the hallway. By the time she got to the phone three, four or sometimes five minutes had elapsed.

Cydney was having trouble staying focused on her work. She had fallen behind a little in her studies and was trying to catch up but her mind was still basking in the limelight. There was no doubt in her mind that she had chosen the right career. She wanted another assignment and soon. She would ask Sam for one when they met the next day.

Cydney tossed the book aside and jotted down a few things she had to take care of. She and Carmen had talked about getting out of the dorm and into an apartment. If she could keep getting some assignments at the paper, she could afford it.

Second on her list was to write a long letter to Uncle Aaron and Aunt Patrice and also to her grandfather and Leta. She realized that she had not been home since Christmas. Ironically, Cydney didn't like to write letters, she would rather call but this arrangement with one phone on the floor was a pain in the butt. She decided to ask her grandfather for a loan to help her get set up in an apartment. She would talk with Carmen about it and maybe they could do it at the semester break.

She was so deep in thought; she didn't hear her name come thundering down the hall over and over. Finally some faceless messenger knocked on her door, "Cydney, are you in there? Cydney? Telephone's for you again."

Cydney threw on a t-shirt and slip-ons and trotted down the hall. "This is Cydney," she said to the receiver.

"Cydney, hello! It's David Duprey. How are you?"

"David!" Cydney said with a startled tone. "I'm very well, thank you. What a surprise."

"Well, in my morning mail I received a copy of the story you wrote about me and I wanted to tell you how flattered I am. It's really a very good article. And you said you were just a beginner."

"A beginner who had an outstanding subject to write about," she said, not wanting to take too much credit. "But thank you very much, now I'm the one who's flattered."

There was an awkward lull in the conversation but David picked it up. "I have some news to share with you - I've been invited back to

UIC for Alumni Day in October. I'll be doing another concert and I was hoping we could have dinner together after that."

Cydney was breathless, "How wonderful, David. I look forward to hearing you play again."

"Is that all? Aren't you looking forward to seeing me again?" he mused.

Cydney wasn't sure how to handle this, "Well, yes of course I look forward to seeing you but your music – it was so," she stumbled for the right words, "so extraordinary."

David laughed, he could almost see her blushing face. Her very pretty blushing face.

"Good, then I'll consider it a date for October 20th, okay?"

"Yes, thank you David, I'd like that."

"Good. And I certainly look forward to seeing you again, Miss Cydney Brown." He laughed again.

Cydney stood motionless, the receiver still in her hand. "My gosh," she said to herself, "I have a date with David DuPrey!" She practically ran back to her room, giggling and jumping around. Too bad Carmen wasn't there to share the news with. She laughed out loud and wondered, "If he could see me now would he still want to have dinner with me?"

Too excited now to study, she tried to rehearse what she wanted to say to Sam in the morning. She would let him know David was pleased with her story. She would hint that he was coming back to Champaign but she wouldn't tell him how she knew. Sometimes you need to keep people guessing. She was pretty sure Sam wouldn't want a second story about David DuPrey, but she hoped that all her accolades would convince him to give her another big assignment. If he didn't offer, she would just flat out ask him.

When Cydney met with Sam at eight o'clock the next morning, she was more than a little nervous. Although he had since calmed down about her accepting this assignment from Evelyn, he presented a gruff façade. Without heaping too much praise on her, he told her how, despite her inexperience, the story was very good. He told her she had exhibited true journalistic qualities. She humbly accepted his praise. She let him know that David had seen the article and was very pleased with it. So pleased in fact, that he was returning to UIC for a second concert. Sam was surprised, indeed. Harland Jefferson's reputation had preceded them and his scheme was to have David perform in as many places as possible for added exposure. David usually didn't do repeat performances, at least not within such a short time frame. Sam didn't understand that move since he was unaware of David's attraction to Cydney.

Finally, Cydney mustered up the courage to ask for another assignment. Sam was not hesitant. He told her he had already met with his publisher and she had been selected to write a monthly feature article about life in a small north woods town. She could write what she wanted to but the article would be reviewed by the city editor before it went to print. Cydney was ecstatic and when she left his office for class she was in a state of euphoria.

October 20th was just a few weeks away and Cydney had to prepare for her date. She wanted to learn more about music so she would be able to carry on an intelligent conversation with David. She had also learned from the first interview that he enjoyed the theatre and jogged for exercise. She didn't have much knowledge about either, so she would have to spend a fair amount of time familiarizing herself with these things as well.

Cydney wasn't the only one preparing for David's return visit. Posters started popping up around campus and it seemed to Cydney that every time she turned around, there was David's handsome face, smiling at her.

About a week before the concert, Cydney received two tickets in the mail from David. They were for front row seating and a note was attached:

> *"Invite a friend to the concert, but not to dinner.*
> *I only reserved a table for two."*

Signed simply, David.

Once again she turned to Carmen for help with her wardrobe and this time the sexy black dress seemed appropriate.

CHAPTER EIGHTEEN

Alumni weekend was a big thing at UIC. There were Friday evening parties at frat and sorority houses. The Saturday afternoon football game was a sell out and the loss to Purdue did not dampen spirits. The concert was at eight p.m. followed by the Chancellor's Ball.

A big black car pulled up in front of Cydney's dorm half an hour before the concert was to start. David said he would send a car, he didn't mention that it would be a limo. Cydney had invited Carmen and they settled themselves into the back seat like two Hollywood queens for the short ride across the campus.

Carmen wore Navy blue satin, which accented her eyes. Her blond hair was held in place by two sapphire hair clips and cascaded down her back. Her jewelry was subdued and she had a natural aura of elegance about her, which only comes from good breeding. Cydney had chosen black velvet from Carmen's extensive wardrobe. It was knee length and form fitted. The bodice had a high neckline, which plunged in the back almost to her waist. She wore her hair piled high on her head with just a few trundles hanging freely. The black heels and sparkly jewelry she chose made her look very much like the sophisticated lady David would expect her to be.

When they arrived at the concert hall, Harland Jefferson met them and suggested that they not go back stage. David preferred to be alone prior to performing. Cydney remembered that David was quite annoyed when she tried to interview him prior to his performance the last time so they simply took their seats in the front row.

Once again Cydney was mesmerized as the lights dimmed and David came center stage. If he saw her there he didn't acknowledge her. In fact, it seemed like he was looking at everyone in the audience except at Carmen and her. The pre-performance routine was the same as last time. He bowed right, then left, then center. He slowly raised his violin, it was like a ritual. He gently laid his chin on the rest and with slow, smooth strokes drew the bow across the taut strings. His body swayed ever so slightly with the music. Cydney watched his eyes. They were so deep, almost like he was in a trance. And the music, it was so sorrowful, yet so sweet. She closed her eyes and let the sound carry her away. Away somewhere with David, who was making those exquisite sounds just for her. When at last the music stopped and she was jolted back to the present, she knew her face was wet with tears. Tears of sheer joy for the wonderful music that filled her heart and soul. David took his bows and once again his eyes darted around the auditorium, passing over her as if she were not there. Cydney was so confused. This man, so intense and so passionate for his music, had invited her to be his guest and the music brought utter pleasure to her, yet as he stood before her amid this raving audience, reveling in their appreciation, he totally ignored her.

Carmen sensed the disappointment her dear friend was feeling. In spite of thundering applause, there was no encore tonight and as soon as the audience realized the concert was over, the hall cleared out. Cydney sank down into her seat, feeling hurt and disenchanted. Carmen sat down, too. "Look Cyd," she said in a conciliatory voice, "you don't know David all that well, maybe that's his usual MO."

Cydney was trying not to cry, "I know, Carmen," she said softly, "but it was like we weren't even here."

"Maybe he didn't see us. Sometimes the stage lights block out the front row."

"Nice try, Carmen. But he gave me the tickets, of course he knew where we were sitting."

Carmen shrugged, no use making excuses for some jerk she didn't even know. "Do you want me to wait with you? Just to make sure he picks you up?" She looked at Cydney and tried to suppress a smile. "Look at us, Cyd, we look like a couple of hookers waiting to turn a trick!" She started to laugh and Cydney laughed with her. Carmen always knew how to make Cydney laugh when she was feeling down.

Harland Jefferson cleared his throat as he came down the aisle of the theatre. "Miss Brown," he said flatly, "David would like you to join him now." Carmen and Cydney snapped to attention, the joke forgotten. He looked at Carmen, "Do you need a ride, Miss?"

"No. No thank you. It's just a short stroll across campus. See you later, Cyd. Have a wonderful time." Carmen exited the side door and left Cydney face to face with the unsmiling Mr. Jefferson. He said no more but turned and walked up the center aisle with Cydney following close behind. Once they reached the exit, he gently took her arm and steered her in the direction of the waiting limousine.

David opened the door and smiling broadly, stepped out to greet her. "You look lovely," he said. "Did you enjoy the concert?"

"Very much so," she replied once again fighting the feeling of confusion looming within her. He helped her into the car and the driver pulled away from the curb, leaving Harland standing alone in the cool October night.

The restaurant was elegant; the lighting dim and discreet. The tables were set with white linens and crystal goblets. The waiters wore black bolero jackets. They were escorted to a table in the rear of the large room, where a bottle of wine was already on ice.

David sensed the tension. "May I say again how lovely you look?" His voice was almost too cheerful.

"Thank you, David. And may I say again that the concert was wonderful."

"Wine?" He summoned the waiter.

"Yes, please." The tension remained. "Thank you for the tickets. The seats were very good. They were right in the front but I suppose you knew that."

"Actually, Harland takes care of those sorts of things. I simply tell him what I want or need and he sees to it."

The wine steward arrived and began his routine of displaying the wine bottle, opening it, presenting the cork to her, pouring the sample for David, who twirled it, sniffed it and then took a sip. He nodded his approval and the steward filled their glasses.

"A toast," David said softly, "to Cydney, my charming critic, my beautiful date." He raised his glass to her. Cydney touched hers to it ever so lightly, her face flushing.

"Thank you."

"You keep saying 'thank you', is that all you can say?" David laughed.

Cydney was becoming annoyed. She was trying to be serious. To delve into his personality and find out just what he felt and thought when he played the violin.

"The concert was a big success," she said. "The auditorium was full."

"Really? I didn't notice."

"David, how could you not notice that the auditorium was full? You scanned the room several times, you bowed, you raised your violin to them."

"You're right. I did all of those things, but I still did not notice how many people were there. Cydney when I perform, I think, see, and feel one thing and one thing only – that's my violin. I hold it, I feel it, I touch it like it was a part of me. It took me many years to reach that level of concentration, of oneness, of the music coming from my soul, not from the violin, but from my soul because when I hold my violin it is me, it's in my heart and soul." As he spoke, his eyes once again blackened with intensity. Just speaking about his violin and his music stirred a passion deep within him. Cydney realized that his violin and music were his true loves.

David drained his glass and the wine steward returned to the table without be summoned, to refill it. Cydney, although having little or no experience with alcohol, was sensible enough to sip hers very slowly.

David had several glasses of wine before he summoned the waiter. Cydney, once again acknowledging her lack of social graces asked David to order for her. She listened intently as he ordered hors d'oeuvres: Lemon herb salmon lox on caper croutons; tomato basil brochettes and spinach and feta strudels. For the main course he selected garlic crusted rack of lamb on eggplant couscous with artichoke chutney and stone ground mustard yogurt jus. Cydney sat demurely, hands folded in her lap, wondering what exactly for sure, she would be eating.

They conversed easily over what turned out to be a pretty good meal and Cydney confessed that she had never eaten in such an elegant place as this. David simply smiled and suggested that they do it more often. When he suggested an after dinner drink she agreed because she only had one glass of wine and had sipped it all through dinner.

David asked about her life on the farm and about Wisconsin. He said he had been to Milwaukee many times but nowhere else in Wisconsin. Cydney told him about her grandfather and Leta, about Uncle Aaron and Aunt Patrice and the twins, she casually mentioned Brock. Other particulars about Gwendolyn and Luke and about her mother could wait. She didn't feel comfortable enough with David to bare her soul to him. If she got to know him better, she might tell him the whole story but not just yet.

Her glass now empty, she declined another and hoped they would go soon. She was finding it difficult to talk with David. He had infinite knowledge about things she had never even heard of. He talked about far away places and exotic things. Lavish restaurants and elite company. She had long ago left her comfort zone. David must have sensed her restlessness. He checked his watch and was surprised at how late it was. "We have to stop at the Chancellor's Ball," he said matter-of-factly.

"Would it be appropriate for me to go there? I'm a student."

"A student who happens to be the date of one of UIC's most famous alumnus," David said sarcastically, "of course, you can go there!"

David took care of the tab and had the concierge summon the car. They rode in silence. David had his arm draped casually across the back of the seat, his fingertips brushing her bare shoulder.

It was late and the Chancellor's Ball seemed to be winding down, but David said they should at least put in an appearance. The Chancellor towered over David as they shook hands and David introduced him to Cydney. If he knew she was a student, he didn't mention it but rather made them feel very welcome. He clapped his hands to get the attention of the other guests and publicly introduced them. The crowd cheered and David raised his hand slightly in acknowledgment. He ordered another drink, Cydney passed. Several other alumni came forward to talk with them and Cydney found herself immersed in conversation with a couple who obviously thought she and David were a real twosome. David finally rescued her and after thanking the Chancellor for a wonderful evening they escaped through the patio door. The car was waiting and when they settled themselves into the back seat once again, Cydney realized David was slightly drunk. She was chilled and David put his arms around her to warm her up.

"Where to?" he whispered in her ear.

"Oh, David, it's late," she said quietly, "and I'm way behind on my studies. I have a test on Monday and have to devote my entire day tomorrow to studying. I think I'd like to go home now."

David picked up the intercom, "Phillip," he said to the driver, "take us to Balsam Rivers, Wisconsin." Cydney slapped him on the shoulder with her evening bag and he started laughing.

"It's Balsam Hills, and you know what I meant, home to my dorm." He kissed her then. On the lips, firmly yet gently. She didn't resist but she didn't return the kiss. He pulled back and looked deep into her eyes.

"Can we try that again?" he asked. This time she did respond but she remembered another kiss a long time ago, that set her insides afire and she knew that this one did not compare.

CHAPTER NINETEEN

Over the next few weeks, David continued to woo Cydney with flowers and telephone calls. He was very persistent and Cydney had to admit that she was flattered.

Cydney had just gotten off the phone with her grandfather. It was so good to talk with him. She didn't realize how much she missed her family. She had not been home since Christmas and she was so looking forward to making the trip over the Thanksgiving holiday, regardless of the long bus ride. She had so much news to share with them.

She started back down the hall to her room and was only about half way there when the phone rang again. She sprinted back to answer it since all her dorm mates where giving her a lot of static about how she never was there to answer the phone and it always seemed to be for her.

"Bradford Hall," she said into the receiver, a little breathless.

"Cydney? It's really you? I don't have to wait five minutes to talk to you?" It was David of course.

"Oh, David, you're exaggerating," she said recognizing his voice. "It only takes me four and half minutes to get here." They both chuckled.

"It's been so long since I've seen you. I miss your smiling face." Not able to yet admit that she missed him, she just laughed lightly into the receiver.

"I'm serious," he said. "I would really like to see you again."

"I'd like that too, David."

"Good, because I'm doing a concert in Chicago on Saturday the 15th of December and I was hoping you could come up and spend the weekend with me."

Disappointment washed over her. "Oh, David, I couldn't. I don't have a car and even if I did, I have never driven in a big city." Carmen had a car, of course, but Cydney would never, ever think of asking to borrow it or driving to Chicago by herself.

"I'll send a car for you."

"David, I couldn't ask you to do that. Do you realize how far away Chicago is?"

"Of course I do and if I didn't really, really want to see you, I wouldn't offer the car. So what do you say? Is it a date?"

Cydney's mind was racing. She knew she didn't have much time to think about it. But she was concerned with sleeping arrangements, clothes, life in the big city, and more importantly, her feelings for David.

"Well, um, David, where would I be staying?" He sensed her apprehensiveness.

"Why in the room right next to mine! Is that okay?" he teased.

She didn't answer right away, knowing he must think her a big prude. "That would be fine."

"Can they be adjoining? I'll get a padlock for you if you think you're in danger," he laughed again.

"Yes, David, they can be adjoining. What's the name of the hotel?"

"I prefer the Drake. Can you come Friday evening?"

"Yes, my last class is at one, so I can be ready to go by three thirty."

"Good. Harland will make the arrangements for the car and the room and get the information to you. You can expect to hear from him in a week or so."

"I'm going home for Thanksgiving, so I'll be gone from Wednesday, the 28th until Sunday, December 2nd. So please don't have him call during that time."

"Do you mean home to Wisconsin?"

"Yes, and I'm so excited. I haven't seen my family since last Christmas and I have so much news to share with them."

"Does your news include me?" he asked bluntly.

"Well, yes, I suppose I will tell them about our relationship."

"What exactly is our relationship?"

"You probably know that better than I do. After all, I'm just a college kid and you, well – you're a sophisticated musician with more talent than anyone else I know in the whole wide world and truthfully, I can't imagine why you're wasting your time on me."

"Quite frankly, Cydney, I hope I'm not wasting my time on you. I hope we can spend a lot more time together and get to know each other much better. I'm hopeful that our relationship, as you called it, will lead to something more intimate."

Cydney was stunned that David was so candid, "You amaze me, David. What are the plans for the daytime in Chicago? What type of clothes will I need?"

"Whatever you want to bring, Cydney. And we'll have fun, I promise you that."

"David?"

"Hmm?"

"Thank you. I really am looking forward to it. It's really nice of you to send a car all the way down here to pick me up."

"How are you getting to Wisconsin?"

"I'm taking the Greyhound." David started to protest but she interrupted him, "I have my ticket already," she said, "so don't get any ideas about sending a car. I've ridden the bus many times before and I'll be fine."

"Give my regards to your family. I hope I get to meet them some time soon. And have a wonderful trip. I'm going to Boston for a few days for business and a concert, so I may not have time to call you before you go. But I'll be thinking about you and looking forward to Chicago."

"Me too! Have fun in Boston. Good bye, David."

"Bye Cydney."

She leaned against the wall to support herself. What was she thinking? Going to Chicago to meet David for a weekend! At least she got one thing straight, they would have separate bedrooms. She liked David a lot but she wasn't ready to jump into bed with him and she hoped he didn't expect her to. They had a long way to go before their relationship escalated to anything close to sharing sleeping quarters. She would be sure to relay that information to her grandfather and Leta when she told them about David.

Carmen came in and slammed the door. She stood there looking like she was about to cry. She just got off the phone with her mother. Her parents decided to stay in the South of France until mid December so no one would be at the house in Jackson for Thanksgiving. Her siblings had been notified too and the housekeeping staff had been given the week off. Her mother assured her they would all be together at Christmas.

Despite Carmen's glum expression, Cydney sprang off the bed, "Perfect!" she shouted. "That's perfect! Carmen you can come home with me!"

"You don't understand, Cyd, we've always all gone home for Thanksgiving. It's like a tradition. I can't believe they're staying in France!"

"Look, Car, I know it won't be the same as going home, but really, we'll have a great time. Leta makes the best Thanksgiving feasts, and you can meet my family and see the farm. Please, Carmen? Please, please, please come with me? It will be so much fun!"

"I've never been on a farm," Carmen confessed, looking a little happier.

"Listen," Cydney commanded, "here's the plan. We leave early Wednesday morning because it's a real long bus ride. You'll need to bring some books or magazines along and we'll make a little lunch. The bus stops quite a few places but never for very long. We'll have time to get a soda or maybe a quick hotdog some place but we need to have some fruit and candy bars with us." Cydney paused and looked thoughtful, "I bet you've never ridden a Greyhound before, have you?"

"Well – "

"Come on Carmen, tell me the truth. You've never ridden the bus before have you?"

"Well, no, not that kind of bus. But Cydney, we could drive up, I'm sure we could get there faster in my car then on the bus."

"I don't know, Carmen, the traffic will be bad because of the holiday and I'm not even sure of the best route and to tell you the truth I think my grandfather would rather have me come on the bus and if we go on the bus, we can relax and gab and have fun. What do you say?"

"If I go to Wisconsin with you for Thanksgiving, will you go to Jackson with me for Christmas?" Carmen questioned.

Cydney shrugged her shoulders. "I don't know. I'll have to see what my family is doing. But please come with me for Thanksgiving!"

"Okay, it sounds great. I know it will be fun," Carmen was smiling now, "and Cydney, thanks, you rescued me from a dismal Thanksgiving alone in the dorm." Cydney just smiled back. She was very excited to have Carmen going home with her. She knew Caleb and Leta would make her feel just like part of the family. That was their way. Her smile broadened at the thought of seeing her family again. She really missed them.

Once again the bus ride proved to be redeeming. The girls talked and laughed and even had the other passengers singing ***Over the River and Through the Woods***. They got off at every stop to stretch and look around and replenish their supply of snacks and candy bars. Cydney thought she had never had such fun on a bus ride before and she could tell Carmen was enjoying it too, although she complained a lot. Cydney knew her roommate well and just let her grumbling go in one ear and out the other.

Late that evening, as the driver roared out the approach of Balsam Hills and the bus pulled into the station both girls were on a natural high in spite of being exhausted from the long ride.

Caleb and Leta were both there to meet them and Carmen had to admit that she had never seen Cydney so excited. She squealed and jumped and hugged first her grandfather, then Leta, then back to her grandfather. Carmen knew this was a very special family and she was happy to be part of it even though it was just for this weekend.

Cydney did the introductions and Caleb and Leta immediately made Carmen feel welcome. Good thing the ride back to the farm was not too long because Caleb thought he had never heard such noise in his whole life. First Leta asking questions, then Cydney and Carmen each answering and giggling and carrying on. He wondered how the bus driver survived.

When they turned on to Apple Road and approached the farm, Cydney asked her grandfather to stop. She and Carmen got out. They could see the house below. The yard light was on and silhouetted the whole house. Soft light glowed in each window thanks to the electric candles Leta always put in place just before Thanksgiving and didn't take down until after the new year. Carmen drew in a deep breath of cold air, "It's so pretty," she said. And although it paled in comparison to her family's Jackson estate, it was in her mind and in her heart, truly pretty. She knew she would have a wonderful time here.

Leta made hot chocolate and they retired to the living room to continue their lively banter. They talked about school and Cydney's job at the newspaper. They talked about Carmen's family and the girls' plans to get an apartment. She asked Caleb if he could loan her some money until they got settled and of course he said yes.

Amid the conversation and giggles no one heard Brock come up the driveway and into the house until his voice called out from the dark dining room, "Cydney?"

"Brock!" She leaped up and disappeared into the shadows. When she reached his side, he put his arm around her waist and planted a kiss on top of her head. A surge of disappointment gushed through her. They came back into the living room arm and arm.

"Carmen," Cydney said, "this is my ......," She stumbled, looking for the right words. Her what? Her surrogate sibling? Her foster brother? The man she would love until she died? What could she say?

Brock simply stepped forward and extended his hand, "Hi, I'm Brock."

"Brock, this is my roommate, Carmen and my best friend in the whole world."

"Hey, I thought I was your best friend?" Brock teased. She swatted him on the shoulder.

Carmen's eyes never left the handsome face. She turned on the southern charm. Cydney was right, he was very handsome; the black,

black hair and eyes, the high cheekbones, the bronze skin. What an Adonis!

"Brock," Carmen sugared, "I'm so happy to meet you. Cydney has told me soooo much about you and she didn't exaggerate when she said you were handsome."

Cydney blushed. Brock was his usual cool self. "I'm glad to meet you, too, Carmen. I bet all the handsome guys on campus are after the two of you." They shared small talk. Where she was born and raised, what she was majoring in.

Caleb interrupted, "Brock, would you like a soda or beer?"

"No, thanks Caleb, I'm tired so I guess I'll go on out."

Cydney glanced back and forth between the two of them. "Out? You mean up, don't you? You're going upstairs?"

"Didn't Caleb tell you?" Brock asked. "I live in the cottage now. I'm fixing up the inside. Ellen and I are going to live there when we get married."

Once again disappointment flowed through her. So that was it. He was really going to marry Ellen. Cydney tried to sound enthused. "That's wonderful, Brock. I'm happy for you."

"Come on out tomorrow and see it." Brock said. "You'll be surprised at how different it looks." Cydney nodded and Brock turned to leave.

Cydney turned back to Leta and Caleb and in a voice loud enough for Brock to hear even as he left, she said, "I have some other news to tell you. I've met someone who's really special." Was it her imagination or just wishful thinking that the door closed a little too hard behind Brock?

Brock heard Cydney start to tell Caleb and Leta about some guy and he did slam the door and he slammed the door to the cottage, too. Damn that woman. Every time he thought he was over her she shows up all smiley and peaches and cream, smelling like a country meadow after a spring rain. When she came to him in the dark dining room, he had all he could do to restrain himself from taking her in his arms. He loved Ellen, he told himself that over and over again. He really did but then there was Cydney, always in his mind, always haunting him. Well, no more. He would get the cottage ready and ask Ellen if they could move up the wedding date. She had already said the wedding would be small. She didn't have much family, nor did Brock. He was convinced that once he and Ellen were married, he could forget Cydney. After all, she obviously was involved with some candy ass guy who played the violin and probably never knew what hard work was. So let her have her big city and high society. That wasn't for him. He was a just a small town guy and that was fine with him.

Well since Cydney had opened her big mouth trying to make Brock jealous, she'd have to tell them now, so she started by telling them again how she met David DuPrey and the first interview. She told them about his second trip to UIC and she and Carmen laughed hard remembering the limo ride from the dorm to the concert hall. She left out the part about Chicago for now. She thought she would present that news at the dinner table tomorrow when there was a crowd present. Her grandfather might not make an issue of it then.

Uncle Aaron, Aunt Patrice and the twins arrived late in the morning. The aroma of turkey already filled the house and Cydney knew it would be a very special Thanksgiving. Carmen immediately felt comfortable with Aaron and especially took to Patrice. The two of them talked for a long time while Cydney and Aaron played with the twins and updated each other on what was happening in their lives.

Cydney had planned to tell Uncle Aaron and Aunt Patrice about David and bring up the Chicago matter after dinner had been eaten and they were all relaxing at the table but Carmen, the big mouth, brought it up before Cydney had a chance to.

"Patrice," Carmen cooed, "have you ever heard of David DuPrey?" Cydney shot her a dagger but Carmen failed to notice.

"David DuPrey, that name sounds familiar." Patrice answered.

"He's a violinist, soon to be very famous."

"Oh, yes. Now I remember. There was a feature article about him in a magazine I was reading at the pediatrician's office last week. After I read it, I remembered that Cydney interviewed him at school. Do you know him, too?" she asked.

"Well, yes, I do," Carmen said with a smirk on her face, "but not *nearly* as well as Cydney does." She left them hanging just like that.

Patrice and Aaron both looked at Cydney with surprise and anticipation. "Cyd?" Aunt Patrice said, "are you dating him?"

Cydney colored a bit and nodded. "Oh my gosh!" Patrice practically shouted, "That's wonderful! The magazine said that he is headed for a great career. He is giving concerts all over. Gosh! Cydney!" They all started laughing.

"Speaking of concerts," Cydney thought she better say something before big mouth did again, "he's playing in Chicago on December 15th and I'm going up there to meet him." She cast a sidelong glance at Caleb who immediately spoke up.

"What do you mean, you're going up there to meet him? How would you ever get to Chicago?" he asked. Cydney was prepared for the interrogation.

"Well, Grandfather, David is sending a car to pick me up on Friday afternoon."

"And where will you be staying?" he continued the questioning.

"We're staying at the Drake Hotel, Grandpa and please don't worry or get upset, I have my own room."

"I should hope so," Caleb retorted, "I think you're a little too young to be spending weekends in Chicago with someone you hardly know." Leta remained silent but reached over and put her hand on Caleb's. "But, then you are 19 years old, so I guess you can do as you choose," he added in a much softer tone. Cydney smiled at Leta, who winked back. So it was done, she broke the news to them. Hopefully, Caleb would tell Brock so he would realize he wasn't the only one who was romantically involved with someone.

By the time the table was cleared and the dishes done, Cydney had told Leta and Patrice everything she knew about David. Carmen admitted that she was jealous and they again had a good laugh imitating Harland Jefferson and his stern antics.

Cydney never did go out to the cottage. At one point late Friday afternoon, she mustered up the courage, but just as she started to open the kitchen door, she saw Brock's truck head up the driveway. She didn't see him again that weekend.

When Sunday morning came and it was time to leave, Carmen felt disappointed. She had had such a wonderful weekend. She never imagined she could have such a great Thanksgiving without her family.

Although, they had just met, she already felt this was her new family, well, her second family and she looked forward to seeing them again.

Cydney regretted telling Caleb and Leta that she would not be home for Christmas. The girls were going to find an apartment and get settled and then go to Jackson for the holidays. They understood that Cydney was an adult and had her own life now. They would stay in touch and she was always in their thoughts and prayers.

So this special weekend ended and it was a turning point for both Cydney and Brock. She knew that he was serious about Ellen and they would be married. She also knew she had to bury any hopes she had of building a life with Brock. She reassured herself that she could learn to love David, even if that love would never measure up to the love she felt for Brock.

Brock, too, was assessing his feelings for Cydney. He knew the love he felt for her had to be suppressed. He had to focus his attention entirely on Ellen and go ahead with his plans to marry her. After all, Cydney had found someone else. Obviously, she would build a life that would not bring her back to Balsam Hills. He had to accept that fact. He had loved her since she was a child. Maybe since the first time he saw her. So what if he was six years older than she? So what if they grew up together? He loved her but failed to let her know it and now she was lost to him. Lost to life in the big city. Lost to this high fallutin' violin player. What really mattered was that she was happy. And it sure seemed that way to him.

CHAPTER TWENTY

When Cydney unlocked her dorm room, the letter she was expecting regarding arrangements for Chicago, was lying on the floor. Someone obviously slid it under the door. She eagerly ripped it open and scanned the pages. Harland had written it, of that she was sure because his sarcasm carried over to the letter.

A car would call for her at four o'clock on Friday, December 14th. The car would take her directly to the Drake Hotel in Chicago. The room reservations were in David's name, but she would have her own accommodations. Harland instructed her to bring both casual and formal attire. David would already have arrived but she was not to disturb him since he may be rehearsing. David would call for her about 9:00 p.m. and they would go for dinner. Attire for that evening would be dressy but not formal. Saturday's daytime activities would be planned by David and her that morning and would probably be casual. They would also have dinner after David's concert on Saturday evening and that would call for formal wear. The car would return her to her residence late Sunday afternoon. If these arrangements were unsatisfactory, she was to call Harland immediately, since David was not to be bothered with any trivials. Cydney showed the letter to Carmen and they had a good laugh.

"I wonder if he helps David get dressed," Carmen laughed, "or if he tells him what to eat, too." She became more serious now. "I don't like him very much, Cydney. Don't let him brainwash you like he has David."

"I don't like him much either, Car, but I think he really cares for David and thinks he's doing a noble thing by overseeing David's career."

"Probably, but stay on your toes."

"Come on, Carmen, do you think I would really take orders from that creep?" They both laughed again but Carmen had some serious doubts, especially since she knew Cydney was bent on pursuing this relationship with David to help her get over Brock.

Between classes and meeting her deadline for the paper, Cydney and Carmen worked on Cydney's wardrobe. She bought a few new things with some of the money she borrowed from Caleb, but relied heavily on Carmen's endless array of clothes and her terrific sense of style.

For the approximately two and a half-hour drive to Chicago, Carmen suggested slacks and a blazer for comfort. She also helped Cydney pick out the other clothes she would take with her and showed her how to pack them so they wouldn't wrinkle.

At precisely 4:00 p.m. on Friday, December 14th, 1973, Phillip, the same driver who had chauffeured Cydney and David around campus in October, rang her floor from the car phone. He asked the unfamiliar voice to please summon Cydney Brown and inform her that her ride had arrived. Cydney was very excited but Carmen reminded her to stay cool and aloof. The girls hugged. Cydney carried her overnight bag, while Carmen struggled with the big suitcase. Phillip was waiting in the foyer and took over as soon as he saw the size of the bag Carmen was sparring with.

The bags tucked safely in the trunk, the girls hugged once more and Phillip helped Cydney into the back seat. It was a car, not a limo, but very plush nevertheless. The black exterior gave way to a burgundy leather interior that seemed to swallow her up and Cydney suppressed a smile when she saw Carmen raise an eyebrow and mouth the words, "Mercedes Benz".

Cydney was striking. She wore soft gray, wool slacks with a mauve turtleneck and herringbone blazer. Her shoes and handbag were a darker shade of gray and looked extremely chic. Her auburn hair hung free and casual. She looked cool but her insides were churning.

The car was so smooth and comfortable that Cydney was able to do some reading and jot down some ideas for her next article for the News/Gazette. It seemed like only minutes had passed when Phillip informed her that they were approaching Chicago. Although it was dark, he suggested that they take the Lake Shore. It would be a little longer, but the city lights along with Christmas lights would make for very pleasant scenery. Phillip asked what she thought of Chicago and she sheepishly admitted she had not been here before. If he was surprised, it didn't show. He just told her about some of his favorite places in what he called one of the greatest cities in the world.

Cydney silently repeated Carmen's words over and over, "Stay cool, don't let them know how excited you are, stay calm. Take deep breaths." She did. In between turning her head from side to side to take in the lights, first on the lake side then on the street side, and listening to Phillip point out certain landmarks, she gulped big mouthfuls of cool air and wondered if the butterflies in her stomach would ever stop fluttering. They drove north on Lakeshore Drive and as they turned west onto Walton Place, she had to restrain herself from shrieking out loud when she saw "The Drake" spelled out in huge pink neon letters atop the building. Phillip was amused at her reaction, "It's part of the city's skyline," he said, "you can always find your way to the Drake."

Remembering Carmen's tips on how to act sophisticated, Cydney stayed put until Phillip came around and opened the car door for her. She accepted his extended hand since there was a small amount of slushy snow on the curb. She left Phillip to handle the luggage and headed for the door, her stomach still aflutter. The lobby was enormous. The oak paneling and crimson carpet reeked of wealth. Phillip had mentioned that Queen Elizabeth stayed here once and now she understood why. It was beautiful. A quiet elegance permeated from every corner. She approached the desk fighting back anxiety and trying very hard to look like she had not just recently left the farm.

The desk clerk greeted her instantly, "Good evening, Miss, and how may I help you this fine evening?"

Deep breath, deep breath! "It is a fine evening, isn't it? I'm Cydney Brown and I believe that Mr. DuPrey has reserved a room for me." Well, now that sounded pretty darn good!

"Ah, yes, indeed, Miss Brown, we've been expecting you. Welcome to the Drake. We do hope your stay with us is most pleasant. And if we can be of service to you in any way, please don't hesitate to contact me personally. My name is Frederick and I always do my best to make Mr. DuPrey and his guests very comfortable."

"Thank you." Cydney flushed slightly at the thought of Mr. DuPrey's other guests. "I'm sure I will be very comfortable here."

She accepted the room key from Frederick, who gave her a lengthy dissertation about their services and then rang for assistance. The bellboy added his pleasantries, gathered the luggage and escorted her to the elevator. Before heading back to the car, Phillip told her he would be available to drive her if she wanted to go any place. She assured him that that would not be necessary but he gave her a number to call, just the same. He also pressed a ten-dollar bill into the bellhop's hand.

Cydney didn't make conversation with the bellboy on the elevator. It seemed awkward at first but he didn't make an effort either so they stood in silence watching the floor numbers light up as they ascended. At the top floor, the elevator lurched to a stop and the doors parted. In a mannerly fashion the young man extended his arm across the doors, as if to hold them open and made way for her to exit. She glanced down at the key because she had no idea what room she had been assigned but the bellboy took it from her and led the way. He unlocked the door and entered first to turn on the lights. He steered the luggage cart toward the rack and hoisted the large suitcase unto it. He set the small case in the bathroom.

Turning back to Cydney, he extended his arm and made a sweeping gesture. "Welcome to the Drake," he said with pride, "Chicago's finest hotel. Five hundred thirty seven rooms of luxury with an exquisite view of the Lake, the Gold Coast and Lincoln Park. Enjoy your stay."

Cydney was impressed and chuckled lightly. "Thank you," she said, "I'm sure I will."

Alone at last, her eyes swept the room. It was furnished in English style furniture and was more of a suite actually, than a room. The bed was king sized and looked very comfortable. It was adorned with a dust ruffle and a large comforter in a bright floral pattern; throw pillows added a homey touch. There was a settee, covered in velvet in a shade of soft peach, which blended with the bedclothes and a huge bouquet of flowers graced a large cocktail table. Two other chairs flanked the coffee table and the drapes, in perfect contrast with the rest of the room, hung in evenly spaced pleats. She drew them back and gasped. The bellboy was right, the view was spectacular!

She opened a door in the sitting area and was greeted by another door, this one knobless. So David had indeed, reserved adjoining rooms.

The bathroom was elegant. The fixtures had bright brass handles. There was a walk-in shower with frosted glass doors and brass trim. In a tiled alcove at the far end of the bathroom, three steps ascended to a claw foot tub large enough for two people and just begging to be used. Thick, plush towels also in shades of peach hung in numerous arrangements. Small bottles of toiletries and sculpted soaps were scattered about.

She wandered back into the sitting area and plucked the card from the flowers. How beautiful! A mixture of all her favorites. They were, of course, from David.

> *I am counting the hours until I see you again.*
> *Relax for a while and if you need anything, just call room service*
> *and charge it to my account.*
> *Meet me in Le Coq d'Or at 9:00 p.m.*
> *We'll drink a toast to a perfect weekend. Love, David.*

Love, David? That seemed a little bold. The last message she had from him was simply signed David and now he had advanced to *Love, David?* Did he expect more from her this weekend than she was prepared to give? She could not let things get out of hand. She was looking forward to this weekend too but she wanted to take things slow. She only hoped David would agree.

She found a brochure in a bureau drawer and learned that Le Coq d'Or was the hotel bar and they claimed to serve the best martinis in town. She had never had one but thought she might like to try one.

Just one, because she knew a martini was pretty potent and she had to be in complete control.

She hung up her clothes and laid out the outfit Carmen had suggested for this evening. It was a lovely tailored dress of soft crepe, with an empire waist. The white top was sleeveless with a high round neckline and the fitted bodice and skirt portion were dark beige. It was topped with a waist length collarless jacket with three quarter length sleeves in the same dark beige. Her shoes and handbag were taupe. Pearl earrings and a small tasteful pearl broach on the jacket would complete the ensemble. Cydney really liked this outfit. Probably because it was hers and she had picked it out by herself. Carmen had looked over her shoulder but Cydney had made the selections and Carmen agreed it was a classy look.

Cydney called room service and ordered a tuna sandwich on toast and a cappuccino. She found herself liking the sound of, "Please charge this to David DuPrey's account." Realizing that she would have to tip the waiter, she dug in her handbag for a five-dollar bill just as she heard a light tap on the door. She reminded herself she didn't have much cash with her for tips so she would have to limit her deliveries. The waiter greeted her politely and steered the food cart into the room. He spread a white napkin on the table and laid out the sandwich as if it were a formal dinner. When she offered him the gratuity he shook his head.

"That has been taken care of, Miss." Cydney was dumbfounded. What was going on? Was someone watching her every move? She reminded herself to ask David about this.

She sat back in a Queen Anne chair nibbling her tuna sandwich and sipping the pecan caramel flavored drink. It was so relaxing; the whole room just had a calming affect. She wondered if David lived like this all the time. This lifestyle was new to her. She had never stayed in such an elegant place in her whole life and she hoped she didn't look or act like a country bumpkin. She read for a while and jotted down a few more ideas for her next column. She showered and polished her nails. She applied her make-up so perfectly that it looked like she wore none at all. She rolled her hair into a French twist, which was one of her favorite styles plus it made her look very mature. Finally, she dressed, hoping that David would be pleased with her looks. She waited until exactly nine before leaving her room because she didn't want to sit in the bar unescorted.

Although the lights in Le Coq d'Or were low, David recognized her silhouette as she paused in the doorway, her eyes scanning the dimness. He rose and walked to meet her, took her hand and pressed it to his lips. Without speaking he led her to an intimate table at the back of the room. A waiter, with a white towel draped over his forearm met them and pulled out a chair, first for Cydney and then held David's while he sat and made himself comfortable.

Cydney noticed that David was already sipping a martini and when the waiter asked, "Madam?" She smiled coyly and said, "I'll have the same."

"A refill for you, Sir?"

"Yes, please." David raised an eyebrow, "You drink martinis now?"

"Well, I've never had one but since it appears this entire weekend is going to be new and exciting, I thought I should be a little adventurous."

David laughed boisterously, which was out of character for him. "You look absolutely stunning," he said brushing his thumb across her cheek. "Your hair, I love it like that. What's that called?"

"Thank you, David. This is a twist. It's easy to do and looks more sophisticated than when I let it hang free."

The waiter returned with their drinks and they fell silent as he served them. David never took his eyes off her. When she looked up and saw him staring at her, she flushed lightly and felt her heart do a little flip-flop.

David raised his glass and she followed his lead. "Just sip it," he said, "they're very potent." She nodded knowingly. They touched glasses. "To us," David said, "to us and a wonderful weekend." They sipped their martinis and stared into each other's eyes.

They ate dinner about 10:30 in the Chicago Seafood Restaurant, one of three exquisite restaurants in the hotel. Cydney was famished. The martini, she only had one and she sipped it, had enhanced her appetite. David saw the look of panic on her face as she scanned the menu, not knowing for sure what to choose. Speaking softly so as not to embarrass her, he said, "May I order for you?"

"Please do," she said her voice filled with relief.

"Do you like seafood?"

"I've never had much other than pan fish or river fish," she said suddenly sounding very back woodsy. "Please, just order anything, I'm sure I will enjoy it." She was becoming flustered. Luckily, she heard Carmen's voice in her head saying, "Stay cool, don't get flustered, breathe deeply." And she did all of the above.

As usual David was so perceptive. "It's okay Cydney, I don't mind ordering for you, in fact, that's the proper way to do it." She only nodded. "Would you like another drink?" She nodded, yes. "Remember," David continued, "just take small sips." She nodded again, she would remember.

At last David summoned the waiter. He ordered two more martinis and for Cydney; seared scallops on squid ink fettuccini tossed with lemon tarragon sour cream sauce and garnished with pastrami lox and confetti peppers. For himself he chose sesame red tail tuna on purple sticky rice and red chili pineapple and citrus soy glaze.

They engaged in small talk while they waited for their dinner. He asked if her ride to Chicago was pleasant and how she liked the hotel. Cydney could hardly contain herself. She talked freely, telling David how the whole afternoon and evening was a new experience. How beautiful the hotel was and how overwhelmed she was that he had invited her to spend this weekend with him. Later they talked about Thanksgiving in Balsam Hills and his concert in Boston.

When Cydney had become extremely comfortable with his presence, she broached the subject of the tip for the waiter who brought her room service. "David," she asked, "how could someone have taken care of the tip, when no one knew for sure that I would order anything?"

"Cydney, Cydney," he said, shaking his head and smiling, "you've got to learn that when you're with me, everything is taken care of. I simply informed the desk that if you requested anything they were to oblige you and charge everything to my account along with a generous gratuity for the staff."

"You're spoiling me," she said, smiling into his eyes.

"I hope so," he said, smiling back.

They shared a piece of white chocolate macadamia nut cheesecake and drank freshly brewed black coffee.

David suggested they move to Palm Court, the hotel's intimate cocktail lounge, for a nightcap. They stopped to admire the opulence of the lobby and then found a table away from the music so they could continue their conversation. They danced a few times and David was extremely light on his feet. He held her so close, she was almost breathless, and she could feel his chest pressed tight against her breasts. His movements were slow and methodical, but his eyes lacked the passion she had seen there when he held his violin.

David escorted her back to her room about 2:00 a.m. It had been a Cinderella night and although Cydney was very tired she didn't want it to end. Obviously, David didn't either. He lingered at the door, holding both her hands in his. He kissed her on the lips a few times, gently at first but then Cydney could feel his passion rising and his kisses becoming more demanding.

"David," she said, pushing back, "it's very late and I'm very tired, shall we call it a night?"

"If you say so," he mumbled planting his lips on hers one more time and then letting his kisses trail down her neck.

"Please, David," she was adamant.

"Okay, okay!" he said, holding up his hands. "I guess this means you aren't going to invite me in?" He smiled then and Cydney relaxed a little.

"Not tonight," she said flatly.

"Good night, then," he said and gave her one more quick kiss. He unlocked the door for her and turned on the lights.

"Good night, David. And thank you so much. It was a wonderful evening." He smiled back and she closed the door.

Alone in her room, Cydney leaned against the door and breathed a sigh of relief. She wasn't quite ready for David's advances. Tomorrow she would ask him to take things a little slower.

She peeled off her clothes and grabbed the thick white terrycloth robe provided by the hotel. She washed her face and undid her hair. It came tumbling down and hung recklessly around her face. She brushed her teeth, put on her nightgown and began putting away her clothes when there was a light tapping on the door between their rooms. She threw on the robe and opened the door. David was leaning against the door jam. He still wore his trousers and socks but he was bare-chested and looked rather appealing. His hair was tousled and he had the beginning of a five o'clock shadow. He looked so cute, Cydney had to smile.

He rubbed his chin with his thumb and forefinger, "I was just thinking," he said, "we didn't make any plans for tomorrow."

"Can't it wait until breakfast?"

"No, because you won't know where to go for breakfast if we don't talk about it now."

"Well, I guess you have a point," she smiled again and pushed the door open wide, "I guess you'd better come in then so we don't starve to death tomorrow."

He laughed and nodded, obviously happy to have gained entry. "Well, let's see," he said rubbing his hands together, "are you an early riser?"

"Well usually I am but since it is already the middle of the night that could change."

"Oh Cydney," he said, "I have so many things I want to show you tomorrow! We have to get an early start. I'll need to be back here at five to get ready for my concert or Harland will have a fit. Can you request a wake up call?"

Before Cydney could answer, David began laying out the plans for the next day. "There's this wonderful Swedish restaurant on the north side that has the most delicious, gooiest, cinnamon rolls I have ever tasted. We'll start there with coffee and rolls, then take in a few sights and then we'll go to Lou Mitchell's for mimosa and brunch. They have these huge omelets and they're just wonderful." He rattled on and on.

"It sounds like the only thing you want to do is eat! How do you stay so fit?"

"Cydney, these places aren't just restaurants, they're the essence of Chicago. We'll have a fabulous day, believe me!" His voice pitched, he was clearly eager to show her the city. "Let's leave here at 7:30. Can you be ready by then? Or better yet, just knock when you're ready."

She nodded her head and smiled. He came to her then and once again engulfed her in his arms. He smothered her with kisses, and brushed his lips against her neck and throat and ear lobes. She responded unknowingly and he sensed it.

She whispered his name and drew away, breathless and flushed. "David, please, can we take it a little slower? I'm so inexperienced, so gullible. I need time."

He looked deep into her dark eyes, "Cydney," he said, also a little breathless, "you can have all the time you need. Just so you know, I can wait."

He left her to the big comfortable bed and sweet dreams.

CHAPTER TWENTY-ONE

Cydney pulled back the drapes to view the early morning Chicago skyline. A light fluffy snow was falling gently and she shrieked in delight.

She showered quickly noting that it was already 6:45. Again, she skillfully applied her make up. This morning she chose navy blue wool slacks, with a yellow turtleneck sweater with cable stitching down the front. She pulled her hair back to the nape of her neck and secured it with a large gold barrette. She added a long gold pendant, small gold earrings and a large gold bangle bracelet. Because of the snow, she chose boots and a navy shoulder bag. It was 7:25 when she knocked on David's door, her navy blue pea coat, thrown over her arm, a plaid navy blue and yellow scarf, hung casually around her neck.

David answered immediately, handsomely dressed in soft brown corduroy slacks and a loose knit beige turtleneck sweater. He flashed her a wide smile displaying his perfect teeth. He was indeed, a handsome man. "Good morning," he chortled.

"Oh David, did you see the snow? It's so beautiful!"

"You never said you liked snow."

"How can a girl from northern Wisconsin not like snow?"

He laughed and nodded in agreement. He came into her room, his brown leather jacket flung over his shoulder and they left for a day of adventure via her door.

Phillip was waiting next to the car as they approached. He greeted her with a warm smile and a friendly hello as he held the door open for them. "You look lovely, Miss Cydney, I hope you enjoy the sites of Chicago."

"Thank you Phillip, you were right, this is a marvelous city." She snuggled near to David in the back seat although the car was already warm and he reveled in her scent.

As promised, the first stop was Ann Sather's Swedish restaurant on Belmont Avenue. David explained that it had been a funeral home at one time and laughed heartily as Cydney curled up her nose at the thought of it. There was a fire blazing in a huge stone fireplace and beautiful murals adorned the walls. Cydney had to agree that the cinnamon rolls were the best she had ever tasted. The coffee was strong and aromatic and she sipped it leisurely while David prattled on about the rest of the day.

"Is there anything special you'd like to do Cydney?" he asked finally.

"I was hoping you would ask. Of course, I don't know anything about Chicago but the snow has put me in the Christmas spirit and I was thinking that it might be fun to do a little shopping."

"You bet we can," David said equally enthused. "We'll fit it in. Most of the shops aren't open yet, so I have a couple of places I want to show you and then we'll do some shopping before we stop for brunch."

The ever faithful Phillip was waiting by the car and couldn't help but smile at her exuberance. David gave him instructions before settling in the back seat beside Cydney and off they went.

They drove south and David told her they were headed for State Street and The Loop, the heart of Chicago's financial industry. Besides being a commercial center it is also a cultural center dotted with landmarks, theatres and smart hotels. "The Loop is the heart of Chicago," David told her. "Weekdays from 6:00 a.m. to 6:00 p.m.," he continued, "it's bustling with business people but on weekends, it's almost totally deserted except for the museum hoppers." David pointed out different buildings like the Reliance Building and Carson Pirie Scott & Company.

"Did he really think they would mean something to me?" she wondered silently but continued to smile and nod since David was so excited about it all.

From the Loop they continued south for a few blocks and turned onto Jackson Drive where a construction site loomed high overhead. "Look!" David almost shouted, "Just look at the size of that building, Cydney. When it's done it's going to be the tallest building in the world."

Cydney was indeed impressed and gasped in amazement. "What is it?"

"It's the Sears Tower," David answered, "and it's going to have 110 floors and from the very top, you will be able to see for miles and miles. It should be completed sometime next year." He was moving from side to side in the car trying to get a better view and then asked Phillip to circle the block a few times so Cydney wouldn't miss seeing it. She laughed again, knowing David was more interested in it than she was but to please him she continued to ask questions and feign excitement to mirror his. When they had seen as much as was possible they headed east to Michigan Avenue to Christmas shop and enjoy the snow that continued to waft slowly to the streets.

Cydney recognized the name Marshall Fields and she was anxious to see the store. However, she was disillusioned when she saw the prices. David noticed the frown. He said nothing, just raised a questioning eyebrow.

"David," she spoke softly, "I can't afford to shop here. Is there a less expensive place where we could go?" He knew her well enough now to know that she wouldn't agree to his buying the items for her.

"Cydney, in the interest of time, why don't I put your things on my account and we can settle up later?"

She nodded, "Only if you promise to let me pay you back." Now he nodded and they linked arms and continued on their shopping spree.

For Leta, Cydney found a lovely vanity set. The brush and hand mirror both were white with delicate pink flowers strewn about. There was a small apothecary jar of clear glass with the same white and pink lid. Cydney was thrilled with it and told David how Leta's hair was so long and black and beautiful and how she brushed it every day. She found a pipe rack and humidor for Caleb and a beautiful gold business card holder for Aaron. She bought Patrice a Gucci scarf and a teddy bear for each of the twins. Carmen was a perfume addict and Cydney found an exquisite cut glass atomizer for her favorite fragrance. David had never seen Cydney so happy. She was pleased with each gift she bought and it was obvious to him that these people meant the world to her. They were headed for the escalator when Cydney stopped dead in her tracks.

"Oh," she said more to herself than to David, "it's perfect." On the wall above them was a painting of a wolf baying at the moon. It was a handsome piece, David had to admit.

"Is that for the half-breed?" He immediately regretted what he said, but it was too late, the words cut her deep. She hurried away, trying to check the tears that were stinging her eyes. David knew of course, about Brock. At least he knew that Brock had come to live with Cydney's family and that they were very close. He didn't know how much she loved him.

He caught her by the arm and turned her toward him. Her face was so sad and pale. "Cydney, I'm so sorry. That was an unkind and cruel thing to say."

"Yes, it was David. Is that what you think of my family?"

"No, no of course not. Cydney, I am so very sorry. Please forgive me. I know how important your family is to you and if you love them all so much, they must be very special people. It was just a thoughtless thing. I couldn't remember his name and that just popped into my head. Forgive me?" He stood looking directly into her eyes and felt her sadness. She in turn, felt his sincerity.

"Yes, I do forgive you. His name is Brock, please try to remember it." He nodded and they went back to purchase the painting. Cydney's heart was pounding as the clerk carefully wrapped it. It *was* perfect because Brock had this thing for wolves. He told her many times, how as a boy on the reservation, he laid awake at night dreaming dreams that he knew would never come true and listening to the wolves howling in the darkness as if they were as lonely as he.

David's crude comment put a damper on her spirits for a while but as they headed for Lou Mitchell's her mood brightened. David

103

had raved about the restaurant's hearty omelets oozing with butter and cheese and a variety of home baked breads. It was very late in the morning and those wonderful gooey cinnamon rolls were already a happy memory.

There was quite a long line, which David said was a usual occurrence, so they just talked while they waited. David, trying desperately to redeem himself, asked questions about her family and northern Wisconsin winters. She, in turn, asked questions about where he lived in New York.

It didn't matter that they had to wait since they both knew dinner would be late. David was performing that evening at Orchestra Hall, home of the Chicago Symphony Orchestra.

"David, may I come to your concert tonight?"

"I'd rather you didn't."

"And why is that?"

"You might distract me."

"Last time I heard you in concert you didn't even know I was there."

"It's different now. I know you better. If I glance up and see your beautiful face, I'll lose all my concentration. Then Harland would be pissed off and the Chicago Symphony would black ball me and I'd never be able to come to Chicago again and I'd probably never get to see you again, and…."

"Alright, alright," she pouted, "sorry I asked."

"But, I'll show you where it's going to be, okay?" Cydney just nodded but couldn't help wondering what the real reason was that he didn't want her to attend the concert.

Satiated at last by a hearty brunch of Lou Mitchell specials, they sipped coffee and planned their afternoon. In addition to Orchestra Hall, David suggested Navy Pier, where they could watch the ice-skaters; the Museum of Contemporary Art with its square metal plates and round bolts making it look like a set of dominos just waiting to topple; the Michigan Avenue Bridge with its impressive sculptures on four pylons representing Chicago's major events; and the State Street shops, Chicago's oldest shopping district.

As it turned out, Cydney was delighted with the tour and when at last they returned to the Drake, tired, but happy and laden with packages, she was glad that she would have some time to rest while David was performing.

David helped her with her packages and hungrily kissed her lips before going to his room via the adjoining door. It was almost 6:00 and he was obviously trying to avoid the watchful eye of Harland. He promised he'd be back about 10:00 p.m. and they would go out for a wonderful dinner. He would be in a tuxedo, so she should dress accordingly.

It had been a wonderful afternoon but Cydney was happy to finally be alone, to have some time to catch her breath and think about the events of the day. So many wonderful things had taken place. She decided to make a journal of her weekend activities so she could share them with Carmen and maybe Leta and Patrice. She stripped down to her underwear and put on the white fluffy hotel robe. She sat down in one of the easy chairs and began writing, smiling the whole time, cherishing the hours of this wonderful day and the time she spent with David. There was so much to write about!

She jolted upright! How long had she been asleep? She looked at the clock and was startled to find it was already 9:15. She stood up and almost fell backwards. Her neck and back were so stiff from sleeping in such an awkward position she could hardly straighten up. She needed a hot bath!

She started the water running in the elevated tub and added some bubble bath. She opened her door and pressed her ear against the adjoining door. All was quiet over there. Good. David wasn't back yet. She left her door ajar just a bit so she could hear him when he returned and hopefully, he wouldn't be angry if she wasn't ready to go but her neck was so stiff, she really needed to relax in the tub for a while.

She piled her mane of hair atop her head, secured it with some pins and lowered herself into the hot bubbles. It was a sanctuary. The steam rose around her, curling wisps of renegade hair and plastering them to her neck. She sunk deep into the water, the bubbles rising up to brush her chin. She laid her head back and felt the pulsating water wash over her.

CHAPTER TWENTY-TWO

David couldn't get his mind off Cydney. He didn't go back out on the stage for his usual encore and Harland was all over his ass. "What the hell's gotten into you?" Harland hissed between clenched teeth. "The audience applauded for a solid three minutes and you didn't go back out?"

"Ease up, Harland. The audience got their moneys worth. So what if I didn't give them an encore? I'm in a hurry to get back to the hotel and pick up Cydney."

"That's what's gotten into you, David, and you know it. It's Cydney. I never did like the idea of you bringing her up here."

"Well you're right Harland, Cydney is on my mind most of the time and if you want to know the truth, you'd better get used to it, because I'm going to be spending a lot of time with her, whether you like it or not."

"I didn't say I didn't like it, David, but you need to stay focused on your career if you want it to continue to skyrocket. You didn't get where you are today by ignoring your audiences."

"Damn it, Harland, I didn't ignore the audience. I gave them my very best performance, as I always do. I will continue to perform to the best of my ability whether or not Cydney is with me, do you understand that?" David was getting angry and Harland knew it.

"Okay, okay," he relented. "Just make sure you get to the cocktail party at the Pump on time. Gloria and Roger are expecting you." Harland said no more.

"Shit!" David said under his breath as he left via the stage door. He forgot about the cocktail party at the Pump Room given by Roger and Gloria Savage. Harland had met the Savages at some music festival in New York four years ago and convinced them to let David audition for them. They were an affluent couple, in their late sixties, who were members of the Chicago Symphony and after they heard David play, they insisted on making arrangements for him to appear at Orchestra Hall. Since that first concert in 1970, he returned to Chicago each spring and fall to perform with the symphony. Roger seemed to think he, rather than Harland, was David's mentor and boasted how he was helping David advance his career. And Gloria, well Gloria flat out loved David and let everyone know it. She flirted with him openly and audaciously. Whenever she had the opportunity, she hung on his arm and smothered him with kisses. David rather disliked both of them but Harland kept insisting that they were good for his career so he put up with them.

Harland told him a week ago about the cocktail party and they had argued about it because David didn't want to go. He preferred to spend the time with Cydney. After much heated discussion, Harland agreed that David would bring Cydney along. The problem was, he forgot to mention it to Cydney. He would have to fill her in on it in a hurry, because taking her there unprepared would be a gross injustice to her.

Phillip drove David back to the hotel. He was very quiet and Phillip didn't ask questions, but he knew something had upset David. He was usually so talkative and pleasant. David was contemplating how to describe Gloria and Roger to Cydney. He had told her he'd be back at 10:00 but it was only 9:25, so he'd have some time to explain it all.

David unlocked his door, threw off his jacket, took off the cumber band, loosened his bow tie, and kicked off his shoes. A bottle of wine was chilling and he poured two glasses. He opened the door adjoining Cydney's room and was surprised to find the second door ajar. He pushed it open a little farther with his knee because he was holding the wine glasses. He called her name softly. No answer. He stuck his head into the room and called her name again. Still no answer. He walked in and set the glasses on the cocktail table. The room was dimly lit but he could see the light in the bathroom was on. As he approached, he could hear her singing softly. That door was also ajar and he pushed it open. She was in the tub, the bubbles reaching her chin, her hair was stacked high on her head with some curls plastered against her damp nape. Her head was back and her eyes were closed. She looked so lovely lying there David had all he could do to keep from undressing and getting in there with her. He cleared his throat and she sat upright, obviously startled.

"David!" she almost screamed it. "What are you doing in here? What time is it?"

"Well, I came back a little early and you left the door ajar. I called your name but you didn't answer. I thought maybe I would have to rescue you." A sly smile crossed his handsome face.

"I'm sorry I'm not ready," she said, calmer now. "I fell asleep in the chair and when I woke up I was so stiff I could hardly walk. I thought a hot bath would help me relax."

"Do you need some help, either bathing or relaxing?" he asked, that roguish grin still on his face. Her face was flushed and he wasn't sure if he had embarrassed her or excited her. He hoped for the latter. "Tell you what, let me get us a glass of wine and I'll tell you where we're going." As soon as he left the room, Cydney made sure there were still plenty of bubbles covering her breasts, which were tingling beneath the surface of the water either in excitement or because of the water temperature, she wasn't sure which.

David came to the side of the tub and gave her the glass of wine. He looked into her eyes and then down into the water, disappointed that she was so well concealed. They sipped the wine in silence for a few seconds. Then he reached into the tub for her bath sponge and started squeezing hot water over her neck and shoulders. "Lean forward," he said, "I'll rub your neck for a few minutes." She did as he suggested. Feeling no embarrassment, she sat up, drew up her knees and clasped her arms around them, hiding her well-rounded breasts from him once again. He continued sponging hot water over her and with the other hand, massaged her aching neck. She groaned with pleasure and he laughed out loud.

"What's so funny?"

"You are," he said without an explanation.

"How was the concert?"

"Another superb performance. I forgot to tell you, we need to go to a cocktail party tonight."

"Tonight? It's already near 10:00 isn't it and I'm famished." She was getting more comfortable with him and said what was on her mind.

"You can eat something at the party because we really do have to go. Your dear friend, Harland will be there," he teased, "and there are some other people I want you to meet."

Her neck was loose now and he stopped rubbing it. He reached for the big, fluffy robe and held it open for her. She blushed. "Thank you, David, just leave it on the floor, I'll be out in a minute."

He shrugged. "Okay, but don't say I didn't offer to help you out," he said over his shoulder as he exited the steamy room. God, this woman was wonderful. She was everything he wanted in a woman and he was aroused by the thought of her stepping out of the tub and slipping into the soft white robe. He finished his wine and went to refill it, closing both doors when he came back. She stood in the center of the room, the dim lights giving her a halo affect. She, too, was sipping her wine. He lowered himself into a chair but never took his eyes off her.

"Sit for just a minute," he said, "and I'll tell you about Gloria and Roger." She sat across from him, her eyes fixed on his. He started his tale but knowing she was naked beneath the robe made it difficult for him to concentrate. Likewise, Cydney was having trouble listening to David. She had never felt so bold in her entire life. She was sitting here with this wonderful man, sipping wine. She was naked under this robe and he knew it. The fact that he knew it rather excited her and she felt a little ashamed of that. She also felt something else, which she didn't quite understand and couldn't control.

She heard the last of David's sentence, "...so that's why we need to go to the party."

He got up and extended his hand to her. She rose and took it. She didn't know for sure what happened next, only that David was covering her lips, her throat, her neck with kisses. Kisses so hot she could hardly breathe. Kisses she knew she responded to. Kisses she wanted to go on and on. His hands slid down and covered her breasts first on top of the robe and then somehow inside it. He touched her so gently she couldn't resist. She was no longer embarrassed or ashamed. She heard him whisper her name over and over. He had untied her robe and it hung loosely around her. His hands were around her waist now and he continued to draw her close. She thrust herself against him. His hands crept down her back and caressed her buttocks. She felt his erection press against her. Tears stung her eyes. These were feelings she didn't know existed and she wasn't sure how to respond. She tried to say his name, to tell him to stop but the words wouldn't come out. There were piercing jolts of passion inside her and as he steered her toward the bed she did not resist. He had just laid her back on the soft comforter when there was a fierce knocking on the door.

"David! David! Are you in there? Where the hell are you?" Harland's voice was like a mad man. "You know you have to go to the party." He continued to bang on the door.

Cydney lay still, afraid almost to breathe. David, hovering just inches above her, let out a sigh. He reached for her hand and helped her stand up. He tied the robe around her again, ran a hand through his hair and yanked open the door.

"For christ sake, Harland, are you crazy? I told you we would get to the party and we will. Cydney's getting ready right now."

Harland looked past David and saw her standing there all disheveled, still wearing her white robe. He muttered something under his breath and stormed off.

David turned back to her. "I'm sorry," he said, "he's like a god damn nanny. Still treats me like a child. Tries to control everything I do. Then when I get pissed off at him he backs off."

Cydney just nodded. "I'll get dressed," she said. "Give me twenty minutes or so, okay?"

"I'll be right next door," he said.

Cydney quickly did her hair up in a twist, knowing David liked it that way. Again, she deftly applied her make-up and slid into her dress. This was the season of long dresses and the one she had chosen for this occasion was elegant. It was black in soft taffeta with a halter top that exposed her lovely shoulders and a high neck. The skirt flared out just slightly at the bottom, accentuating her trim body. She chose black patent leather shoes and bag, silver earrings and bracelet. The dress didn't require a necklace, just a small silver pin at the neck. She knocked on David's door without using up the allotted twenty minutes. David had retied his bow tie, readjusted his cumber band and put on his jacket and shoes. When Cydney turned around and indicated she needed help with her zipper, she could feel his hot breath on her neck.

"I wish we could stay here," he whispered.

"Me too," she said, blushing slightly at the thought of what would have happened if Harland hadn't come knocking at the door. David called Phillip to bring the car around and arm and arm they headed toward the elevator.

The Pump Room was an icon of Chicago nightlife if ever there was one. The restaurant was established in 1938 and boasted of catering to Hollywood royalty. Big round tables were surrounded by black and white glossies of an array of celebrities and the reputed Booth One was off limits to almost everyone but the biggest and brightest stars. Gentlemen were required to wear a tie and jacket so the atmosphere was always upscale. The din was almost deafening, so Cydney was surprised when a hush fell over the crowd and heads turned when she entered the room on David's arm. Harland watched from the back of the room and had to admit that they made a handsome couple. But it was Roger and Gloria who approached them first with outstretched arms. Roger to embrace Cydney, whom he had yet to meet and Gloria to smother David with kisses, as usual. David untangled himself from Gloria's clinch and made the introductions.

"David," Roger said, still holding Cydney's hands in his, "Harland said you would be late and now I understand why. Where have you been keeping this lovely creature?"

"I'm absolutely green with envy," Gloria said with raised eyebrow. She sized Cydney up from head to toe while freeing her from Roger's hold and then led her away, chatting pleasantly the whole time. They sat at a small table near the back and Gloria hijacked a passing waiter. She somehow managed to order champagne for both of them but never stopped talking. Cydney liked Gloria immediately and was amused by her barrage of comments and questions, which she never gave Cydney the opportunity to answer. Roger and Harland joined them at the table. Harland nodded ever so slightly to Cydney who acknowledged him in turn. Roger and Gloria continued to gush over Cydney and dashed any hopes Harland had that they might disapprove of her. David continued to make his way to the table but was stopped several times along the way by friends and well wishers. His eyes rested on her as he advanced through the crowd and he was taken aback by her refreshing beauty and innocence. David had to settle for sitting next to Gloria, who refused to relinquish her spot next to Cydney. He continued to glance her way until their eyes finally met. He saw the look of panic and abruptly rose. He took her arm and helped her to her feet.

"Are you all right?" he said softly.

"David, I've had two glasses of champagne and I feel a little dizzy. I haven't eaten since Lou Mitchell's and I'm afraid I'll get sick if I don't eat soon." He didn't answer, but simply steered her toward a buffet set up especially for guests of the Savages'. David carried her plate and spoke in a low voice to the waiters who wore high white caps and crisp white jackets and manned the food line. There was so much to choose from but of course, Cydney knew little of what David was selecting for her. When again they were seated, and he had managed to displace Gloria, he discretely labeled the medley for her. First there was gorgonzola puff pastry napoleon with arugula and red pepper puree; escargot sautéed with pancetta and pearl onions; brie on focaccia toast points with tart apples, grapes and roasted garlic relish. There were crisp won tons with sesame-ginger vinaigrette and an abundant display of cheeses and peppered beef. Harland watched in horror as they ignored their hosts and sat side by side nibbling from the same plate and talking in a low whisper. Apparently, this girl, this child, whom David was fixated with, had no manners whatsoever. Hopefully, Roger and Gloria and their other guests, many of whom were well known in the Chicago music circles, were not offended by David's lack of socializing. After all, Roger and Gloria had given this party in his honor. First, Harland had to remind him of the party, then he catches them involved in some hanky-panky in the hotel room, then they show up late and now, they disregard the other guests and sit in the back of the room like two lovesick teenagers. Well, David would hear about this brash behavior in the morning!

When at last the party ended, it was indeed very early in the morning. The delicious hors d'oeuvres had done their job. Cydney was feeling better but exhausted. David looked chipper save the five o'clock shadow on his handsome chin. They stood beside Roger and Gloria bidding a good evening to the few remaining guests. Harland, lurking in the background, was trying desperately to squelch the jealously he felt as one after another complimented Cydney on her good looks and expressed sincere pleasure in meeting her. David beamed with pride and assured them all that they would surely see her again.

Even Roger and Gloria, obviously charmed by Cydney, seemed reluctant to say good night and insisted that they all meet tomorrow for lunch. David was hesitant but agreed because he had no choice. David summoned Phillip and ignoring Harland's sulking, invited him to ride back to the hotel with them.

Harland didn't speak until he exited the vehicle, and then only to remind them that lunch was at 1:00 p.m. at The North Pond Café. "Try to be on time," he barked as he slammed the car door. David and Cydney waited discreetly for a few minutes to allow Harland time to make his way through the lobby. He obviously was upset and surely didn't want to share an elevator with them.

At her door, Cydney once again foiled David's advances. After a few kisses, which she returned without much ardor, he agreed that it was time to call it a night.

"Sleep in as long as you want," he told her, "we'll make our plans in the morning." He planted one last kiss on her lips and let her slip away.

CHAPTER TWENTY-THREE

In her dreams, Cydney was sparring with Harland. Every time he hit her and knocked her down he shouted an obscenity at her. When at last she was too tired and battered to get up, he leaned over and warned her through clenched teeth to stay away from David. She would ruin his career and thus, his life.

She awoke drenched in perspiration and disliking Harland more than she did before. Her negative feelings for Harland really bothered her because Cydney was a *love thy neighbor* type of person and she liked almost everyone she met. It was like a sixth sense. If she did dislike someone when she first met them, she seldom changed her mind, even after getting to know them better. This time had been no exception. She didn't like Harland from the moment she met him and it was weighing heavy on her decision to build a lasting relationship with David.

She felt rested so she must have slept well prior to her dream. It was 6:45 a.m. She kicked back the covers and sat up smiling in anticipation of what this day would hold in store for her. The last two days had been an exciting adventure. A taste of a lifestyle she had only read about or heard about from Carmen. Oh, yes, Carmen! She would be waiting at the door when Cydney came home, expecting a full report and there was plenty to tell her.

She showered and did her make up. She toyed with her hair and again decided on a twist, since she knew David favored it. She chose a deep purple crepe pantsuit. The jacket was long sleeved with fitted cuffs.

It buttoned down the front and had a white insert at the neck. Purple was Cydney's favorite color and she wore it well. She chose gold jewelry and black suede pumps. She looked stunning as she rapped lightly on David's door. He didn't answer, so she rapped again, this time a little harder. She could hear his voice so she knew he was up. She pressed her ear to the door just as his voice reached an angry crescendo. The phone slammed and just a few seconds later David opened the door. The smile on his face didn't hide the throbbing temples and the furrowed brow.

"Cydney, you look marvelous." He wrapped his arms around her gently so as not to disturb her hair. His lips sought hers and she returned his kiss.

"David, what's wrong? Why are you so angry?"

"It's nothing for you to worry your pretty head about."

"It's Harland, isn't it? David, I know he doesn't approve of me and truthfully, I don't think much of him either." Their eyes met and this time when David smiled she saw the angry lines disappear.

"He just read me the riot act. He thought we were rude last night, sitting cheek-to-cheek, noshing and sipping wine. I think he's jealous because he doesn't know what it's like to be in love."

His words caught her by surprise. "Do you? Have you ever been in love with someone?"

"Yes." His smile widened. "Cydney, I am in love with you. And I want you to love me in return, but as we talked about on Friday, you can take as much time as you need. If you say you love me, I want you to be sure. But let me warn you, I won't give up easily, I will continue to pursue you and make advances toward you and do everything in my power to win you over. Never mind Harland, concentrate on me."

They kissed again and she knew his words echoed his feelings. She wondered how she would know if she truly loved him.

They chose The Oak Terrace inside the hotel for a light breakfast of crepes and coffee and David laid out the details for another adventurous day.

Phillip was waiting just inside the main entrance of the hotel and greeted them with enthusiasm. He held the door as David led her to the waiting car, which was already warm inside. David instructed Phillip where to go.

The first stop was Union Station. David insisted that the 10-story skylighted waiting room was worth seeing and he was right even though the steps from Canal Street were very steep. The Corinthian columns and gilded statutes sparkled under the December sun causing Cydney to draw in her breath. She was equally intrigued by the Rookery, another Chicago showpiece, built in 1885 and featuring a bird motif on the exterior. She felt a surge of pride when she learned that famous Wisconsin Architect, Frank Lloyd Wright did some renovations in the two-story lobby and light court in 1905. The white marble mezzanine stairway was laden with intricate incising and gold-leaf gild and Cydney had to admit she had never seen such beautiful buildings. Her favorite stop, however, was the Art Institute, which houses some of the world's most famous paintings. The two lions that flank the museum's main entrance are said to be the most photographed in the world and Cydney and David both laughed out loud to see Christmas wreaths around their massive necks. Inside, Monet, Renoir and van Gogh are featured along with lesser known artists. David had been to the museum many times but never with anyone quite as ecstatic as Cydney. She led him from place to place, wanting to see it all, drinking in the beauty. He watched her every movement. And every step, every spin, every turn, only made him love her more.

In the Thorne Miniature Room she was like a little girl playing with a dollhouse. At the Rubloff Paperweight Collection she was like a kid in a toy store and when David told her it was time to leave, he saw the disappointment in her eyes. He gently rubbed her cheek with his thumb and promised they would come again soon. But for now, they had to keep Harland happy so it was off to the North Pond Café.

Situated once again in the warm and comfortable Mercedes, David explained that the North Pond Café was once a warming house for Chicagoans ice-skating on Lincoln Park's North Pond. Now the Sunday brunch and lobster bisque were a conversation piece.

David and Cydney arrived before the others. The ordered mimosa and drank a toast to a wonderful weekend. Cydney beamed as she relived the happenings of the morning to David, as if he had not been there.

Once again Harland found them sitting cheek to cheek and he wondered if they were lovers. Of course, he would never ask. Roger and Gloria came in soon after. Cydney's rosy cheeks and bright smile were infectious and when asked about the morning she was not hesitant or shy about relaying the wonderful events that she had experienced.

David was right, the lobster bisque was to die for and she ate lavishly on delicacies she had never tasted before. Her mind and heart full of Chicago, she was content to sit back and listen to Roger and Gloria's stories about life in this magnificent city, knowing it would end all too soon. David sat silent too, but more interested in watching Cydney than listening to Roger and Gloria's tales. Harland also was very quiet. Not only did he watch Cydney, but he watched David, and he knew by the restrained smile on his face and the twinkle in his eyes, that he did, indeed, love Cydney.

When at last they returned to the hotel, David sat in her room while Cydney packed. Again, he watched her graceful movements and elegant demureness. He knew Phillip was waiting and that the drive back to Champaign was long, but he was reluctant to see her go.

"Cydney, will you go out with me on New Year's Eve?"

"New Year's eve?" she laughed. "How can I go out with you on New Year's Eve? You'll be in New York won't you?"

He just nodded and then reached inside his jacket pocket and drew out a large envelope. He walked over to her and pressed it into her hand. She looked down, confused.

"What's this?" She opened it. "David! Is this what I think it is? Is this an airline ticket?"

He laughed, too. He picked her up and spun her around. "Please come Cydney! Come to New York for New Year's Eve. We'll usher in the New Year together. Please?"

"I don't know what to say."

"Then say you'll come. You said you had a wonderful time this weekend and New York will be even better. Please come. I don't have any concerts scheduled between Christmas and New Years. My last performance is the 23rd so I'll have lots of free time."

Such emotion rushed over her. She did have a wonderful weekend. She loved the time they spent together. She loved being with David and experiencing how he lived. But New York! That was a lifetime away from Balsam Hills, Wisconsin, from her grandfather and Leta, from Brock and the farm. But her grandfather always said life was an adventure just waiting to happen. She looked at David and saw the excitement brimming in his eyes. She was so choked up she couldn't speak. She just nodded and David let out a holler and swept her up in his arms. She was coming to New York!

Saying good-bye was difficult and time was so limited. Phillip had already collected her bags and was waiting patiently in the lobby when David escorted her down to the car. He kissed her lightly several times and they shared one final lingering kiss. She laughed out loud when he whispered something in her ear as he helped her into the car. As it sped away from the curb, she turned and saw him waving. She waved back and then rested her head on the back of the seat. Unknowingly, a smile crossed her lips.

Several times during the drive back to Champaign, she opened her handbag just to make sure the plane ticket was still tucked safely inside.

CHAPTER TWENTY-FOUR

Carmen was eagerly waiting Cydney's return. She wanted to know each and every detail, no matter how small, about the weekend and she wanted to tell Cydney about the fabulous apartment she found for them.

They sat on their beds, cross-legged and facing each other, drinking a beer. "Start at the very beginning," Carmen prompted her, "I want to know *everything!*" They laughed together and Cydney started her story. She glazed over a few details about the bathtub and how close she and David had come to making love. But the color in her cheeks betrayed her and Carmen sensed that there was more. "Are you lovers?" she asked boldly.

"Carmen!" Cydney acted shocked.

"Well, are you?"

"No, we aren't. At least not yet."

"What does that mean?"

"Carmen, David has invited me to New York for New Year's Eve. He even gave me an airline ticket."

"Well, I hope you're going! You are, aren't you?" Cydney just nodded. "Great!" was Carmen's only reply. They talked on and on and Carmen could tell from Cydney's expressions and the twinkle in her eye that she was falling for David.

"I owe you so much, Carmen." Cydney continued, "You helped me with my clothes and taught me some of the social graces. Actually,

I probably will need more help. David knows all the right places to go and the right things to say and do. I usually watch him and I think he catches on and is subtle about it. Most of the time he orders for me because I don't even know what half of the stuff on the menu is. Besides, he said it's proper for a gentleman to order for a lady. I guess you could say I'm a modern day Pygmalion. You will help me some more won't you Car?"

"Only if you promise that I can be in the wedding." Carmen giggled like a little girl and Cydney blushed at the thought of it.

"Deal," she said, and they each leaned forward and touched their beer cans together.

The next morning as they left to look at the apartment, Cydney was still on a natural high. She had slept well but memories of Chicago and the upcoming trip to New York for New Year's Eve filled her with excitement.

The apartment turned out to be only two short blocks from campus and it was perfect for them. It was the second floor of an old Victorian style house. It had a huge living room with a fireplace that burned on natural gas, a small kitchen, two good-sized bedrooms and an enormous bathroom that had the toilet and shower in one room and a vanity with two sinks in an adjoining room. The whole apartment was painted a pale green but neither of the girls minded that. They signed the lease and Carmen paid the security deposit. Cydney promised to reimburse her for half when she got the money her grandfather was sending. She had called and asked him for another loan and he agreed. Cydney still didn't know about the trust fund Mr. Hathaway had set up for her years earlier. It had a substantial balance due to high interest rates and Caleb planned to tell her about it and give her the rest of the money on her twenty-first birthday. In the meantime, Caleb let her believe the money was a loan.

The girls stopped for lunch and yakked about all the things they had to do before Christmas. Plus, this week was finals! They both had their work cut out for them.

First thing on Cydney's mind was getting her Christmas gifts mailed home, after that she would hit the books and after her last test on Thursday, which would be December 20th, they would get ready to go to Jackson. They would come back to Champaign on Wednesday, the 26th and shop for some things they needed for the apartment. They planned to move on Saturday and Sunday, the 29th and 30th. Monday morning, the 31st Cydney would be flying to New York.

While they ate, they made notes and penned a layout of the apartment, jotting down what pieces of furniture would go where and what accessories and incidentals they would need to furnish the place. They could start shopping right away because Carmen had a charge card and her father paid the balance without ever questioning any of her purchases. Cydney thought she had never been so excited. Life was good!

When they left the restaurant, a bitter wind from the north stung their faces and a driving snow was falling. It was piling up fast and Cydney hoped it wouldn't last long enough to interfere with their plans for the upcoming week. The streets were getting slippery as they made their way to the post office, Carmen crawling along at a snail's pace.

David, God bless him, had arranged for Marshall Fields to package her purchases for shipping and she was so grateful now that he had insisted on doing that. The bulkiest one was, of course, the painting for Brock. In spite of the ice and snow, she managed to get them all to the window in only three trips from the car and was overjoyed when the mail clerk informed her that the packages would arrive at their destination before Christmas. Back in the warm car, a thought hit Cydney like a ton of bricks, "Carmen!" she virtually screamed, "Oh, God, Carmen." Carmen trying desperately to concentrate on driving on the treacherous roads was confused.

"What? Cydney, what is it?" She glanced back and forth from Cydney to the slush covered streets.

"Oh God, Carmen, I didn't get anything for David for Christmas. I never even thought of that. What am I going to do?"

Carmen started laughing, "Must be true love!"

"That's not funny, Car. David helped me shop for all my family and I didn't even think about a gift for him. How awful of me! I feel just terrible!" She buried her face in her hands.

"Come on, Cyd, take it easy. Let's get out of this weather and then will figure something out. Do we have any beer or wine in our room?"

"I don't think so. Why?"

"Why? Because I always think better with a drink in my hand, that's why. Let's stop and get a bottle of wine. I'm sure we can smuggle it up to our room along with all this other stuff we have." Carmen pulled to the curb when she saw a liquor mart, grabbed her purse and ID, "Come on," she said, "let's stock up and ride out the storm."

Cydney knew nothing about wine, so she chose the snacks, got some small paper plates and napkins while Carmen picked out the wine. The clerk was watching a small TV set on a shelf behind the counter. "Getting ready to settle in for the night? Looks like this ones gonna be a doozey," he said nodding toward the black and white weatherman. "Sez to stay home if you can, he's not recommending traveling in this."

"How long is it going to last?" Carmen asked as she flashed her driver's license at him. He scanned it and looked at her over the top of his nose-pinched glasses and nodded approval.

"Probably gonna go on most of the night. You gals students?" They both nodded and gathered up their packages. "You should probably go right back to campus," he said sounding fatherly, "they say the roads will be almost impassable in a few hours. Pretty little gals like you don't want to be stranded alone in weather like this." He winked, shattering the fatherly image.

They thanked him and ventured back to the car. They decided to take his advice because Carmen admitted that she didn't have a lot of experience driving on snow and ice. She was, after all, from Mississippi, where icy roads and snow are rare.

Although it was against the rules, most students brought beer and other alcohol into the dorms. No one ever seemed to check and for as long as Cydney and Carmen had been at Bradford Hall no one had ever been caught. Actually, neither of the girls knew what the penalty was, so it wasn't even an issue with them.

Back at Bradford, the students were rowdy. Many of them were outside throwing snowballs and one couple was building a snowman. Some of the dorm windows were open and Christmas music filtered down. A scenario that would excite anyone: end of semester, close to Christmas, first measurable snow fall of the season.

They lugged their packages upstairs and both changed into sweats. They, too, opened the window a little, turned on some Christmas music and cracked open the wine. They both knew they needed to study but first they had this other problem to deal with; what to do about David's Christmas present, or lack of one.

"First of all, what would I ever buy someone like David?" Cydney asked.

"Well, kiddo, you know him a whole heck of a lot better than I do."

"Well, one good thing, he knows I don't have any money, so it doesn't have to be expensive. Just meaningful."

"How 'bout a pack of condoms?" Carmen shrieked with laughter and ducked as Cydney threw a pillow at her.

"That's not funny! Come on, I need your help. How am I ever going to explain that I forgot to get him something?"

"Look, Cyd, I don't know what you can get him, but why not call him and say that you didn't want to mail his present because you wanted to give it to him personally, then you can get something and give it to him on New Year's Eve."

"That's a great idea, Car. Thank you, that's exactly what I'll do. Now I just have to concentrate on what to buy for him."

"What are some of his interests? I mean beside music? What does he do in his spare time?"

"Well, I know he jogs and he's really into the arts. He likes to read and he plays chess and — Carmen, I've got it! What if I bought him a book, a really nice book about Wisconsin? Its history, its people, its interesting places. And he'll know that I want him to know what Wisconsin is really like." She sat cross-legged (Brock style) on the bed and stared into her roommate's face, waiting for a reaction.

Carmen sat cross-legged, too, (Cydney taught her) with her hands held out like two scales of justice, "Let's see," she said alternately moving her arms up and down and trying to suppress a smile, "condoms or a book, condoms or a book." They both burst out laughing. "Truthfully, Cyd, that's a great idea." They clinked their plastic wine glasses together and drained them. With that major problem solved, they refilled their glasses, and hit the books.

By morning the storm had abated and the air was clean and fresh. The sun shone and light, fluffy snow clung to the trees and bushes. It was a beautiful sight. The girls dressed in warm clothes and even put on boots to trek across campus in the foot-deep snow to take an economics test. "Just keep telling yourself that in just four more days we'll be basking in the sun by the pool," Carmen reminded her.

Cydney knew Carmen was not very fond of the cold and snow and she was really looking forward to going home for Christmas, especially since she hadn't gone home for Thanksgiving. By mid-afternoon the December sun had warmed enough to melt most of the snow on the streets and sidewalks, creating a slushy mess. The Bradford Hall snowman was standing at a precarious angle but Christmas music could still be heard and the excitement was still running high. Students who had already completed their exams were saying their good-byes and going home. Carmen and Cydney knew they would soon be among them.

They ordered a pizza for supper and studied most of the evening. Carmen had one test on Wednesday and two on Thursday. Cydney didn't have any on Wednesday, but two on Thursday. They snacked and drank more wine and fell exhausted into bed about eleven, one day closer to Jackson.

The girls were a little worried when they woke to snow on Thursday morning but by noon, when they were both done with exams, the snow ended and the sun came out. They hurried back to their dorm room, packed their clothes and Carmen's car and with the radio belting out ***Jingle Bell Rock*** they headed south toward Christmas in Dixie.

CHAPTER TWENTY-FIVE

The bright red Mustang sped along the road, Carmen handling it well. Together they sang Christmas carols and enjoyed the sun, already warm on their faces. They had left the snow just south of the Kentucky, Tennessee border where they spent the night at a Holiday Inn. Carmen wanted something classier but Cydney convinced her they would only be sleeping there so why spend the extra money. Now as the gap between them and Jackson narrowed, Carmen became more excited and talkative. She told Cydney about her parents. They were sixtyish but didn't look it, especially her mother. They drank too much and enjoyed entertaining, especially when the kids brought college friends home. Her oldest brother, Donovan was working on his PhD at a small school in upstate New York and he was bringing his girlfriend home for the holidays. Geoff, her other brother, also older, was working on his masters in veterinary medicine at Texas A&M in Galveston and he was bringing home a college buddy.

"No, he's not gay," she said when Cydney threw her a sidelong glance, "in fact," Carmen continued, "he's the biggest pain in the ass there is. Thinks he's a real ladies man, so watch out. When he sees you, he'll be blown away. He'll have his hands all over you."

"Hey, that thought never crossed my mind," Cydney said in reference to her gay statement. "Have you ever fallen for any of his friends?"

"Yeah, once I did and that was a big mistake. It was summer right after high school graduation and my parents were having a big party.

I had too much to drink and thought he would love me forever, you know? Then after we snuck away and – well you know, after we did it, he went back to the party and never looked my way again."

Cydney gasped, "You mean you – you lost your virginity to him and it was just a one night stand?"

"It was more like a one hour stand," Carmen laughed. "Don't worry about it, Cyd, you're just naïve. Wait 'til you get to New York, you'll see what the party scene is like. Lots of drinking, drugs, the whole shebang! I'm really surprised you didn't get a taste of it in Chicago."

"Drugs? I would never do drugs! You don't, right Car? I mean we've known each other quite a while now and I'm pretty sure you don't use, right?"

"Right, I don't - but I did, once or twice and it just didn't do much for me."

"What did you try?" Cydney wanted to know.

"Well, pot a couple of times and then once I took a snort." Carmen could see the look of disapproval on Cydney's face. "Hey, I swear, it was just those few times that same summer that I got laid and I vowed I would never do it again and I haven't. I'm more mature now and have some goals to meet"

"Good," Cydney said. "I'm sure David's too mature for such a thing, too. Although, musicians sometimes are a little weird. I'll ask him when I see him again."

The road was now parallel with a white rail fence and Carmen hooped, "We're almost there!" Just ahead, Cydney could see two stone pillars that rose about eight feet high with a white wrought iron gate and an overhead inscription that read simply *Prather Estate*.

Carmen reached below the dash and with a flick of her wrist, the gate swung open wide. The large oak trees that lined the blacktop driveway formed a canopy that stretched ahead of them for at least a half mile. When the mansion came into view, Cydney drew in her breath. It was gorgeous.

In the middle of the circle drive, was a white marble cherub, his head back, his arms stretched heavenward, spewing water from his mouth. It cascaded down his naked body into a swirling fountain of exotic fish.

The house itself was tall and elegant. Four white pillars graced the front entrance, two on each side of a semi-circle of tile steps leading to the double front door. Above the pillars were three balconies jutting out from the second floor bedrooms, French doors were visible on each balcony. To the left was a veranda with a tile floor and huge potted palms. Pine, magnolia and more oak trees shaded it. A perfect spot to relax on a hot afternoon. To the right was a screen porch with white wicker furniture and more potted plants. Carmen pulled around to the left side of the house explaining that the garages and riding stables were in the back. Cydney was speechless. Never had she seen such a beautiful house. She couldn't imagine living here. Carmen noticed Cydney's eyes darting back and forth, taking it all in.

"Well, what do you think?" Carmen asked, "Is it suitable for a Christmas party?"

"Oh, Carmen," Cydney let out a long, low breath, "it's like Tara Mansion. It's so beautiful. Going home with me at Thanksgiving must have been a real let down for you."

"Nonsense!" Carmen reassured her, "It's not the outside that matters, Cyd, it's what's inside and let me tell you, things aren't always rosy on the inside here. Your family was genuine and sincere. You might find that lacking here. We always start out okay but then someone says something which offends someone else and before you know it we're all shouting at each other and someone gets pissed off, but, hey, they're my family no matter how dysfunctional they are." She laughed and Cydney guessed there were things Carmen wasn't telling her.

A butler came out, greeted Carmen with a warm smile and collected their bags.

"Andrew, Cydney. Cydney, Andrew," Carmen nodded. The white haired gentleman again flashed the warm smile, this time at Cydney.

"Charmed, Missy. I hope you enjoy your stay here."

"Thank you, Andrew," Cydney managed to say although her mouth was still gapping. "I'm sure I will."

In the kitchen, which was just behind the veranda, two women in black dresses and aprons were busy preparing food. "Hi!" Carmen practically shouted as the girls came in. Both women, recognizing the voice turned and came forward to greet them.

"Carmen, dear, welcome home," black dress number one said, kissing Carmen lightly on the cheek.

"So good to see you, dear," black dress number two added holding up her hands that had just been plucking at a large head of lettuce. She touched cheeks with Carmen and together they stood sizing up Cydney.

"This is my dear friend, Cydney Brown. We room together at college. I spent Thanksgiving with Cydney and her family in Wisconsin so I wanted her to celebrate Christmas with us."

"How wonderful, dear. So nice to meet you Cydney," said black dress number one.

"We do hope you have a pleasant holiday here at Prather," added black dress number two.

"Cydney," Carmen said gesturing toward the uniformed ladies, "this is Louise and Luella. They have worked for my parents for years. In fact, they mostly raised me and I love them dearly," she said hugging both at once. "And tomorrow I will ask them to make my very favorite dessert."

"I'm very pleased to be here," Cydney managed to say still in awe of her surroundings.

The girls headed for the foyer and Carmen looked over her shoulder and blew the women a kiss. Carmen took the wide, curved staircase two steps at a time and soon she was showing Cydney the second floor. Three bedrooms faced the front of the house and four more faced the back and while the back rooms lacked the balconies that the front rooms had, the back rooms had huge windows that looked out over a kidney shaped swimming pool and a vast area of grassland and pastures. In the distance a small river cut through the property. Carmen rambled on, pointing out pieces of art and crystal ware that she knew Cydney would recognize by name. There were four bathrooms on this floor along with a large sitting room. Carmen showed Cydney to her room, where Andrew had already deposited her bags. Then they went on to Carmen's room. It was a typical little rich girl's room. A canopy brass bed and large armoires filled the room. The curtains were lace as well as the coverlet of the big oversized bed. There was a TV set and several easy chairs. One entire wall was closets and the exterior of the doors were full-length mirrors. Cydney knew how many clothes Carmen had so this was no surprise.

"Darling, you're home!" came a deep voice from the doorway.

"Mother!" Carmen yelped. "Yes, I'm home! Merry Christmas!" The two embraced but Carmen pulled back quickly knowing her mother had already been drinking. "How was France?" Carmen went on.

"France was lovely dear, but we can talk about that later. Come, introduce me to your friend."

"This is Cydney Brown, Mother. We room together and she was nice enough to invite me to Wisconsin to celebrate Thanksgiving with her family, since mine deserted me." Cydney noticed the mother's smile faded ever so slightly and her left eyebrow shot up almost to her hairline.

"Cydney, this is my mother, Angeline Prather."

"Welcome, Cydney," Mrs. Prather said with a genuine smile and handshake. "Is this your first visit to Mississippi?"

"This is my first visit to just about anyplace, Mrs. Prather." Carmen was right about her mother, she didn't look sixty-something. In fact, she looked quite young. Her bottle blonde hair was short and pert. It was swept back from her face in a feathery brush cut with a few strands casually dipped down on her forehead. She was slim and graceful. Her nails were perfectly manicured and she had applied her make up with great care. She was truly an attractive woman.

"Thank you for having me. Your home is so beautiful."

"Thank you, dear. I hope you will be comfortable here and that you have a wonderful Christmas even if you cannot be with your family."

"Have the boys arrived yet, Mother?" Carmen was referring of course, to her brothers.

"Not yet, but I expect them before dinner."

"And where's Daddy? Is he here or at his office?"

"He's at the office now, but I expect him shortly. Why don't you girls get unpacked and then freshen up. We'll all meet in the living room at six," Angeline headed for the door, "And again, Cydney, welcome to our home. We're so happy to have you."

"Thank you, Mrs. Prather." She left the room and closed the door quietly behind her.

"Carmen, your mother is beautiful."

"Yeah, she is, isn't she?" Carmen laughed. "But wait until tonight, when you see her all sloshed. She won't be quite so charming."

They toured the rest of the house, up and down and then returned to their respective rooms. Cydney unpacked, showered and just finished dressing when she heard squeals from the hallway. She opened the door and looked out but the hallway was empty. She could tell the racket was coming from the main foyer so she walked to the top of the staircase. Below Carmen was jumping up and down excitedly, hugging a whole group of people. The five of them made quite a din. Finally, one tall, handsome man looked up and saw Cydney watching them. He let out a low wolf whistle.

"And who do we have here?" He planted one foot on the first step and the other on the floor. His light brown hair hung down a few inches on his collar. He wore cowboy boots and khaki pants and a pale blue crew neck sweater, the collar of a plaid shirt peeked out the top. He displayed perfectly straight, white teeth when he smiled and Cydney knew this had to be Geoff.

"Cydney, come down and meet my brothers and their friends," Carmen shouted.

Cydney started her descent. She tried to walk straight and tall. She had chosen a pair of gray woolen slacks and a soft white sweater with small black beads and sequins at the neck, waist and cuffs. She wore small pearl earrings and had her hair arranged in a twist. Geoff never took his eyes off her and she could feel her face starting to flush. When she reached the bottom step they stood eye to eye. He didn't wait for any introductions. Instead, he took her hand and helped her down the last step.

"Hello," he said smoothly, "I'm Geoff Prather."

"I know," she said. "Carmen described you perfectly." They all laughed.

Carmen finished the introductions. Geoff's friend Tony, Donovan and his girlfriend, Victoria. The group moved into the living room where they shared stories about their respective colleges and got better acquainted. Cydney was relaxed and comfortable thanks to the bottle of wine that Donovan opened and passed around. They drank a toast to getting an education, to being together again and to new friends.

"Another new experience," Cydney said to herself. "I think I'm going to like it here."

At precisely 6:00 p.m., Angeline and her husband entered the living room arm and arm. Carmen literally flew into her father's arms. He picked her right off the floor and swung her around. They hugged and kissed and then hugged again. Angeline stood off to the side watching father and daughter embrace. Cydney thought she saw a twitch tugging at the corner of Angeline's mouth.

Finally, Carmen pulled free, "Daddy, I want you to meet my dearest friend, Cydney Brown."

Mr. Prather advanced toward Cydney, his snow-white hair impeccably groomed. His skin tanned and healthy looking. He was a big man with drastic features that gave him a certain aura. When he spoke, his voice was deep but gentle.

"Cydney," he said smiling down at her, "welcome to our home. If you can put up with the likes of my impetuous daughter you must be a saint, indeed. And a beautiful saint, I might add. Hasn't Geoff cornered you yet?"

"Thank you Mr. Prather. I cherish the friendship I have with your daughter, and yes at times she is impetuous. As far as Geoff goes, Carmen warned me about him, so I think I can handle it."

"Let's all have something to drink then," he said much louder. Angeline rang a small silver bell and Andrew came in with a large bucket of ice and a tray of glasses. One of the black dresses also appeared but Cydney couldn't remember if it was Louise or Luella. She carried a large silver serving tray full of attractively arranged hors d'oeuvres. Cydney remembered what both David and Carmen taught her. If you're going to drink, you have to eat.

Mr. Prather, Charles, as he asked everyone to call him, prided himself in making the best cocktail in Mississippi, so he started the task while the rest of them talked quietly among themselves. Cydney looked around the vast room. It was aglow with Christmas lights and numerous decorations. The ceilings were high and trimmed with crown moldings, the windows were tall and draped with fashionable dressings.

Everything looked expensive. In fact, Cydney thought, the whole place reeked of money. In spite of that, she was enjoying it.

When dinner was finally served at 9:00 p.m., Cydney could feel the effects of the drinks she had consumed. She reminded herself to slow down. Geoff conveniently seated himself next to her at the long table, but she didn't mind. When he reached over under the security of the tablecloth and put his hand on her knee, she simply brushed it away. The second time he did it, she pinched the back of his hand as hard as she could. He let out a little squeal but obviously got the message.

"So, Cydney, what does your father do in Wisconsin?" Charles asked.

"Well, sir, uh, Charles," Cydney stammered, a little embarrassed. "I lived with my grandfather." She hadn't expected this question and wasn't sure what to say so she opted for the truth, "You see, my mother was very young when I was born and my father never married her."

"So it was just the two of you?" The other conversations had stopped and everyone was listening, but Cydney just went on, they would have to accept her for what she was, like it or not.

"Well, no. My mother couldn't care for me because she was trying to finish high school so my grandfather hired an Indian woman to care for me and my grandmother, who was ill at the time. She died when I was six and then my mother left, so Leta, that was who my grandfather hired, just stayed on and cared for us."

"An Indian, you say?" Angeline interjected in a shrill voice.

"Yes, an Indian," Cydney confirmed.

"Well," Angeline went on, "I guess everyplace has its low life to contend with. I mean, we have the blacks here in Mississippi and you have the Indians."

"You don't understand," Cydney's voice was rising along with her emotions. "There are several Indian reservations in Wisconsin. Leta is a Chippewa. Indians are very intelligent and astute people and they are an integral part of Wisconsin and its history."

"Whatever you say, dear," Angeline said in a patronizing manner. "But to me, the very word *Indian* conjures up an image of wild savages."

"That's very narrow minded of you, mother," Carmen interrupted. Angeline once again raised an eyebrow at her daughter and then turned backed to Cydney.

"Where is your grandfather now?" Charles asked.

"He still lives on the family farm. Leta lives there, too. She just stayed on when we all left."

"And what does he raise on the farm?" Charles seemed genuinely interested.

"Well, when he was younger he had dairy cows, some chickens and beef cattle, but now he does mostly cash cropping." Cydney's temperament had mellowed and she no longer found it necessary to be defensive.

"May I ask how old your grandfather is?" Charles inquired.

"Yes, of course, well, let me see, he's uh - 59 years old." Cydney said, doing the math in her head.

"He must be in very good physical condition," Charles went on, "farming is hard work."

Cydney had an answer for all their questions, "He is in good shape. But he has a hired man who helps him out." Of course, she was referring to Brock.

"Is he an Indian too?" Angeline asked.

"Yes, as a matter of fact, he is." Cydney remained calm, "Actually, half Indian, his mother was white."

"Down here," Charles stated flatly, "the blacks don't consort with the whites. It's heavily frowned on."

Again, Cydney held her composure, "Wisconsinites aren't segregationists," she said in an even tone. This time Charles raised an eyebrow.

"But is your grandfather able to make a decent living on a small farm in Wisconsin?" Angeline put in, her words slurred from a steady consumption of whiskey.

"Mother!" Carmen shouted, "How rude of you!"

The rest of the group ate in silence. Victoria kept her eyes fixed on her dinner plate. She could feel the tension in the air and she knew what Cydney was going through since she too, had been the subject of an interrogation last Christmas, which was her first visit to Prather. She wondered sometimes why she came back, but of course, it was because of Donovan.

"Please excuse my mother, Cydney," Carmen said. "She tends to drink when she should be eating." The girls exchanged glances, each feeling embarrassed for the other.

"How dare you make apologies for me!" Angeline shrieked, rising from her chair. She started to tip but Charles was right there to take her arm.

"Please excuse us," Charles said steering Angeline out of the dining room and up the gracefully curved staircase.

When their parents had left the room, Donovan, Geoff and Carmen all apologized again to their friends. Victoria leaned over and kissed Donovan on the cheek, Tony was silent.

"Happens all the time," Geoff said just shrugging his shoulders, "but if you come again," he said directing this statement to Cydney, "she'll leave you alone. Just ask Victoria." Cydney looked her way and Victoria just smiled.

"Well, hell," Donovan said, "let's not let this ruin our evening. Let's eat!" He reached for the little silver bell that was now sitting by Angeline's place. He shook it several times and Andrew appeared with a fresh bottle of wine. He moved silently around the table filling the glasses. One of the black dresses also appeared again bearing dinner rolls and salad. The group sat quietly while they were being served. When they left the room, Donovan raised his glass in a toast. He smiled and looked around the table. "To a Merry Christmas." They all raised their glasses, sipped the wonderful cranberry wine, and started eating the first course.

CHAPTER TWENTY-SIX

The sun was already high in the sky when Cydney woke. The wine and whiskey had obviously thrust her into a deep sleep. They were also slowing her down this morning. Her head throbbed slightly and she hoped some coffee and breakfast would ease the pounding. She had one of the back bedrooms that overlooked the pool and the grounds and she could hear conversation coming from the pool area. She opened the large window and leaned out.

"Good morning," she called down. Geoff and Tony were already poolside. The temperature was rising quickly and the pool, on the south side of the mansion, captured all available sunshine.

"Hey Cyd," Geoff called up to her, "get on your suit and come on down. It's really warm down here."

"I just got up!" she said. "I need some coffee."

"Too much whiskey?" chided Tony.

"No, that would have been Angeline," Cydney mused back.

"Come on down," Geoff continued, ignoring her comments. "I'll have Luella bring your breakfast out here. Is Car up yet? Tony wants to see what she looks like in a bikini!"

"If she isn't, I'll get her up and we'll be right down." Cydney was anxious to get out in the warm sun.

Carmen heard the clamor from the pool and had the comforter pulled up over her head when Cydney knocked on the door. "Don't come in unless you have a pot of black coffee and some aspirin," Carmen's voice was muffled.

"Come on Car, the pool looks great. Geoff said he would order breakfast for us poolside."

"I know, I heard. Oh God, Cyd, my head is pounding. What time is it anyway?"

"Mine is too, Car, but I think we'll feel better after we eat something. It's already 10:30."

"Guess we can't chastise Mother too much." Carmen laughed. "I think by the time our little party broke up last night, we were all a little tipsy. Have you seen or heard anything of Donovan and Victoria?"

"No, I only know that Tony is waiting to see you in a bikini. Come on Car, get up. Give him something to look at." Carmen spilled out onto the carpet. Cydney was surprised to find her naked and let out a little gasp.

"Oh, sorry," Carmen said. "I couldn't find my nightgown and anyway, I like to sleep naked." She threw on a robe and retreated to the bathroom. "Go ahead, go on down. I'm going to stop off in the kitchen and order dessert."

Cydney went back to her room and put on her swim suit. Although it wasn't a bikini, it was two pieces and the top was quite scanty. It showed enough of her lovely body to intrigue any man. She took a towel and her cover up and headed for the sunshine. Once again, Geoff let out a long, low whistle as she approached, his eyes boring into her. His smile widened and he pulled out one of the chaise lounge chairs for her.

"Good morning, gorgeous," he said. "Breakfast will be here shortly. Sit down and enjoy the sun. It's really warm already. The weatherman says record warmth for the weekend. That means you can go back to school with a tan."

Cydney settled into the long low chair just as Donovan and Victoria appeared. They both wore short white terry cloth robes; their arms around each other, their bodies close. They looked and acted like lovers, who shared an intimate secret. Cydney felt a little twinge. She thought of David. She had to admit she missed him and would be anxious to see him and New York.

Carmen showed up, carrying a pot of coffee, one of the black dresses in tow, with some breads and rolls neatly arranged on a silver serving tray. Andrew followed with a tray of assorted juices and milk. They spoke with everyone and it was obvious to Cydney that they enjoyed the presence of the young people very much. Maybe more so than the parents did. Cydney wondered, in fact, where the parents were.

"Will your parents be joining us?" she asked to which ever Prather child was listening. Donovan, Geoff and Carmen all looked at each other and started laughing.

"Nah, I don't think so, Cydney," Geoff said, "truth is Mother's probably still sleeping and Father left for the office very early. Mother will be up by noon and it will take her a good share of the afternoon to get herself together and presentable for tonight. Charles will be back just in time for cocktails and then we'll probably have a rerun of last night."

"It's Saturday. Does your father go to his office everyday?" Cydney thought it was her turn to ask the questions.

"Well, let's see," Donovan put in, "today's the 22nd, he'll be home on the 25th for Christmas and probably on December 31, New Years Eve, New Years Day and oh yeah, maybe tomorrow since it's Sunday." They all laughed again, but Cydney could tell, it was really no joke.

"That's right," she told Carmen, "It's the 22nd. I need to call the farm this afternoon. Everyone will be there for the holidays and it's the twins' birthday today. I wonder if there is snow." The last sentence was more to herself than anyone else and she felt a pang of loneliness stirring in her gut.

It was late afternoon and Cydney had retreated to her room to make that special phone call. She was showing signs of a tan and just needed some time alone. The young people had truly enjoyed each other's company. After basking in the sun, they went horseback riding and had a late lunch on the veranda. Cydney had to ward off Geoff's advances several times but she had to admit she was flattered and enjoyed his company. Carmen and Tony hit it off quite well, although they had met before and Carmen didn't seem interested in him then. Donovan and Victoria, well, it was obvious, they were in love.

"Uncle Aaron!" Cydney almost shouted into the phone, "Merry Christmas."

"Cydney! We miss you! How are things in Mississippi?"

"Well, it's quite warm here. We sat by the pool this morning and I got a little bit of a tan. Is there snow?"

Aaron could tell she was a little homesick. "Had a dusting on Thursday and a couple of inches last night. But it's pretty cold, so I'm sure the snow will stick around and we'll have a white Christmas."

"How're Aunt Patrice and the twins?"

"Well after we're done visiting, you can talk with all of them. School going good?"

"Yes, that last week of tests was pretty grueling, but I think I did good."

"And David? You still see David? I heard you're going to New York? You're becoming quite a worldly woman, Cyd." It was so good to hear his voice. She missed them all so much.

In turn she talked with Aunt Patrice, her grandfather and Leta. The gifts she sent had arrived safely and everyone was anxious to open them on Christmas Eve. They, in turn, had sent gifts to her, which would probably be waiting for her at the dorm, when she returned to school. They talked about the new apartment and she gave Leta her new address. She would call with a phone number as soon as the phone was installed.

"Well, I really should hang up now," Cydney was saying to Leta. "I'm calling from Carmen's parents' house and it must be expensive. Leta, I miss you all so much. Please tell everyone how much I miss them and I hope you all have a wonderful Christmas. Give the twins a big hug and kiss for me."

Leta was saying her goodbyes too and then, as an after thought, "By the way, Cyd, Brock and Ellen got married last weekend. It was just a small, simple ceremony. Brock seems very happy, he asked me to tell you."

Cydney felt her throat tighten, she didn't know if she could speak. "Oh, that's great," she tried to sound cheerful. "Tell Brock, I'm so happy for them." She cradled the phone, tears stung her eyes. She took a deep breath. Well, she knew it was going to happen. Brock was smart and handsome and single, (well single no more) of course some woman was going to latch onto him. And if she hadn't left Balsam Hills, she could have been that woman. Instead she chose college and career, so she would just have to live with it. Brock was married. No need for her to think about him anymore or to fret about it. She showered and dressed. It was almost cocktail hour.

On Sunday, Carmen and Cydney drove into Jackson to go shopping. It was just two days before Christmas and the malls were packed. Carols rang out over the loudspeaker system and colorful decorations were everywhere. Cydney had never spent a Christmas away from home and never one without snow. She was having a difficult time getting psyched up. Cydney had already purchased all her gifts but she wanted to buy a little something for Carmen's parents to show her appreciation. Carmen said it wasn't necessary but when Cydney insisted, she suggested a certain kind of confectionary that her parents dearly loved. They didn't buy it very often because they preferred to drink their calories but Carmen thought it appropriate to splurge at Christmas time.

And Carmen was adamant about buying Cydney an evening dress for New York. She wouldn't take no for an answer so reluctantly, Cydney agreed.

"How can I ever repay you, Car?" Cydney asked. "You have taught me so much and I will always be grateful to you." Carmen shrugged it off and continued looking through the rack of dresses. "And someday maybe I'll have enough money to repay you."

"Anything catch your eye, Cyd?"

"Not yet."

"Well keep looking, we're buying you a new dress for New Year's Eve and that's final." Carmen was obstinate.

Finally, Cydney held one up. "This one," she said confidently.

Carmen caught her breath. "It's beautiful!"

Cydney carefully removed the plastic covering and closely inspected the dress. She found her way to a fitting room to try it on. Carmen waited patiently to critique it but when Cydney appeared she could only gasp. It was a beautiful dress and Cydney wore it so well. The bodice was covered in dark navy blue sequins that sparkled no matter which way she turned. It covered only one shoulder exposing the slightly sun tanned skin of the other. The crepe skirt, also dark navy, hung straight in soft folds and fell to her ankles. A slit on the side exposed her right leg to mid-thigh.

"Wow, Cyd," she said in a barely audible tone, "you look just stunning. David will never let you out of his sight."

"It is pretty, isn't it?" Cydney turned from side to side in the three-way mirror, looking at herself from every possible angle.

"Pretty! Pretty doesn't begin to describe it. It's indescribable. No telling what will happen when David sees you in that!" The girls both agreed that this was the perfect dress for Cydney and although it was very expensive, Carmen seemed nonchalant about it. She laughed when Cydney told her that all the clothes in her closet didn't cost as much as this one dress.

When they had shopped until they were ready to drop, they lunched and then Carmen gave Cydney a tour of Old Jackson and some of its attractions. There was Jackson State University, the Old Capitol Museum, the Smith-Robertson Museum and Cultural Center, the War Memorial Building and Mississippi Agriculture and Forestry Museum. Of course, they couldn't forget to visit the Mississippi Symphony Orchestra building so Cydney could tell David all about it.

Cydney remembered that today, the 23rd, was David's last concert of the year. She would call him in the morning to wish him a Merry Christmas and finalize her travel plans.

The girls were on a natural high, as young ladies are after a day of shopping and sight seeing, but they were eager to get back to Prather to freshen up and join the group. Cydney now knew the routine was cocktails in either the living room or on the veranda, depending on the weather, followed by dinner in the exquisite dining room just off the foyer where Andrew, Luella and Louise would once again have prepared a feast.

After the first evening of intense interrogation by Carmen's parents and jibes and innuendos between mother and daughter, things went pretty well. However, Cydney did feel that Angeline Prather was a bit of a snob. She lacked the warmth and sincerity that Carmen, Geoff and Donovan all seemed to have.

While the house was aglow with Christmas lights and candles and holly berry and greenery were everywhere something was lacking. Several times during the evening, Cydney swallowed hard to rid her throat of the lump that kept her from truly enjoying the evening. She looked out the large dining room windows at the still-green grass and yearned for the snow and cold of Wisconsin, the warmth of the old farm house and the smell of Leta's coffee meandering through the rooms.

Later, alone in her room, she opened the window to let in the pleasant night air. She got in bed and pulled the comforter high around her neck to ward off the chill. Thoughts of home still plagued her and just before she drifted off to sleep, a solitary tear rolled down her cheek as she murmured his name. "Brock."

CHAPTER TWENTY-SEVEN

David sat in the study in a big leather recliner drinking a soda. He was glad to be alone. Harland had left earlier in the day for upstate New York to spend the holidays with relatives and they hadn't parted on the best of terms.

David had given a stellar performance last night and this morning that gossiping bitch from the New York Times wrote another article about him. Like a previous article, it implied that he was gay because he was, after all 28 years old and single. Harland was again pressing David about squelching that rumor but when David brought up Cydney's name, all hell broke loose. Apparently, Harland didn't think Cydney was good enough for David and they argued. David told Harland to mind his own business. Harland told David *he* was his business. Whenever they had a disagreement, which was quite frequent these days, Harland brought up the promises he made to his dear, departed sister, David's Mother.

"You fulfilled your obligation to my mother, Harland," David would say. "I'm all grown up now, see?" But David's capriciousness only made Harland angrier and when David reminded Harland that Cydney would be coming to New York for New Year's Eve, he stormed out.

"Just as well," David said to himself, "he needs time to cool off." He laid his head back and closed his eyes picturing Cydney in New York for the first time. A smile crossed his face. She would be so overwhelmed. They would have such a wonderful time. He reminded himself that he couldn't push her too much. She had told him repeatedly, she wanted to take things slowly. He also reminded himself that she was only 19 years old, which is exactly what Harland said. Too young, too inexperienced, too naïve. David preferred to look at it differently. Young, yes. Naïve, maybe a little. Fresh and exciting – definitely. And she had certainly swept him off his feet. He only wished that he could do the same with her. He was so deep in thought he didn't hear the phone ringing right away.

"David DuPrey here."

"David! Merry Christmas!"

"Cydney! I was just sitting here thinking about you."

"You must have been sleeping, the phone rang about eight times. How are you?"

"Lonesome, and I wasn't sleeping. I was just day dreaming about seeing you again and thinking about all the fun we'll have. Are you still in Mississippi?"

"Yes and David, it's beautiful here. You know I haven't been many places but this is very nice. Carmen's family is very wealthy. They have a mansion and it's warm and sunny and I even got a bit of a sun tan and Carmen's family is very nice, especially her brothers, Geoff and Donovan and their friends. I mean Geoff has a friend named Tony and Donovan has a girlfriend actually, I think they're engaged. Her name is Victoria. But Geoff isn't gay, in fact, he's quite a ladies man...."

"Hold it, Cydney, slow down. You're babbling. You can tell me all those things when you arrive here. Right now I want to know about you. How was the trip to Mississippi?"

"Oh David, I'm sorry, of course. It's just that, well it's just a whirlwind of excitement. We had an uneventful drive, which I guess is good. It was snowing Thursday morning but by the time we reached the Tennessee border the snow was gone and it got pretty warm. I'm fine, David, really I am. A little lonely. This is the very first time I've ever been away from home at Christmas."

"Did you talk with your family yet?"

"Yes, I called on the 22nd because I knew everyone would already be at the farm and it was the twin's birthday. I talked with Grandfather and Leta, with Uncle Aaron and Patrice. They got all the gifts I sent.

Speaking of which, I didn't mail your gift, I wanted to give it to you in person, so you'll just have to wait until I get there."

"Oooh, I can't wait. What is it, Cyd?" They both laughed.

"You have to wait, too," he said referring to the beautiful gold and jewel-studded watch he bought for her at Saks Fifth Avenue. "Cydney, listen! Your plane comes into LaGuardia about noon. Just stay at your gate and I'll be there to meet you, okay? Don't try to go to the baggage claim. You might get lost. The airport will be very crowded. Bring warm clothes. It's supposed to be very cold."

Cydney responded with an "okay" to each command until finally David had finished giving her directions.

"David, do you have decorations and a Christmas tree?"

"Well of course, I do. It's Christmas isn't it? Do you think I'm a scrooge or something?"

"No, I don't. It just seems rather strange that two bachelors, who spend so much time away from home would put up decorations and a tree. Are you going to church tonight?"

"Church? I don't think so, Cydney. I can't remember the last time I went to church."

"It *is* Christmas Eve, you know."

"Yes, I do know that it's Christmas Eve. How about if we go on New Year's Eve, before we go out on the town?"

"That would be lovely, David. You said Harland was going away. Is he gone already?"

"Yup, he left this morning for upstate New York. Going to visit some of his relatives, wanted me to go along but I said no. I don't know many of my mother's relatives and I guess I don't care to know them."

"But then you'll be alone for Christmas!"

"Actually, I won't be Cydney. Roger and Gloria Savage are flying in tomorrow morning and I'm picking them up at the airport and then we're going to have brunch at The Rainbow Room. They'll spend Christmas Day with me and stay the night. Wednesday afternoon, they leave for Rome. So don't worry about me, I won't be lonesome."

"With Gloria Savage there, I should worry about you."

"Jealous are you?"

"Yes, I guess I am. Gloria gets to catch you under the mistletoe before I do!"

"Cydney! You surprise me. I will hold you to that, you know."

"David, I have to hang up now. I'm running up quite a phone bill for Mr. and Mrs. Prather. I'm so anxious to see you, David. To see your home, to see New York. Give Roger and Gloria my best. Please tell them I hope to see them soon. Merry Christmas!"

"Merry Christmas to you darling," David said in a low, sexy voice, "I'm counting the days until you arrive."

When at last they said their good byes, David again sunk down into the recliner. He would have to mend fences with Harland. In spite of his overbearing nature, he was a good manager and agent. He seemed to have unlimited contacts and if it weren't for all the bookings he secured for David, the name David DuPrey would not be the household word it had become. Somehow he would have to get Harland to accept Cydney because David intended to marry her. Of course, Cydney didn't know that yet but that was all part of his plan. Lure her to New York, wine her and dine her and let her know how much you care for her. Be irresistible, be charming, take it slow. Propose. He smiled again.

The soda had lost its appeal so he poured himself a scotch on the rocks. He thumbed through the rolodex on the desk in the study and found the phone number of the New York Times. He dialed and waited for the after hours operator. He asked for Marilyn Shields. Of course she wasn't in. He didn't expect she would be. He asked if he could leave a message.

"Go ahead, sir," the voice said in true operator nasal jargon.

"Please tell Miss Shields that if she would like another story on David DuPrey's social life, she should hit all the high spots on New Year's Eve." He abruptly hung up. There! That might please Harland! For David was confident that when Marilyn Shields saw him with Cydney, she would certainly get the message that he was not gay. In fact, he intended to start some rumors of his own. Rumors that he was engaged to be married. Rumors he hoped would soon be coming true.

He drained his glass and refilled it. Wednesday, after the Savages left, he would have to get busy and find a Christmas tree and get a few decorations up. He returned to his recliner. The solitude was bliss. He closed his eyes. There were no visions of sugarplums. Just Harland stomping out of the house and then Cydney running into his outstretched arms at the airport.

CHAPTER TWENTY-EIGHT

"I just want you to know, Cydney, so you won't be surprised or embarrassed," Carmen was referring to her family's Christmas Eve ritual, "It's not even anything special," she continued, "we all congregate in the living room at six, just as we always do, then my father rings the little silver bell, three times, that means all three of them, Louise, Luella and Andrew are all supposed to answer. They bring in the usual things: ice, glasses and hors d'oeuvres, then Father fills all the glasses with champagne and gives one to everyone including the three of them. He proposes a toast to them for all the years they have served our family. He tells them they are dedicated and loyal employees. We sip our drinks and then Father gives them each an envelope with money in it. After they return to the kitchen he repeats the performance for each of us. He will give you an envelope too, so don't be humble or proud, just take it."

"I couldn't do that," Cydney interrupted, "I can't take money from your parents!"

"Sure you can," Carmen said without hesitation. "They have tons of it and they like to give it away. I guess it makes them feel big."

"But, Car, I hardly know your family."

"Just take the envelope, Cyd, or my parents will both make a big stink. Just ask Victoria. My mother even called her ungrateful, but of course that was after several drinks. He isn't going to give you a million bucks or anything Cyd, probably a hundred."

"A hundred dollars! Carmen, I can't take it."

"Yes, you can." Both girls were raising their voices, "Please, Cydney, for my sake, just take it." The arguing continued until at last, Cydney relented. She would take the money and put it in the collection basket at church.

Cydney was grateful, indeed, that Carmen had prepared her for the evening. It went off pretty much like Carmen had predicted. However, after Charles had handed out the envelopes, he once again rang for Andrew and informed him that he and Angeline would be having dinner in their room and the young folks should be served in the dining room. Carmen, Geoff and Donovan all looked incredulous as Angeline gathered up a few small gifts from under the tree, including the confectionary that Cydney had purchased for them, and staggered toward the staircase.

When they were out of sight, Donovan just shrugged his shoulders. "Let's drink a toast to a wonderful Christmas, with or without them."

Geoff was indifferent, Carmen was angry, "They do this all the time! What gives them the right to be rude to our friends?"

"Forget it, Car," Donovan said softly.

"No, I can't forget it. How many times did they encourage us to bring our friends home? Then they treat us like shit. Every year it gets worse."

"Let's not let it ruin our Christmas," Donovan again, the mediator. He filled the glasses. "Does anyone have any gifts to open?"

They all started chattering at once. Carmen and Cydney both headed for the staircase. "Don't anyone open anything 'til we get back," Carmen called over her shoulder. In a flash both girls were back down stairs, each bearing a few presents.

Geoff and Tony exchanged gifts and of course so did Donovan and Victoria. Cydney gave Carmen the perfume and cut glass atomizer and she could tell by the look on Carmen's face that she truly loved it. Carmen gave Cydney two gifts, the first, a beautiful cashmere sweater in a soft beige tone. "It will accent your beautiful hair," Geoff said as she held it up against herself. When Cydney opened the second package, she squealed with delight. It was a book on etiquette and manners, the dos and do nots of fine dining. Cydney held it against her and twirled around.

"Oh, thank you, Carmen. You, above everyone else, know how much this means to me. How much I need it." The girls exchanged hugs.

When they moved to the dining room for dinner, everyone was in a festive mood. They had rack of lamb with mint julep sauce and all the trimmings. They sang carols between courses and truly reveled in each other's company, minimizing their wine consumption and when at last they had all eaten their fill, including caramel flan, Carmen's favorite dessert, they got ready for church.

Cydney didn't mind the fact that she would be attending midnight mass instead of the Balsam Hills First Presbyterian Church, and as she sat reverently in the church, bedecked with dim lights and candles and with ***Oh Holy Night*** floating up softly from the organ, she closed her eyes and felt the presence of her family. She prayed for all of them, and for herself, that she would find her own happiness. A happiness like Brock had found with Ellen. And, as promised, when the collection plate was passed, she discretely dropped the hundred-dollar bill in it.

Although she had been up late, Cydney woke early. It was Christmas Day and she suddenly felt very lonely. She missed the hustle and bustle of the big kitchen at the farm. She missed the smell of Leta's cooking and the heavy pine scent of the balsam boughs that Caleb always gathered and laid across the big wooden mantle. She missed the snow and even the cold. She had never spent a Christmas away from her family or without snow and she longed for it now. She knew she should be grateful that Carmen had invited her to spend Christmas in Jackson. She also knew she had to hide her feelings. She couldn't let Carmen know what a cold and calloused image her parents portrayed. Although, Cydney had an inkling that Carmen knew. She also knew that in spite of her family's obvious wealth, they could not measure up to Cydney's family.

It was late morning before there was a knock on her door. Cydney was reading the book Carmen gave her last night and was intrigued with how many things she had already learned. Things that would certainly help her in New York and prove to both David and Harland that she was more than just a country bumpkin.

"Come in," she looked up from her book.

"Merry Christmas!" A handsome young face with an infectious smile peaked around the door. It was Geoff.

"Geoff, what a surprise! Merry Christmas to you. I was expecting Carmen."

"I know. That's why I popped in. Carmen and Tony have gone off for a horseback ride. She didn't know if you were still sleeping and asked me to let you know where she was. Want some company?"

"Sure, come in. Sit down, please. I was just brushing up on my manners."

"Maybe Carmen should have given our parents a book like that. Cydney, I'm so sorry that they were so rude. Mother drinks too much, which doesn't justify her actions, but at least explains them. Father caters to her every whim, which again is no excuse."

"Please don't apologize, Geoff. They must find it difficult to have the likes of me here. A farm girl, who consorts with the Indians." He cast her a wary glance. "I'm sorry, Geoff. Now I'm the one being rude. I'm just a little homesick today. I've never been away from my family at Christmas and we have all these wonderful traditions and there's snow on the ground and the whole house smells like pine and there would be a fire roaring in the fireplace," her eyes were distant and he knew her thoughts were, too.

"I'm jealous," he said and meant it. "One thing about being part of a wealthy family — there are all these standards to live up to. All anybody ever worries about is trying to out do the other guy. What will so and so think? What will the help think? That's all we ever heard when we were growing up. We could never do what we wanted to do. We always had to do what our parents deemed proper."

"Oh, come on, now. Carmen told me about some of her escapades and it sounds to me like she did plenty of things that weren't so good and proper."

"Well, you're right there, I guess we all did. But all the crap we pulled we did behind someone's back and when we got caught, which we did sometimes, our parents just ignored it and thought it would go away, because we were Prathers. If it didn't go away, my father paid somebody off. Now that we're adults, there aren't too many fond memories to look back on."

"Paid someone off how?" They were both comfortable now and the talk came easy.

"Well, I remember one time, I got drunk at one of their parties, and drove off with the neighbor's car. It was a pretty cool little MG, and I slammed into a tree. Lucky for me, I didn't even have a scratch. But my father couldn't let it get out that a Prather kid was driving drunk so he paid the cop to lose the police report and then of course, he had to pay old man Fellows for the car. Boy, I got my ass kicked that time!" Cydney looked wide-eyed and Geoff continued, "And if Carmen told you about some of her pranks, did she tell you about the guy who came to one of the parties and took her off into the woods?"

"Yes, as a matter of fact, she did."

"Well, dear ole Dad paid him off, too. Never to show his face around here again or he'd have his ass for statutory rape."

The talk continued. Geoff detailing one scenario after another and Cydney listening intently. It wasn't her idea of how to spend Christmas Day but the time passed quickly and soon they were being summoned to the veranda for lunch. As Geoff escorted her downstairs, a feeling of pity rushed over her. She would endure one more night here. She refused to let Mr. and Mrs. Prather intimidate her. She was who she was. Fatherless - yes. Poor - by Prather standards, yes. But richer by far than these people could ever imagine because her family knew love. She thought of all the times she had been jealous of Carmen. She had all these beautiful clothes and unlimited spending, but she didn't have what really counted.

"No more," Cydney told herself, "I will never be jealous of her again. In fact, I need to be more cognizant of her feelings. I need to try to help her stay grounded and normal."

Mr. and Mrs. Prather did not make an appearance at lunch but they showed up at precisely 6:00 p.m. for cocktails. Cydney thought this seemed like a broken record. The same scene played over and over again. Angeline looked lovely, Charles was debonair. They both talked incessantly, as if they had been the perfect hosts. As if they were sorry their guests would be leaving in the morning. Cydney noticed that Angeline didn't drink as much as usual. In fact, she made it all through dinner and even complimented Luella and Louise on a delicious meal.

"So, did you enjoy your stay in Jackson?" Charles directed this question at Cydney and snapped her back to reality.

"Yes, thank you, Charles, I had a wonderful time. You have a lovely home. I was very comfortable."

"You seem distant tonight, my dear. Did you really enjoy it?" Angeline's voice was cold.

"Yes, of course, I did. I'm just a little homesick. This is the first time I've been away from home at Christmas."

"What could possibly be so special about Christmas in the north woods?" The cold voice questioned. Cydney bit her lip to restrain herself.

"Mother!" Carmen was on her feet as her voice rose, "You are so rude!"

"Sit down, Carmen," her mother ordered, "I just think Cydney could show a little more enthusiasm. After all, we welcomed her into our home with open arms and she sits here sulking like a spoiled child."

Carmen had remained standing and clenched her fists at her side. "Cydney is anything but a spoiled child. If anyone is spoiled and sulking it's you, Mother. You want all of us to make a big fuss over you when we come home but then you treat us like shit! Every time I bring a guest home, this same thing happens. If we don't kiss your ass, you don't show up for lunch, you get drunk before dinner even starts and then you make a big scene. I hate it here!" She burst into tears as she fled the dining room and took the steps two a time. Tony excused himself. Donovan and Victoria sat silent. Geoff was embarrassed. Charles cleared his throat.

"Please accept my apologies, Cydney. We don't see each other for months and still we have our difficulties. Surely, you understand what it's like with family."

"No, sir, I do not," Cydney said with a lot of dignity. "When I go home my family is happy to see me. And, Angeline, as far as Christmas in the north woods of Wisconsin is concerned, it's everything this place lacks. It's love and laughter, genuine love and laughter. It's brilliant white snow and deep green pine trees. It's my home, the best place in the whole world." She folded her napkin over, as she had learned in her new book, and laid it beside her plate. "Please excuse me," she said. She rose and left the table.

Geoff started clapping and soon Donovan and Victoria joined in. As she ascended the stairs with her head held high, she smiled to herself.

Carmen and Cydney left early the next morning without seeing either Mr. or Mrs. Prather. Carmen was still filled with rage and Cydney was just happy to be leaving. But she would do the right thing; she would send them a note thanking them for their hospitality, just as the book suggested.

CHAPTER TWENTY-NINE

Cydney had never flown before and she told herself that after this trip she would never fly again. The 40-minute trip from Champaign to Chicago was like a roller coaster. No wonder, considering the size of the airplane. It was so small, Cydney didn't think it would get off the ground. But nothing could have prepared her for the size of O'Hare. Carmen tried to explain it, but she gave up, telling Cydney she would have to see it to believe it. Carmen was right!

Standing motionless in the middle of one of the concourses, trying to take it all in, she looked every bit the tourist she was and since she didn't know where exactly she was supposed to go, she decided to take Carmen's advice and ask for assistance. Cornering the first person she saw wearing an identification badge, ticket in hand, she looked like a small, lost child. The handsome, black man who helped her was amused. With a wink of an eye and a wicked grin, he gave her very explicit directions and wished her well as she dashed down the concourse toward her connecting flight.

This plane was huge! But Cydney was ignorant regarding air travel and she didn't understand the meaning of first class. She only knew the seats were plush and comfortable. She was given a pillow and a warm blanket; she was offered a glass of wine or other beverage of her choice. She got comfy as the stewardess scurried about catering to the every whim of her charges. As soon as the plane was airborne she would take a nap. It would probably be a very late night. She had a wonderful view.

Thoughtful David had reserved a window seat, knowing how excited she would be about flying, yet another new adventure.

She reflected on the past few days. They left Jackson on Wednesday and arrived in Champaign late Thursday afternoon. The weather was cold and snowy for the last leg of the trip, slowing them down considerably. Carmen had calmed down but spent much of the drive home, telling Cydney about some of her mother's other antics. They slept late on Friday morning. Most everyone was gone from the dorm and it was very quiet. They went out for lunch and shopped most of the afternoon. Saturday they moved. Their friend Allen helped and it didn't take long, since they didn't have too much stuff to take with them. They were able to sleep at the apartment Saturday night and they drank a champagne toast to independent living. Sunday was a day to get organized and as usual, Carmen helped her choose the right clothes to pack. The navy sequined dress was on the very top of the suitcase and she had specific orders from Carmen to hang it up as soon as she arrived.

Cydney listened intently as the stewardess gave her safety demo then took a deep breath as the plane glided upward. A smile crossed her face as she watched the people, cars and buildings below fade into oblivion. Although it was a cold day, the sun shone brightly and here above the clouds it seemed, to Cydney, even brighter. Only a few people were in the first class section of the plane so Cydney was able to ease her seat back and close her eyes. Thoughts of David filled her mind. What were his intentions this time? She knew Harland was away and she never asked David about sleeping arrangements. She only hoped that she would have her own room. She thought about her grandfather. He certainly wouldn't approve of her spending a few days alone with David in his apartment, even if she did have her own room. She smiled, thinking how Leta would say, "Caleb, this is the 70's and after all, Cydney is 19 years old."

She also wondered what David had planned to ring in the New Year. She intended to hold him to his promise of going to church. She also intended to move slowly and not let him talk her into anything. She blushed as she remembered their close encounter in Chicago. If Harland hadn't come pounding on the door, they probably would have had sex. Carmen was pretty sure, they would "do it" (as she liked to call it) this time and she asked Cydney what she used for birth control.

"Birth control!" Cydney shrieked, "What a joke. I'm a virgin, for heaven's sake, why would I think about birth control?"

"Well you better think about it, Cyd," Carmen said seriously, "He's not inviting you to New York to play Old Maid you know."

"So what do I say to him?" Cydney asked, also serious now, "and when?"

"Well, if things are getting hot and heavy, you have to tell him you don't have any protection. If he's any kind of a gentleman, he'll either say he'll take care of it, or else he'll stop. Just remember, Cyd, it only takes one time and contrary to what so many girls believe, you *can* get pregnant the first time. And if he doesn't have a condom, I don't think you should chance it. But hey – that's my opinion!"

"Oh, Carmen, I'm so dumb about these things. What if we get started and can't stop. I mean, I've heard girls say that – he couldn't stop – what if that happens?"

"You can't let it happen. Before things go that far, you have to tell him, you don't use any type of birth control. And while you're at it, you'd better tell him you're a virgin. Or does he know that?"

"Well, he probably suspects it, given my history. One night when we were talking seriously, he asked me about other men in my life. What an embarrassment to say they were none. Although, in hind sight, he seemed happy about it."

"Well of course he was happy. That pretty much told him, you didn't sleep around. So yeah, you're right, he probably knows you're a virgin. Like I said, if he's a gentleman, he'll be prepared. Especially since you'll be on his turf. Hey, what did he say about other women in his life?"

"Well, he was pretty vague. He said there was only one serious relationship and that didn't work out. David says he's too busy practicing and performing to have much of a social life. In fact, some gossip columnist is writing that he's gay because he's 28 and still single. I hope he's not just using me to prove the newspaper wrong."

"I don't think you have to worry about that, Cyd. If he needed a show piece he could have picked up anyone in New York, he wouldn't come all the way to Champaign to prove a point."

"Yeah, I guess you're right. At least I hope you are. Car, I really am excited about going to New York but I'm also a little scared."

"Listen, Cyd, before this goes any farther, you better ask yourself, are you excited about New York and the life style or are you anxious to see David?"

"Well, both. Is that wrong? You know what a sheltered life I've led. Of course, I am excited about the extravagant life style but I also am very fond of David. To be honest, Carmen, right now, I don't love him. But I think I could fall in love with him if we spent more time together. Maybe this will be a test."

"How long are you staying?"

"Well, I'm not sure. My ticket doesn't have a return date on it."

"Hey kiddo, that's a good sign." Carmen grinned, "It's called an open-end ticket, which means you can come back whenever you want to – in two days or two months."

The sound of their laughter echoed in her head and she dreamed of all the wonderful things she had read about New York. She didn't stir until the pilot announced they had begun their descent into LaGuardia.

CHAPTER THIRTY

David was right; the airport was enormous! But he was nowhere in sight and she felt something stirring in her gut. Panic! For the first eighteen years of her life in the north woods of Wisconsin she never felt anxiety. Now, three times in the last few months she had this gut-wrenching pain: when she first encountered David DuPrey backstage at the campus theatre in Champaign; when she checked into the Drake Hotel in Chicago; and, at the dinner table on Christmas Day at the Prather estate in Jackson. Once again her stomach knotted! Her eyes scanned the swarms of people – no David.

"He said he would be waiting for me," she told herself. "What if he doesn't show up?" She sat down, trying to clear her head. Quite frankly, she was a little frightened. Alone, in New York! She felt like crying but of course that would be very childish. She needed a back up plan. She checked the clock; she would wait for one hour. If he wasn't here by then she would call him. If she couldn't reach him she would retrieve her bag and take the next flight home. Carmen said it was an open-end ticket, she could return anytime she wanted to.

She drew in deep breaths but the stale air did little to calm her. She picked up a discarded copy of the *New York Times* and pretended to read it, every now and then looking over the top at the crowds of people, all in a hurry, pushing their way down the concourses like cattle being sent to slaughter. The clock on the wall ticked louder and the crowd thinned slightly. Time was almost up. She looked around for a phone and rummaged in her bag for David's number in anticipation of making the call.

When she looked up again, he had emerged from the masses and was headed in her direction, hands stuffed in the pockets of his leather bomber jacket. A hint of a smile just beginning to erupt. Relief rushed over her but so did anger. Everyone else seemed to be in a big hurry, why wasn't he? Didn't he realize that she might be uncomfortable waiting for him, alone – in New York? He tried to embrace her but she held him at bay. He saw the frightened look on her face.

"Sorry I'm late," he said casually, "but that's New York. Traffic jams everywhere – 'tis the season." He tried to be light and make her smile. She didn't.

"David, don't joke," she said seriously, "I was really frightened when you weren't here to meet me." Again, she had to restrain herself from crying.

"I'm here now," he said gently, "no need to be frightened." He hugged her and she clung to him. He kissed her lightly, then took her elbow and steered her toward the baggage claim area. They exchanged small talk: the return trip from Jackson, the weather, the new apartment.

"You travel light," he said as he picked her bag from the carousel.

"Well, I'm only going to be here for a few days."

"We'll see about that," he grinned and displayed those straight, white teeth that she noticed the very first time she met him.

"And now, my dear," he said as he guided her toward the line of waiting taxis, "another new adventure for you – a ride in a New York taxi!" The driver chuckled out loud as he put her bag in the trunk. David helped her into the back seat and settled in beside her. It was a cold day, but the taxi was warm and David, close beside her, warmed her even more. The panic was gone. David's mere presence had calmed her considerably. He noticed.

"Feeling better?"

"Yes, I am. I'm sorry David. It's just that I expected you to be waiting for me and when I didn't see you, I panicked."

"What can I say?" His mood was still light, "I'm a New Yorker. New Yorkers' lives revolve around the traffic. You'll learn the meaning of a New York minute." He gave her a peck on the cheek. She saw the driver's eyes in the review mirror and he nodded in agreement. The incident was forgotten.

It was mid afternoon and as the taxi headed down the Brooklyn-Queens Expressway towards Queens Boulevard, Cydney could see and feel the excitement of the city, alive with people, traffic and lights. She couldn't contain her enthusiasm, turning from one side of the street to the other. It was like Chicago – but bigger. Much bigger!

David was both amused and happy. He wanted this night to be perfect. He had planned it carefully. They would hit some of the clubs early; have an elegant dinner near Times Square. Dance 'til the wee hours and finally go home to his apartment, his bed.

David lived in a posh penthouse apartment on the Upper East Side, just off Fifth Avenue, with a magnificent view of Central Park. The public elevator didn't go all the way to the penthouse, so when it stopped, David had to insert a key and enter a series of code numbers to get up one more floor.

"What if I don't have a key or know the code?" Cydney asked, "how do I get in?

"Then you need to use the intercom," David said. "Here, let me show you." He just finished explaining the entry system when the elevator doors opened onto an elegant foyer.

Thick carpet with an abstract design in muted shades of mauve and navy stretched before them. Queen Anne chairs and a love seat in contrasting fabric, cherry wood tables bedecked with huge floral arrangements and artwork with ornate frames graced the room. The walls had just a hint of a mauve hue and the windows were draped with heavy brocade in yet another shade of mauve. The soft, low lights gave it added appeal. Cydney drew in a breath.

"Like it?" David asked, pleased with her expression.

"Oh, David, it's beautiful." Cydney was feeling very relaxed. She knew Harland was away and David told her the kitchen staff was also on holiday.

"Let me show you the rest of it." He unlocked a heavy cherry wood double door then stood aside so she could enter. The carpet and color scheme from the foyer continued into the living room, which yielded a breathtaking view of the park. The furniture, elegant but comfortable, was expensive; that she could tell and David had to chuckle as she stood in the center of the room and slowly turned in a circle, her mouth gapping, taking it all in. She squealed in delight when she saw a huge Christmas tree with brilliant white lights and exquisite crystal ornaments in the far corner of the room. It must have been fifteen feet tall, for it brushed the ceiling. David could tell by the look on her face that she loved it.

"I'm afraid that's the extent of my Christmas decorations," he said, "seemed like a waste of time to put them all up, since I was here alone for most of the holiday."

"It's beautiful," Cydney said. "It reminds me a lot of the Christmas trees we have at the farm. My grandfather would go out right after Thanksgiving and cut the fullest, tallest tree he could find and drag it home on a sled and…"

"Cydney, you're babbling again," David said with a bit of disinterest. "Let's move on."

He steered her toward the next room. The apartment occupied the entire top floor of the building and was bigger than most houses. David explained that the right wing was Harland's. There were two guest rooms, each with a bathroom, Harland's bedroom and bathroom and a study. The left wing, exactly like the right, was David's private quarters. In between was this huge living room, a den that the men shared for business purposes, a kitchen, dining room and two small guest bathrooms. They toured the whole apartment, save Harland's quarters. It was all so luxurious and each room yielded a surprise. In the den it was the leather furniture in dark burgundy and a ladder on wheels to access the bookshelves that stretched all the way to the ceiling. The kitchen was a gleaming mass of stainless steel and Cydney wondered how long the house staff had been gone because there was not one dish or cup or crumb in sight. Cydney's favorite room was the dining room. A chair rail divided each wall, the lower portion wainscoted and the upper half wallpapered in an exquisite floral design in muted shades of pink and mauve. A huge crystal chandelier hung over a massive cherry wood table with matching side board and china cabinet. It was a beautiful room and Cydney thought it had a bit of a feminine touch.

She followed him down the hall into his private quarters. He had picked up her bag and showed her to one of the guest rooms. Like the rest of the apartment it was massive. There was a huge four-poster bed, several armoires, a dressing table, an easy chair, and a fireplace, with a marble facade. The bathroom was stark white with fuchsia accents and gleaming brass fixtures, a hot tub, a walk in shower and mounds of gargantuan towels.

"Oh, my," she was a little breathless, "this looks just like the Drake."

"A little more private," David said. She blushed at the innuendo, both remembering Harland's intrusion.

"Oh, I almost forgot!" she said spying her bag on the chair. She opened it, shook out her evening dress and hung it up while David let out a low whistle.

"I'm not taking you out in public if you're wearing that," he said trying hard to be serious.

She smiled her beautiful smile. "I bought it just for you."

"That's why I won't take you out, I want you all for myself."

"There's just one problem, I only have this one coat and I don't think it's formal enough to wear with this dress. Hopefully, we won't see anyone you know. I wouldn't want to embarrass you."

"You could never embarrass me. But don't worry, I can take care of that problem."

Before she could ask any questions he took one step forward and she was in his arms. His kisses were sweet and gentle, but she could feel his passion rising so she gently eased herself out of his grip.

"What are the plans?" she asked. "I mean after church, where are we going after church?"

"You really want to go to church?" he asked.

"Yes, David, I do. I always go to church on New Year's eve. Just to reflect on the year and all the things I have to be thankful for." Once again she got coy, "This year I have one more thing to be thankful for."

"And what would that be?" he teased.

"Well, I'm mighty thankful you picked me up at the airport!" she said, playing his game.

He showed her the rest of his quarters and she blushed once again when he suggested that his bed was roomier than hers and the view from his room more appealing. He also reminded her that they were alone and this time there would be no interruptions.

They walked arm and arm back to the living room. David knelt before the huge marble fireplace, flicked a switch and watched as the fire sprang to life. He excused himself but was back in an instant with a bottle of wine, some sandwiches and some small canopies.

"Hungry?" He poured the wine and set the food on the cocktail table in front of them.

"Where were you hiding this?" Cydney asked, "the kitchen was spotless."

"The deli just around the corner takes real good care of me when Sophie and Gracie are gone. Have I told you about Sophie and Gracie? They're my housekeepers. Gems, real gems."

The afternoon sun was low and pleasant and filtered into the room. Cydney sank into one of the easy chairs, nibbled a ham on rye and sipped the wine, which had an immediate calming affect.

"You never said what time church started?" She wasn't going to let him get out of going.

"Well let me call Phillip. I'm sure he can find out where to go, and at what time." He rose and headed for the study.

"Phillip?" she asked in surprise, "Phillip, your driver? You mean he's here?"

"Well of course he's here, Cyd, he works for me, remember?"

Cydney was exasperated, "With all due respect, David, if Phillip was here, why didn't he pick us up at the airport? Then maybe you would have been on time!"

David didn't get upset with her, "It's Monday, Cyd. Monday is Phillip's day off. That's why he didn't drive me to the airport. Besides, I wanted you to ride in a New York taxi."

"If it's his day off, why is he driving us tonight?"

"Phillip's lived in New York long enough to know that it's next to impossible to get a taxi on New Year's Eve. So he said he'd drive us. Personally, I think he just wants to see you again." He threw his head back and laughed that infectious laugh.

David returned shortly with explicit instructions. Phillip would call for them at seven. There was an eight o'clock mass at St. Patrick's Cathedral.

"I hope you don't mind going to a Catholic church but everyone who comes to New York must see St. Patrick's. The 5th Avenue Presbyterian Church is just down the street from St. Pat's but I don't think it could compare."

"That's fine, David," again, she wasn't going to let him bow out of church, "I went to a Catholic church on Christmas Eve in Jackson and it was very nice." She thought she saw a frown but he didn't reply.

"Well then," he finally said, "we have some time to relax." He refilled their wine glasses. "Remember, if you're going to drink, you have to eat." He passed the sandwiches and canopies to her and she added some more to her plate.

"I won't be drinking much now," she smiled, "can't go to church smelling like a tavern."

"You obviously think I need saving," he said lightly, "you keep pushing this church thing."

"I'm sorry," she said blushing slightly. "I grew up going to church and it's very important to me."

"Then it's important to me, too." He flashed her a sincere smile.

"Oh, there's something else!" She hurried toward her room, returning with a brightly wrapped yet somewhat crumpled package. She held it out to him. "Merry Christmas, David, a little late and a little rumpled but I hope you like it."

He grinned like a little boy while he carefully unwrapped the present. Cydney stood by his side, watching his expression, hoping he would like it.

"A book!" he said as he pulled away the last of the paper. He turned it to the front and ran his hand over the glossy finish. Across the top **_Wisconsin_** was written in large gold embossed letters. Below was a scenic forest alive with autumn colors.

"I hope you like it David." She was a bit sheepish yet obviously bursting with pride, "I want you to learn all about Wisconsin. It's such a beautiful place."

"I love it, Cyd. And I do want to learn all about Wisconsin. In fact, I hope we can go there for a visit sometime soon." She felt her heart flutter and she could tell that David did, indeed, like the book.

"Well, it's not much," she admitted, "but since I went to Jackson and then moved, and since I still owe you money from our shopping trip in Chicago, it's all I could afford right now, I'm sorry."

"Don't be," David said sharply. "You should never apologize for a gift. If it was chosen with sincerity and thoughtfulness, it doesn't matter how much it cost. What matters is how you feel about the person you're giving it to and how that person feels about you."

She nodded in agreement, "I know you're right, David, but there is such a sharp contrast between us, I mean such a difference in our backgrounds, I hope you don't think it a trivial or meaningless gift."

"Cyd, really, I meant what I said. I love the book. But enough about that. I have a gift for you, too." He left the room this time and returned with a small package, elegantly wrapped in silver foil paper. She knew from the box that it was jewelry and her fingers shook with excitement as she unwrapped it. Inside was a black velvet box and inside that was the exquisite diamond studded watch.

She gasped, "Oh, David, it's gorgeous. I'm speechless, I just don't know what else to say."

"I'm glad you like it. Here let me help you put it on." She held up her arm. He undid the silver plated bracelet with the pair of geese in flight that dangled from her wrist and fastened the watch in its place. "Now you won't have to wear this cheap thing anymore," he said tucking the discarded bracelet into her hand.

Emotion swept over her and she fought back tears. "Maybe it was cheap," she said. "but I love that bracelet. It means the world to me."

He could see the hurt in her eyes and he knew his words cut her deep.

"I have a way of always hurting you, Cydney. I don't mean to, really, I guess I just don't think sometimes before I speak."

His words were so sincerely spoken, the tears spilled down her cheeks. "It's okay, David, you didn't know. The watch is beautiful and I really need one." He reached up and gently brushed away a tear with his thumb and kissed her ever so lightly.

David realized Cydney was right. There was a vast valley between them, socially and economically and he would have to weigh his words more carefully. Things that he considered trivial and insignificant were important to her. He guessed that the bracelet may have come from her half-breed so called brother but of course, he could not let on. And he tried desperately to understand how some cheap piece of costume jewelry could move her to tears. If he planned on winning Cydney over, and he did, he would have to spend a lot of time teaching her about the power of money. He contemplated all this as he held her close and apologized again for his lack of sensitivity.

As he held her in his arms and apologized, Cydney wondered about his double standard. He had painstakingly explained the merits of gift giving and yet in the next sentence made disparaging remarks about her bracelet. She wore it all the time, surely he must have realized that it had sentimental value. Meeting David's standards would be difficult. She knew he was wealthy. What she didn't know was just how wealthy!

Cydney retired to her room at five thirty with a promise from David not to disturb her. She would be ready to go at seven when Phillip arrived but she needed time to rest and get dressed. Alone in her room, she unpacked the rest of her bag and arranged her cosmetics and toiletries in the bathroom. She didn't realize that she was smiling as her fingers traced the face of her beautiful new watch. She laid it on the dressing table and meandered around the room, admiring each piece of furniture, each piece of artwork, each delicate vase and statuette.

She ran the tub full of steaming hot water and sank down in it contemplating what nightlife was like in New York City.

David was standing by the bar sipping a vodka martini when Cydney emerged from her room a little before seven. Their eyes locked and he felt a catch in his throat. She was so lovely. He set his glass on the bar and walked toward her. She stopped as he advanced. The soft lights only enhanced her beauty. Her auburn hair, piled high on her head was flecked with tiny little sparkles that twinkled almost as much as the sequins on the bodice of her dress. Her right shoulder was bare and her skin had a healthy glow thanks to the sun tan she got poolside in Jackson. The dress rose up over her left shoulder and then plunged down her back to the right side of her waist. The crepe skirt, dark navy, hung straight in soft folds and fell to her ankles. The slit on the side exposed her right leg to mid-thigh. She wore navy blue suede pumps. The design of the dress didn't warrant a necklace, but her earrings and bracelet sparkled like her dress and she wore her new watch on her left wrist.

David took her hands in his. "You're beautiful," was all he could say.

"Thank you, so are you." She smiled back. That made him laugh.

"I've never been called beautiful before. But thank you." They stood there in silence, admiring each other. To her David was a beautiful sight. His black suit was meticulously tailored with silk lapels. His shirt was perfectly pressed and starched. A silk tie, colorful but subtle, was held in place by a diamond tie tack. His teeth were as pristine as his shirt. His hair and nails, perfect as always. Even his black shoes gleamed. The smell of his cologne made her heady.

The intercom buzzed and before David had time to steal a kiss, Phillip entered the room from the kitchen door. He had come into the apartment via the door that led from the foyer directly into the kitchen. He was uniformed and handsome. He removed his hat, smiled broadly, and welcomed her to New York. He assured her she would enjoy it more than Chicago. He carried a big white box, which was about three feet square and tied with a red ribbon. He set it on the sofa and retreated toward the kitchen.

"Please let me know when you're ready to leave," he told David, who only nodded in response.

David walked to the sofa, untied the ribbon and opened the box. Cydney tried to peer around him but he stood between her and the sofa, blocking her view. When at last he turned around, he was holding a fur jacket.

"See if this fits," he said nonchalantly.

"You're kidding!" Cydney said a little too loud.

"No, I'm not. You said you didn't have a proper wrap for tonight, so try this on."

"So you just had Phillip run out and buy a mink coat?" Her voice and expression were both incredulous.

"No, silly, and it isn't mink. It's silver fox and I got it on loan from a friend who is a furrier." He continued to hold the jacket up so that she could just slip her arms in it. "Come on," he joked, "you don't want to be late for church do you?"

Still shaking her head in disbelief, she walked to him, turned around and slipped her arms into the jacket. David gently brought it up over her shoulders. She grasped the lapels with both hands and drew it close around her.

"Oh, my! It's gorgeous. It's so soft and warm. I didn't know you could borrow a fur. Are you teasing me?" Her eyes sparkled as she continued to caress the elegant fox jacket, which fit her perfectly.

"No, I'm not teasing. It's yours to wear tonight. But if you spill on it or damage it, I'll have to pay for it and then I might make you repay me." This time he was teasing but he tried to hide it.

"David, you know I could never afford to pay for this!" She was falling right into his trap.

"Then, I may have to take it out in trade," he continued, his eyes bright with laughter.

She realized now that he was bantering with her so she played the game, "Then I'll be very, very careful."

He called for Phillip, who met them at the elevator in the foyer. Cydney felt like the luckiest person in the world. She had so much to be thankful for. She would reflect more on that at church but for now excitement overtook her. New Year's Eve in New York lay just ahead.

CHAPTER THIRTY-ONE

The cold, gothic exterior of the Cathedral deceived her for she found the inside warm and welcoming. Despite its enormity, soft organ music filled the church, dim lights illuminated the aisles. Soft candles danced among the religious icons. Two colossal Christmas trees shimmered with tiny white lights. David knew nothing of the history of this magnificent structure, but Cydney would learn later that construction began in 1859 and it was consecrated in 1879. It wasn't completed until 1906 and was home to the city's Irish Catholics. The interior was so impressive. The St. Michael and St. Louis altars came from Tiffany and Co. of New York, and the St. Elizabeth altar, honoring Mother Elizabeth Seton, the first American-born saint, was designed by Paolo Medici of Rome.

Heads nodded in greeting as they walked arm in arm down the center aisle midway to the altar. Cydney genuflected as she entered the pew, as she knew all Catholics did, but David did not follow her lead. And when she knelt in prayer, he remained seated. Once she glanced at him and thought he looked either annoyed or bored, she couldn't tell which. However, she ignored him and went about participating in the mass, as best she could given her lack of knowledge of the Catholic faith. And in this most solemn setting, Cydney once again was overcome with emotion. In the silence of her heart and mind, she recited her childhood prayers of gratitude. She asked God to watch over her family and keep them safe, wherever they might be at this particular time. She asked for a prosperous new year; she asked God to help her make the right decisions regarding her future; and finally, as she had for the past thirteen years, she asked God to make Brock happy.

David watched her intently, not fully understanding why she wanted to be here and why she found it necessary to kneel for so long on that wooden plank, atoning for her sins like some common street urchin. He had to admit, however, that she looked a damn sight more beautiful than any woman he was ever attracted to. This only strengthened his resolve. He wanted to make Cydney his wife. Harland might not be happy about it right now but when he saw how Cydney would help David's career and his image, he would change his tune.

When Mass was over and they returned to the waiting car, Cydney felt both renewed and happy. She sat close to David, their arms locked together. She didn't speak, choosing instead to bask in her happiness.

Finally, David laid his hand on hers and smiled, "Church is over," he said, "no need to be so quiet."

"Just enjoying the sights and this luxurious ride." She saw Phillip smile at her in the rear view mirror.

"May I ask what you were thinking about all that time you were kneeling?" David asked seriously.

"I wasn't thinking, David. I was praying."

"For what?" He surprised her with the question. "Why do you have to pray for things? Just tell me what you want and I'll take care of it!" She laughed, thinking he was joking.

"I'm serious," he said. "What ever you want, just tell me and I'll get it for you."

"Some needs, and wants aren't material, David. Don't you believe in praying?'

"Not really. I have everything I want. Except you. So there really is nothing to pray for."

"What about your career, your health, the health and safety of all your friends?"

"Well, in my opinion that's kind of a waste of time. My career is soaring, my health is exceptional and my friends can all take care of themselves. So why do I have to pray?"

"Well, if you want to—" she stopped. "David, let's not spoil our evening by having this discussion. We'll talk about it some other time, okay?" He nodded in agreement, but he could sense that she was annoyed.

Cydney wasn't annoyed. She was hurt, deeply hurt, to think that the man she thought she could love, had such materialistic values. She remembered his little speech earlier about gift giving and realized he did indeed, have a double standard. He also had a big pocket book, and a big ego. She might have to reconsider her feelings for David. Tomorrow.

Phillip eased the car to the curb at the Copacabana. They were silent for most of the ride, which seemed long even though Phillip knew all the best and quickest routes. He slid out of his seat the minute the car stopped and hurried around to hold the door for her. He offered her his hand and she stepped out gracefully, feeling David's tender hand at the small of her back. People were lingering on the street and several glanced their way, wondering if this emerging beauty was a star. David had a developed a good following among the classical music set, but was not often recognized on the street. Tonight seemed to be an exception because the crowd parted as they advanced, David still steering her. She heard murmuring from the crowd and when she slowed her step, she felt David's hand press firmer.

"Keep moving," he said flatly, "and smile." She turned slightly and glanced at David, a grin perpetuating his lips. A camera flashed, but David continued forward. Inside, the doorman unlatched the velvet rope to allow them to enter and greeted David by name. Other staff members nodded and smiled, David returning each greeting and adding a personal touch.

"Hey, Martin, how are you tonight?" to one of the waiters.

"Jacqueline, you look stunning as always," to the cigarette girl.

"John Henry, is the wine chilled?" to the wine steward. He was obviously a regular.

Cydney was becoming uncomfortable. She didn't know the protocol. "David," she half whispered, "what about the fur jacket?"

"Keep it on for now," he said softly as he continued to steer her, "you may be chilly and besides, I don't want to risk checking such an

exquisite wrap. It's not ours, remember?" They followed the maitre d'
to their booth and only after they were seated did he lower the jacket
from her shoulders and tuck it away.

Martin appeared immediately, and David ordered hors d'oeuvres.
John Henry materialized out of nowhere and began pouring the wine.
Apparently, David had a preferred brand or had ordered it in advance.
When at last they were alone, Cydney could not contain her curiosity.

"David, did you see that flash outside? Someone took our
picture!"

"I know," he seemed smug, "I hope it was someone from the *Times*.
They published two articles about me recently and both of them implied
that I was gay. Maybe now that I've been seen with a beautiful woman,
they'll think differently." He kissed the back of her hand and she smiled
at him.

"I remember you telling me about that but how would anyone know
we were here?"

"I don't know," David lied, "but on holidays and special occasions
lots of entertainers come to the Copa. They usually have to dodge the
press outside, but once they get in, they usually have some privacy."

"I gather you've been here before seeing as how you know all the
staff," she teased.

"Jealous, are you?"

"Only of Jacqueline. Unless what the *Times* wrote is true, then I
suppose I have to be jealous of Martin and John Henry as well." He
continued kissing her hand and her forearm and she felt her pulse
quicken.

"If you want to go back to my apartment right now, I can prove
the *Times* and Marilyn Shields both wrong. Dead wrong." She felt his
tongue hot on her arm.

"What happened to the guy who was going to show me all the hot
spots in New York tonight?" her voice was low and alluring.

"He's got a hot spot of his own," he whispered as he pulled her close
and transferred his lips from her arm to her neck. She laughed out loud
then, her face almost as red as her lips.

Martin cleared his throat discreetly and David's head jerked upright. Martin slid the platter of delicacies to the center of the white linen, nodded and backed away, a smile inching across his face.

This time David laughed when she taunted, "I thought you said there would be no interruptions this time." Their love making put on hold, they sipped wine, nibbled fripperies and spoke softly, their heads touching now and then. Suddenly, another flash! David rose, pretending to be angry, and insisted that the young photographer be escorted out. He did not, however, ask anyone to confiscate the film.

David suggested that they dance and he was extremely agile. Cydney once again was self-conscious. But David came to her rescue, counting out the steps and gently but firmly steering her around the floor. She was a good student and soon was able to follow his gait without stepping on his toes.

"I'll call Phillip, let's move on," David said as they made their way back to the booth, "I want you to see more of the wonderful clubs in New York and I want the clubs to see you."

"How *do* you call Phillip?" she asked. David pulled a small black square from his inside pocket.

"Press it." He held it out to her. "It's a pager. It just vibrates a little and in ten minutes Phillip will be waiting by the front entrance." Once again she was baffled. She didn't know there was so much to learn about life.

The next stop was the Café Carlyle, an intimate and swanky cabaret on the Upper East Side. The staff here was also very familiar with David. Cydney was delighted with all the special treatment they received but David brushed it off. It was not unusual, he said, after all, the Carlyle was the essence of Manhattan. David ordered a seafood sampler and more wine. He was getting more affectionate and even suggested that they cut the evening short and return to his apartment, which was only a few blocks away. Again, she dismissed his advances and continued her barrage of questions about New York and what else the evening held in store for them.

The next stop was LaBernardin, a French seafood restaurant, and although Cydney didn't realize it, this place was a real splurge even for the wealthiest patrons. The room was gorgeous, the service impeccable and when Cydney told David she wanted to try something exotic for dinner, he suggested the black bass ceviche awash in cilantro, mint, jalapenos and diced tomatoes. He chose the herbed crabmeat in saffron ravioli. Cydney had never consumed so much wine in her life and although David thought she was a bit talkative, she was in fact, just excited about experiencing New York to its fullest.

While they waited for their dinner, they made plans for the next few days. David assured her they had only just begun. There was no end to the fun that awaited them. They would visit Rockefeller Plaza and Lincoln Center, Grand Central Station and The Empire State Building. They would walk the bridges if it wasn't too cold and of course he would show her Carnegie Hall and other museums and galleries. David went on and on.

Finally, Cydney held up her hand as if to say stop. "How long do you think I'm going to be here?" she asked.

"Well, I was hoping you'd stay a week or two."

"A week or two! Are you crazy? I can't stay for two weeks!"

"Why not? You don't have class again until the end of the month. You probably would be bored back in Champaign. Here we could do something new and exciting every day."

"Don't you have some performances lined up?"

"Yes, I do. But at this stage of the game, I really don't need to practice too much, Cyd. I usually spend an hour or so before a performance just warming up. Quite frankly, I play many of the same songs over and over. And if I introduce a new piece, I have it down pretty good in my mind, so as I said, I really don't have to practice much."

"When is Harland coming back?" she questioned.

"Probably mid-week. But don't worry about Harland. I'll take care of him. Oh, and Sophie and Gracie will both be back on Wednesday, and I really want you to meet them. They will love you."

"I didn't bring enough clothes along for two weeks," she said knowing full well he wouldn't take that for an answer.

"Well go shopping then," he said. "You'll love shopping in New York."

"David, when are you going to realize, I can't afford to shop hardly anywhere, much less in New York."

"Then I'll shop for you." He said no more, implying it was the end of the discussion.

When she was about to object, a throng of staff people, led by the wine steward approached their table and showered them with attention while they served dinner. Cydney thought she had never seen food presented so elegantly.

"It's almost too beautiful to eat," she said in her naivety. She noticed that David frowned slightly and one of the waiters raised an eyebrow at her. She thought it best not to try and explain herself. Instead, she folded her hands in her lap, smiled and sat demurely, while the wait staff finished their work. She focused on her meal and when at last she thought she would burst, she sat back in her chair, satiated with both food and wine. They ordered hot steaming coffee and frozen rum-scented chestnut soufflé' for dessert. Now Leta was a very, very good cook but her best efforts could not compare with this gourmet feast that Cydney had just devoured.

"It was just wonderful," she told David.

"Then I suggest you tell the waiters to give your compliments to the chef. They always enjoy hearing that and it will make up for the faux pas you made about the food looking better than it would taste." He was once again, teaching her proper etiquette.

It was nearing midnight and David suggested they stay at LaBernardin because the crowds in Times Square would be mobbish. When they had finished their coffee and dessert, David ordered champagne for a New Year's toast. The wine steward filled their flutes and when the clock struck the magical hour, David proposed a toast to their future. The celebration was reaching a loud crescendo, so Cydney, too dumbfounded, too star struck, too tired to protest, simply clinked her glass to David's and nodded in agreement.

"Let's go dancing," David said matter-of-factly- like it was only 10:00 p.m. instead of one a.m.

"Oh, David, I'm really tired."

"You can sleep all day tomorrow. We can't cut short your first New Year's Eve in New York, now can we?" Again, she gave in but she thought she had never been so tired in her whole life.

The final stop of the evening was the infamous Rainbow Room on the 65th floor of Rockefeller Plaza. The Art Deco design was pure opulence. A live orchestra played and couples, all dressed in their New Year's Eve finery, whirled gracefully around the floor. David nodded to several people as they were escorted to their table in a secluded corner. As soon as the wine steward had served them, David took her hand and led her to the middle of the dance floor amidst smiles and greetings from other patrons.

His right arm encircled her entire waist and their hands entwined snuggly between their bodies. Her cheek brushed his, already sporting a fine, dark stubble. They danced for what seemed like an eternity as the orchestra moved from one song to another with no interruption. David hummed softly in her ear and their bodies swayed gently to the music. The rest of the night was a blur. The combination of wine and fatigue began to take its toll, and the last thing she remembered was David drawing the covers up around her neck, kissing her forehead and wishing her a happy New Year as he softly closed her bedroom door.

CHAPTER THIRTY-TWO

She *did* sleep until noon and even a little beyond. She wondered if she had put her pajamas on by herself or if David had helped. It really didn't matter. She had been so exhausted and she knew David had simply tucked her into bed. She remembered that much – the fragrant sheets, the thick warm blanket.

She was ravenously hungry and the smell of coffee whet her appetite. She was in the bathroom untangling her hair and brushing her teeth when David knocked just once on the door and then pushed his way in, carrying a huge tray. The smell of eggs and bacon and fresh brewed coffee filled the room. A section of the morning edition of the *Times* was tucked between a carafe and a vase, which held a single red rose.

"Breakfast!" he announced.

She peeked around the corner of the bathroom door, "Good Morning." Her voice was light.

"How about, good afternoon?"

"What time is it?" she asked and then before he could answer, she continued on, "I don't think I have ever been so exhausted in my entire life!"

"You fell asleep in the car," he was trying to sound serious, "and Phillip and I had to carry you up here and put you to bed."

"David, that's absurd. Surely you didn't let Phillip carry me up here?"

His grin was devilish. "Of course not. You don't think I'd let Phillip get a look at that body, do you?" he asked nodding his head at her. "Come and eat while it's still hot." He continued holding onto the tray. She scrambled back up onto the huge bed, settled herself cross-legged (Brock's style) against the big fluffy pillows and tucked the covers around her mid section. David adjusted the tray over her and sat down at the end of the bed.

"Did you make this?" She smiled at him; her hair half up, half down. She looked enticing sitting there nibbling on a piece of toast.

"Of course I made it," he said, trying to sound indignant. "Do you think the only thing I can do is play the violin?"

"Well you do that better than any one else, can you cook that well too?"

"You tell me." He poured them each a cup of coffee, "Breakfast is my specialty."

"Does that mean that you do this often? I mean serve breakfast in bed to lots of women?"

"Only special women get this pampering."

"And how many special women have there been?"

"Two, counting you." Then changing the subject, "Look," he said sounding conceited, "we made the gossip column in the morning paper." He folded it over and handed it to her. A large picture of them stared back at her. It was the one taken as they were entering the Copa. Almost a profile shot but the smile on both of their faces was clearly visible.

The caption read *David DuPrey and mystery woman light up the night.* There was a brief article speculating about her identity and what their relationship was. Below was a smaller picture, the one from inside the club. They were sitting close, heads together, looking intimately into each other's eyes. The caption under that picture read *Anonymous Beauty squelches rumors regarding DuPrey's sexual orientation.* The story, written by none other than Marilyn Shields, went on to report that David and his "mystery woman" had been seen at the Copa, the Carlyle and the Rainbow Room and it was obvious that they were in love. She described how they danced, and what they ate and drank. She reported in detail what this mysterious woman was wearing and questioned who the designer was. It was an exquisite dress, she wrote, but she could not put the style of dress with any particular designer. She even went so far as to ask the fashion house that designed the dress to call her so she could give them the credit they so deserved. Cydney was amused and flattered. She had never been the subject of such intense scrutiny.

"Did someone actually spy on us?" she asked naively.

"That's usually how they get their information." David was also amused but probably more pleased. "I hope Shields drops this gay thing now." He tossed the paper aside.

"Don't throw it away!" she sounded alarmed. "I want to keep it for Carmen. She helped me pick out the dress and she will be fascinated that it was such a conversation piece."

"I think the person in the dress was the conversation piece." David smiled at her, "What should we do today?"

"What's the weather like?" She turned her gaze toward the window but the drapes were still drawn. David got up and opened them. Although her room faced the north, she could tell the sun was shining brightly. "Is it cold?"

"Weatherman said it will get up around twenty." He refilled her coffee cup.

"I'm still very tired. Maybe we could go for a short walk and then stay in this evening. I'd offer to cook you dinner, David, but the truth is, I don't know too much about cooking."

"Well, I do and that's a splendid idea. Let me see what's in the freezer. It's a holiday you know, so the markets won't be open."

They finished eating and David cleared the tray away. "I'll check the freezer. When you're ready, I'll be in the study catching up on my mail." David blew her a kiss without using his hands and she retaliated.

When he was gone she stretched and slid down under the blankets. She was so happy. Happy to be in New York, happy to be here with David and happy that he was not pressuring her. She lay there deep in thought, wondering how long she should stay and what other excitement and surprises lay ahead.

David busied himself in the study for at least an hour, scanning the mail, checking the calendar, reviewing a contract for an upcoming performance. Finally, he heard her call his name and he swiveled around in the big leather chair just as she entered the room. She was wearing brown wool slacks topped with the cashmere sweater that Carmen had given her for Christmas. Her hair was casual, brushed off to one side and secured with a large barrette. The copper hues were highlighted by the soft beige sweater just as Geoff had predicted. She wore a bright scarf at her neck and gold earrings. The diamond studded watch sparkled at her wrist. He sat still for just a moment admiring her.

"You are so lovely," he said, his voice breaking with emotion. "I don't think I want to take you out today, I don't want to share you with anyone."

"I thought we were going for a walk?"

He let his shoulders droop and feigned defeat but she saw the sparkle in his eyes, "If you insist."

"I do insist. I want to walk in Central Park."

"Then we shall." He was acting gallant now, getting to his feet and bowing.

The walk was slow and relaxing but the air was colder than they had anticipated and it didn't take long before Cydney's cheeks were bright red and her teeth were chattering.

"Let's turn back now," David said. "We'll have a drink by the fire before dinner."

"By the way, what are we having for dinner?" she questioned.

"How does a Caesar salad and shrimp linguini sound? It's my specialty."

"I thought breakfast was your specialty?"

"Breakfast is my morning specialty, dinner is my evening specialty."

"Any other *specialties* I should know about?" she asked with a twinkle in her eyes.

He raised a brow, "Well, I've got a terrific late night special, if you're interested?"

"And do I have to order now or can I wait 'til later?"

"Whatever suits you," he said as he led her toward the elevator.

Before long she was seated on the floor right in front of the blazing fireplace. She had kicked off her boots and with her arms back to support her and legs stretched forward she wiggled her toes to warm them. David was at the bar observing her graceful movements. As he approached she straightened up, drew up her legs and crossed them like a pretzel in front of her.

He was amused. "I've seen you sit like that before. It looks uncomfortable."

"It really isn't," she answered, "in fact it's quite comfortable. Brock, my – um, well you know, Brock, he taught me to sit like this. You should try it."

"I should have guessed that," David said without thinking, "It's called *Indian style* right?"

Once again the smile faded from Cydney's face. "David," she said quietly, "that was very thoughtless of you."

"What! I can't say the word Indian because what's his name's part Indian?"

"We've been down this road before," Cydney said, the hurt in her voice very obvious, "and, his name is BROCK!"

"Yes, yes, I know, Brock. I'll try to remember that." But he sounded insincere and Cydney felt stinging pain once again in her heart and she now realized that David was not always as kind or considerate as he pretended to be. He handed her a delicate cocktail glass.

"What are we drinking tonight?" she asked trying to put aside the hurt and not spoil the evening.

"Vodka martinis," he said. "But sip it, it's real potent. You have to acquire a taste for it and it usually takes people awhile so give it a chance."

"I thought there was gin in a martini."

"Gin is for school girls," he said laughing into her beautiful dark brown eyes, "this is a serious drink."

She raised her glass to his, "Then I will be very serious when I drink it." David threw his head back and laughed. As he had suggested, she slowly sipped her drink. At the first taste of it, she turned up her nose and David laughed again. The second sip went down easier. They sat in silence sipping their martinis and enjoying the warmth of the fire with soft music as a backdrop.

"What would you like to do tomorrow?" He asked.

"Give me some choices. I love galleries and museums and shopping and I need to see all the touristy things."

"Well, yes, of course, but we don't have to do it all in one day. It's not like you won't ever come to New York again, right?"

"Well, since you put it that way, I guess you're right. I'd love to visit again. Maybe when it's warm outside."

"Whenever you want to come here, you just tell me. After dinner we'll plan our day. Tomorrow morning is still play time but I expect Harland home late in the afternoon and then we will have to be on our best behavior." David laughed again and Cydney with him but she already felt a churning in her stomach. How was she ever going to cope with Harland?

"And by the way, we probably will be having dinner with some friends of mine on Wednesday evening. I hope that's okay?"

"Of course it's okay, David. You don't talk much about your friends so I am very eager to meet some of them."

"Well to tell you the truth, I don't have many friends. I'm usually too busy to socialize much. But it will just be Harland, you and I, and Tom and Joyce Caprock. Tom is actually my attorney so he's really more a business associate then a friend but we do socialize occasionally."

"Will it be formal or dressy casual or what because I didn't bring too much eveningwear? Actually, I don't *have* much eveningwear. Most of the clothes I took to Chicago belonged to Carmen. Most of the clothes I wear belong to Carmen. Lucky for me, we wear the same size. She just happens to be a bit taller."

"Then we'll go shopping tomorrow." He took her glass and returned to the bar. The vodka had warmed her insides so she moved away from the fire and sat on the plush sofa. David returned and sat beside her.

"Tell me about some of your friends." His eyes and voice were inquiring.

She laughed, "How ironic, because like you, I don't have many friends. Back home, we didn't have close neighbors and I didn't have many friends at school. I got teased a lot because I didn't have a father, or a mother for that matter. My mother left when I was only three. Then Leta cared for me. I guess my only true friends are Carmen and you. And Brock. Brock is my friend, too." David raised an eyebrow and wondered who she was trying to convince, herself or him because he noticed the way her eyes lit up whenever she mentioned Brock's name.

"I want to be more then your friend, Cydney."

"Are you familiar with the old saying, 'you have to be friends before you can be lovers'?"

"Touché, my dear, touché." He stood up and extended his hand to her, "Come on," he said, "Don't think you can get away without helping with dinner." They walked arm and arm into the kitchen.

"Do you want to eat in the dining room or in here?" David asked, gesturing with his head toward the breakfast bar while he sautéed the shrimp.

"Why don't we eat by the fire?" she questioned.

David hesitated. "But Sophie and Gracie would not approve. They're very rigid."

"Sophie and Gracie aren't here," she said matter-of-factly.

"You're right, again," he said, "the vodka must have sharpened your wit."

David moved the sleek, glass coffee table closer to the fireplace while Cydney laid out two place settings. David instructed her as to proper placement of silverware and glassware. When at last they were satisfied that it was both cozy and functional, David brought in the salad and a bottle of chardonnay. Cydney served the salad while David uncorked the wine. They situated themselves at their makeshift table in front of the fire, toasted the new year and began eating, still conversing about their respective pasts and their hopes for the future. While David retreated to the kitchen to serve the main course, Cydney went to her room to retrieve the book that Carmen had given her on the proper way to do just about everything. Over the linguini they thumbed through the book, Cydney asking questions and David answering them.

"What's the proper way to set the table?"

"Easy," he answered, "just remember solids to the left, liquids to the right. So the bread plate goes on the left, just off the tip of the silverware and the glassware goes on the right. If you're not sure which utensil to use first, watch someone else, whom you know to be well versed in the matter, like me!" His laugh was boastful.

"Is it true it's improper to bite into the bread?"

"Absolutely! Break off a bite size piece."

"Can I tip my soup dish to get to the bottom of it?"

"Yes, but tip it to the back, away from you and don't worry if you leave a little in the bottom."

"How do I let the waiter know that I don't want him to keep refilling my wine glass?"

"When you've had enough just don't drink any more of it. You don't have to say anything."

"What about reapplying lipstick at the table?"

"Oooh, that's my pet peeve. Gloria Savage does it all the time and it's a no-no. So rude. If you must freshen your lipstick or makeup, excuse yourself and go to the powder room."

"What about ordering? What if I don't recognize some of the menu items?"

"Well that's easy if you're with me. Actually, it's proper for a gentleman to order for his lady but most people don't adhere to that rule. If you ever want me to order for you, just let me know but do it discreetly, of course."

They had finished their meal, and now sat side by side on the sofa, looking through the book. David had casually put his arm around her shoulder. He looked intently at a page, pretending he was really reading it. "Does it say anything about kissing immediately after you eat?"

She thought he was serious and when she turned her face to look at him, he did just that. He kissed her. Gently, but long and she responded. His mouth covered hers and his tongue gently eased her lips apart. He explored the deep recesses of her sweet mouth and felt her go limp against him. At last he eased his grip and their mouths separated. She looked up at him with eyes full of rapture.

"You are a devil," she shrieked, "and I'm gullible enough to fall for everything you say."

"Well, I just wanted to make sure that you knew the proper way to thank your host for preparing such a delicious dinner."

"It was delicious, David but I have another request." Again she looked so appealing, with her head cocked to one side and a twinkle in her eye. He didn't respond, just raised a questioning eyebrow. "Will you play your violin for me?"

"Now?"

"Yes, now. Please David. Play just for me?"

He sat silent for just a minute or two, studying her face, her eyes, and finally got up and went into the study. She leaped up and shut off the stereo system, her heart was pounding. David was back in just a few seconds, carrying the sleek leather case. She dimmed the lights.

He didn't speak. He just laid the case out on the sofa with great care. Cydney noticed how his hand slid affectionately over the surface of it before he unlatched it. The room was silent and Cydney thought she could hear her heart beating. But David was so intense; maybe it was his heartbeat she heard! He carefully lifted the delicate instrument from the case. He assumed a pose, as if on stage and drew the violin slowly upward until his chin rested on it. Still, he did not speak. He lifted his bow; his eyes were black and fervent. Cydney closed her eyes and laid her head back. The sweet sounds poured forth. And while David played, Cydney felt tears cascading down her cheeks. Still she sat silently, listening as he made a smooth transition from one song to the next. Finally, she opened her eyes and peered at David. Like the other performances she had witnessed, David eyes were open although he was transfixed. His nostrils flared, his body language erotic. Cydney knew, at that very moment she knew, that David's first and true love was his music.

Cydney was the one who was now spellbound. Her emotions had run a gamut She admired his dedication to his work. She appreciated his talent. She adored the music but she had a difficult time accepting the fact that David placed his music over and above everything and everyone else in his life. She understood why he had no friends; she understood why the public questioned his lack of an intimate relationship; she understood his difficulty with personal bonds. David was a loner. His lover was his music and right now she was having a problem understanding why he wanted her in his life and she was confused about her feelings for him.

David played several songs before he lowered his violin. Sweat beaded up on his brow, a shock of hair had fallen forward and lay limp across his forehead. His eyes, alive with passion, were blacker then she had ever seen them. He didn't speak until he had encased the instrument. Then he softly spoke her name and advanced toward her. He held out his arms. She put her hands in his and he lifted her to her feet. He led her to his bedroom.

CHAPTER THIRTY-THREE

The lights in the bedroom were very dim. David reached down to the bedside table and soft music floated upward, his eyes never leaving hers.

"Cydney," he said with a voice as passionate as his eyes, "I have dreamed of making love to you, since the day we met. That's what I want to do now. I want to make love to you."

Before she could answer, whether to protest or agree, he again covered her mouth with his and Cydney could feel the longing in his kiss. When the kiss was over and she opened her eyes, his intense eyes were staring deep into hers. He had placed his hands on her shoulders, when he drew her near and kissed her, and he let them slide forward now, over her breasts. Those same slender, fragile hands that played the sweetest music in the world, now rested on her breasts and she found her breath coming in short gasps. David's hands lingered there, his thumb gently stroking her nipples and she felt them harden under the soft cashmere. She was breathless. And when she tried to speak her throat was dry. Tears stung her eyes. She was a little bit embarrassed, a little bit frightened and more aroused then she wanted to admit. David sensed she was uncomfortable.

"Don't be afraid," he said in the softest, gentlest voice she had ever heard, "we'll go slowly. I won't hurt you. I would never hurt you." Again, she could not speak. She simply nodded her head. David took his hands from her breasts and wiped her tears with his thumbs. He gently caressed her cheek. He kissed one eyelid, then the other. The beating of her heart echoed in her ears. He unknotted the silk scarf at her neck and tossed it aside. His hands traveled downward until he reached the bottom of her sweater. He lifted it up and she automatically raised her arms. He eased the sweater over her head while she pulled her arms free. He undid the large barrette and unleashed her hair. He wound his fingers through the coppery mass and then buried his face in it, basking in the sweet fragrance. Cydney stood before him, not knowing what to do. David didn't mind, for she seemed to be taking his cues. When he faltered trying to unhook her bra, she helped him. He noticed how her hands trembled and was overjoyed to think that she wanted him as much as he wanted her. The lacy bra fell to the floor and he drew in his breath when he glimpsed her bare breasts, ample for such a small person. Her nipples were still erect and her skin was flushed.

"You are so lovely," David said just above a whisper. "This is exactly how I dreamed you would look standing here before me." They kissed again and he crushed her to him. When he released her, their eyes remained locked together. He began unbuttoning his shirt.

She smiled shyly, "Let me." She finished the task with shaky fingers. He pulled his t-shirt over his head and let it fall to the floor where the other clothes were piling up.

"My turn," he smiled back at her. His hands encircled her slight waist until he found the button and zipper of her slacks. He undid them and got to his knees. David began pulling her slacks down to her ankles while he planted tiny kisses on her tummy. She stepped out of her slacks and with one foot, kicked them off to the side. David stood up and waited. Cydney reached forward and loosened his belt. She unhooked the clasp on his trousers and opened the fly, her hands still aflutter. She pushed his trousers down. He helped her and then, as she had done, stepped free of them. They continued to exchange kisses. Cydney was wearing only her lace panties now and David had to restrain himself from throwing her down on the bed and taking her by force. He opened the bed and turned back to Cydney. This time when they kissed he manipulated her around and lowered her onto the bed. He threw the covers back further so she could stretch out. David towered over the bed and with great agility, slowly removed her panties. Then, still standing, he removed his shorts.

Now the girls' dorm rooms had been full of pictures of handsome, naked young men in various stages of arousal, but Cydney had never seen a real, live, naked man before and while she wanted to tell David that he, too, was a handsome man, she found herself speechless.

David didn't seem to care. Most men in his position wouldn't. He had one thing and one thing only on his mind right now. He wanted to get inside her and fast. But as he promised, he took his time. They lay together, a tangle of legs and arms, exploring each other's bodies with eyes and hands, with kisses and tongues.

Only then, did Cydney remember what she and Carmen had talked about.

"David," she said in a startling voice, as she pushed herself up on one elbow, "what about birth control? I don't use any form of birth control."

Once again, David seemed oblivious to her concerns, "It's okay," he said, his voice hoarse with passion, "trust me, it's okay. Just trust me."

She tried to speak again, wanting an explanation, but David's mouth covered hers. His tongue pried her lips apart and with rhythmic thrusts delved into the recesses of her sugary mouth. Her body told him she was ready to receive him and he could wait no longer. He parted her legs and positioned himself between them. With their eyes still embracing each other, he moved forward and gently entered the private most part of her.

The pain was sharp but brief. She wrapped her arms around his neck and hooked her legs over his, eager to receive him, eager to please him. David's voice came in soft whispers. He spoke her name over and over. He murmured wild words of passion, he instructed her on how to move to help them both achieve the maximum pleasure. Cydney felt alive. So alive! She tried to do just as David asked. She was no longer embarrassed or afraid. She was enjoying their lovemaking. And just when she thought she had never experienced such bliss, something at the very core of her being burst forth. Lights exploded before her eyes, blinding her. So intense was the feeling, a low moan escaped her lips. She tried to focus on David's face but it too, was awash with passion.

His fervent, rhythmic movement increased and then suddenly stopped. He slowly thrust himself forward, deeper and deeper into her, and then at last, buckled silently over her.

He shifted his weight so he now lay next to her. Cydney's eyes were closed but she had a smile on her face. David couldn't help but smile, too. They lay together in silence for several minutes. Finally, David pushed himself up on to an elbow and looked down at her.

"Cydney, you're wonderful."

She opened her eyes and smiled up at him. "I felt so awkward," she said sheepishly, "I didn't know what to do. This is the first time --." He pressed his fingers to her lips and she stopped talking.

"Some things come naturally," he said with a smile, "I think lovemaking is one of them. Would you like a glass of wine?" Cydney was so emotional, she could only nod. David got up and put on his under shorts. "Never know who you might run into in the kitchen," he said with a grin.

When he returned with a bottle of Riesling and two glasses, Cydney had propped herself up on the pillows and pulled the sheet up over her breasts. She held the glasses while David poured the wine. He set the bottle on the night table and slid into bed beside her. She gave him one glass and kept the other. Without speaking, they touched their glasses together. The fine crystal made a melodious sound. They sipped.

"What kind of wine is this?" Cydney asked, "It's very good. A little sweet."

"Yes, it is," David agreed. "It's a good Riesling. It's a dessert wine. It seemed appropriate, because I feel like I've just had a feast!" She laughed at that. "You have the most wonderful laugh," he told her. Cydney was so content lying here next to David, sipping wine. She felt so fulfilled. So alien to the life she knew just a few short months ago.

"So," David continued, "do you think having sex is wonderful?"

"I don't know," she said with sincerity, "I've never had sex, but I think making love is fabulous!"

This time David laughed, but he quickly grew serious, "I didn't hurt you, did I?"

"It hurt for just a second, but the pleasure far out weighed the pain." She was serious, now too.

"The next time, it won't hurt."

"Prove it," she challenged.

Without hesitation, David took the wine glasses and set them on the night table. He shimmied out of his under shorts. He pulled her atop him and began fondling her face, her neck, her breasts. She returned his caresses. Running her fingers through the thick dark hair on his chest and tracing it down his stomach to his penis, already hardening under her touch. They kissed, they played, they enjoyed each other's bodies. David sat up and retrieved the wine bottle. He let just a few drips run down her breasts and quickly lapped it up. She straddled him and watched in delight as his facial expressions reflected his pleasure. They switched positions and David, slow and methodic, gentle and loving – proved it!

When they were again satiated they drank more wine. Amid the dim lights and soft music, they fell asleep.

David stirred. What was that sound? He was used to being alone in bed and something was different. Oh yeah! He smiled before he even opened his eyes. The room was bright so he knew it was morning. He forced open one eye and caught sight of the clock. Six twenty. Only six twenty? And what was that noise? He turned over, Cydney was gone. Still fighting grog, he leaned forward on his elbows and looked around. The bathroom door was ajar and he could now identify the sound. Cydney was taking a shower. Still naked, he tiptoed silently toward the bathroom. He could just make out her silhouette through the beveled glass and steam. She was humming softly. He yanked open the glass door and roared. Cydney screamed! Through the steam she couldn't identify the intruder and tried to cover her breasts with her arms. He stepped into the shower.

"Last night you were begging for me and now you scream at me?"

"Oh, God, David, you scared me!"

"Who did you think it was, Harland?" He laughed uncontrollably.

He stood as far back as he could and watched the water cascade over her beautiful body. She had pinned her hair up haphazardly, soap bubbles drifted downward and whirlpooled at her feet. David took the bar of soap from her and began rubbing her skin with it. She tossed her head back and gave him free range. His hands moved deftly over her body and when she opened her eyes she could see he was aroused. She took the soap from him and lathered his body, heightening his desire. He unpinned her hair and watched it fall and mat against her neck and back. He pushed her to her knees, reached for the shampoo and applied some to his hands. He worked it into her gnarled hair. As he gently massaged her head, she found a new way to pleasure him.

CHAPTER THIRTY-FOUR

When Sophie and Gracie arrived at noon on Wednesday, no one was at home. But their instincts, along with empty wine glasses, a few dirty dishes and a display of fabulous feminine toiletries in one of the guest bathrooms told them David had a guest, and they sincerely hoped it was the young lady they had heard David and Harland discussing, or if the truth were known, arguing about.

Meanwhile, David and Cydney were out shopping. David insisted they go to the big department stores, where they probably would be recognized by some of the locals. David insisted it was not for his ego but for his career. He told Cydney to choose whatever she wanted and that he would pay for it. His gift to her for the New Year. David knew her taste was impeccable and she would choose just the right thing to impress the Caprock's as well as Harland at dinner tonight.

She proved him right. When she exited the fitting room at Bergdorf Goodman wearing an elegant, cream colored crepe jump suit with fitted cuffs at the wrists, taupe hose and alligator skin shoes, with her hair piled high and held in place with rhinestone clips, and topped with an alpaca cape in muted brown tones, even the clerks were spellbound. Cydney was comfortable with the intimate setting Bergdorf provided. It was quiet and somewhat secluded, which suited her just fine. The clerks showered her with attention and although the prices were out of sight as far as Cydney was concerned, David sat quietly in a Queen Ann chair, enjoying the one-woman fashion show and sipping a cup of tea. He took pleasure watching the glow in Cydney's eyes as the clerks brought one outfit after another for her to try on. She paraded before David in each one and selected only the ones he gave an approving nod to.

From Bergdorf Goodman to Barneys to Bloomingdale's, Cydney shopped until she was exhausted and she never concerned herself with the cost of anything.

When she confessed as much to David later, he only laughed, "Now you're beginning to act like I want you to, like a wealthy New Yorker. You don't need to be concerned about the price of anything. I'll take care of that."

Inside she felt a little guilty but on the outside she was very happy because she had never, in her whole life, had such exquisite clothes to wear. David was happy, too, because he could see that Cydney was developing a taste for the good life and he vowed that he would use whatever resources he had to win her.

From the moment David introduced Cydney to Sophie and Gracie, they adored her and they doted on her like two cows mothering a newborn calf. Since they didn't have to prepare dinner Wednesday evening, they squandered their time in the kitchen asking Cydney questions and listening to her chatter. She told them all about Wisconsin, about how she met David and the wonderful weekend they had spent together in Chicago. And both Sophie and Gracie could tell by the twinkle in Cydney's eyes that she and David were more than just friends. They in turn answered her questions about their years of service to David and his family; about David's childhood and teen years and of course, because they loved him like their own child, they didn't hesitate to paint a very rosy picture of the Jefferson and DuPrey families. These two lovable old ladies were at Cydney's beck and call and she couldn't help but bask in their attention.

Harland also returned mid-afternoon on Wednesday looking rather dapper. Cydney noticed that he had the New Year's Day issue of the *Times* tucked under his arm and when she found him in the kitchen with Sophie and Gracie with the newspaper spread out on the wide marble counter top, she had to admit he seemed pleased and he was even pleasant to her.

"Lovely picture, Cydney," he said with a bit of a spark in his eye, "Bet the Times will back off now and leave David alone."

"Maybe not," Sophie interjected. "Maybe they'll be on a mission to find out who this – quote- mystery woman is."

"Maybe we should tip them off," Harland suggested. "David might get more ink that way because I'm pretty sure Marilyn Shields will want the whole story. If I didn't know better, I'd think she was after David herself." They all laughed and Cydney couldn't help but join in.

"You look well, Harland," Cydney said in her most pleasant voice.

"As do you, my dear. And may I ask how you are enjoying New York?"

"Well, I haven't seen much of it. We walked in Central Park yesterday and today we went shopping at all the fabulous stores I've heard about but never dreamed I would be shopping at. Tomorrow I want to walk the Brooklyn Bridge and David said there are lots of museums to visit."

"How long will you be staying?" Sophie asked.

"Well, I'm not sure, Sophie, I don't have to be back for class until second semester, which starts on January 28th. Of course David thinks I should stay for weeks, but to be honest, Carmen, that's my roommate, and I just moved into a new apartment, well actually, it's not new, but an apartment and I didn't even have a chance to get settled. But maybe I'll stay for a few extra days."

"Oh, my dear, I hope so," Gracie interjected, "we haven't seen David this happy in a long, long time." Cydney blushed a little, but smiled broadly at both Sophie and Gracie. Even Harland seemed pleased to have her there.

Dinner with Harland and Tom and Joyce Caprock went very well. When Phillip deposited them at the entrance to the Tavern on the Green and David took her cape, all eyes rested on her as the host led them to the Crystal Room. She looked stunning in her new outfit and David was bursting with pride. He was eager to introduce her to his friends and was very pleased to see that Cydney was immediately comfortable with Tom and Joyce, and even Harland, which surprised him. The women talked quietly over a glass of wine while the gentlemen discussed a small business matter.

Cydney liked Joyce and Joyce liked Cydney. They both agreed that they should get together again before Cydney went back to Champaign. Of course, Joyce would never be so rude as to ask Cydney's age, but she looked quite young in spite of being very sophisticated and Joyce was flabbergasted to learn that Cydney was still in college.

After the men had completed their business, they ordered more wine, and Tom proposed a toast to Cydney.

"An angel, who makes the devil smile," he said holding his glass in the air and nodding toward David as he spoke the word devil. The crystal chimed as they saluted each other.

As the conversation buzzed around him, Harland sat back, surveying the group. He had to agree with Sophie and Gracie, David had not been this happy for months. The stories Marilyn Shields had printed about him weighed heavy on his conscience. Harland and David had argued several times about the matter because David's Uncle Jonathon, Harland's brother, had been gay. At that time in history, a gay man, from a wealthy family, which was often in the limelight, did not bode well. Under pressure from his peers, he came out of the closet and was immediately shunned by family and society and when he could bear the burden no longer, took his own life. Harland often lamented about their family. Yes, they were very wealthy, but they lacked harmony. They lacked sincerity. They lacked love. David told Harland he was determined to break that mold and from the moment he laid eyes on Cydney, he hoped that she would be the one to help him capitulate the stigma of indifference.

David glanced at Harland, who gave an approving nod. David nodded back, so pleased with his uncle. His eyes drifted over to Cydney; young, sweet, beautiful Cydney, still chatting away with Joyce and he was more determined then ever to take her as his wife.

Cydney talked incessantly on the way home, drawing an amusing smile from both David and Phillip. Even Harland, who pretended he wasn't listening, had to grin. She loved the wine, the food was irresistible, the restaurant was divine, Joyce was a saint. She adored New York, and on and on.

She slapped him on the shoulder and stopped talking only when David leaned forward and said to Phillip, "Is this the same lovely lady you drove home on New Year's Eve?" Their laughter filled the silent void.

CHAPTER THIRTY-FIVE

After several days of endless shopping, sightseeing and fun, and nights filled with passionate lovemaking, Cydney moved her things into David's room and she wasn't even embarrassed that Sophie and Gracie knew it.

This night had been special again. They had taken in a poignant off-Broadway drama, had a late dinner at The Copa, one of David's favorite restaurants, and mulled over the play for hours, sipping wine. Cydney learned to love the late nights. It was their time. David never seemed to be in a hurry to get home and when they did, they engaged in intimate but meaningful conversations. This night had been no exception. It seemed like they had known each other forever instead of the meager six months since they met. David was already in bed, propped up against a pillow with his hands clasped behind his head. Cydney sat cross-legged on top of the thick comforter. She was so comfortable with David, they seemed like an old married couple as they discussed the days ahead. David was so easy to be with and Cydney had to admit that she was in love with him in spite of the fact that he often hurt her feelings, either consciously or unconsciously.

David told her they would spend the rest of the week sightseeing, but on Wednesday, January 9th, he would have to think about getting back to work and concentrate on his music. There were tours to book and new arrangements to work on. Although he would be busy during the afternoons and some evenings, he wanted her to stay for a few more weeks. She finally agreed to stay until Saturday the 19th. Then she would have to get back to Champaign and prepare for the next semester of school and try to get back in Sam Ezpazito's good graces.

She had called Sam shortly after she arrived in New York and told him she wanted some time off. He ranted and raved as usual and said she would be looking for another job if she didn't send her article in and fast. She sent the article she had written along with a note that she would not be submitting any more material in the foreseeable future. Right now her life was full of David and the wonderful time she was having discovering New York. The job at the newspaper could wait!

David started reading. Cydney began touching up the nail polish on her toes. She wore new silk pajamas in a pale green color and as she reached toward her toes, her hair fell forward, partially covering her face. The loose fitting pajamas exposed her lovely breasts as she stretched out her arm to dab her pretty toes. David was having a hard time concentrating; he put the book aside.

"Want a glass of wine and a snack?"

She pushed her hair back and hooked it behind her ear, not stopping to look up at him. "Do you always drink and eat in bed?"

"Yes, actually, I do quite often. When I get home from a concert I usually make some notes about how well the performance went. Which songs I played, how the audience reacted, that sort of thing and I usually mull it over with a glass of wine. It helps me relax."

"I've had quite a bit of wine already." She looked up at him now and saw him staring at her.

"Well let's have some more. It will help you relax, too."

She laughed now, "I'm very relaxed, David. But yes, I'll have a glass. Do you have more of the Riesling? That was my favorite." As he was getting up and preparing to go to the kitchen for the wine, she surprised him. "Are you going to make love to me tonight?"

"Why do you ask? Do you want me to?"

"Yes, certainly I do, but I've heard that if a man drinks too much he may have difficulty getting aroused. Is that true?"

He walked around the side of the bed to where she was sitting and wound his hand in her hair. "Well, I guess it is true sometimes, but I'm pretty sure that won't happen to me tonight, Cydney, just the sight of you makes me hot." He released the handful of hair and she kissed his wrist as he backed away.

When David returned with the wine, Cydney had finished her repair work and again sat cross-legged on the bed. She had removed her pajama top, her arms were extended behind her and her bare breasts jutted outward, the nipples not yet taut. She accepted the wine glass and waited for him to get situated beside her. She leaned over and kissed him hungrily. His free hand sought her left breast and gently caressed it. Her free hand found his growing erection and she fondled it. They continued to sip their wine and stroke each other.

Cydney pulled back abruptly, "David, I need to ask you something. The other night when I told you I didn't use any birth control you said it was okay, I should trust you. What exactly did that mean because I really don't use any birth control? Up until now, I've never had a reason to."

"Do you trust me?" he asked.

"Yes, of course I trust you, but I'm just curious. We've made love several times and we didn't use any protection. I don't want to get pregnant, at least not right now! Is there something I need to know?" David was hesitant and she thought he seemed a little embarrassed but she continued to press him.

"David? What is it?"

Finally he answered her, "Well, if you must know, when I was a teenager I had a very bad case of the mumps and the doctor said that it usually causes sterility, so you don't need any birth control as long as you're with me."

"But are you sure? Have you ever been checked?" Cydney was more sympathetic now.

"Yes, Cydney, I was tested."

"Under what circumstances were you checked? I mean, why?"

"You're pretty damn nosey. If you weren't so beautiful and desirable, I'd throw you out." He kissed the tip of her nose. "Remember when you asked me about serving breakfast in bed to other women and I said two counting you? Well, that's true. I was serious with a woman several years ago. We were even contemplating marriage. She wanted desperately to get married and have a family. So I told her that it wasn't possible for me to have children and she suggested that we get tested. Well, the results were as the doctor predicted; I had a very, very low sperm count. She ran scared. I guess she only wanted my money and my name for her child. She didn't really love me!"

"Oh David, I'm so sorry," Cydney's voice was soft and understanding. She leaned forward and kissed him again. This time he took her glass and set it on the nightstand along with his. He pulled back the thick down comforter and together they slid into bed.

"I'm not," he said, "if I had married her I wouldn't be here with you." She needn't have worried about David's ability to perform. He did a fabulous job and they drifted off to sleep in each other's arms, satisfied and smiling.

When Cydney woke the next morning, David was already gone. She remembered that he said he needed to get back to work so she took her time showering, choosing her outfit and updating the journal she had started when she first arrived in New York. Then she made her way to the kitchen, where Sophie and Gracie were cleaning up the dishes and already preparing lunch.

"Good morning," Cydney said cheerfully.

"Good Morning, dear," they said in unison and immediately began fluttering about her, pouring coffee and preparing a place setting for her.

"Just coffee, thank you," she said with a smile, "I see it's almost lunch time. I didn't realize I was so exhausted."

Sophie and Gracie both gave her a shy, knowing smile. "That's what vacations are for, dear," Sophie said, "so one can sleep late and get rested."

"Well David likes to stay up very late," she told them, "and I'm not use to that."

"It's New York, dear," Gracie interjected. "The city comes alive late at night and David has always enjoyed that. You'll get used to it." She said it matter-of-factly, as if it were a given that Cydney would become a New Yorker.

"Is David about?" Cydney asked. "Or has he gone out?"

"He's in the study with Harland. I think they're working on the spring concert schedule," Sophie said.

"They've been in there for quite awhile and apparently are having another disagreement because I could hear them shouting at each other more than once. They certainly have been at odds with each other lately," Gracie offered.

"Maybe he would like a break." Cydney got off her perch and headed toward the study.

Sophie and Gracie exchanged glances. "David doesn't like to be interrupted when he's working," one of them said, but Cydney was already half way down the hall.

She paused at the door and listened to their voices, muffled but harsh so she was pretty sure they were having another argument. She thought David really would need a break. She rapped lightly on the door and then entered.

"Good mor---," she began.

Harland was behind the desk and looked up in surprise. David was seated with his back to the door but instantly swiveled around.

"How dare you!" he hissed at her, cutting off her greeting, "How dare you interrupt me when I'm working!"

Her smile disappeared and the color drained from her face.

"I knocked," she said trying to justify the intrusion, "I thought you might ---"

He rose to his feet and came toward the door, again cutting her off. "We're working," David said almost shouting, "I don't care what you thought." Cydney backed out of the room and David slammed the door. She stood there for just a split second, shocked, embarrassed and very angry. Then she turned and ran to the bedroom, tears spilling over her rosy cheeks.

She grabbed her suitcase from the armoire, the suitcase she brought with her. To hell with the bigger one David bought for her. She threw it on the bed and started packing her things, the tears still stinging her eyes. Enough of this place. Enough of this man, who loved his music over anyone and anything else. She was muttering to herself as she jammed things into her bag and she didn't hear David enter the room. He took her arm and spun her around to face him, a look of utter anguish on his handsome face.

"Cydney, oh, Cydney, God, I'm so sorry," he tried to put his arms around her but she pushed him back.

"Don't!" she said trying to keep her voice from quivering. "Don't come in here all sweet and nice and try to apologize."

"But I'm sorry. Really, I am." He did sound sincere.

"That was totally uncalled for. I've never been so humiliated in all my life. You had no reason to shout at me like that just because you're angry with Harland!" He could sense the anger in her voice.

"You're right, I was entirely out of line. Please, come here, give me a hug."

"No David!" Her anger was not subsiding. "You can't do this all the time. You can't hurt my pride and hurt my feelings and then just say you're sorry and think that that's going to make everything all right."

"What can I do to make it right?" David realized now how badly he had hurt her.

"Maybe, just maybe, you can't this time." He looked shocked.

"What does that mean?" He continued to try to put his arms around her and she continued to resist.

"You're used to always getting what you want, David. You say what you want, you do what you want and you think being wealthy and being half-assed famous makes it all okay. Well it doesn't! Do you know what you're problem is?" She didn't let him answer. "Your ego, that's the problem! And you know what else? You said you love me and I think you do, ***but*** you love your violin, and your music and yourself more than you love me or anyone or anything else." She slammed the suitcase shut. "Please call Phillip for me, I need a ride to the airport." David continued to look at her in disbelief. She went into the bathroom and continued gathering up her belongings. He followed her and blocked her exit.

"I said I was sorry and I said you were right, I was way out of line. I don't know what else to say." She could see the pain in his face. "And another thing you're right about, Cydney, I do love you. Regardless of how you feel about my career, I do love you and I intended to ask you to marry me before you left New York. Give me another chance. I'll try harder to put you first, I promise! I'll change."

"When you do, call me." She ducked under his arm and went back to packing. "I'm going home. Please call Phillip."

CHAPTER THIRTY-SIX

Cydney stood before the full-length mirror in her bedroom in the old farmhouse. On her left, Leta made some last minute adjustments to the wedding dress that she had custom made for Cydney. On the right, Carmen put the finishing touches on Cydney's massive copper curls.

Late September was a wonderful time to have a wedding. The weather was cool and sunny, the leaves in the north woods were already boasting color and the fall concert tour had not yet begun.

"Leta," Cydney said, "thank you again for making my wedding dress. It's just what I wanted. It's so beautiful!" Leta was so overcome with emotion that she could not speak.

They had sipped coffee at the table in the big kitchen and sketched out a design. They had shopped together for the fabric and the beading and the material for the veil. Cydney was like her own daughter and she was so proud to play such an important role in this, the biggest day of Cydney's life. And the dress *was* beautiful. It was ivory colored with puffy sleeves that ended just above the elbow and a square neck, which showed just the right amount of cleavage. The edge of the sleeves and the neckline both were peppered with tiny sequins, each one sewn on by hand with love. The bodice was fitted and came to a "v" in the front. Below that the skirt flared out in soft folds and fell to the floor, the hem sparkling with the same tiny sequins.

Her hair was pulled high on her head and a sequin-studded tiara, with a veil attached in the back, fit over it, allowing some tresses to hang free. As always, her make-up was perfect and there was an aura about her that was befitting a young woman on her wedding day.

Carmen, her only attendant, wore a satin gown of soft mauve with sleeves and neckline similar to Cydney's dress. Leta had made Carmen's dress too, and she was stunning. Her blond hair was pulled up and entwined with Baby's Breath; her skin so tan from the Mississippi sun.

It was difficult to say which of the ladies was most excited: bride, makeshift mom or maid of honor. Each of them was beautiful; each of them so perfectly coiffed, Cydney teased that Carmen or Leta would steal the show. Of course they denied that possibility, since all eyes would be on the bride.

The three of them had spent hours behind closed doors preparing for the four o'clock ceremony and in just thirty minutes Caleb would drive them to the Balsam Hills Presbyterian Church in his brand new 1974 Plymouth. There, with a lump in his throat and bursting with indescribable pride he would lead his granddaughter down the aisle of this small country church that held so many bitter sweet memories.

The guest list included Uncle Aaron and Aunt Patrice, Brock and Ellen and a few other locals. Donovan and Victoria had come and so did Tony. In fact, he was Carmen's escort. Geoff had come stag, hoping to charm some unsuspecting local girl into being his escort for the evening. Sophie and Gracie had come to help with the food and there was Phillip. Dear, sweet Phillip. Also, the Savages and the Caprocks, and of course, Harland, the best man.

"Leta! Cydney! Come on or we'll be late." Caleb was standing next to the car, reaching into the window and honking the horn as he called to them.

"Five more minutes," Leta hollered back.

The horn honking continued intermittently until at last the three came down the back steps, dresses held high to avoid the dusty driveway. It took another five minutes for them to get settled into the car.

"Grandpa," Cydney said, "you look so handsome in your tuxedo. Maybe we should have a second ceremony for you and Leta." Leta and Caleb exchanged glances.

"I think one wedding today is enough," Caleb said, his eyes still focused on Leta.

The new car moved gracefully up the driveway and turned right onto Apple Road.

They rode in silence. Cydney's head turning from side to side, drinking in the sight of the lush green fields and the trees, alive with color.

As she reflected on these sights from the past, she also reflected on the last few months.

She had left New York in a huff, no question about that. Cydney had never felt such anger in her entire life and now she could relate to the anger Carmen felt for her mother the day they left Jackson.

When David realized he could not convince Cydney to stay, he called Phillip as she had asked. He watched in silence as she finished packing and went back to the kitchen to say a solemn good-bye to Sophie and Gracie. They didn't ask questions, but they surely knew she was leaving in anger.

David escorted her to the elevator where he turned her over to Phillip, but Cydney did not speak to him. No good-bye, no thank you, nothing. She simply stared straight-ahead, lip quivering as if she might cry at any moment. David thought it best to give her time to cool off.

Phillip, too, was silent as he wove his way through the streets of New York up Queens Boulevard and back toward the Brooklyn Queens Expressway to LaGuardia. He whistled softly to himself and occasionally glanced at Cydney through the rearview mirror. At the airport check-in, he helped her from the car and hailed a porter. Phillip gave him instructions and then turned to Cydney. He placed both of his hands on her elbows and kissed her gently on the cheek.

"He loves you Cydney. He really does. He just has his priorities mixed up. I wish you'd give him another chance." Cydney could no longer contain herself. Tears rolled down her cheeks and made droplets on her new suede jacket, a gift from David. Mustering up a smile, she turned and walked through the doors just behind the porter.

Phillip watched in silence just to make sure she went to the right ticket counter and then maneuvered his car back into traffic. He wondered what had happened and how David could have let her go.

"You stupid son-of-a-bitch," he said out loud as if David was within earshot.

Cydney called Carmen from Chicago just as they were announcing her connecting flight.

"Wait up for me," she told Carmen, "I don't have time to explain but I'll be there in a couple of hours."

Carmen was pacing the floor by the time Cydney arrived in Champaign and there was a huge bouquet of flowers waiting for her along with a card of apology. Carmen grabbed her around the neck and hugged her tight. She jumped up and down bubbling over with excitement. She wanted to know every detail of every day, every kiss, every sexual encounter.

She was amazed when Cydney collapsed on the sofa, a mass of nerves and tears. Carmen didn't patronize her. She let her babble on between sobs. When the tears abated, anger again ran its course. David was, according to Cydney, an egotist, as well as a conceited arrogant, self-centered bastard. How could she have been duped by his charm, taken in by that charismatic smile? How could she have given away her precious virginity to this self-indulgent snob?

Hours later, finally calm, they sat sipping wine. Cydney filled in the blanks, painting a rather distorted picture.

"There must have been some good times?" Carmen asked.

"Yes, I guess there were. Quite a lot actually." Cydney raised her glass, "He taught me about wine. Good wine." A slight smile crossed her tear-swollen face, she dug in her handbag, still lying on the sofa, "And there's this." She tossed the New Years Eve pictures from the *New York Times* in Carmen's direction.

"Oh Gosh, Cyd! Look at you. How beautiful you look!" Her eyes scanned the pictures, the captions and the related story before she flung it back at Cydney. "If you ask me," she went on, "anyone with half a brain can see by the way he's looking at you that he's in love with you."

"Maybe he is," Cydney said softly, her eyes filling again, "but I'm not number one, Carmen, his work is. And that doesn't cut it for me."

"Do *you* love *him*? I mean have you really searched your soul and asked yourself that big question? Are you better off with him or without him?"

"That's a non-issue. Of course I'm better off with him. He's rich. I'm flat broke. He can buy anything he wants – but there in lies the catch. He can't buy me. He tried, the whole time I was in New York, he tried. And obviously, he's still tying. Just look at the flowers."

Both pairs of eyes looked to the huge bouquet in an exquisite crystal vase, overpowering an end table in the small living room.

"Cyd, look at the big picture. Of course you'd be better off financially, but what about your heart. What's your heart telling you to do?"

"That's what's so confusing, Car. The wonderful dinners, the theatre, the excitement of New York, they all were part of the romance. It's hard to sort out!"

"Well," Carmen went on, "what about this. When you weren't with him, did you miss him? Did you look forward to the time when you'd be together? Just the two of you?"

"Those were the best evenings, Carmen. We'd go out to dinner or to the theatre and when we got back to his apartment, we'd drink wine in bed and talk about our evening. Or any number of things. It seemed like we had so much to talk about. Then we'd make love. That's the David I want to be with. That's the David I love."

"It sounds to me like you have sorted it out. Now you just need to make David understand."

"I guess that's why I left so abruptly. Maybe such drastic action will make him rethink things."

"I hope so Cyd, because you deserve the best and you deserve to have the lavish life style that David can provide."

"That's not important to me, Carmen. My grandmother died when I was six and right after she died, grandpa and Leta became lovers. I didn't know it then but I know it now. I know that grandpa loved Leta even before my grandma died. He loved her because she was caring and gentle and good. Because she worked hard and didn't complain, because she took care of grandma even though she obviously had feelings for my grandpa. She gave her all to earn the love and respect of our entire family. That's what makes her so special. I want David to love me like grandpa loves Leta."

"Then tell him. Tell him how you feel and what you want. Tell him what you expect of him. If he truly loves you, he will change his way of thinking."

They talked on and on, late into the night and by that time Carmen was convinced that Cydney really loved David. But Cydney had to convince herself.

The next day another bouquet of flowers arrived. And the next day and the next. On Saturday, Cydney was forced to call David and tell him to stop sending flowers. They didn't have any more room in the apartment. David was somewhat aloof on the phone but reluctantly agreed to no more flowers. She kept one bouquet and delivered the other three to a local nursing home.

On Tuesday, a package arrived. Cydney undid the plain brown wrapper to reveal a black velvet box tied with silver string. Inside was a dazzling pair of earrings. Small, round, just her style. This was David's way. A spontaneous surprise, yes and that was thoughtful but it was a very expensive way to say he was sorry. He was again using his wealth to try to win her back. Why not just call and say, "Cydney, I love you. I can't live without you!"

Like the flowers, the gifts continued for several days. A pair of leather gloves, a cashmere scarf, a silk teddy. Each with a romantic innuendo attached. Once again, Cydney called David to tell him to stop sending the gifts. This time he sounded much happier on the phone.

"Only if you'll say you'll give me another chance," he said.

"I'll consider it if you change your priorities. If you want me back David, I have to be number one."

"You are," he said emphatically.

"No, I'm not," she argued. "Your work is, David. Your work is your life."

"My work is what makes my life possible."

"Wrong!" she snapped. "Your work makes your life *style* possible."

"So what are you saying? I have to change my life style to get you back?"

"Do what you wish. I'm just telling you that I don't care about the lavish life style. I care about you!"

"Ah ha! You admit it then. You do care about me," he chuckled thinking he had tricked her.

"That's my point, David. If what we have is true love, it wouldn't matter how lavish our life style. We would find contentment in each other."

"Cydney, I've lived like this my entire life. I can't just throw it all away."

"You don't have to David. Just rearrange your priorities."

"Then what?" he persisted.

"Then call me." He knew the conversation was over and pressed her no more.

Weeks passed and there was no word from David. With no more flowers and gifts, Cydney was able to focus on school. She even charmed Sam Ezpazito into giving her another assignment. She stayed up late, studied hard and immersed herself in her work. In spite of all that, she realized late one night, while sipping a glass of wine and studying for an economics test, that she missed David, terribly.

"Call him." Carmen urged.

"No Car, I can't. I told him to call me when he had his priorities straight. I can't cave now or things will never work out."

Several more weeks passed and Cydney was struggling now to keep her grades up and Sam was on her ass again. She missed another deadline. She started to cut classes. Some days, when the alarm rang, she just pulled the covers up over her head and refused to get out of bed. She cried often.

It was a beautiful spring day in early April and Carmen was running out of patience. This was the third morning in a row that Cydney refused to get up. Finally, Carmen stormed into Cydney's room, grabbed the blankets and flung them back. Cydney was curled up in a fetal position and let out a wail when her security was snatched away.

"Cydney Brown," Carmen almost screamed, "get your ass out of bed!"

"No Carmen, please, leave me alone."

Carmen was furious. She grabbed Cydney's arm attempting to pull her to a sitting position. "Get up! You're really pissin' me off! Get up!" Cydney pulled away, continuing to ignore Carmen. "Look at you!" Carmen went on. "If you're so damn love sick, call him! You can't go on like this. You're failing in school, you're on the verge of losing your job and you've been a real pain in the ass to live with." Carmen was exasperated. She stood there gasping for breath, tears streaming down her face. "Either you call him or I will!"

"No Carmen! You wouldn't!" Cydney bolted upright and looked at her dear friend. Her mentor, her confidant, the sister she never had.

"Yes, I will. Don't you see, Cyd? You obviously love him and since he hasn't called you, you have to call him. If you don't, you'll crack up."

Cydney started sobbing uncontrollably. Even as Carmen sat beside her on the disheveled bed and wrapped her arms around her, the tears would not stop. Her shoulders shook, her breath came in short gulps and her lips quivered. All she could do was shake her head and when she was finally able to speak, she said, "I won't call him. I'll be all right, Carmen, really I will. Thank you for being such a good friend, for seeing me through this misery. I'll pull myself together, really, I'll be okay."

And Cydney held true to her word. She studied for finals and eked out passing grades. She quit her job before Sam fired her and as soon as she finished her last test on Wednesday, May 10, she packed her things and headed for Wisconsin.

She cried on Leta's shoulder as she had on Carmen's. But Leta, in her infinite wisdom, offered no advice. She just listened and when the tears stopped once again, Leta sat her down at that big blue kitchen table and made her eat.

"Everyone thinks better on a full stomach," Leta said, "and just look at you. Nothing but a rack of bones." Leta was right. Cydney had lost at least ten pounds and the lack of sleep that plagued her night after night was evident in the dark circles lying thick beneath her sad eyes.

It was good to be home. So good. There was so much to talk about. Just Leta and grandpa and her. She poured her heart out to them at dinner over cole slaw made fresh while they talked, baking powder biscuits saturated with honey, pot roast with carrots and onions, mashed potatoes, creamy and smooth and topped with thick brown gravy. No fancy wines, no exotic foods, just good ole' home cooking. And just when she thought she couldn't eat another bite, out came the apple pie, bubbling over with sweet crabs from the tree in the front yard. They lingered over coffee and then continued their conversation while Caleb puffed contentedly on his pipe and Leta and Cydney did the dishes.

The next morning she woke refreshed. What is it about coming home? What is it about crisp, clean sheets smelling like fresh air and sunshine? What is it about home that makes your problems disappear and makes you wish you had never left in the first place? What is it about home that makes you lonesome in your heart for days gone by? Cydney was unbelievably calm. There were no more tears. She shimmied into a pair of jeans and topped them off with a *"fighting Ilini"* sweatshirt, slid on her sling back loafers and headed for the kitchen. She could smell breakfast and in spite of her late night pledge that she would never eat again, she was ravenous. She could hear Caleb and Leta's voices drifting up the stairs. There was a third voice mingling with theirs; one she didn't recognize until she reached the kitchen door. Brock! It was too late to turn back.

"Cydney!" He came toward her, genuinely pleased to see her. His huge arms encircled her petite frame and lifted her right off the ground. "How are you? You look great!"

"And you're a damn liar," she said returning his hug and planting a kiss on his cheek. "I look like crap but I slept so well and I feel much better this morning. How are you?" She realized she was happy to see him, too.

"Were you sick?" He looked more serious now and before she could answer Caleb interjected.

"Love sick. That's what she is. Love sick."

"Grandpa." Cydney said in a voice trying to discredit his statement. Leta raised an eyebrow in his direction. Caleb knew by now that when that left eyebrow goes up, he'd better pipe down. So he said no more.

"I'm fine, Brock. Really, I am. I just wanted to come for a visit. A nice long visit."

"How long?" His questions were blunt.

"Well, I'm not on any schedule this summer, so I can stay as long as I want to."

"Good," he nodded, "maybe will have some time to catch up." His smile was still captivating. She hadn't seen him in months but it seemed like only yesterday.

"So how's married life?" Cydney went on.

"Good. It's good," Brock looked down and shuffled his feet around. He said no more.

"I hope I have a chance to meet Ellen."

Brock looked up, his eyes meeting Cydney's. "She's not here right now. She went to visit her sister over at Mason. Her sister just had a baby so it seemed like a good time for her to go. You know – to help out and all."

Cydney nodded. "The coffee smells good," she shifted her gaze to Leta, who busied herself with breakfast.

"Have you eaten, Brock?" Leta asked.

"No, but I'm heading over to Bad River so I'll catch a bite on the way."

"Nonsense!" Leta retorted. "You'll eat with us." That matter settled they all sat around the table making small talk.

"I couldn't get along anymore without Brock," Caleb said more to Leta than to Cydney, "my age is really catching up with me."

"Grandpa," Cydney said, "you're as fit as a fiddle." She felt herself blush at the pun but only Leta picked up on it and a trace of a smile crossed her face.

"No Cydney, I'm not. I really need to slow down some and Brock knows everything there is to know about Oakwood. He's in charge now. He manages all the crops and fields. He decides what gets planted where and what goes to soil bank." Cydney looked at Brock. He was the one blushing now as Caleb continued to heap praise upon him. He returned Cydney's smile and just shrugged his shoulders. After Caleb and Brock went outdoors, Leta refilled her coffee cup and Cydney's, too. They still weren't talked out. Leta gave more details about Brock taking over.

"Your grandfather's having some health issues, Cydney. That's why he wants Brock to manage Oakwood. He made Brock promise to stay on as manager for as long as Oakwood Acres is in the Brown family."

"And did Brock agree? That's a huge commitment to make," Cydney look concerned.

Leta nodded, yes. "It was only a verbal agreement but Caleb and Brock are like father and son, so I know that they will both keep their word. Brock can always live here at no cost to him. Caleb pays him a good wage and of course Brock is worth every bit of it. He works very hard and is very smart when it comes to farming."

"What's wrong with grandpa?" Cydney asked.

"Well, it's a heart problem of some sort. The doctor wants him to go over to that clinic in Minnesota for more tests but he refuses," Leta looked concerned, too.

"Refuses? How can he refuse? Can't you make him go, Leta?"

"No Cydney, I can't. I've talked till I was blue in the face but he just won't do it. He keeps saying he's fine for now and if he gets worse, he'll go."

"What symptoms does he have?"

"Well, he gets tired out pretty quickly and every once and awhile he breaks out in a cold sweat. But he says he doesn't have any chest pains, never has. I think he's telling me the truth." Leta was philosophical about it.

"It's not only chest pain you need to be concerned about. It's shoulder or arm pain, even neck pain."

"Well, I'm tired of arguing about it with him. He promised he would go to Minnesota if he has other signs or if the ones he has get worse." Leta was exasperated, "Your grandfather is a very stubborn man." Cydney could see the love in Leta' eyes, as well as the pain and she opted not to press her anymore. She knew full well that Leta would do everything in her power to keep Caleb alive and well. "So," Leta continued, "in the meantime, he's making sure Brock knows everything he needs to know about the farm."

"Is there really that much involved?"

"I think so," Leta said. "Some of the land is rented out to neighboring farms, some is in soil bank, we use some. Brock knows all about the crops, the latest in farming technology, pesticides, crop rotation – all the things necessary to produce a bumper crop and keep the farm productive. Plus, he can build just about anything. You should see how he fixed up the cottage."

Cydney absorbed it all and instead of being apprehensive about her grandfather's health and the future of the farm, she was secure in knowing that he had taken measures to insure that Leta, Cydney, Uncle Aaron and his family, and Brock, yes even Brock, would always have this place to call home.

By the second week of June, first crop hay was ready for baling and Cydney was thrilled when Brock agreed to let her drive the tractor. She handled it pretty well, driving along side the wind rows, while the baler scooped up the hay and spit the bales out onto the wagon, where Brock and Caleb neatly stacked them. Early June peas and the strawberries were ready for harvest too, and she spent hours in the garden helping Leta. Cydney enjoyed the farm. She didn't realize how much she missed her family.

The summer sun bronzed her skin and added yet more copper hues to her already brilliant hair. She took long walks in the fields, lay in the hay mow like she had as a kid, and sat for hours beside the pond watching a family of geese strut single file along the sandy shore.

It was on one of her walks, on a cool, breezy morning that she met Ellen. Cydney had left early and walked the eastern perimeter of the farm. It was cooler than she expected and further, too, so she cut to the northwest back through a field of blossoming alfalfa. Deep in thought, drinking in the heady aroma of the alfalfa, she almost missed the slender woman sitting silently on the ridge overlooking the pond. She was clad in jeans and a t-shirt topped off with a frayed flannel shirt. Her hair hung free blowing softly in the early morning breeze. She wore no make-up. She didn't need any. She was a natural beauty. She sat on the ground, knees drawn up, her elbows resting on them. Her eyes, blue as the sky, focused somewhere in the distance. So silent was she that had Cydney not caught the movement of her sandy hair in the wind, she may have passed her by unnoticed.

"Good morning," Cyndey called out. The woman jumped to her feet and spun around to face her. "I'm sorry if I startled you," Cydney went on. "You must be Ellen."

"Yes, yes, I am," Ellen answered nervously, "and you're Cydney, I expect."

"That's right." Cydney advanced toward her and extended her hand. Ellen reluctantly accepted it. "I'm so happy to meet you, Ellen," Cydney said. "Beautiful morning, isn't it?"

"Yes," the still nervous Ellen answered, "but a bit cool. Do you always get up so early? I mean, I usually do and I've never seen you out here before."

"This is very early for me," Cydney chuckled, "but I couldn't sleep – guess I'm all caught up on my rest now. I usually don't walk until later in the day."

"What else do you do all day? I mean, if you don't mind my asking." Ellen looked her up and down obviously drawing a conclusion of some kind.

"Well, to be honest with you, I really haven't been doing much of anything. I walk, read, help Leta. I came home because I needed some time to sort some things out in my life. I was on the verge of a - well, let's just say, I needed a rest."

"Must've been a guy," Ellen said sort of under her breath.

"Excuse me?" Cydney said.

"I said, it must have been a guy," Ellen repeated louder and slower.

"What makes you think that?" Cydney questioned.

"Well, who else can cause a woman so much grief?"

"I guess if I were honest, I'd have to say, I caused my own problems," Cydney said.

"You mean there was no guy?" Ellen looked surprised.

"I didn't say there was no guy. I just said *I* made a mess of things."

"Because of a guy."

"Well, yes, I guess it was because of a guy," Cydney conceded. There was an awkward pause then.

"I'm sorry I got so personal," Ellen said still eyeing Cydney, "It's just that I feel like I've known you for a long time. Brock and Leta talk about you all the time."

"Only good things, I hope," Cydney smiled.

"Of course," Ellen brushed off the question. "So have you sorted things out? Have you decided what you're going to do?"

Cydney hesitated, not wanting to answer, and then realized Ellen probably knew most of the story anyway. "It's not what I'm going to do. It's what he has to do. He has to decide if he wants me back."

"And why wouldn't he? I mean you're beautiful and Leta said you're very smart and have a heart of gold and Brock says you're sweet and honest and true."

"They're my family. Of course they're going to say nice things about me. They're prejudice," Cydney laughed.

"Brock's not really your family," Ellen said, their eyes meeting.

"Well no, not biologically, but we grew up together, he's sort of like my brother."

"Is he?" Ellen sounded perturbed. "I have brothers and let me tell you, none of my brothers worship me like Brock worships you."

Cydney felt herself flush. "I think you're mistaken. Brock and I have been close since childhood. Naturally, we're very fond of each other."

Now Ellen laughed, "To say the least. When I first met Brock that's all I ever heard. Cydney this – Cydney that. Truthfully, I got kinda tired of hearing it."

"I'm sorry," Cydney said trying to put Ellen at ease. "I remember when Brock first met you. He was head over heels crazy about you and he talked about you a lot, too. I guess that's just his way." Then trying to change the subject. "Do you work, Ellen?"

"Of course I work. Someone is this family has to have a real job." Cydney caught the sarcasm in her voice. "I work at the market in Balsam Hills, just part time, 20 to 30 hours a week." She kept rambling – "Brock says he wants to start a family but we can't afford a baby unless Brock gets a job where he can earn more money."

Cydney was growing uncomfortable with this conversation. Yet, she felt obligated to defend both Brock and her grandfather. "I think grandfather pays Brock quite well."

"Yes, I suppose he does as long as we stay home every single night, never go out to dinner, never go to a movie and never go on a vacation."

"Brock's a pretty basic guy. A real homebody." Cydney was defensive again and still trying to change the subject. "Brock told me your sister just had a baby. Boy or girl?"

"Girl," Ellen said abruptly. "And I don't even want Brock to see her because then he'll start with that family business again."

"Don't you want a family, Ellen?" Cydney asked.

"I want to have some fun. Go places, do things. We can talk about babies later."

Cydney fell silent. How ironic. She was trying to get David to focus less on material things and more on her. Ellen obviously wasn't satisfied with her life and wanted more than Brock could afford to give her. Cydney, once again, came to Brock's defense.

"Brock's always been the happiest when he's working on the land. He sticks pretty close to home and family's very important to him. Maybe because he lost his family when he was so young."

Ellen's eyes were distant once again, "Well, being stuck out here, not doing much of anything is not what I want outta life. It's not what makes me happy." Cydney realized that Ellen and Brock had problems and she didn't want to be involved in them. She had enough to deal with. She needed to end this conversation.

"I think I'll continue my walk now. I'm glad we finally met. Hope to see you soon." Cydney hurried down the hill, happy to leave the discontented Ellen behind. She was deep in thought as she made her way back to the house. She would ask Leta to fill her in on the situation. But then Cydney realized she shouldn't concern herself with Brock and Ellen. David was still on her mind.

Cydney continued to enjoy her days of leisure on the farm. She thought no more about Brock and Ellen until one afternoon Leta announced that she had invited them for dinner.

Cydney showered and put on a bright colored sundress with spaghetti straps. It showed off her tan. She wore sandals and pulled her hair, now bright chestnut from the summer sun, into a ponytail and added a matching ribbon. She looked fresh and cute, like the young farm girl she was. She borrowed Caleb's car and went into town to buy a bottle of wine. Cydney was getting pretty good at making the proper selection. This time she chose a chardonnay to go with the stuffed catfish Leta was making for dinner. It was one of Brock's favorite meals. Cydney remembered that from their childhood.

Brock and Ellen arrived looking fresh and happy. Ellen in shorts and a t-shirt with her lovely hair hanging free. She too, had a beautiful tan. Brock, in jeans and a t-shirt as usual, hair still damp from a recent shower and muscles bulging from under the sleeves, rolled up to his shoulders.

They made small talk during dinner and raved about the fish. Leta was such a good cook. Cydney noticed that she seemed to be the only one enjoying the wine. During dessert, Ellen said bluntly, "So Cydney, tell us about David. That's his name isn't it? David?"

Caleb, Leta and Brock all seemed to hold their breath until Cydney finally answered.

"Yes, his name is David. There's not much to tell. He's a New Yorker and a violinist. He tours, actually mostly in the east and mid west. He's becoming quite well known in New York."

"He must be rich," Ellen said.

"Sometimes musicians struggle to make ends meet," Brock said looking directly at Ellen, "and just because he's from New York doesn't mean he's got money." Cydney didn't answer. She didn't think David's financial status was any of Ellen's business.

"How did you ever meet him?" Ellen persisted, "I mean, after all, a farm girl from Wisconsin and a musician from New York!"

"He performed at my university," Cydney was a bit curt. "Actually, he's an alumnus."

When Cydney said no more, Leta picked it up. "Cydney was working for the local newspaper and she did a story about him."

"Love at first sight?" Ellen questioned.

"Not exactly," Cydney was trying not to sound annoyed.

Again Leta rescued her. "If it had been love at first sight, Cydney probably wouldn't be here pondering her future."

"Did he propose?" Ellen blurted out.

Again, Cydney found it difficult to keep her temper in check. "Why don't we concentrate on all the things that have happened around her since I visited last. I don't want to bore anyone with things that don't concern them." That went right over Ellen's head.

"You never answered, Cydney. Is he rich?"

"Yes, I suppose he is," Cydney said this time showing some irritation.

"Well, what's to ponder then? You're being pursued by a wealthy musician from New York and you're hung up on what to do?"

Now Brock intervened. "Ellen, some people believe that money can't buy happiness. Slack off!"

"Well, it can buy a hell of a lot," she went on. "I can think of all sorts of things I could buy that would make me real happy." Cydney got up from the table and retrieved the wine. Everyone declined, so she filled her own glass. Brock looked embarrassed and Cydney's heart went out to him. Ellen had delivered a low blow. Cydney was relieved when Brock pushed back his chair and stood up.

"Thanks for dinner, Leta," he said planting a kiss on her forehead, "It was delicious." Then turning to Cydney, "We're going into town. Want to come along? It'll be fun."

"No thanks, Brock. I'll stay and help Leta clean up. You and Ellen go and have a good time."

Ellen thanked both Leta and Caleb, nodded to Cydney and left. The screen door slammed behind her as she hurried down the steps to Brock's truck. Weeks passed and Cydney didn't see Ellen again.

Cydney woke feeling rested and fresh. She lay in bed, eyes scanning the room: old fashion floral wallpaper, hardwood floor with a worn area rug, brass bed, two huge armoires, a dressing table and a full length framed mirror, all antique. She loved this room! Simple, functional, like her. Cydney was convinced that she was over David. She didn't need his wealth to make her happy. She was happy with this simple life.

Summer was half gone. The fourth of July was just a few days away. In small farming communities, the Independence Day celebration is a big deal, and Balsam Hills was no exception. There would be a big picnic over at the fire station organized by the Ladies Auxiliary and the volunteer firemen would shoot off fireworks as soon as it was dark enough. Cydney was really looking forward to it.

She got up. She hoped she could talk Leta into going shopping with her. Balsam Hills didn't have much but they could drive up to Ashland. Maybe Cydney would treat herself and Leta too, to a new outfit for the 4th and they could have lunch.

However, Leta was already busy making strawberry jam. "You go ahead," Leta said, "this will take most of the day."

"But I was so hoping we could go together," Cydney said with a little whine in her voice, "I don't want to go alone."

"Maybe you should, dear," Leta went on, "I think you're getting restless."

"Restless? What do you mean?" Cydney felt deep down in her gut that Leta was right.

"Well, when you arrived it was obvious that you were a basket case. You needed some TLC. Now you're rested up, you look healthy and fit and I think you're getting restless. This life style doesn't fit you anymore, Cydney." Leta's words were soft and kind. "You were away a long time. Two years. You got used to another way of life. I'm so happy you came. Caleb and I have truly enjoyed the time we've spent together, but I think, maybe subconsciously, you're missing the big city life." Leta glanced over her shoulder. Cydney was sitting at the big blue table with a mug of coffee. "Am I right?"

"I don't know," Cydney said, deep in thought. "Maybe I am restless. I have been thinking about school and if I'd be able to get my job back, but quite frankly, I doubt that Sam would give me another chance."

"And what about your relationship with David?"

"Well, I guess I've accepted that fact that David has chosen his work and fast paced life over true love. What I don't understand is why. Sophie, Gracie, even Harland all said that David was much happier when he was with me." Cydney was talking to herself as much as to Leta.

"Think about it, dear," Leta answered, "from what you've told me, David's parents died when he was very young and Harland took over. Maybe David does love you, a lot, but he doesn't know how to express it. Maybe showering you with expensive gifts and fancy dinners is his way of saying he loves you."

"But I told him that's not important to me. I enjoyed the dinners and the gifts, I really did, but what I want is a stable home and a man who loves me for who I am, even if I don't know what utensil to use first and which wine goes with what food." Leta just listened and went about her jam making. She didn't need to give any more advice. She had already spoken her mind.

"Maybe you're right, Leta," Cydney went on, "but since I haven't heard from David, I assume he's no longer interested and I've accepted that." She drained her coffee mug. "I think I will drive up to Ashland and do a little shopping and right after the 4th, I'll head back to Champaign."

The warm summer wind whistled through Cydney's hair and cleared her mind as it always did. It had been years since she had been to Ashland. The city had grown some. There was a new mall, the latest architectural wonder of the 70's, with lots of boutiques. She shopped, lunched and had her split ends trimmed. It was late afternoon when she headed back home anxious to show Leta her purchases.

When Cydney turned into the driveway from Apple Road she noticed a strange car parked in a strange place. The neighbors usually drove all the way up the driveway and turned around in the yard, car facing back toward the road. This car was parked where the driveway actually expanded to become the "yard" and it had Minnesota license plates on it. Cydney's curiosity was peaked. Leta hadn't mentioned that she was expecting anyone. Maybe it was Uncle Aaron and Aunt Patrice!

Cydney gathered up her packages and hurried up the steps. "Leta," she called out, "wait 'til you see what I bought you." She pushed the screen door open with forearm and stopped dead in her tracks. David was sitting at the kitchen table drinking a cup of tea. Leta sat across from him, the fresh strawberry jam, now sealed in Ball jars and capped, creating a buffer between them. They conversed easily, like old friends getting reacquainted.

"David!" Cydney was taken back. David smiled broadly, displaying his pristine teeth. "What are you doing here?"

Leta excused herself and discreetly disappeared into the dinning room.

"Carmen told me you were here. I called so many times but you were never there. Finally she told me where you were." He stood up. Cydney looked stunned. She stood by the door, still clinging to her packages.

"You look great, Cyd."

"Why did you come here?" she asked.

"I came to try and convince you that we belong together. That we can work out our differences. I miss you so much."

Cydney bit her bottom lip so David wouldn't see it trembling. "Don't cry," she told herself, "don't let him see you cry." She regained a bit of composure, "I'm surprised, David."

"Why?" Now David looked stunned.

"Why? Because I gave you an ultimatum and after three or four weeks, I gave up on ever hearing from you again," her voice was strained.

"It took me this long to realize how much I love you." David sounded sincere. "I thought I could go on without you but I found out I was wrong."

"So what have you been doing all this time?" she asked.

"Thinking about you. And you?"

"Thinking about you." She smiled finally and David felt a little more confident that his decision to come here, to this north woods outback had been the right thing to do.

"Now what?" David asked.

"Well," Cydney said, putting down her packages, "how about another cup of tea?"

Before David could decline, she reached for the teakettle and began filling it. Once on the stove, she busied herself with the tea bags and a cup for herself. She knew David liked lemon with his tea but there was none. She looked exasperated.

"There's no lemon," she said trying to conceal her nervousness.

"Never mind the lemon, Cyd, it's okay. The sun and fresh air must agree with you. You look great." They stood facing each other, the ten feet between them, a huge chasm.

"How did you get here?" Cydney asked.

"I flew into Minneapolis and rented a car."

"So what do you think of Wisconsin?"

"I haven't seen much of it," David said trying to sound cheerful, "but there certainly are a lot of pine trees. It's a lot like upstate New York."

The teakettle started screeching and startled both of them. David sat back down. Cydney refilled his cup and added a fresh tea bag, then filled her own. She slid into the chair vacated by Leta and watched the tea swirl as she stirred it.

"What does this mean, David?"

"What does what mean?"

"You know what I'm asking. You came all this way to see me. Why?"

"I already told you why, Cyd. I need you. I thought I could make it without you. I can't. I need you as much as I need food and water. Which means," he smiled at her, "I can't live without you."

"So what's changed?" she pressured.

David shrugged. "Maybe nothing. I'm not sure. I only know I've been miserable since you left. I can't eat or sleep. I can't concentrate on my work. Everyplace I go, everything I do reminds me of you. I love you and that's all that matters."

Cydney's heart pounded so loudly, she thought David would hear it. Those were exactly the words she needed to hear – *I love you, that's all that matters.*

"Are you sure, David?" Cydney asked. "Are you sure that it doesn't matter that I'm a farm girl who doesn't know that white wine is served in flutes and red wine in goblets? Or which utensil is for dessert and that I never heard of escargot? A farm girl who goes to church and believes that people can be happy even if they aren't rich?"

"I've asked myself those same things over and over and if I weren't sure I wouldn't have left Harland mad as a pole cat with a hot poker up his ass and come all this way to find you." David looked hard into her eyes.

"What now?" Cydney asked.

"Well, it's pretty simple, I think. I love you. Do you love me?"

She nodded before she answered. "I do, David. I do love you."

"Enough to marry me and move to New York?" He was smiling now.

"Enough to marry you, yes, but New York scares me."

"You'll learn to love it, I promise." They were still sitting at the table facing each other. Finally, David got up and came to her. He knelt down next to her chair and took her hand. "Cydney, marry me, please, I beg you. Even if we can't have a family, please marry me. I love you so much." Tears spilled from her big brown eyes. She kissed his forehead and he buried his head in her lap. He had missed her so much. She was finally his.

CHAPTER THIRTY-SEVEN

"So when do you want to get married?" David asked tucking a wisp of fiery hair behind her ear. They were sitting at the edge of the pond enjoying the warm morning sun. Leta had assigned David the room next to Cydney's and he had to admit he slept very well. It was so quiet. He laid awake for quite awhile wondering if Cydney would come to his room and when she didn't, he toyed with the idea of going to her. But then he remembered her grandfather – not exactly the welcome wagon- talking at dinner about the morals of the younger generation, so he opted for yet another night of celibacy. Through the open windows he heard the crickets and the whippoorwills and the drone of a distant train. Sounds foreign to a New Yorker. The next thing he knew it was morning and Cydney was at his door with some fresh brewed coffee. After a huge breakfast of ham and scrambled eggs and biscuits dripping with honey, they made their way to the pond. Cydney always said it was her favorite place to just sit and relax.

"I don't know when," Cydney answered him, "but I know where."

"Where?" David said. "I guess I just assumed we'd get married in New York."

Their eyes locked. "I want to get married here David, in my church." His eyes shifted to some invisible place across the pond.

"Harland was so pissed off at me when I told him I was coming here to propose to you. The only thing that redeemed me was when I reminded him that the press would make a big deal of it. You know how Harland loves publicity."

"Isn't famous New York violinist running off to marry a farm girl a big deal? Pretty romantic, too," Cydney commented. He sat silent and continued to stare across the pond. Finally, his gaze returned to her.

"Well, I guess we have the ___where___, so now we need the ___when___," David smiled.

"You pick the when since I got the where."

David rubbed his chin. "Well, let's see. How about tomorrow?"

"Tomorrow? That's impossible!"

"Why?" he asked.

"Why? Because I only intend to get married once and I want to make it perfect," Cydney smiled at him.

"How perfect can it be if we get---". David stopped mid-sentence and watched Cydney's face fall.

"Married here? Is that what you were going to say?" David knew he had hurt her yet again and found no words to erase the pain. They both sat silent now. Cydney remembered Leta's words. Maybe David really did love her but she was still convinced that she would always be competing with his love for his music and his lavish way of life. A way of life that he constantly rubbed under her nose.

"How about the end of September?" David was gentler now. "The fall tour starts the middle of October so we would have a few weeks to honeymoon."

"If the minister has an opening then it would be fine. We can go to town this afternoon and see him."

"Will you fly back to New York with me tomorrow?" David asked.

"No." Her answer was abrupt. "You go and I'll make as many of the arrangements as I can without you. I'll come in a couple of weeks. Okay?"

"That's good. I don't know anything about planning a wedding anyway, so you just go ahead with it."

"Well, you'll need to have a best man. You might want to give that some thought."

"Harland," David said without hesitation. "It will be Harland. And you? Who will you have?"

"Carmen, no question about it," Cydney said. "And tux. You'll need tux - how stupid of me - you have them. We need to decide about the wording on the invitations and I'll talk with Sophie and Gracie about the food when I get to New York."

"There's one more thing, Cyd," David said reaching into his pocket. The ring was indescribably gorgeous and when he slipped it on her slender finger it sparkled and shimmered in the early July sun. Cydney was flabbergasted. She had never seen such an exquisite piece of jewelry.

"Thank you, David," her voice was just a whisper. "I've never seen anything so beautiful."

David leaned over and kissed her forehead. "Remember," he said, "these are the kinds of things a lot of money can buy." The remark was like a knife stuck in Cydney's heart, but she chose to ignore the pain.

That evening, Leta made a very special dinner and they toasted the happy couple with apple cider because, much to David's dismay, there was no wine. The next morning he left for New York.

CHAPTER THIRTY-EIGHT

Two weeks later, Cydney again flew into LaGuardia. This time David was there to meet her. As Phillip picked his way through traffic, he occasionally glanced in the rear view mirror at the handsome couple. Cydney, talking non-stop and David, with his arm flung casually over her shoulder just nodding in agreement, brought a smile to his face.

"Sophie, Gracie, even Harland, are all waiting to welcome you back." David told her, "There's just one thing."

"And that is?" a now confident Cydney inquired.

"Well, I told them when the wedding was but I didn't tell them where." Now it was David who seemed a little meek. "I know they just assume it will be in New York."

"Are you embarrassed that we're getting married in Balsam Hills?" Cydney was incredulous.

"No, not really. I just know that Harland will be pissed and Sophie and Gracie will be crushed."

"Well," Cydney sighed, "first of all, I'm not marrying Harland, I'm marrying you. Secondly, most weddings take place in the bride's church and finally, it is my intention to have Sophie and Gracie come to Wisconsin to help with the festivities and the food." David just nodded. He should have known she would have it all worked out. But he still had to break the news to Harland.

Harland was a little stand-offish, but Sophie and Gracie were overjoyed to see Cydney and when dinner was served it was veal parmigiana, one of her favorites, with all the trimmings. Harland, a gentleman in spite of his obvious dislike of the situation, proposed a toast to them.

"Cydney. David," he said with just a hint of a smile as he raised a flute of pinot grigio. "Here's to both of you. Cydney, I know you will be very happy with David. He's a stable person, caring and generous. He will be a wonderful husband." Then a little lighter, "Thank you for taking him off my hands." Then turning his gaze to David. "David, I trust your decision and hope that you can concentrate on your work now that your quest is over."

Cydney felt the knife again cutting her deep but she said nothing as the crystal glasses clinked together. The rest of the conversation was small talk. But while they sipped wine and waited for dessert and coffee, Cydney decided to take the bull by the horns.

"So Harland," she said sweetly, "are you looking forward to going to Wisconsin?"

"Wisconsin?" He didn't grasp the innuendo.

"Have you ever been there?" she persisted.

"No and why would I go?" he asked.

Now it was Cydney's turn to drive home her point. "Why for the wedding of course. It's really quite beautiful in fall." She took another sip of wine and watched over the top of her wine glass as Harland blinked in disbelief.

He swallowed hard, trying to absorb the words that took his breath away. Harland's face was ashen, his heart was pounding, his temples throbbed. He put the wine glass down so Cydney and David wouldn't notice how his hand suddenly started to tremble. He looked from Cydney to David. "Wisconsin?" His voice was an octave higher than usual as he tried to conceal his anger. "You're getting married in Wisconsin?"

"Most couples get married in the bride's home town," David said, remembering Cydney's words, "and we'll only be there for a few days."

"I'll need Sophie and Gracie to arrive there on Tuesday," Cydney put in, "to help Leta clean the house and prepare the food." Sophie and Gracie were now serving the coffee and dessert and were privy to this part of the conversation and they were ecstatic. Harland continued to look from David to Cydney with his mouth agape. Revenge was not part of Cydney's nature, so she felt guilty taking pleasure in Harland's obvious discomfort. When it was apparent that he couldn't find words of rebuttal, he dabbed his mouth with his linen napkin and as he excused himself from the table, he threw it down on the chair in disgust.

Silence loomed for a few seconds until Cydney cheerfully said, "Sophie and Gracie, I do hope both of you will do me the honor of going to Wisconsin and helping with the wedding reception." Both ladies beamed with pride. "There's not much for caterers in my home town," she went on.

"Cydney dear, money's no object," David was patronizing. "We can have the food flown in."

"Nonsense!" Cydney said sharply. "I think Sophie and Gracie would enjoy the trip and meeting my family." Then turning to them, "Wouldn't you?"

"Oh yes, dear," they replied, almost in unison.

Much later, in the privacy of David's bedroom, Cydney asked the question that had been troubling her since she accepted David's proposal.

"Will we continue to live here after we're married?"

"Of course, Cyd. I own the place."

"What about Harland? Where will he live?"

"Well, I expect he'll continue to live here, with us. Is that a problem?"

"Are you blind, David? The man obviously despises me." Cydney was becoming irritated.

"Aren't you exaggerating a little?"

"Am I David? You tell me."

"Do you want me to talk to him about it?" David asked.

"Not for my sake. But I can tell you this, if my family were so blatantly rude to you I would certainly let them know that it was unacceptable and that it was a total lack of respect toward someone I love dearly."

"Ah, Cydney, wonderful, you love me dearly." He was watching her brush her hair.

"This isn't funny, David." The strokes got quicker and harder now. "Does his wealth give him the right to treat me with such disrespect? What about the toast he made to us. His inference certainly was that although he didn't like me, he would go along with your decision to marry me."

"Why do you always have to bring our wealth into the conversation?"

Cydney was silent for a moment as she pondered the question. "Well, maybe because when I was growing up, I was taught that being wealthy wasn't important if what was on the inside was good and kind. That's not the case with Harland. He thinks he's better than I am and maybe he is in a lot of ways. But I know in my heart that I'm a good person and if I were wealthy I would not look down on people who didn't have all the material things that I have or weren't as well versed in the social graces."

"Well, you better practice what you preach," David said, planting a kiss on her cheek, "because after we're married, you will be wealthy."

"And, I will still practice the golden rule!" Cydney was emphatic.

"Which is?" David questioned.

Cydney was taken back. "You don't know the golden rule?"

"Can't say that I do."

"David, you must have learned – *do unto others as you would have them do unto you.*"

"Sounds like some of your church stuff."

"It is church stuff. The golden rule, handed down by Almighty God."

"The only thing that's almighty to me is the almighty dollar," David said, straight faced.

Cydney laid her hairbrush down and turned to face him. Her shoulders fell, her face brimming with sadness. "Oh, David," she sighed, "are we doing the right thing? Getting married, I mean. We're worlds apart."

"You have so many beliefs," David answered. "Don't you believe that love conquers all?"

He came to her then and reached for her hand, which she freely extended. Cydney stood up. David encircled her tiny waist and pulled her close. His kiss was hard and hungry. He had been without her for so long. David continued to hold her with his left arm while his right hand crept beneath her silk pajama top and caressed her soft flesh. Slowly his hand moved upward and found her breast. He felt her nipple harden under his touch as she slumped against him, succumbing to her own passion.

Locked in each other's arms, they made their way to the bed. David's kisses peppered her neck as he unbuttoned her top and she wiggled free of it. He lowered her to the edge of the bed and slid her pajama bottoms down over her sleek legs. Cydney knew he was aroused and moved seductively as she shimmied to the center of the bed. David was already bare-chested and it didn't take him long to shed his boxers. Cydney spent a few minutes admiring his hard body before David dimmed the lights and came to her. Their separation had left them desperate for each other and neither of them could restrain themselves.

"Hurry," Cydney whispered, her voice laced with passion, "please hurry." David slid his arms beneath her and raised her hips to meet him. Her hands clutched his neck, trying in vain to pull him closer. They melded together, working themselves into a heated frenzy, which they both knew could not last. David whispered her name over and over until he shuddered and unleashed his love potion.

They slept in each other's arms for several hours. When Cydney woke, the first streaks of morning were visible in the sky. She freed herself from David's arm, trying not to wake him and rolled onto her back.

Her eyes scanned the textured ceiling with its ornate lighting. Everything here reeked of money. Cydney folded her hands and prayed for some direction. She told herself that she truly did love David. She told herself that she could learn to enjoy luxury and hang onto her values. She told herself this was the life she wanted. She thanked God for sending David to her and asked His help in making her a good and loving wife.

Cydney snuggled up to David's naked form. Beneath the covers, her hand sought his manhood, now limp as the rest of his body. Gently, she began stroking it. She smiled to herself as it began to grow hard in her hand. Instinctively, David stirred and turned onto his back. Cydney smiled again. That was exactly what she wanted. She straddled his firm body just as he opened his eyes.

CHAPTER THIRTY-NINE

Driving a new car can make a man feel like a king and that's exactly how Caleb felt today. Ignoring the jabber of the women, he focused on the dashboard and all the dials and gadgets. It would take him quite awhile to learn what they were all for.

Caleb knew his friends and neighbors thought he was just like them – a farmer who suffered through lean years and rejoiced in good years. In the lean years you complained about the hard times and in the good years you bought that new piece of machinery or the new car you've been wanting for awhile.

Truth was, Caleb was different. Caleb had money! He always had money. He just didn't flaunt it. In fact, Caleb was frugal. Some of the money had come from his father and in reality, Caleb never knew how his father came to have it. But Caleb was a good, shrewd businessman and he loved poring over his books and accounts, keeping track of his income and expenses. The money Caleb inherited from his father had grown to a tidy sum, due to Caleb's diligent business deals and he was proud of it. Plus, Caleb always had what he called his "rat hole money". One never knew when some extra cash would come in handy. Caleb remembered a night a long time ago, when he pressed some money into Aaron's hand giving him the opportunity to spread his wings. He also pictured Sarah, asking for a new outfit for homecoming. Ah, yes. Sarah's junior year homecoming. The beginning of the end. But now he had Cydney and he was about to set her free. Caleb smiled to himself recalling the night before Cydney left for New York.

They had just finished dinner. Leta got up and started clearing the table. Caleb opened his humidor and began tamping his pipe.

"Cydney," he said, heading for the living room, "let's have a talk."

She followed him. "Grandpa, I thought you weren't supposed to smoke anymore."

"Who told you that?" He settled into his worn and comfortable rocking chair and pushed the footstool toward Cydney. The sweet aroma of pipe tobacco filled the air as Cydney took her place at Caleb's feet. As usual, Caleb took his time before speaking. He drew on his pipe and blew the smoke out in rings. Something he had done many times when Cydney was a child. And like then, she giggled, a little girl giggle and tried to stick her finger through the rings.

"Cydney," he said, looking deep into her eyes, "you've made a decision. A life changing decision and I want you to look me in the eye and tell me that you're confident you've made the right choice."

Cydney didn't hesitate. "I am Grandpa. I love David and I know this is the right thing to do."

Again Caleb was silent, studying her lovely face. "Are you sure this isn't your way of getting even with Brock?"

Cydney flushed. Partly because she was embarrassed and partly due to anger. But her love and respect for Caleb dictated that she not raise her voice to him.

"Why would I want to get even with Brock? Brock is married now. He made his choice and I've made mine."

"Cydney," Caleb's words were slow and deliberate, "maybe you don't even realize how much you love Brock. I watched the two of you grow up together. From the day that Brock joined our family, you loved him."

"You're right, Grandpa, I do love Brock. I love him like a brother."

"Do you?" Caleb goaded her, tested her.

"You know I've always had aspirations of a career and life in a big city. You also know that Brock is a country boy. Our worlds are different." Cydney tried to sound persuasive.

"And isn't David's world different from yours?"

"David's world is becoming my world, Grandpa, and I won't regret my decision. Please believe me."

Caleb seemed satisfied. "I believe you, Cydney. I just want to know in my heart that you'll be happy." His eyes scanned the room. "When I'm gone you and Aaron will own Oakwood but I promised Brock that as long as Oakwood Acres is in our family, he can live here. In exchange, he will take care of the place when no one is here. But what I want from you now, Cydney, is a promise that you will do your very best to keep the farm in our family."

Cydney's eyes welled up with tears. "I promise, Grandpa. I will never part with this place."

Caleb was silent again for a few minutes. "Another thing," he said as last. "This is yours." He handed Cydney a large manila envelope and watched quietly as she opened it. She gasped.

"There's money in here. Where did it come from?"

Caleb took a deep breath. "When Sarah found out that she was pregnant and the young man would not own up to his responsibility, I needed to be sure you would have a secure future. The young man's father and I made an agreement. His father established a trust fund for you and in return we agreed not to name the boy in a paternity suit and thereby released him from obligation or involvement in our lives."

Cydney looked down at the envelope again and then back at Caleb. "There's a lot of money here, Grandpa."

Caleb suppressed a smile. "I know, Cydney. And remember those couple of times you asked me for a loan? Well, you were actually borrowing money from yourself. It's the balance of your trust fund." Caleb said nodding toward the envelope.

Now Cydney sat in silent contemplation. Caleb rocked and puffed on his pipe, waiting patiently while she absorbed the enormity of his words. "Grandpa," she said at last, "being married to David, I will never be in need of money. He is very wealthy. So, I'm going to keep this money as a sort of slush fund for the farm. Whenever we need repairs or if we want to change something, we'll always have funds available."

Caleb's face lit up. "Good girl! And maybe some day you'll have children who will look forward to coming to the farm for holidays or a summer visit." He seemed content now and laid his head back on the rocking chair. After a few minutes he sat forward again, "So," he said, "tell me more about David and New York."

Cydney chose her words carefully, telling her grandfather only the things she knew he wanted to hear. She purposely avoided mentioning Harland. Caleb would get a taste of his acrid personality soon enough. And she made no reference to having children, who would someday look forward to coming to the farm. Instead, she spoke of David's blossoming career, his posh penthouse apartment with its captivating view of Central Park. Cydney raved about Sophie and Gracie and how they treated her like royalty and catered to her every whim. She talked of the Savages and the Caprocks and how they would all come to Balsam Hills for the wedding.

"By the way, Grandpa, what would you think about me asking Brock to be the usher? He's so dear to me and I want him to be part of my special day."

"What does David think about it?"

"David is leaving all those details up to me. He doesn't have time right now to plan a wedding. But we do need an usher and Brock, well, he knows all the local people. He'll know the ones he doesn't recognize will be David's friends and relatives. What do you think?"

"Well," now Caleb would say the words he knew Cydney wanted to hear, "if you're comfortable with it and David's okay with it, then I say, go ahead. I think Brock would be honored to be part of your wedding." He was flattered that Cydney still valued his opinion.

"Grandpa," Cydney said, "I love you so much. Thank you for everything you've done for me. Both you and Leta, I love you both so much."

Now it was Caleb whose eyes filled with tears. He had done all that he could for Cydney and he had done it with all the love he could muster up.

So, as they discussed, early the next morning, Cydney tracked Brock down and asked him to be her usher and of course, he accepted. Then she flew off to New York.

CHAPTER FORTY

Caleb eased the new car into the parking stall reserved especially for them, right in front of the church. He hurried to help Leta out and together they helped Carmen and Cydney untangle themselves from the backseat with their fancy dresses in tow.

It was such a beautiful fall day. The white church steeple pierced the azure blue of the sky. The trees on the grounds were dressed in their finery of brilliant yellow, burnt orange and deep scarlet. The double doors of the church were open and the organ music floated into the warm September afternoon.

Brock stood by the door, handsome, although uncomfortable, in his tuxedo. He came forward to escort both Carmen and Cydney to the church while Caleb extended his arm to Leta.

"Cydney," Brock said, "you're breathtaking." He lightly kissed her cheek. "I wish you much happiness. Ellen sends her regrets, she couldn't be here — she had to go to Mason again."

"Thank you," Cydney said kissing Brock back. There was nothing else to say.

Cydney, Carmen and Caleb all waited in the vestibule until the last of the guests were seated. Then at Cydney's request, Brock walked Leta down the aisle where she proudly took the envious position of mother of the bride. Whispers passed among some of the locals but Cydney didn't care. Leta deserved, no - Leta earned the ranking.

The wedding march began and Caleb and Cydney, arms linked in love, followed Carmen down the aisle. Past their friends and neighbors. Past Uncle Aaron, Aunt Patrice and the twins. Past Donovan and Victoria, Geoff and Tony. Past Gloria and Roger. Past Tom and Joyce. Past Sophie and Gracie. Cydney smiled at each of them and Caleb beamed with pride.

David waited nervously, flanked by the minister on his right and Harland on his left. His eyes never left Cydney as Caleb gracefully steered her toward him.

Even Harland was impressed with her beauty. Surely this would make the society page of the New York Times!

At the foot of the altar steps, Caleb and Cydney stopped. He kissed her cheek and then placed her hand in David's. When the minister asked, "Who gives this woman to be married to this man?" the lump in Caleb's throat made his response almost inaudible.

Cydney listened intently as the minister spoke of giving and taking, of caring and sharing, of the end of me and the beginning of us. Of all the things it takes to have a successful marriage and she tucked them away in the deepest recesses of her heart.

David, on the other hand, paid no attention. He couldn't believe he had agreed to this church wedding. It was hot and stuffy in here. A judge could have married them. He had to admit Harland was right when he referred to this place as "god forsaken". There wasn't even a decent restaurant in town. The rehearsal dinner had been at the Knights of Columbus Hall for christ sake. Cydney had done her best in selecting three different entrées but David was not impressed with a grilled chicken breast, an 8-ounce rib-eye steak or deep fried fish. And wine – what a joke that was. The group had only consumed three bottles when the house informed them they were out. Out! They ran out of wine! He couldn't wait to get back to New York and he vowed it would be a long time before he returned. Yes, it was quiet. Too quiet. And when the wind was out of the south, the whole house smelled like the barn. He really would have to apologize to the Savages and the Caprocks for subjecting them to this. He wondered what the wedding dinner would be like. Hopefully better, because he knew that Sophie and Gracie were involved in the preparation of it and Sophie and Gracie knew David's taste and they always did their best to please him.

David's mind snapped back to the present as Cydney squeezed his hand. The minister was already directing Cydney, "Repeat after me."

She looked deep into David's eyes and began reciting her vows. David listened now and then took his turn. At last he heard the words he had been waiting for, "I now pronounce you husband and wife." David looked at Cydney standing beside him. She was radiant. She was also oblivious to the impression this hick town was making on his friends. A few more prayers and they'd be outta here. He was really getting antsy.

They knelt and the reverend raised his arms and showered God's blessing upon them. They stood up and arm and arm turned to face the smiling congregation. David smiled back but Cydney's expression was solemn. She noticed that Brock's seat was vacant.

CHAPTER FORTY-ONE

Brock slammed the door of his truck and kicked, first at the dirt and then at the tire. His face was as red as the September sumac. He had shed his jacket when he left the church. Now he jerked at the bow tie and opened the neck of the shirt. Finally able to breathe and free of the god damn monkey suit!

He had spun the tires in the gravel in the church parking lot, desperate to escape. He hardly remembered driving here but knew he had thrown caution to the wind. When he crossed Arrowhead Road the speedometer read 85 and he hardly slowed down at Preacher's Bend, the hairpin curve by the Lutheran church, just two miles below this place, his new sanctuary.

Brock no longer sought refuge at the pond. It reminded him of Cydney. Now, when he needed to think, when he needed to do some soul searching or clear his mind, he came here, to Breezy Point Lookout. High above the trees, now drenched in brilliant color, where he could see all the way to the Bad River.

Brock rested his elbows on the hood of this truck and even pounded his fist on it once or twice in frustration. What was he thinking? Agreeing to be an usher in her wedding! Stupid! A stupid thing to do! Did he really think he could just sit there and watch her marry that rich, smart ass son-of-a-bitch?

Sure, he was married to Ellen and when he married her he truly believed he loved her. But Ellen had since become disillusioned with

him and she told him so. She wanted more than he could give. She
agreed he was handsome and strong. He was virile and sexy. Ellen
wanted all that. And more! She wanted someone who would take her
away from this meager life. Someone with fame and fortune. Someone
who could offer excitement. Brock was content living the simple life.
He loved working the land and being in tune with nature. He wanted
to live here for the rest of his life and he wanted to raise a family here. If
he were truthful, Brock would have to admit that he was first attracted
to Ellen because she reminded him of Cydney. In looks, at least. Not
personality. Ellen started complaining and whining right after they got
married and she never stopped and when she left for Mason yesterday
she hinted that she might not come back and Brock really didn't care
if she did!

He pounded the hood of the truck one more time, rolled up his
sleeves and retrieved a bottle of rye whiskey from under the seat. Brock
sat down beside his truck, the warm afternoon sun just starting to wan,
and took a long pull on the bottle, the amber liquid burning its way
to his belly. When did he first realize that he loved Cydney? Hell, he
watched her grow up! He loved her from the get-go. Brock closed his
eyes. He could see lanky arms and legs, a freckled nose giving way to
a beautiful, graceful young woman.

He remembered that kiss on her high school graduation day and
the bittersweet good-bye kiss when she left for college. What about the
night she came home for Thanksgiving break with her roommate and
came to him in the dim dining room? He had to restrain himself from
pulling her close. Instead, Brock held her at bay and planted a kiss on
her forehead.

The whiskey was tasting better, the memories growing more vivid.
Her smile, her laugh, her silky, chestnut hair. Brock scooped up a
handful of sandy soil and let it sift through his fingers, imagining she
was there beside him. A gulp of whiskey, a glimpse of the past. Again
and again until Brock could neither stand nor speak.

Ashland County Deputy Sheriff, Everell Hanson patrolled Breezy
Point on his nightly rounds and he found Brock sprawled in the dirt
beside his truck. A sight he had seen before. And like before, to spare
his friend trouble and money, Deputy Hanson helped Brock into the

cab of his truck and confiscated the keys. Just before he locked the door and slammed it shut, Brock, in his drunken stupor vaguely remembered hearing him say, "I'll be back at the end of my shift, Roberts, with your keys."

CHAPTER FORTY-TWO

David was so happy to be on the plane returning to New York. He turned and looked at Cydney, her eyes closed, a smile tugging at the corners of her shapely lips. He would never admit it to Cydney, but the wedding had been a source of embarrassment to him. Something men usually don't concern themselves with, but the Savages and the Caprocks had been there and they would surely discuss the wedding with other friends and acquaintances. If such gossip got back to Cydney, she would be crushed. For David it was simply a matter of pride. He was a millionaire many times over and yet, because he let Cydney take over the wedding plans, there was no fine china or crystal goblets; there was no gourmet food or exotic wines. In retrospect, a big mistake! He should have overseen the plans. Instead, Cydney hired a "local" to do a pig roast. Oh, it was exciting for the townspeople and between Sophie and Gracie and with the help of Leta, there were a wide variety of side dishes and finger foods, along with sauerkraut and potato salad. And a wedding cake. David had to admit, the cake was nicely done. But he should have insisted that a wedding planner be hired and all the amenities brought in from New York. David never stopped to consider that to Cydney's family and friends in Balsam Hills, this was the social event of the year and they would be talking about it for a long, long time, in the barbershop, at the general store, and before Sunday services at the Presbyterian Church.

Cydney stirred and reached for David's hand. He interlocked his fingers with hers.

"Never mind the wedding," he told himself, "you have her now."

Still, Harland had already voiced his negative opinion and reiterated several times that he hoped Marilyn Shields didn't get wind of the news or she'd have a field day with it. Again, David and Harland were not on the best of terms right now. They had argued off and on regarding living arrangements for several days prior to the wedding. David had suggested that because Harland didn't care much for Cydney, he might want to find other housing. But Harland too, was a man of great pride and he held his ground. In the end, David relented. Harland was staying.

Harland knew Cydney didn't like him either but he was content knowing David was happy. Still, driven by his pride, he had no intention of making peace with Cydney. Rather, he chose to live under the same roof and play the part of martyr. He was polite, but he was not going to accept her as family! At least Harland would have a few weeks to come to terms with Cydney invading his space. David and Cydney would spend only two days in New York and then leave for their honeymoon. During that time, Harland would remove all of his personal belongings from the common living area, giving way to Cydney's unsophisticated taste. He wondered how long it would be before David woke up and realized that all the prompting, all the mentoring, all the coaching in the world, could not instill in Cydney, the one thing usually bred into the wealthy – class! Harland agreed, Cydney was beautiful. She was coy, she was an avid student of the social graces but in his opinion, that one thing – class – was lacking. Of course, David disagreed, another source of contention between them, and David was convinced that by the time they returned from their honeymoon, Cydney would be able to assume the roll of a wealthy New York socialite, because now, as his wife, she was one.

CHAPTER FORTY-THREE

Just leave it to David to find the perfect romantic hideaway for a honeymoon. Cydney was overwhelmed. She had never even heard of this place – the Yucatan Peninsula in Mexico.

Just coming into its own rite as a tourist attraction in 1975, the Yucatan separated the Gulf of Mexico from the Caribbean Sea. David booked a suite at a resort in the seaside city of Cancun. Still relatively unknown to American tourists, there were, at this time, only a few high-rise hotels along the beach but like always, David selected the biggest and the best.

They left Balsam Hills on Monday morning and drove to Minneapolis. From there they caught a flight to New York City and arrived mid afternoon. Their plane for Cancun would leave early Wednesday morning so there wasn't much time for reminiscing about the wedding. They could do that lying on the beach later in the week. Instead, Cydney concentrated on unpacking and then repacking, while David tended to business, returning phone calls and confirming dates.

Harland made himself scarce and Sophie and Gracie were busy with laundry, cleaning and a lot of day dreaming about what they thought was an absolutely wonderful wedding. For now, the household was in harmony.

Although the Cancun airport was undergoing a major expansion project, the private jet that David rented from Tom Caprock glided smoothly to a stop on a secondary runway. Even David seemed excited as they carefully descended the steep steps. Of course, there was a car waiting for them. David saw to everything. It was hurricane season in the Caribbean but the weather forecast for the next two weeks was perfect, as were the accommodations.

The hotel had an impressive open-air lobby, tile floors with mosaic inlays, stucco pillars and beveled mirrors. Exotic flowers and plush greenery in terra cotta urns adorned the entryways to the hotel's restaurants as well as the steps that led to the pool and the white, sandy beach. Mexican men in white bolero jackets waited the tables on the verandas while others, in navy blue uniforms, tended the walkways and green areas, which were meticulous. Most of the staff spoke English un pocito, *"a little"*, which gave Cydney a chance to practice her Spanish. She looked around, drinking in the beauty of the turquoise water and the azure sky, the brilliant sun and cotton ball clouds and she knew at that very moment, that she would want to come back again and again.

Everyday was a new adventure! They traveled the Yucatan, touring the dense rain forests in the south and the costal city of Tulum. They visited other Mayan ruins at Tikal and Uxmal and the pyramids, observatory and ball court of Chichen' Itza.

They shopped in the open markets for souvenirs, and for hammocks, hats, tote bags and sandals made from a Mayan agave fiber.

They visited huge haciendas, once owned by wealthy Europeans and saw peasant farms that still produced corn, beans, squash and sweet potatoes. Cydney loved to try new things and she delighted in the pleasant sweetness of the starchy tapioca tubers called maniocs.

They sunned themselves in the heat of the day and frolicked in the shallow water as the tide crept in. And yet, each day, they found time to make love. Wild, wonderful love that knew no geographical boundary or social class. Just sweet, savage love that both Cydney and David vowed would last forever.

CHAPTER FORTY-FOUR

It took five years, but as David predicted, Cydney learned to love New York. At first there was no time to explore. She had thank you notes from the wedding to write and grade transcripts to transfer. She enrolled in NYU and took extra classes so she could earn her degree early. And then there was the household. Cydney had to learn to deal with Harland on a daily basis and she quickly realized that it was best to just ignore him. Sophie and Gracie were her salvation. They continued to dote on her and mother her. They were the ones who listened intently to her babbling when she was on top of the world and wiped her tears when life seemed overwhelming.

David often ignored her for days (and nights) on end. Then, mysteriously, he would surprise her with an expensive gift or an elegant night on the town and once again become the intimate wine-sipping husband and ardent lover. When Cydney questioned him about it, he was vague.

"You know how devoted I am to my music and my career, Cyd. Sometimes they have to come first," he would say nonchalantly.

"You promised me I would always be number one, remember? That's why I agreed to marry you."

"Don't be childish and selfish," he would say, "you know how much I love you."

"Don't patronize me, David. You know I don't interfere with your music. In fact, I want to help with your career."

"And how do you propose to do that?" he asked, arching a brow.

"Well," Cydney said excitedly, "I've been thinking about that. We could have a cocktail party. I've been practicing my cooking with Sophie and Gracie and I could make some hors d'oeuvres and we could invite the—"

"Cydney! Stop! You leave the cooking to Sophie and Gracie and the cleaning and ALL the chores."

"But David," she argued, "I have to do something. You don't want me to get a job, what am I suppose to do all day?"

"Relax, have fun, shop, get acquainted with New York. Just stay out of the kitchen and stay our of Sophie and Gracie's way."

"I'm not in their way," Cydney pouted.

"Well Harland says you're in the kitchen bothering them all the time. Leave them alone so they can get their work done."

"So Harland spies on me now does he?" Cydney was outraged.

"Just find a hobby or something," David said over his shoulder, leaving Cydney steaming.

They had the same argument over and over. Cydney felt depressed and alone. She had no friends in New York except Joyce Caprock. Of course, there was Leta, and Patrice, whom she spoke with on a regular basis, but she would never hint to either of them, or to Joyce that she was disenchanted. She was David's wife and that was that. She would just have to make the best of it.

Cydney also corresponded and regularly spoke with Carmen, now married to Tony and living in a suburb of Dallas, Texas, where Tony was a vet and Carmen worked for the local newspaper.

"Cydney," Carmen said one evening as they talked on the phone, "do you know what has happened in these couple of years? We've flip-flopped. You're the wealthy socialite and I'm a small town working girl."

"Oh, Carmen, I envy you," Cydney said with a sigh.

"Is that discontentment I hear?"

"No, no Carmen, it's not. It's just that David is so busy and sometimes I get so lonesome."

"Cydney," Carmen said in a firm voice, "you're the only one who can change that."

Cydney pondered that thought one pleasant August afternoon as she sat on the balcony basking in the sun with a best seller from the New York Times list. Carmen was right, Cydney could continue to feel sorry for herself or she could make the most of it.

The next day the adventure began!

Cydney joined an aerobics class at the "Y". She joined a book club at the library. She enrolled in an advanced Spanish class at a junior college and signed up to volunteer at St. Vincent's hospital.

Every chance she had, Cydney rode the Grey Line bus. She visited all the tourist attractions. How she loved Times Square with its bright lights and bustling crowds. She rode the Hansom Cab through Central Park. The next day she walked it and one day she biked it, Eight hundred acres, plus. Why it was like Caleb's entire farm smack dab in the middle of New York City! She walked the streets of Greenwich Village enjoying the elite shops and storefront galleries. She rode the Staten Island Ferry and spent hours visiting Lady Liberty, watching and observing. Was it really true that all incoming planes tipped their wing to her?

Cydney shopped the Madison Avenue luxury shops as well as Saks and Macy's, all seventeen levels. She visited Grand Central Station with gleaming marble floors and lines and lines of commuters. Like any good tourist, she over indulged in cheesecake at a Times Square deli and another in the West Village and then walked the Brooklyn Bridge to even the score.

Cydney couldn't get enough of Broadway and the Theatre district. She often attended performances alone, since David always seemed too busy now to go with her. SoHo, China Town, Tribeca, each district, each day, each different. Yet all part of what endeared her to New York. And with all Cydney saw and did, she made friends. Lots of friends.

Cydney met Brenda Carrigan at the hospital. They both enjoyed delivering newspapers and reading to the patients. They visited often over coffee and found they had a lot in common. Brenda's husband was a gynecologist so she was alone a lot, too.

One day Cydney casually mentioned a Broadway production she was interested in seeing and Brenda suggested that they go together. As it turned out, the show was fabulous and they decided to critique it over a piece of cheesecake and a cup of coffee at a deli on Broadway.

The next day, they visited the Guggenheim where Brenda introduced her to Loren, an artist who lived in the West Village. Brenda mentioned that Cydney was looking for a piece of art to display in her home so when Loren invited them to view his paintings, they eagerly accepted.

Loren's studio consisted of two storefront windows and a partition to display his works. He lived behind the partition in one large room and obviously concentrated mainly on his work and not on his living conditions. Cydney had already learned that the "Villagers" are a breed onto themselves, so she ignored the sour empty pizza boxes, the slimy sushi containers and the slight smell of marijuana lingering in the air. Instead she concentrated on the beautiful paintings suspended on the pegboard partition. Cydney made her selection and bartered on the price. She told Loren she would come back the next day to pick up the painting.

"I can deliver it to you," he suggested.

"Oh, Loren, would you? That would be wonderful, because I have no way to transport it."

The next afternoon, Loren arrived with Cydney's purchase under his arm, two or three days worth of stubble on his face, a dirty t-shirt and jeans with big gaping holes in the knees.

As luck would have it, Harland answered the intercom and was surprised and curious to learn that a man was asking for Cydney. Reluctantly, Harland summoned her and hovered in the background as Cydney buzzed Loren up. Cydney welcomed him with a hug, while Harland sneered at Loren's appearance. David would surely be appalled to hear that Cydney was allowing this despicable person to enter their home and hear it he would! Harland would see to that.

Cydney was admiring her new painting, hanging low over their bed, when David came charging through the door.

"What kind of people are you carousing with?" he demanded, his voice loud.

Cydney was expecting this outburst because she had seen the smirk on Harland's face as she welcomed Loren into the apartment, but she stood her ground with David.

"First of all, I'm not carousing with anyone but if you're referring to my friend, Loren, he's an artist who lives in the West Village."

"The West Village? God, I hope you don't hang out in the West Village! It's a terrible place and how in the hell did you meet someone from the West Village?"

"My friend, Brenda introduced us." She was going to make David work for every piece of information.

"And Brenda is from the West Village, too?"

"No David, Brenda volunteers at the hospital with me. Did you know that I do that?" Her voice was dripping with sarcasm. "Did you know that I volunteer at St. Vincent's Hospital twice a week?" David was silent. He didn't know, but he kept his gaze fixed on her. "Brenda's husband is a doctor. Is that good enough for you? Is it okay if I carouse with a doctor's wife?" She turned her back to him then and focused again on the painting, angry but also a bit ashamed that she had been so flip. But it was true; David knew nothing of her comings and goings.

When they had cocktails before dinner, Harland was usually present and the conversation was general. Neither of them ever asked her about her day. And when David and Cydney were alone, David talked mostly about his latest accomplishments both on and off the stage; or, they made love and then drifted off to sleep. He had no idea how Cydney occupied her time. David said no more, just turned and bolted from the room, slamming the door behind him.

Cydney was adamant. Even if David was indifferent to her most of the time, and he was, she would keep her marriage vows, but lead her own life. She had, by now, acquired a close-knit circle of friends, which included Loren and she wasn't about to let David tell her who she could and could not associate with. Her friends would sustain her during the times when she was lonely and if David chose to occasionally surprise her with a night on the town, or lure her to his bed, she would remain at his beck and call. Because, in spite of the fact that David's feelings for her had changed, although he would not admit it, she remained in love with David and she still firmly believed that some day she would have his full and undivided love.

Cydney and Brenda began spending more time in the West Village with Loren and his partner, Harold. Loren had taken Brenda on as a protégé of sorts and she was dabbling in oils. Harold was writing an off Broadway play and Cydney was collaborating with him. He had a great story line but no writing skills and he valued her input.

On one of these visits, Cydney became quite ill. The smell of stale smoke and spoiled food turned her stomach. They all assumed she had eaten something gone bad but a few days later it happened again.

"Maybe you should see a doctor," Brenda suggested.

"A doctor?" Cydney questioned. "I haven't been to a doctor since – well – since I don't know when. For years! I don't think I need a doctor, just some fresh air; and besides," Cydney added over her shoulder as she headed outside, "I wouldn't even know who to go to."

Brenda followed her into the chilly February air, "Cydney go to see Carl. Please! I know you aren't feeling well, I can tell and you look so tired."

Cydney smiled, "Carl's a gynecologist, Brenda."

"Well," now Brenda smiled, "maybe you're pregnant!" Their eyes locked.

"I don't think so Brenda, really, I – David-," Cydney searched for words, "well, we can't have any children."

"I'm so sorry, Cydney, I didn't know."

"It's okay, Brenda. I've accepted the fact. But you're right, I'm just not feeling well, but a gynecologist?"

"Hey, you're a sexually active female. You should be seeing a gyno guy every year."

"Okay, Okay," Cydney gestured palms down, "I'll make an appointment."

Cydney sat across the desk from Carl Carrigan. He was a tall man, fit and healthy looking with smooth skin, bright blue eyes and salt and pepper hair. He was a soft-spoken, kind man and Cydney couldn't muster up an image of him and Brenda together. They seemed worlds apart, just like she and David.

The exam had been simple and painless and he waited patiently in his office until she dressed and joined him.

"Mrs. DuPrey," he said with a smile and a hand gesture, "Cydney. May I call you Cydney?"

"Please do," she smiled back.

"Cydney, when was your last period?"

Cydney looked surprised, her mind calculating. "Well, let me think. I really don't keep track – but I'm pretty sure it was just a few weeks ago. Why?"

"Why? Because, Cydney, I'm happy to tell you that you're pregnant." His smile was genuine and mixed with anticipation of her reaction.

Cydney bolted up straight. "That's impossible, Doctor!" she said firmly.

"Cydney," he said again. "You're pregnant. Why do you think it's not possible?"

Her mind raced back to another time when Carmen taught her how to breathe deeply to calm herself and she did so instinctively, at the same time she felt tears welling up. Dr. Carrigan recognized her emotional trauma. He sat patiently, giving her a few moments to absorb the information and compose herself.

"Whatever you tell me Cydney, is strictly confidential. Trust me. You can trust me." His eyes were kind, his smile warm.

She continued to sit silently for a few minutes. When she spoke her voice shook with emotion. "Before we got married, David, that's my husband, well he told me that he was unable to – well – that he was sterile."

"And did he tell you how he became sterile? How he knows that he's sterile?"

Again, Cydney searched her mind. "Well, yes. He had mumps as a young adult and later was tested. The results were a very low sperm count."

Dr. Carrigan smiled again, "Well, there you have it! A low sperm count is not the same as sterility. It only takes one sperm cell to fertilize an egg. You're pregnant! But before I can give you a due date, we need to know when your last menstrual was."

Cydney tried to remember how long she had been feeling poorly. It was February now.

She felt pretty good over the holidays, she remembered that. She had a period just before Christmas. Then January came. What all happened in January? Oh yes, Harland's 50th birthday. She didn't feel well and David accused her of feigning illness so she wouldn't have to go to the party. Cydney went to the party but she didn't have a good time and in the morning, still feeling ill, David insinuated that she was hung over when in fact she only had one glass of wine. She remembered now, thinking she didn't feel well because she was going to get her period. It never came and the raw emotions that plagued her were blamed on PMS. Dr. Carrigan quietly observed Cydney as she made her mental calculations.

"December," she finally said. "I had a period in December, just before Christmas."

"Good." He continued to smile as he jotted down some notes. Dr. Carrigan looked up from his paperwork. "Everything looks very good, Cydney. You're a healthy, young woman and I'm confident you'll have a beautiful, healthy baby at the end of September."

Again, Cydney was silent. An involuntary smile crossed her face in spite of her moist eyes as she listened intently to Dr. Carrigan's words.

A baby! A baby to love and to symbolize their love. A baby to cement their family together and carry on David's legacy. A baby. How wonderful! Now she would have to convince David.

CHAPTER FORTY-FIVE

Cydney tapped lightly on the study door and waited until she heard David bid her enter. She had learned her lesson that January day on her first visit to New York and she would never again enter his office without being summoned.

David looked up and smiled. "Well, well. Look who's here. What brings you a callin'?" He was obviously in a good mood.

Cydney smiled back, "I was wondering what you're doing for dinner tonight. It seems like weeks since we've had a nice quiet dinner together at home."

"Sorry, Cyd. Not tonight." He sounded rueful. "I have an early rehearsal with the Julliard School orchestra."

"It's okay." She wandered around the room, straightening piles of books and newspapers, adjusting picture frames. "Isn't it a beautiful day?" He watched her circumvent the room. She looked very pretty today. Actually, she always looked great but today she had an aura about her. "The sun is warm, the air is fresh…"

"Something on your mind, Cyd?" He continued to eye her.

"Yes, David, actually there is."

"Sit down." He gestured. Cydney slid into the upright armchair right across from David and their eyes met and held.

"You look lovely, Cydney." She nodded a muted thank you. Their eyes were still locked and Cydney smiled.

"What is it?" he asked.

"We're going to have a baby!" She tried to control her emotions but her heart pounded and her temples throbbed. She continued to look directly into David's eyes.

He sat motionless, expressionless. His pupils blackened and his eyes became mere slits. "I see," he said at last, still showing no emotion. "You're going to have a baby."

"No David, **WE'RE** going to have a baby."

He stood up then and she saw that his knuckles were white as he clasped the edge of his desk for support. "You know that's impossible!" he hissed. David was not a violent man but Cydney could feel the rage welling up in him. "I told you a long time ago, I'm sterile. Whose baby is it?" His voice was rising and he slammed his fist on the desk.

Cydney stayed seated and again fixed her eyes on David's. "Are you accusing me of infidelity?" Now her anger was surfacing.

"What else can I think?" His voice was malicious.

"David, I've seen a gynecologist. I asked the same questions..."

"I don't want to hear about it." He was almost shouting now.

"Yes! You will hear me out!" Cydney stood now and leaned forward, leveling the battlefield. They were almost face-to-face. "David," she said again, softer now, "David, you told me you had a very low sperm count. Dr. Carrigan said that's different than sterility. It only takes one sperm."

"So you discussed our personal life with a stranger?" David was still enraged.

"For heaven's sake, David, he's a doctor. I needed to see a doctor. This is why I haven't been feeling well."

They sparred verbally behind closed doors for hours. David hurling accusations at her and Cydney trying desperately to defend herself. He paced the room and continued to berate her until at last, emotionally and physically exhausted, she collapsed in a cauldron of uncontrollable sobs.

"David," she begged through muffled cries, "please believe me. I have not been unfaithful to you."

"Are you sure your friend, Loren isn't involved in this?" He was sarcastic now.

Cydney was both livid and exasperated. "Loren's gay, David. But of course, you wouldn't know that, since you never took the time to meet any of my friends. But as God is my witness, I have not been unfaithful to you. Believe it or not – like it or not, we're going to have a baby. And if you need proof that this child belongs to you, you can get a paternity test."

David sat down, trying to absorb Cydney's words. He had to admit, Cydney didn't lie and she never gave him reason to believe she was unfaithful. Yet, he had listened to Harland complaining about her comings and goings and her friends, and just as Cydney pointed out, he never took the time to meet any of them. David recalled that he was the one who told her to make some friends. He was the one who was too busy to indulge her. What's more, Cydney stood here before him and called on God to be her witness. Cydney, who never cursed or swore or took God's name in vain. Surely, she would never call on God to witness a lie!

Cydney sat down, too. The pent up emotion spewed forth again and she started to cry. "I'll talk with Dr. Carrigan," she said between sobs, "and he can arrange a paternity test."

David swallowed hard. "That won't be necessary." He rose from the chair and knelt beside her. His hand gently stroking that beautiful chestnut hair. She rested her head on his shoulder and the tears subsided.

"I'm so sorry, Cydney," he said just over a whisper, "I've been busy, I've neglected you. I've ignored you." He continued stroking her hair. "But I did keep one promise I made," he said trying to smile, "I've given you everything money can buy."

"Oh, David," she said, their eyes meeting once again, "I don't want everything money can buy. I just want you. And our baby."

Harland was speechless. Sophie and Gracie let out shouts of joy.

In the days and weeks that followed, pictures of David the baby, David the toddler and David the young boy began cropping up around the apartment. Obviously, one thing this baby would have was good looks.

Cydney loved being pregnant and pregnancy was so becoming to her. Sophie and Gracie doted on her more than ever and Cydney was so pleased that David began taking an interest in her pregnancy and was devoting more time to her.

She continued to see her friends and she continued to work with Harold but now Cydney and David spent more evenings together, especially over the summer months when David's schedule was not so demanding. As September approached and Cydney grew in girth she began staying closer to home. The fall concert tour didn't start until mid-October so they had time to decorate the nursery and many evenings they pored over books of names and found in each other, a joy, they had lost somewhere, somehow over the last five years.

CHAPTER FORTY-SIX

David was doing a benefit concert in Atlantic City, New Jersey when Cydney went into labor. She called the number he left but she couldn't reach him. After three desperate attempts, Cydney gave up and called Brenda because her labor pains were regular now and only about ten minutes apart. She was frightened. Brenda told Cydney to take a taxi to the hospital, she would call Carl and they would meet Cydney there.

Cydney was admitted to the hospital, assigned a birthing room and prepped for delivery before she had a chance to try to call David again. This time, Harland answered.

"I need David," she told him. "I'm at St. Vincent's. I'm in labor."

"I see," he replied showing no emotion at all.

"Please, Harland," she pleaded, "have David call me right away." She gave him the number. Cydney half expected him to offer some words of encouragement, to say something nice. Something to show her he wasn't such an ass after all. But he hung up without saying anything else.

Maxwell David DuPrey was born on Tuesday, September 30, 1980 after a long and difficult labor, with Brenda, and only Brenda at Cydney's side.

The disappointment and anger Cydney felt toward David were somewhat diminished as she peered into the face of her precious baby. He had David's eyes, both shape and color and wisps of chocolate down atop a perfectly shaped head. Cydney now knew the meaning of unconditional love. It was mid-morning on Wednesday, when David finally called.

"Cydney!" He sounded breathless and excited. "I called as soon as I got your message. Harland said you thought you were in labor." The sound of David's voice brought instant tears to Cydney's eyes yet she struggled to control her anger.

"I was in labor yesterday, David and thank God Brenda was here." David was silent now, finally beginning to realize just how cunning Harland was.

"Oh, Cyd, I'm so sorry, I ...." Before he could finish Cydney interrupted.

"We have a son, David," her voice was so full of hurt and emotion, "and you weren't here. His name is Maxwell. Maxwell David." With trembling fingers, she hung up the phone. She laid her head back, her beautiful chestnut hair fanned out over the pillow. Silent tears meandered down her cheeks. God forgive her. She hated Harland.

David arrived on Friday morning to drive them home and Cydney had to admit she was overjoyed to see him moved to tears as he held his son for the first time. Sophie and Gracie met them at the door. Harland feigned indifference in the background. He knew David was enraged and now regretted not immediately relaying Cydney's message to him.

Several bouquets of flowers were scattered about the apartment. The nursery was ready and waiting. Cards welcoming the new baby were stacked on the nightstand. Cydney and David stood hand in hand admiring their tiny creation, now comfortably asleep in his crib.

Cydney was filled with joyful anticipation of the years ahead. She hoped and prayed that she could be a great parent. Parents like Caleb and Leta were to her. Thoughts of Sarah flashed through her mind but she quickly dismissed them. She would love Max with all her heart and soul. She would protect him from all harm, if possible and yes, she would lay down her life for him. Being a mother was going to be an exciting and rewarding job.

Although David had shed tears the first time he held Max, he told himself it was because he was so overwhelmed. No question, Max was a handsome child. His baby pictures mirrored David's. There was no longer any doubt in David's mind. He had accepted the fact, he was Max's father and he would see to it that, like Cydney, Max would have everything money could buy. But since David found it very difficult to display affection, to profess his love to anyone but Cydney, or to show emotion, he once again went on the defensive. He armored himself against this child, who would want David to be all the things he couldn't be and who already had stolen Cydney's love and attention. Being a father was going to be a complex and difficult task.

When Max was just one year old, Cydney took him to Balsam Hills for the first time. David refused to go and Cydney didn't even care. It gave her a chance to relax, visit with her family and enjoy Max without David's strict authoritarian figure.

David decided Max should begin taking music lessons when he was only three. The Suzuki method was proven most affective for children and it was time for Max to have some structure in his life. Max showed no interest and he had no talent. David was livid.

Max cried on his first day of kindergarten and David called him a sissy and punished him.

When Max was eight he got into a fight at school. David called him a bully and again, punished him. At age nine, Max fell out of a tree in Central Park. David said he was clumsy and the broken arm was enough of a punishment. Cydney did her best to counter David's negativity and strict discipline. As a result, Max adored his mother and he was indifferent and ignored his father. In later years, Cydney would look back on Max's childhood with deep regrets.

CHAPTER FORTY-SEVEN

Sarah sat at the kitchen table in her small, shabby apartment, a letter from Patrice and a cup of brackish coffee in front of her. It was not good to the last drop, she had re-heated it one too many times but she couldn't afford to dump it out. Tears and cheap mascara dribbled down her cheeks and dotted the letter. She had received it just today but already read it several times.

Chicago was a lonely place. She had no friends. Well, there were the women she worked with at the Top Notch, a hair salon on the east side but they weren't really her friends. In fact, some of them looked down their noses at her so she kept pretty much to herself. The shop had several affluent clients but they all had their regular stylist. Sarah was not well established as a hairdresser, but like everything else in her life, she didn't put a lot of effort into it. She preferred during manicures, but apparently didn't do a good job at that either because most of those clients didn't come back to her. Sarah knew that if she didn't start to bring in more business, she might be let go.

Today, Patrice's letter full of mostly good news did nothing to lift her spirits. Patrice wrote about Aaron's successful architectural firm and how they were going to be taking on a new apprentice to increase their business. Evan and Elizabeth were fifteen years old already and Patrice had just recently gone back to work to supplement the family income. And of course, she updated Sarah on Cydney.

From previous letters, Sarah knew that Cydney married David and they had Max. In fact, Patrice kept her well informed about the whole family and often pleaded with Sarah to swallow her pride and return to Balsam Hills. Until now, Sarah had refused. She remembered one of her mother's sayings about people gone astray, "You make your bed, you must lie in it."

But mingled with the good news was word that Caleb continued to have health problems. After all, he was 73 years old now. So Sarah sat there looking over the letter and contemplating Patrice's suggestion. Maybe Sarah should at least go for a short visit before it was too late.

Caleb, like Patrice and Aaron, was nonjudgmental about Sarah and she appreciated that. Of course, she would never forgive her mother, or Leta, whom she blamed for alienating Cydney's affection for her.

Sarah was proud of the things she read about Cydney and she hoped that someday Cydney might forgive her for abandoning her. Sarah hoped she could somehow be part of Cydney's life again. Also, she had an unexplainable urge to meet Max; to let him know that she was his grandmother. Some of Patrice's letters hinted that since Max was born there was some friction between Cydney and David. Sarah wanted desperately for Cydney to be happy. If only she could help, but the truth was, she didn't know just how.

So Sarah decided. She would become the prodigal daughter. The next morning she called the farm in Wisconsin. Leta was surprised to hear from her and said they would welcome a visit. Sarah didn't bother to phone Top Notch to say she was quitting. They could kiss her ass! Things were finally going to work out for her. Sarah had a plan. She would spend some time at the farm and get back in Caleb's good graces. Then she would ask him for a loan. Surely, he wouldn't refuse. Once she had some money, she would head for New York. She'd find Cydney and Max. He was eight years old already and it was about time he got to know his grandmother. With a lot of luck, maybe Cydney would ask her to stay. After all, she had a swanky apartment and a lot of money. Sarah would just have to play her cards right. She might have to take some shit, especially from David. Seems like he could be a real jerk and his uncle an even bigger one. And if Sarah ever found out that David had mistreated Cydney, she'd find a way to get even with him. Sarah was tough and she would do whatever was necessary to come out on top. Hopefully, with some cash!

Caleb was sitting on the porch, puffing on his pipe, rocking back and forth, enjoying the warm summer afternoon when Sarah came sauntering up the driveway. He recognized her immediately but he didn't get up. Likewise, she spotted him but did not quicken her pace.

Sarah had taken the Greyhound as far north as her money permitted and from there on she thumbed it. She didn't have any trouble hitching a ride, mostly from truckers. Sarah looked pretty good for 50-something. She was petite with bottle blond hair and she had a skill for applying her makeup. From a distance she looked quite young and once a trucker stopped it usually was too late to change his mind. Sarah would never admit to 51. She was a flirt and a smooth talker and there never was a trucker who regretted giving her a lift.

"Hi Papa." She stood before him looking pretty and coy, hands clasped behind her back, her blond hair pulled back in a ponytail with a few curls hanging free. She wore jeans rolled up to her knees, sandals and a white peasant blouse, now a little dusty.

"Hello Sarah."

"How are you Papa?"

"Well, that depends on who you ask." A smile crossed Caleb's face. "If you're asking me, I'm fine. If you ask Leta or Brock, they'd tell you I have one foot in the grave." He continued rocking and puffing, sizing her up. "How are you?"

Sarah avoided his glance. She looked up the driveway to the south. "I don't know, Papa. I guess I made a real mess of things." She tried to sound sorry. "I've missed you. It's been a long, long time." She looked back at him now and saw a little mist in his eyes.

"I've missed you, too. Patrice kept us updated on your whereabouts."

"Me too," Sarah smiled, "and Cydney and Max, too."

"He's a fine boy," Caleb said grinning broadly now, "and he loves it here at Oakwood. When he's here, he's like a calf let out to pasture in the springtime." Caleb chuckled, remembering how uninhibited and free Max was at the farm.

Leta came out, drying her hands as the screen door slammed behind her. The women's eyes met. Leta spoke first, "You look good, Sarah."

Sarah looked uncomfortable, fidgeting in the pea gravel, raising a cloud of dust, which settled on the duffle bag sitting at her feet.

"Everything looks the same," she said after a few minutes.

"It's not," Caleb said, "most everything needs repair. Thank God for Brock. He can fix anything and he's working on it everyday. Gonna take awhile, but he can do it."

As if on cue, Brock came around the corner of the house wiping his brow. In spite of his dirty jeans and t-shirt, tousled hair and the smell of sweat, he looked irresistible. Sarah's heart skipped a beat. No one made any introductions, none were necessary. Brock simply acknowledged her with a nod and began talking to Caleb.

Sarah was slighted. Men didn't usually ignore her. She picked up her duffle bag, walked past Brock, close enough that her arm brushed his, cast a seductive look in his direction and followed Leta inside.

Caleb was right. The house, though spotless, was in a state of decadence. Yet it looked like heaven to Sarah and a flood of precious memories washed over her.

The next few weeks went well. Leta was friendly and Sarah was friendly back. Caleb, as before, was the buffer. They reminisced about years gone by and talked about Cydney and Max. Sarah talked pretty freely, but was not totally truthful about her life. Oh, she made sure Caleb knew how much she was in need of money. And she told them how difficult it was to keep a job with no high school diploma. But Sarah omitted the stories about the men, the drugs, and the drinking; the real reason she was broke.

Sarah got reacquainted with the farm; walking the fields, visiting the now empty barn and lying in the sand by the pond. While she enjoyed the quiet laid back life style, she did her best to make sure that she ran into Brock everyday, but he continued to ignore her.

One particular day, while he was working on the John Deere in the shed, she boldly approached him. Sarah was wearing tight red shorts and a tight white t-shirt with no bra. She was tan and trim and as usual perfectly made up. She looked at least ten years younger than she was.

"Working hard?" she asked circling the tractor and looking sensual.

Brock kept his eyes on his work. "Yup, as a matter of fact, I am."

"Don't you know the old saying about all work and no play?"

"Nope." He was still ignoring her.

"Then let me tell you." Her voice was gravelly. "All work and no play makes Brock a dull boy." She was close behind him now and on her tiptoes, almost whispering in his ear.

"I've always been pretty dull." Brock was oblivious to her.

"I find that hard to believe." She laid her hands on his upper arm bulging with muscle.

"A big, strong, handsome guy like you must have all kinds of excitement in his life."

"You grew up in these parts," Brock said, "you know the hottest thing around here is the temperature in July."

Sarah laughed, thinking she was breaking the ice, "Why not take a break? We could walk down by the pond and cool off."

"No need to," Brock said, "I'm not hot."

"I am," Sarah said a little breathless. She was close to him again and rubbed his arm with a red-tipped finger.

Brock stopped what he was doing and took a step backwards. Sarah held her ground and fluttered her eyes at him. Brock was brutally honest. "Look Sarah, I'm not interested in you. I don't want to talk to you, I don't want to listen to you and I don't even want to look at you. If I wanted a woman, which I don't, you would be my last choice." He turned back to his tractor.

Sarah stormed out of the shed, dragging her wounded pride. "Enough of this place!" she said to herself. "Time to move on."

Breakfast seemed like the perfect opportunity to approach Caleb about money. Sarah came to the table in faded jeans and a threadbare sweatshirt with the sleeves cut off. She wanted to look like the needy person she was. She waited until Leta served the scrambled eggs, ham and sticky warm cinnamon rolls and Caleb said grace.

"I've been reading about New York," she said casually, "there's a lot going on there this time of year." Neither Caleb nor Leta replied so she pressed on. "This might be the time for me to go there. That way

I can have some time to spend with Max before he has to go back to school."

Leta interjected, "You should call Cydney and let her know you're coming so she can explain things to Max."

"No, I'm not going to call her yet because I don't know exactly when I'll get there. I might make a couple of stops along the way. I'll call her when I actually get to New York." Sarah knew Caleb was looking at her but she could not meet his gaze. She was not a good liar. Instead she concentrated on stirring her coffee.

"How do you propose to get there?" Caleb asked, still eyeing her and wondering why she seemed so nervous. Sarah finally looked up, knowing Caleb was scrutinizing her.

"The Greyhound."

"That's an awfully long bus ride."

"As I said, I'll probably stop along the way."

"Why?" Caleb asked, "I thought you were in a hurry to get there?"

"To visit friends," Sarah lied again.

Caleb fell silent and went on with his breakfast. He had a keen insight into people and he had to admit, if only to himself, that he didn't believe his own daughter. During the weeks she had been at Oakwood, Caleb observed her closely and he knew she was not being honest with him. The silence was awkward. Finally, Leta excused herself and left the kitchen. Some things were just none of her business.

"Papa," Sarah leaned forward and covered his hand, wrinkled and bronzed, "I'm sorry that I disappointed you. But I'm not the only one to blame for the way things turned out." Caleb remained silent. Sarah was stirring up a lot of unhappy memories. He preferred to focus on happier times. Sarah went on, "I mean, if Mama had been able to cope with losing Luke, a lot of things would have been different."

Caleb freed his hand. "Don't blame your mother. She couldn't help herself. No one is to blame. It's life – it's just how life is. Things happen – good things and bad things and we have to deal with the things that happen to us. Some people deal with them better than others."

Breakfast was waning down and she had yet to make a pitch for money. "I'll try to do better," she said trying to steer the conversation.

"I'll be leaving tomorrow. I hope I didn't inconvenience you and Leta. You've been so kind."

"Of course you didn't inconvenience us. You're my daughter, you're family. Families stick together. They help each other out."

"Well actually, I do need some help, Papa. Financial help that is. Could you borrow me some money?"

He knew she would ask. He didn't know when, but he was prepared. "How do you propose to pay me back?"

His question surprised her. "Well, uh, I don't know." Sarah was fumbling for words.

Caleb took over, "I mean, you have no job and it appears you don't have any prospects."

Sarah was getting pissed off but she knew she had to keep her composure.

"Look Sarah," Caleb said, "I'm old. Let's face it; we may never see each other again. I won't loan you any money." Sarah was taken back by his blunt statement. She started to speak, to tell him he was an old fool. A cold hearted old fool, but she didn't have a chance. "I don't want you to owe me any money. Tell you what; I can spare three hundred dollars. No loan. A gift." Sarah couldn't believe her ears. This was better than she expected – way better. She would take the money, oh yes she would, but she wouldn't buy a bus ticket with it that's for sure. She would thumb her way east and save the money for something fun!

271

CHAPTER FORTY-EIGHT

Jeremiah Walker was a rambling man and he didn't have a lot of ambition. That's exactly why he loved his job so much. Jeremiah drove a tri-county area of northern Wisconsin in a white panel truck with the words J E W E L   T E A   C O.   on both sides in a perfect semi-circle, selling everything from dry goods to cleaning products and clothing.

The first two weeks of each month Jeremiah was close to home but when he traveled to the northern most parts of Ashland County during the third week of the month, it was prudent to stay up there. That suited Jeremiah just fine! He didn't have to listen to his fat-ass wife nagging and bitching at him for no reason and to four bratty screaming kids. Hell, he didn't even know if that last kid was his. Yes indeed, Jeremiah loved the third week of the month! At the end of the first day, he usually checked into some sleepy hollow. He'd get a good "home cooked" meal at some country tavern and after a few beers, he'd try to pick up a woman. If there were no prospects, he'd just take a six-pack back to the motel. He'd flop down on the bed, surrounded by total peace and quiet; turn on the TV and pop open a beer. Jeremiah could smoke in bed, he could belch or fart, if it suited him and no one – no one – complained.

Jeremiah was born and raised in Georgia but came north after a brush with the law. He was not a particularly handsome man but he had an abundance of southern charm, which he lavished upon the rural housewives he visited on a monthly basis. Jeremiah considered himself lucky. After all, it wasn't rocket science. These women were just so damn gullible! After he yammered briefly about the weather, brought in last month's order and collected his money, he recited the new monthly specials, peppering the whole conversation with hollow compliments, a toothy grin and a wink here and there. By the time he brought out the new order form, Jeremiah usually made a pretty lucrative sale.

This third week was off to a great start! On Monday Jeremiah packed it in early, about 3:00 p.m. because his last stop at the Harris farm was a doozey! Irene Harris was a good-looking woman and by the time he got done telling her how great her new hairdo looked and what a great sun tan she had, her purchase was much larger than usual. And best of all, he even managed to brush his arm across her ample breasts as he reached for the order form.

Back at the motel, he drank a couple of beers, smoked a joint and took a nap. When Jeremiah woke up, he was starving. He showered, put on a clean shirt, slicked back his hair and headed for the Bad River Saloon. He woofed down the Monday Night Special and drank a couple more beers. The jukebox was playing the latest country hits and Jeremiah was feeling a little melancholy. He lit a cigarette, inhaled deeply and eyed a cute little red head at the end of the bar. She was young and sexy and obviously pleased at the attention she was getting because she smiled back at Jeremiah. Before long, she slid off the bar stool and headed his way. It didn't take Jeremiah long to make his move and after only five minutes or so, they left the bar together. Jeremiah just couldn't believe his good luck! He didn't even have to take her back to the motel. She was one hot item and he screwed her right there on the front seat of the white panel truck. Christ, she didn't even ask his name! That's exactly how he liked it – no strings attached – no obligations – just slam, bam, thank you ma'am.

When Jeremiah headed back to the motel he thought if the rest of the week were only half this good, he'd be a happy man.

Tuesday dawned sunny and warm. Jeremiah was still on a high from last night. He expected to have another good day and he planned to go back to the Bad River Saloon tonight. Maybe he could get another piece of ass from red. His first sale wasn't that great but Jeremiah didn't let that dampen his spirits. He was cruising west on Arrowhead Road, the radio blaring and the windows open when he saw a petite blond woman walking on the side of the road. From his vantage point, she looked real shapely and when she heard the truck approaching she turned around and stuck out her thumb. Jeremiah screeched to a halt, leaned over and pushed the passenger side door open.

"Good morning, sweetie." He flashed her a big smile, "Jeremiah Walker at your service. Where you headed?"

"New York." She seemed reluctant to climb in.

"New York? New York's back that way, a long way back that way," Jeremiah pointed to the back of the truck.

"Well, where you headed?" she asked, a little sheepish.

"I'd drive to the ends of the earth if I could get a pretty little thing like you to ride along."

She got in. "I'm Sarah Brown."

"Well, Sarah Brown, what are you doing in these parts?" Jeremiah was looking her over real good and she sure didn't look like a country housewife to him. He judged her to be about 40. Pretty, nicely made up. A twinkle in her eyes. She wore tight jeans, a tight white t-shirt and he could see her nipples outlined against the cotton fabric. She carried a black duffle bag, which she tossed over the seat as she got in.

"I grew up out here," Sarah said, "and I was just visiting my Pa before I head east."

Jeremiah pulled back onto the pavement, driving slowly now. "Well, like I said, that could be a problem, because right now you're heading west, same as me."

"Maybe one of us will have to change our plans." Sarah gave him a suggestive look, "What's west?"

"My route is west. What's east?"

"New York. Fun and excitement." Sarah was looking straight ahead now, "Maybe fame and fortune." At the mention of money, Jeremiah's ears perked up.

"How so?" he asked.

"Maybe I have a rich relative there!"

"How rich?"

"Rich, rich." She flashed Jeremiah an irresistible smile.

"Suppose you're telling me the truth. What's in it for me if I drive you to New York?"

"Could you do that?" Sarah was surprised.

"Maybe I would. Depends." Jeremiah turned his eyes back to the road.

"On what?"

"You. Me." Now Jeremiah was the one to flash a wicked grin.

"Don't you have any obligations?" Sarah asked.

"Don't you?"

"Nope. I'm free as a bird. Nothing's going to stop me from getting to New York. But you didn't answer my question. I mean, aren't you working right now?"

"What makes you think that?"

"The truck's a dead give away, Jerry. Is it okay if I call you Jerry? And don't keep answering my questions with a question."

Jeremiah nodded. Jerry. He liked the sound of it, Jerry. And he liked the way she said it.

"When I'm out here, I'm my own boss," Jeremiah said. "No one tells me what to do. If I decide to drive you to New York, then I will."

"Look, Jerry, I can't pay you to drive me to New York. If I had enough money to get there on my own, I wouldn't have been hitchin'. I've got a couple a hundred bucks. That's it."

"Maybe we can work something out." Jeremiah winked at her.

"Why Jerry, you scoundrel! What are you suggesting?" Once again, Jeremiah pulled the truck to the shoulder of the road and turned to face her.

"Listen sweetie, I only have a couple a hundred myself but if we pool our resources and head east, we could probably have a real good time." Jeremiah had his hand on her shoulder as he spoke and he let his fingers slowly creep up her neck and play with a few wayward strands of blond hair. Sarah was enjoying the attention and his fingers parading up and down her neck set her heart to racing.

"What if we run out of money?"

"We'll cross that bridge when we get to it. What will we need besides gas and lodging? We've got a whole truck full of stuff including some food." Jeremiah nodded his head toward the back of the truck.

"Beer! We could use some beer. It's getting hot out. And how about a joint? I could use a joint, too. Bet you don't have any of that?" Jeremiah laughed but continued to play with Sarah's curls, ear lobes and neck. She was getting hot and he knew it, but he was hot, too.

"As a matter of fact, I have just what the doctor ordered." Jeremiah reached over, fumbled in the glove compartment and came out with a couple of sticks. He lit one and pressed it between Sarah's lips. She inhaled deeply, closed her eyes and laid her head back. Jeremiah lit his joint and did the same. They were both silent now, enjoying getting high. Jeremiah looked over at Sarah. She was so pretty and her tits! Man, they were really sticking out. He sure wanted to touch them. She sensed he was looking at her and opened her eyes. He smiled at her.

"Want a beer?"

"You got some?" Sarah was excited.

"Hey, I told you, I got a whole shit load full of stuff in this truck." He turned around, reached over the seat and produced two cans of cold beer.

"Man, Jerry, this is great. You're right you do have everything we need in this truck." She took another pull on her joint and a big gulp of beer. Jeremiah was more interested in getting his hands on her nipples. He moved closer to her.

"Enough to get us all the way to New York," he whispered in her ear.

"Are you sure you want to go with me?" Jeremiah brushed his lips across her cheek and found her full, sensual lips. After all, maybe she does have a rich relative in New York.

Sarah didn't hesitate. She kissed him back and even parted her lips as his tongue shot into her mouth. After all, he might be her ride to New York. Sarah pushed back just as Jeremiah's hands slid down her shirt and pressed against her breasts.

"Maybe we should get started," Sarah said, "we can save this for later." She took his hands and moved them. Jeremiah grinned. Just the thought of screwing Sarah gave him a hard on. He slid back behind the wheel, did a U turn and headed east. Sarah moved close to him and tucked her arm through his.

"Jerry," she said, "just one more question. What about the truck? Isn't someone going to miss it? It's pretty darn easy to spot with all the lettering on it!"

"We'll have it painted," he said. He reached for her hand and placed it in his throbbing crotch.

CHAPTER FORTY-NINE

Cydney bolted upright in bed. A ringing phone in the middle of the night usually means bad news. She snatched up the receiver on the third ring.

"DuPrey's."

"Cydney?"

"Yes." Then, "Brock?" His voice was shaky and almost unrecognizable, coupled with the fact that she hadn't spoken to him in months.

"Yes, it's Brock. Cydney, it's Caleb."

"What happened?" Cydney's stomach did a flip-flop.

"He died in his sleep, Cyd. Leta came pounding on the cottage door about 1:00 a.m. We tried to revive him but he was already gone."

"What time is it now, Brock?" Cydney looked around the room, momentarily losing track of things.

"Well, it's about 3:30 here. We called the paramedics, but they couldn't bring him back either. They've already transported him to Balsam Hills. When can you get here? Leta wants you to make the arrangements."

"How is Leta, Brock, and you – how are you?"

"We're okay. I'll stay here with Leta but she's already talking about going back to the reservation."

"Don't let her leave. I'll be there as soon as I can."

"We tried to revive him, Cyd."

"I know you did everything possible, Brock. But we all knew he had a bad heart. Have you called Aaron and Patrice yet?"

"I'll call them as soon as we're done." Brock was calmer now.

"I'll see you later today Brock, and thank you for taking care of Leta."

David was already awake and he knew what happened from the bits of conversation he heard. Cydney hung up the phone and sat numb on the edge of the bed. David rolled toward her and sat up. He kissed her neck and started massaging her shoulders.

"How did it happen?" His voice was gentle.

"In his sleep. He just went to sleep. I guess that part is good. He obviously didn't suffer."

Cydney got up. "Will you be coming with us?" She already knew the answer but she asked anyway.

"Oh, Cyd, I'm sorry. I can't go. You know how I hate canceling concerts." She just nodded. She got up and headed for the bathroom. David stayed lying in bed, propped up on the pillows. When Cydney came out of the bathroom, the news had been absorbed and silent tears slid down her cheeks. She retrieved a travel bag from the closet and starting packing.

"How long will you stay?" David asked.

"I don't know, obviously Max can't be out of school too long, fourth grade is so important."

"Maybe Max should stay here," David suggested.

"Absolutely not!" Cydney was emphatic. "He adores Caleb. He needs to see him. He understands dying, he'll need some closure." They said no more. There was no need to.

When Max woke up, Cydney gently broke the news to him and like most nine year olds, he didn't cry, at least not in front of his parents. But the truth was that Max was devastated by the loss of Caleb, the most positive role model in his life. Maybe Brock could replace Caleb because heaven only knows, David didn't fill the bill.

Cydney booked the earliest available flight out of LaGuardia and 4½ hours later they landed in Minneapolis, they took a connecting flight to White River and arrived at the farm about 5:00 p.m., central time. Aaron and Patrice, Evan and Elizabeth had already arrived and together, with Cydney and Max, Brock and Leta, they celebrated the life and mourned the loss of their beloved Caleb. No one knew how to reach Sarah. Neither Patrice nor Leta had heard from her since she left the farm that July day, two years earlier, claiming she was headed for New York.

Friends and neighbors came from miles around to bid farewell to Caleb, a most respected member of the community and when, two days later, he was laid to rest between Gwendolyn and Luke, Cydney felt an unbelievable sense of peace.

Caleb had lived a full and meaningful life. He loved his family and he loved the land he worked. He made the best of what life gave him and he did it with dignity and kindness. Max sensed the aura of calm that engulfed Cydney and that helped him to close this chapter of his life.

There were so many things to take care of. Cydney put Max on a plane back to New York and called David.

"I'm staying on for several more days. There's so much to tend to. Max is arriving on United Flight 1137 at 4:30; you ***must*** be there to pick him up. Don't be late! This had been a very trying time for him."

"I'll send Phillip," David said nonchalantly.

"Why can't you pick him up? Just this once, can't you be there for him?"

"Oh sure, Cyd, I'll drive all the way out there to pick him up and he'll sit in the back seat and not say a damn word all the way home."

"Any idea why?" She was getting angry. She, too, had been through a lot and her patience was wearing thin. She needed some support right now. Obviously, it wouldn't come from David.

"Jesus christ, Cyd, Give me a break. I've tried to --- "

She interrupted. "Don't curse at me David. You haven't tried. You want the truth? Do you know what you've given Max? A name, that's all you've given him, your name."

"Cyd, you're wrong, listen, when you get back we'll talk it over. We'll ... "

"I'm not going to argue with you now, David. I'm tired, I'm emotional and I'm not up to discussing your relationship with Max right now. Just pick him up!" She hung up. She stood staring at the phone, wondering how things between them had changed so drastically. Cydney was choking back tears when a firm but gentle hand touched her shoulder. She knew it was Brock. She covered his big brown hand with hers and squeezed it softly. She turned to face him. His eyes were as sad as hers. She laid her head on his chest and quietly sobbed, while he stroked that beautiful chestnut hair.

Cydney had instructed Max to call her when he got home, which he did. "How was your flight, Love?" Cydney tried to sound cheerful.

"It was great, Mom. I had a couple of cokes."

"Did you use your manners?"

"Yes, Ma'am, in fact one of the ladies said I was a polite young man." Max was pleased with himself.

"And was Dad on time to pick you up?" Cydney asked.

"Phillip picked me up and all the way home he asked me questions about the Mets and I knew almost all the answers." Max was a diehard Mets fan and he and Phillip were buddies. Cydney was so grateful to Phillip for the time he spent with Max but for now she was seething with anger toward David. She didn't want Max to know how livid she was, but David would hear more about this when she got home.

"I'll call you tomorrow, Max, when you get home from school. Give my love to Sophie and Gracie, okay?"

"To Dad, too?"

"Yes, of course, Max, Dad, too."

Leta had prepared a wonderful dinner, her forte'; and the seven of them ate in a subdued atmosphere, sometimes recalling funny things Caleb did or said. Their sadness was tempered with humor knowing Caleb would want it that way.

After dessert, Aaron spoke up. "Evan, Elizabeth, please excuse us, we have some business to discuss." The twins were eager to leave the table. The spring evening was calling them and their seventeen-year-old spirits were responding. Brock got up as well.

"No Brock, you stay. You're part of this family and you need to be in on this conversation. Leta, you stay as well." All eyes were on Aaron as things turned serious. Aaron continued, "Leta, thank you so much for all you did for Caleb. Even though he never married you, we all know how much he loved you." Leta usually strong and stoic struggled to maintain her composure. "Brock, you were like a son to Caleb. He loved you, too and I know that the two of you had an agreement about the farm. Right?" Brock only nodded. "Leta, Brock told us you were planning on going back to the reservation?" This time Leta nodded. Aaron went on. "You know that you are welcome to stay?"

"Yes, I know that, Aaron," Leta said, "and thank you, but there's nothing here for me now."

Aaron turned to Cydney, "Cyd, I know we both promised Caleb we would keep the farm in the family if possible and I know you want to keep that promise. So do I, but Patrice and I are not in a position to put any money into fixing the place up, right now. The truth is, the twins will be going off to college in fall and we're a little strapped financially. They'll be eighteen in December and once they move out, we plan to downsize to a smaller house or condo and I just stuck more money into the business, too. So for now, we just can't afford it." Cydney listened intently to Aaron's words and while he continued talking, a plan was already forming in her mind. She sat silently observing all of them. Cydney was adamant. She would not give up the farm. She would keep her promise to her grandfather. Aaron sat back, emotionally drained, like the rest of them. Cydney could tell he was saddened by the situation. Oakwood had been his home, too! It seemed like Aaron was waiting for Cydney to speak, so she did.

"Oh, Aaron, I can see how badly you feel about all of this. But I really want to keep the farm in the family." They had already read a copy of Caleb's will. Aaron and Cydney got the farm in equal shares. Leta got some cash, so did Brock. Sarah was not mentioned.

"Let's have an appraisal done to see the worth of the farm," Cydney went on, "then if you and Patrice are in agreement, I'll buy your half."

Patrice and Aaron exchanged glances, Cydney pressed on. "You will always be welcome here, Aaron, just like before. You may come anytime and stay as long as you want. In return, I would like you to do some architectural work for me to make some updates to the house."

Next, she turned to Brock. "Brock, I too am aware of your agreement with Caleb and I will certainly honor it. I hope you will honor it as well and agree to stay here and care for the farm. Leta let me reiterate what Aaron said. You are welcome to stay on here as long as you wish." Leta nodded, still so overcome with emotion that she could not speak.

Finally, Brock spoke up. "Caleb was like a father to me. He brought me here and gave me a home. He taught me about life and everything I needed to know to be a good farmer. I'll stay here at Oakwood and take care of things, for Caleb, for you, for as long as you need me. I'll do whatever needs to be done. I have no place else to go."

Leta had composed herself now and she too, spoke up. "Tomorrow Brock will drive me up to Bad River but let me assure you, Cydney, Aaron, Patrice," she looked at each of them as she spoke their names, "I remain forever in your debt and at your beck and call. If you plan on coming to the farm, just give me a call a day or two in advance and I will come back, get the house is order and stay here during the time you're here. You are, indeed, my family. Cydney, you're like a daughter to me and I will be here for you and Max, at anytime."

So things were decided and they were all in agreement. Oakwood Acres would stay in the family for everyone to love and enjoy.

Cydney's next big challenge was to confront David. She thought about it all the way back to New York. She realized she would have to give him an ultimatum. He would have to improve his relationship with Max and support her decision to renovate the farm house or she would see to it that he got some very bad publicity. Cydney didn't believe in blackmail, but she would not allow David to continue to ignore Max and she would not give up the farm. She didn't think David would call her bluff because David and Harland surely didn't like bad ink!

All Cydney would ask was that David spend more time with Max. Max was such a dear child and if David spent more time with him, Max would surely win him over. But all David thought about was work. In truth, David would never have to work another day in his life. He had vast wealth even before his career took off. David kept telling Cydney how much he enjoyed playing the violin, seeing the response on the faces of his audiences and knowing that he gave each of them pleasure. Cydney did not dispute that. After all, she had been mesmerized the very first time she heard David play at UIC back in 1973. She was overcome with emotion by the beautiful sounds and swept off her feet by the musician himself. Still, she thought she could change him. That his love for her would come before his music and she would be number one in his life. She was wrong! Although he promised her she would always be first, she was second to his violin, which he cared for and handled like a fragile young nymph crying out for love.

When Max was born, Cydney actually thought David would rethink his priorities. At first, it seemed like he was trying, but there was Harland, constantly pushing, constantly pressuring David to work harder, book more concerts, make more contacts. David no longer doubted that Max was his child. The brown hair and eyes, the captivating smile, left no room for doubt, but if Cydney was second, then Max was surely third. David approached his son with the same indifference he now gave to his marriage. At this time in their lives and after almost sixteen years of marriage, Cydney didn't expect things to change in her favor, but she still hoped and prayed, every night, that David would become a loving father to Max. Cydney recalled Leta's words from many years ago, "Some people love you a lot, but they don't know how to show it."

So once again, Cydney would forgive David for not picking Max up at the airport. Forgiveness was in her nature. After all, Max got home safely and even enjoyed the ride with Phillip and besides, Cydney had more pressing matters to think about now. Cydney knew that if she didn't have enough money in her trust fund account to purchase Aaron's half of the farm, David would give her the money. That was the one thing David always wanted her to have; plenty of money! If for some reason, David refused to give her financial backing, she would threaten to get a job. He would hate that. He would not allow that! Cydney was not being sly; she was just reviewing her options. She would do anything to keep the farm.

Cydney had already discussed the renovations with Aaron and in just two weeks the blueprints arrived for her to look at. First, Brock would open up the west wall of the master bedroom and add a patio door and deck. That way she could overlook the pond from her bed. She also wanted the upstairs sitting room to over look the pond so the deck would have to be two levels. Brock would also have to repair crumbling plaster and rotting wood, refinish the hardwood floors and paint the house, both inside and out. A monumental task that would take months to complete but she knew Brock would do it. If not for her, then for Caleb.

CHAPTER FIFTY

David was receptive to Cydney's idea about buying Aaron's share of the farm. He knew that if he could keep her busy with the remodeling project, she would get off his back about Max and the long hours he spent away from home. Besides that, according to Cydney, the renovations could take months, since Brock would be doing most of the work himself and squeezing it in between tending the crops and his other chores. That could only mean the Cydney and Max would be spending a lot of time in Wisconsin, especially during the summer months.

Not that David wanted to get rid of them. He was just overwhelmed sometimes and at age 45 he was experiencing some feelings of restlessness. A mid-life crisis so to speak. David was content with his career; it was Harland who kept pushing him. David was now recognized on the street and he was much in demand on the concert circuit and that was enough for him. When he took center stage – anywhere- when he raised his violin, when the beautiful sounds spilled forth, he was filled with sheer joy and consumed with passion. Nothing else in the world mattered. Just David and his violin. He loved performing.

Harland thought David's career was stagnant and he was constantly pressuring David to book more performances, to even branch out to an international tour. Gracie had a stroke and could no longer work and Cydney was constantly interrupting him with trivial tales of Max's accomplishments. Consequently, he began spending more time by himself. He was a successful musician, how could he be such a failure as a father? Truthfully, David never really bonded with Max and now, well, the boy was at the awkward age. His two front teeth protruded slightly and he was all arms and legs. He was reaching puberty and David found it quite annoying. Of course, he couldn't discuss this with anyone. How could he? What would he say? "By the way, I don't like my son. He annoys me just by being in the same room with me."

At one time David would have told Cydney anything, the deepest, darkest secrets of his soul. But he couldn't discuss Max with her. As far as Cydney was concerned a parent's love is unconditional, unflappable, unwavering. But then how would she know? Her mother abandoned her. Thus, David's anxiety continued. Bickering with Harland, pacifying Cydney and ignoring Max. He found it difficult to come directly home after his concerts, knowing that Cydney would be waiting for him. Not to talk about his performance, sip wine and make love but to prattle on about some silly or insignificant thing Max had done that day. So the cycle continued.

He needed some solitude. A place to call his own. Someplace away from Harland and the hectic life he led. When Cydney finally confronted David about the change in his personality he denied that there was a problem saying only that she should concentrate on getting the remodeling done at the farm. So she did. But there was something else, Cydney noticed. Almost as if David were hiding something from her.

Cydney and Max made several trips to Wisconsin over the months following Caleb's death. Each time they returned she excitedly reported to David how the project was progressing and she noticed that each time he was less interested.

September came and Max returned to school, a fifth grader now and ten years old. It had been a whirlwind summer with so many trips back and forth to the farm and he was ready to settle down. Caleb was now a precious memory tucked away in Max's heart. Max and Brock had grown very close over the summer. Max followed him everywhere and helped with the chores and the remodeling. And Brock had to admit Max was quite a guy, considering who he had for a father.

Cydney was full of admiration for Brock. He catered to Max. He never lost his patience or made Max feel like he was in the way. He answered all his questions and sometime asked some of his own. Max loved Brock and she knew Max would be unhappy when she decided to go to the farm without him in late September.

"Why can't I go along?" he questioned, his bottom lip pouting.

"Max, you've only been in school three weeks. When you have a break we can go again. Maybe we can even go at Christmas. But not this time." Max didn't argue with his mother.

CHAPTER FIFTY-ONE

Cydney rented a car at the airport and took her time driving out to the farm. She never tired of the scenery. The trees shone yellow, orange and red against an azure blue sky and she could hardly wait to see what Brock had accomplished since she had been here in mid-August. When she crested the hill and turned onto Apple Road, the old house came into view and her heart pounded. This place would always be home!

Cydney planned to tell Brock that before winter set in, he should move into the big house. The cottage was not well insulated and it seemed wasteful to heat both places. Furthermore, she thought the cottage might hold some unpleasant memories for Brock since that was where he and Ellen had started (and ended) their married life.

Cydney turned the car around in the yard and parked. She hurried up the back porch steps calling Brock's name as she entered the kitchen and rid herself of the bag of groceries she picked up at the local market. The house was silent. No hammering, no saw buzzing, no radio blaring as was usually the case when Brock was working. She stuck her head into the master bedroom, now brightened by the patio door leading to an enormous deck. No Brock. She took the steps two at a time and again called his name. From the new upstairs deck door she looked out over the pond. No Brock. She went into one of the bedrooms and looked out over the yard. His truck was there. He must be somewhere. Cydney looked around; admiring the upstairs much lighter now by opening up that north wall and then she hurried down. She was so happy with the work and she couldn't wait to tell Brock how great it looked.

She approached the cottage, hoping to find him there. She pushed open the screen door and once more called his name then stopped dead in her tracks. Brock was sitting on the floor in the kitchen area, leaning up against the cabinets. He looked up when he heard her come in. His eyes were red and bleary. He wore filthy jeans and a t-shirt stained with sweat and God only knows what else. His hair, now long in the back, was gnarled and dirty. He clutched a bottle of whiskey in his hand. Cydney had never seen Brock drunk. In fact, she didn't know he even drank. She didn't know about all the nights he sat alone, pouring his guts out to Jack Daniels while the voices of Merle and Reba comforted him from the boom box on the kitchen counter top.

"Brock!" Cydney could hardly believe her eyes.

"Hey beautiful," he slurred back.

"You're drunk!"

"Yup, I guess I am. Wanna have a snort with me?" He leered at her as he raised the bottle in her direction.

"Brock, stop it! No, I don't want any. Get up! What's the matter with you? Why have you done this?"

"Okay baby, anything you say. You're the boss now." He tried to get up and stumbled forward, grabbing hold of Cydney and looking right into her eyes. "Why?" He continued to be very close to Cydney and she could smell his acrid breath. "I'll tell you why. Because it's lonely here. Damn lonely. No one to talk to, no one to keep me company. Everyone I've ever loved has left me."

"That's not true, Brock. You have friends, lots of friends."

"Lots of friends maybe, but no one to love. My parents left me, Caleb left me. Ellen left me. Even you, Cyd, you left me, too." Cydney was getting desperate.

"Stop it Brock! You're drunk! You don't know what you're saying!" Brock slumped back down to the floor and once again leaned against the cupboard. He picked up the bottle of whiskey and took another pull.

"You know who I'm like, Cyd?" He didn't wait for her answer. "I'm just like drunken Ira Hayes. Do you know that story? Only I'm a Chippewa. Worse yet, I'm a half breed."

Cydney continued to plead with Brock, to tell him to stop. But Brock ignored her. Instead he took another pull from his bottle and broke into song, slurring his words singing about the Pima Indian, Ira Hayes and looking off into the distance. "I am like Ira Hayes, Cyd, not a Marine at war but a nobody at war with myself. Trying to find some ..."

"Please, Brock, stop it!" Cydney cut him off. "You're just having a bad day. We all have those kinds of days."

"I bet you never get lonely. You have Max. And David. David, Ha! I never did like that son-of-a-bitch. He took you away from me, Cyd." He turned and looked up at her now. Tears welled up in her eyes and she saw that his eyes were moist as well. Their eyes locked and Brock got to his feet. He put the bottle of whiskey on the counter top and reached for her. She didn't fight him and he pulled her close. He held her to him and she could hear his heart pounding. She closed her eyes, savoring the seconds that he held her close.

"I love you, Cydney," he said barely over a whisper. "I've always loved you."

"Of course we love each other," she replied, "we're family."

"No!" he said sharply. "I don't mean like family. I love you. I truly love you and I let you get away from me." She pushed back then and once again looked into his dark eyes.

"Brock, you can't love me! You mustn't love me! I'm married." She turned and ran from the cottage. When she reached the back porch of the house, she stopped to catch her breath. She tried to shake off the words but they echoed in her mind and crept into the corner of her heart. He loved her! Now what?

The evening chill had set in and Cydney built a fire in the huge fieldstone fireplace in the living room. She poured herself a glass of wine, settled into one of the old rockers and watched the flames leap to life. Brock's words marched back and forth across her mind, confusing her and clouding her usual practical thinking.

"He didn't mean it," she told herself over and over, "he was drunk and he didn't mean it. Why, tomorrow he won't even remember what he said." She rocked and sipped the wine and tried to relax but all sorts of hypothetical situations kept cropping up. What if she hadn't married

David? Would she and Brock be married? Would they have a son like Max? She closed her eyes and pictured Brock and Max working in the fields together or playing catch in the yard. Brock would be a wonderful father. She pictured herself in Brock's embrace while he peppered her lips and throat with kisses.

"Cydney! Stop it!" She bolted upright and scolded herself again. She got up and wandered into the kitchen. She made a sandwich, refilled her wine glass and headed back to the living room by way of the master bedroom. From the new deck door she peered into the night. The cottage was dark and quiet. She wondered if Brock had passed out on the floor or if he still sat there wallowing in self-pity. Maybe she should go and check. Just to be sure he was all right.

"No! You're not going out there!" Her conscience was really keeping her in line. "Brock's a big boy. He can take care of himself. Going out there would only add fuel to the fire."

Cydney sat in front of the fire far into the night, reminiscing about her childhood and picturing Brock chasing her across the yard and down through the sea oats that grew beside the pond. When at last she snuggled beneath the thick quilt on the big four-poster bed in the master bedroom, stars were visible through the new door. What a wonderful job Brock had done! She would remember to tell him in the morning.

Brock tapped lightly on the screen door. "Good morning," he called out before letting himself in. Cydney was at the stove frying bacon. Apple muffins were cooling on the counter and the aroma of freshly brewed coffee filled the kitchen.

"Come in. Have some breakfast." When she turned to face him she felt her face flush. Brock didn't seem to notice. He had showered and wore clean clothes. His thick black hair was slicked back, clean and shiny. He poured himself a cup of coffee and then looked at Cydney. "Want some?" She nodded and turned back to the bacon. "Cyd, I'm sorry about last night."

"What are you sorry for?" She wanted to know if he remembered what he said to her.

"For getting drunk and pouring my guts out to you, that's what. But I meant what I said—" Cydney held her breath until Brock finished his sentence, "—it's very lonely here. I love it when you and Max come. How is Max anyway and why didn't he come along?"

"School has started. He's in fifth grade now and can't afford to miss. He's struggling with some of his subjects and with his relationship with his father, or I should say his father's lack of a relationship with him. We hope to come at Christmas."

"What about David? I know he hates this place but won't he want you in New York for Christmas?"

"David isn't big on holidays. Christmas in New York is lovely, but Max would really enjoy Christmas here. I'm sure of that and he'll have time off from school then, too. He was a little upset that I was coming without him this time but when I said he could come at Christmas time, he was excited and I'm sure he'll hold me to it." Cydney served the bacon and muffins. Brock refilled the coffee.

"How did you sleep?" Brock asked. Cydney was still a little uncomfortable.

"Pretty good, thanks. And you?"

Brock threw back his head and laughed, that deep throaty laugh that Cydney loved. "I don't think it was sleep, it was more like I passed out. Anyway, sometime during the night I got up and went to bed so I guess I slept pretty good."

"Do you have a headache?"

"Nah, I guess the sleep took care of that." They ate in silence and Cydney felt pretty confident that Brock didn't remember that he had professed his love for her. She wouldn't mention it – to anyone.

From across the table, Brock flashed her a smile. "Well, how do you like it? Does it look like you pictured it?"

"Brock, it's absolutely beautiful. You did a wonderful job. I love how the doors brighten up the bedrooms, and the deck," she paused and let out a little giggle, "It's – well it's –, I'm speechless."

"All I have left to do is paint the two smaller bedrooms upstairs and I'll get them done in the next few weeks. After that Leta's going to come and clean good so when you come home - er- come here at Christmas, it will all be spic and span."

"When you finish painting, Brock, close up the cottage and move into the house. The cottage isn't very warm in the winter as you probably already know and there's no point in heating both buildings. You can take the largest bedroom and Leta can take the south one. Max can have the small one. Why don't you have Leta clean the cottage good, too and then we can always open it up for extra rooms if anyone else comes at Christmas."

"Good idea. You're right; the cottage can get pretty nippy on a cold and windy night. Especially, when you've got no one to warm you up." Brock laughed again and Cydney blushed a little. "How long are you staying?"

"Well, I need to go over the bills with you and get them paid. Pay you and Leta and maybe when you have time we can talk about anything else that need's fixing or replacing. Okay?"

Brock nodded, finished his coffee and stood up. "I'm going to town. Need anything?"

"What are you doing for dinner tonight?" Cydney asked, a little flirtatiously. "I could make us a nice dinner."

"I thought you couldn't cook?"

"Well, I can't cook much, but I can try!" She smiled at him.

"How about if I cook the dinner?" Brock suggested. "I'm sure I know more about it than you do! What would you like?"

Cydney shrugged and laughed, "Surprise me." He returned her smile and left her standing in the kitchen, still not knowing how much of last night he remembered.

Cydney spent the day poring over the books, checking invoices and paying bills. She relaxed in one of the freshly painted white wicker chairs on the porch in the warm afternoon sun. She called Leta and then Max and finally, she took a long walk through the fields, no longer green with summer crops. The tree tops, blowing in the still warm September breeze, showed brilliant color against a cloudless blue sky. Cydney took it all in from the crest of a hill overlooking the pond and she decided that there was no place on earth quite as beautiful as this. She sensed the presence of Caleb and from way down in her soul, she knew why he, and now Brock, could never leave here.

As Cydney approached the house, she could hear Brock once again singing the heartbreaking ballad of Ira Hayes and when the words escaped him, he hummed or whistled but this time there was no sadness in his voice. No slurred words. He sang loud and clear and it was joyful. Once again, Cydney wondered if Brock recalled more of the details of their conversation last night.

The kitchen was warm and smelled wonderful. Cydney was surprised that Brock knew his way around a kitchen so well. He didn't stop singing when he heard her come in. He just cast an enormous smile her way and gestured for her to sit down. She obeyed and sat opposite the place settings he had already laid out on the table. Cydney enjoyed watching him work, just like when they were children and she followed him around the farm. When she offered to help he seemed put out.

"Absolutely not! If there's one thing that can turn a man and a woman against each other, it's trying to cook together!" he said with amusement.

"Now who told you that?"

"It's just a known fact. Men and women don't belong in the kitchen together."

"Okay, okay," Cydney held up her hands, "offer withdrawn. But what's for dinner? It smells heavenly!"

"Well, Madam," Brock said with a sweeping, gallant gesture toward the stove, "we shall begin with a fresh spinach salad, tossed with apples, walnuts and vinaigrette dressing. Then there's oven roasted chicken and baby red potatoes, corn muffins and pie for dessert."

"Pie? Surely, you didn't bake a pie?" Cydney was surprised by how well he had planned the meal.

"Well, I **ordered** the pie. That should count for something. And wine, I got some wine. I asked at the liquor store what kind of wine is served with chicken and they gave me this." He handed her the bottle. Cydney realized that Brock had done this just for her and she was moved. She examined the bottle. It was an inexpensive, fruity chardonnay.

"It's perfect, Brock." He looked pleased.

They talked all through dinner, which was very tasty, and far into the night.

"Did you ever hear from Sarah?" Brock asked over pie and coffee.

"Never," Cydney answered.

"Well, when she left here, Caleb said she was going to New York to look you up. She wanted to meet Max."

"She never contacted me. Probably furious because you rejected her advances," Cydney said with a grin.

"How'd you know about that?"

"Leta. Let me tell you, Leta is a very smart lady. Maybe not well educated, but very smart. Leta can see into a person's heart and soul. She can read their minds. She knows what people are thinking and what they're going to do before they do it. Leta knew the moment she saw Sarah look at you, that she'd try to seduce you. Leta said Sarah was fuming when you didn't pay attention to her." Brock just shrugged it off and changed the subject.

"So will you and Max come for sure at Christmas?" Cydney nodded, savoring the last bit of her pie.

"How long are you staying now? Should I drive up to Bad River and pick up Leta?"

"No, Brock, I can't stay long. I have to get back to Max. Also, I'm looking for another housekeeper. Gracie retired and there's too much work for Sophie, what with Max and all.

Brock noticed that she never mentioned David. He thought about what he said to her last night and decided not to bring it up because Cydney hadn't mentioned it either. But he was happy that he finally told her how he felt. Although, Brock had to admit, had it not been for the Jack Daniels he probably wouldn't have said anything about his love for her. They cleared the table in silence.

"I'll wash the dishes in the morning, Brock. It's late and I'm too tired to do them now."

He reached for her and drew her close. He felt her stiffen under his caress. She pushed herself back from his embrace.

"Good night, Brock. Thank you for a wonderful evening." She turned and walked away leaving him alone in the kitchen. A few moments later, she heard the kitchen door slam and Brock's tires churning up gravel as he pulled out of the driveway at a high rate of speed.

Although Brock continued to be friendly and talkative, he made no more advances toward Cydney. When she left two days later, it was Cydney who stood on her tiptoes and planted a kiss on his cheek.

"I'll see you at Christmas," she said with a smile. Brock smiled back and waved as she drove up the driveway and turned right onto Apple Road.

CHAPTER FIFTY-TWO

It was late and the roads were snow covered and slippery when Cydney pulled the rental car into the driveway. Max was asleep now. Their flight from New York had been delayed due to weather and Cydney would have preferred canceling the trip. But Max begged and pleaded. He was so looking forward to Christmas at the farm. So she relented not anticipating how nasty the weather would get.

The yard light went on and Brock appeared out of nowhere. He lifted the sleeping boy from the car and carried him into the house while Leta held the door. She lovingly brushed her hand over Max's head and quietly hugged Cydney. Brock continued up the steps and tucked Max into bed. The kitchen was warm and smelled of fresh brewed coffee. In the living room, a fire blazed and the pleasant aroma of the burning wood mingled with the smell of paint, still lingering slightly in the air.

Cyndey had spoken with Brock on the phone just days before. The remodeling project was complete and he was very pleased with the results. Brock hoped Cydney would feel the same. He was anxious for her to see it.

Cydney asked Brock if he would go up to the attic and find the Christmas decorations and then cut a tree. He agreed to bring the trimmings down but suggested that they wait with the tree until she and Max arrived so Max could go with him to pick out a tree.

"That's a wonderful idea, Brock," Cydney said, "Max will love that. Thank you for thinking of him."

How could Brock tell her that he thought about them all the time? That sometimes he pretended that Max was his son and after they tucked him into bed at night, they made love in the big four-poster bed, in front of a roaring fire or weather permitting, beside the pond.

"Is David coming?" Brock asked.

"No he's not." Cydney sounded disappointed. "I told you, David's not big on holidays. I hoped I could lure him there by telling him the renovations were completed. I thought he might like to see the place, but quite frankly, Brock, he's not interested."

"I'm sorry, Cyd," Brock said, but in reality, he was elated that David wasn't coming and he could have Cydney and Max to himself for Christmas. He had shopped for them and bought Max a remote control race car, which he tried out on the new kitchen floor and it really moved.

Finding something for Cydney was harder. He didn't have much money. He finally settled on a wine rack, made out of copper and hammered into a design of scrolls and branches by one of the talented Chippewa men. He also bought some bottles of wine to fill it. But this time, he did his homework and bought quality brands from the Alsace and Rhone Valley and Northwest names like Woodward Canyon and Panther Creek. They included Rieslings, Chardonnays and Bordeauxes; and last of all, he bought a corkscrew.

Leta and Cydney were drinking coffee and eating Christmas cookies when Brock came back to the kitchen. Cydney flashed him a smile, but not her usual one. Brock wondered why.

"Is he still sleeping?" she asked.

"Like a baby," Brock smiled back. "He hardly stirred. You okay, Cyd?" He was genuinely concerned.

"Tired, stressed. Otherwise okay. I didn't realize how bad the weather was. I just didn't have the heart to cancel. Max was so excited about spending Christmas here. Especially when I told him the two of you would be going out into the woods to cut a tree tomorrow."

"Let's all get a good night's sleep," Leta said. "We have a lot of cooking and decorating to do tomorrow. Aaron, Patrice and the twins will be here on the 23rd." She got up and cleared the table except for their coffee cups, planted a kiss on Cydney's cheek and headed for the staircase.

Alone with Brock, Cydney felt a bit awkward. They had spoken on the phone several times since her September visit but Brock never mentioned anything about that night. Surely, when he sobered up he had forgotten what he said to her. Why then, couldn't she forget it?

They made small talk. Brock got up and dumped his cold coffee in the sink. He came up behind her and placed his strong hands on her shoulders beneath her coppery curls. She stiffened. Without saying a word, he began massaging her neck and shoulders. She closed her eyes and exhaled deeply.

"That's it," he said quietly, "just relax." His touch was so soft. She felt her headache fading. She loved the feel of his big hands on her neck and back. It had been a long time since anyone touched her so gently. His hands were like magic, erasing the tension, relieving the stress. When she realized she had moaned with pleasure, she opened her eyes and sat up straight. Brock stopped massaging but kept his hands on her shoulders until she pushed her chair back and stood up.

"Thank you, Brock. I feel so much better now. I think I'll turn in." She turned to face him but he didn't speak. His eyes, dark with passion, said it all. He looked deep into her eyes and set her heart on fire.

"Good night." Her voice was soft and terse and once again she left him standing alone in the kitchen.

By morning the snow had subsided and the pines, laden with the fluffy powder, sparkled in the morning sun. Cydney was astounded by its beauty. Max talked non-stop about all the things he wanted to do today, which besides cutting a Christmas tree included having a snowball fight with Brock and making a snow fort. Brock was silent, every now and then laughing at Max and tousling his unruly mop of brown hair. He kept his eyes averted from Cydney because he couldn't let the wild desire hidden there, betray him.

Right after breakfast, Brock and Max hooked a wagon to the back of the tractor and headed out in search of the perfect Christmas tree. They tried to entice Cydney to go with them, but she opted to stay and help Leta. There was a lot to do and by the time Max and Brock returned, red-cheeked and shivering, it was lunchtime. Max spent the afternoon playing in the snow and although he was exhausted from all the fresh air, he insisted on staying up late to help trim the tree. What a wonderful time they had. A fire crackled, they sang carols and drank hot chocolate and before they tucked Max into bed, the tree and house were ablaze with lights. Cydney knew this was a Christmas Max would remember forever and she vowed that they would spend other holidays at the farm and build some family traditions, with or without David.

That's exactly what they did. For the next five years, all the major holidays were celebrated in Wisconsin. If David disapproved, he didn't show it and Cydney was extremely grateful that he didn't complain about the money she spent on airline tickets. But then, why should he? He was the one who, years ago, kept telling her she had to learn to accept his wealth.

On each Easter Sunday, they had an Easter egg hunt and sometimes there was still snow on the ground. Memorial Days meant parades and church picnics. The Fourth of July was a trip into Balsam Hills for the Firemen's picnic and a fireworks display as well as their own impressive fireworks over the pond. Max never liked Labor Day because it signaled the end of summer and back to school, but then he had Halloween, Thanksgiving and another Christmas to look forward to. And he really did look forward to all the time he spent at the farm. Max and Brock grew so close. No wonder they were all so devastated when near the end of summer of 1996, David dropped a bomb!

Max, at age 15, was very handsome. Like David, he had dark brown eyes and hair but he was tall and slim like Caleb. He was mature for his age and started showing an interest in girls and sports. It was then that David decided that Max should attend a private school, 100 miles from home instead of PS 19, just down the street. Cydney pleaded and cried and carried on but to no avail, David would not relent. There was no way he was going to deal with the raging hormones of a teenage boy. Max would go to Wayland Academy in Kingston. End of discussion!

David's decision to send Max away to school was life changing for Cydney. Not only did she miss Max with all her heart, his absence created a riff between her and David. A cancer, that ate away at her love and respect for him, and could not be cured.

Max resigned himself to boarding school with the same indifference he used to deal with his father but he dearly missed his mother. He entrenched himself in his studies and excelled in all of his classes. He made friends easily and had a lot of them, yet he was lonely. He lay awake many nights wondering about his parents. What brought them together? What kept them together? He knew it was his mother. She was loving and caring. Always more concerned with others than with herself. She was beautiful and full of life and she adored Max. David, on the other hand, was cold, at least to Max and he never seemed happy or interested in anything Max did or achieved. He had an air of superiority about him and generally looked down his nose at other people.

So, like Cydney, Max grew up having everything money could buy: a cool car, an expensive wardrobe, a generous allowance. But also like his mother, he would have preferred David's love and attention. He just wouldn't admit it.

He was still able to join his mother at the farm for most holidays. It was just a big inconvenience, having to leave school, get home and then go to Wisconsin. It actually cut down on the amount of time he could spend there and Max viewed it as a sort of silent punishment from his father, who knew how much he loved spending time at the farm.

CHAPTER FIFTY-THREE

The Bleecker Street Deli was crowded. But then it usually was. Cydney came here often with Brenda, Loren and Harold. They had remained friends over the years, had in fact become closer and ever since David sent Max off to school they were Cydney's salvation, her consolation. Even though none of them knew David, they all disliked him immensely. Not that Cydney ever said anything bad about David. She didn't. She never complained. But they all knew. It was there in those big sad eyes. Eyes that once danced with excitement. Eyes that had once mirrored the joy in her heart. She still smiled and chattered lightly but those mournful eyes with the dark crescents beneath them betrayed her bright facade. They knew – Cydney was unhappy.

They ordered lunch, opting to share the humungous sandwiches, a trademark of a New York deli, so there would be room for dessert. Who could resist the assortment of cheesecakes and other succulents almost too pretty to eat?

They all listened intently as Loren explained his latest project and Harold expounded on an idea for a new play. Enjoying each other's company and their lunch, they were oblivious to the woman in the booth at the back of the shop.

Obscured by the dim lights, dark glasses and a scarf covering her straw-like hair, she sipped ice tea and pretended to be absorbed in the Times. Sarah had been in New York eight years now and although she never contacted Cydney, she felt she knew her well. Sarah followed

Cydney all over New York, stalked her if you will, and several times almost mustered up the courage to speak to her, only to back down. Sarah knew Cydney's routine, her friends, her likes and dislikes; and like Brenda, Loren and Harold, Sarah sensed that Cydney was unhappy.

An article in the Times rather confirmed Sarah's suspicion. An interview featured David and his young, attractive protégé. There was a picture of them standing side-by-side, shoulders almost touching, looking over some sheet music. Sarah recognized the look in David's eyes. It was lust!

As Sarah eavesdropped on the conversation and scanned the Times, she reconfirmed the vow she made to herself that July morning in 1988 when she left the farm. If David did anything to hurt either Cydney or Max, she would find a way to get even with him. From the looks of things, now might be the time. The only problem was, Sarah didn't have a plan. She would talk it over with Jerry. Surely, he could think of something. Heaven knows he was devious enough.

Sarah let her mind wander. She was growing tired of Jerry. Oh sure, he got her to New York but it took almost a whole year. They stopped in every two-bit town along the way. Jerry would get some minimum wage job or find some woman to sweet talk and then con her out of some cash. They'd stay just long enough to get money to buy beer and drugs and then move on.

Jeremiah drank a lot and went from marijuana to the hard stuff. Sarah was proud of herself, she stayed away from the really bad drugs. The booze and joints had already taken their toll on her. She was no longer attractive. She looked hard, used. But after Jerry came up with a plan of some kind, a plan to put the screws to David, she would dump him. She'd get sober, clean herself up and then contact Cydney. Hopefully, Cydney would welcome Sarah into her life and they could build a relationship. A mother, daughter relationship. After all, she was only 60 years old. There was still time for her to enjoy her daughter and her grandson. It was a lofty goal but as Sarah continued to listen to the conversation coming from the other end of the deli, her resolve was strengthened.

Sarah missed the good life. Especially at times like this when she was feeling nostalgic. She had been raised in a Christian home with morals and she was ashamed that she had spent the last nine years of her life doing drugs, drinking too much and cheating good and honest people. She knew God would forgive her if she asked Him to but right now she focused on Cydney. She wanted desperately to make herself known to Cydney and she would. When the time was right.

Jeremiah sat on a bench in Battery Park and watched his next mark. He guessed her to be in her late forties. This was the third day in a row she had been in the park with a small boy, probably her grandson. The woman doted on the child running to his side every time he whimpered and Jeremiah knew that if he was patient he would have a chance to grab her purse and run. He had done it many times before: in Central Park, at Grand Central Station and in Times Square. And one of these days, Jeremiah would hit the jackpot! He just knew it! He just needed to be patient. And when the time came, he'd take the money and run. Run by himself. Christ, Sarah kept yappin' about her rich relative and how some day they'd all be one big happy family. Well, shit, he'd been waiting for nine years and he hadn't seen any money yet! Sure, in the beginning they had fun together. Drinking, getting high and having wild sex as they worked their way east. But once they got to New York, Sarah changed. She wasn't in a hurry to contact her daughter and she had her nose in the air most of the time like she thought she was too good for Jeremiah. Well, he'd show her. When he struck it big and split and she found her sorry ass alone, then she'd regret it. But for now, Jeremiah just had to be patient.

The running child fell down and the woman literally flew to his side, forgetting the purse, perched on the now empty park bench. Jeremiah moved! In only seconds he grabbed the purse and as he ran south toward the Staten Island Ferry he dug the wallet out and discarded the rest, along with the beret and glasses he wore as a disguise. He jammed the wallet into his pocket, slowed his pace, did an about turn and blended in with the crowd of people just exiting the ferry.

CHAPTER FIFTY-FOUR

David sat alone in his study, elbows resting on his knees, his faced buried in his hands. He was miserable. At age 54 perhaps he *was* experiencing a mid-life crisis. But if that were the case, he would have to take responsibility for all of his misery and he preferred to blame some one else. David stayed away from home as much as possible. Harland was seventy years old and still lived with them. He continued to act as David's agent, doing bookings and handling the press. They argued often. Mostly because Harland thought David never lived up to his potential but every once in awhile Cydney's name still came up during an argument. She and Harland never did see eye to eye.

Sophie was just plain too old to work anymore. Cydney had taken over most of the household chores, which David agreed to thinking it would fill up her time and keep her from missing Max so much. Even the ever-faithful Phillip left him. He told David he was tired of big city living and was moving to a small town in Florida but David knew Phillip was leaving because he disapproved of how David treated Cydney and Max.

Cydney was 45, and still a beautiful woman. Just a few weeks ago, when once again trying to cover up his shortfalls he picked a fight with her. He told her she needed to lose some weight and color her hair. She was livid, but as usual, she would not argue with him. She just walked away, looking hurt and unhappy.

Max was almost nineteen and had gone off to college and Cydney missed him even more. But Max had a car so he could come home or go to Wisconsin as he chose.

David realized now that he had been extremely cruel. He loved Cydney with all his heart. He tried to feel the same way about Max, but he just couldn't. If this was the time for self-confession, then he had to admit, he was jealous of Max because Cydney loved him so much and doted on him. David felt neglected. But he had to stop blaming Cydney and put the blame on himself, where it belonged. He knew now that he had hurt Cydney very, very deeply when he sent Max off to school, when he shut her out of his life and when he failed to be part of hers.

All this weighed heavy on his conscience and maybe it was too late to make amends because the worst sin he had committed was adultery. Several months ago, he had taken on Natalie as a protégé. They had been introduced to each other by a musician from the New York Symphony. She was a brilliant young woman with an abundance of musical talent and he was immediately drawn to her. He knew they were spending too much time together but he did nothing to change that. He knowingly led her on and then he seduced her. She was young and naïve, just as Cydney had been and also like Cydney, she had been taken in by his charm and good looks. How he regretted it now! And to think that when Cydney, having heard the rumors and after seeing the pictures in the newspaper, confronted him about it, he lied to her. In this very room, where almost twenty years ago he had accused Cydney of being unfaithful to him, he lied about his own indiscretions. Once again, Cydney just walked away, devastated and distraught. She knew he was lying. And he knew, she knew. He sat there alone, dejected and ashamed. He heard the sound of the vacuum cleaner and knew Cydney was diverting her anger to the carpet.

Cydney, who seldom lost her temper or even raised her voice. Cydney, unselfish, loving and faithful. Cydney, who stood by him all these years even as he shut her out. She put on a bright smile for his fans and their friends and somehow managed to cover up his temper tantrums and indiscretions to the press without ever telling a lie. She predicted in the very beginning that he loved his music more than anything else. She recognized that they were of different worlds but she never lost sight of her values. David now understood that Cydney had been right all along. He loved his career, the limelight, and the money and he did whatever was necessary to clench it. Never mind who he stepped on along the way. That was another thing he was jealous of; Cydney had ethics - he had none.

David needed to clear his head. He didn't want to talk to anyone right now. He changed into jogging clothes and scribbled a note: *gone for a run.*

Central Park was David's favorite place to run. The afternoon sun was warm for late September and the park was abuzz. He entered the park at 79th street and headed west toward Belvedere Castle and then south to Strawberry Fields. It didn't take David long to get into his rhythm and soon he was running at his usual brisk pace, ignoring bicyclists, pedestrians and mothers with baby strollers, expecting them, as they usually did, to step aside for him. Sweat beaded up on his forehead and poured down his face. He ran harder and faster, trying to rid his mind and body of Natalie and focus on Cydney's beautiful image. He would make things right. He would confess. He would strive to be the husband she longed for. David was oblivious to his surroundings as he pounded on. He was on autopilot; not knowing specifically where he was but subconsciously knowing where he was going. His pace quickened, the sweat increased. He was in a zone as he exited the park at 59th Street and headed back to the east. So spaced out that he never saw a vehicle coming around the corner. He never broke stride, didn't have a chance to. The impact hurled him into the air. People gathered around his limp body lying askew on the pavement. Someone dialed 911. Murmurs passed among the spectators when someone recognized him but no one was able to get the license number of the green blur that sped away.

CHAPTER FIFTY-FIVE

Cydney poured herself a cup of tea and sat on one of the stools at the kitchen counter. Since she had taken over the household chores, she had grown to love the kitchen. It was quiet and peaceful and she always kept a candle burning, which filled the room with intoxicating scents. The apartment was spotless. She had vacuumed herself into a state of exhaustion. She sipped her tea and worked the crossword puzzle from the morning paper. She was engrossed in what she was doing so she heard nothing but sensed a presence in the room. She turned slowly and saw Harland standing nearby, a piece of paper clenched in his fingers. His face was ashen.

"Harland," she said sliding off the stool, "what is it? What's wrong?" His eyes were glazed and looked beyond her.

His voice was barely audible but cold and abrupt as always. "There's been an accident," he said. "David's dead."

Time stood still. The words reverberated around the room. Neither of them moved nor spoke. Cydney finally had the presence of mind to steady herself.

"How? Where?" She shook her head already rejecting the possibility.

"He was jogging and he got hit by a car." Harland still was motionless.

"That's impossible! He's in the study!" Harland stretched out his hand and the crumpled note fell to the floor. Cydney took a few steps to retrieve it and as she looked at the familiar writing scrawled on the paper her mind and body went numb. Once again she steadied herself at the counter. Even this terrible tragedy could not bind them together. Neither reached for the other. They both were immobile and silent. After a few minutes, Harland turned and left the room. Cydney somehow made her way to the study. She had to see for herself that David was not there. She could no longer hold herself up. She sank to her knees. After that, everything was blurry.

Cydney didn't know exactly when Max arrived, but when he did; she was able to let her grief pour out. Max would take care of everything. Max would take care of her.

In addition to their anguish, they had to deal with the press and the police investigation. So many questions asked. So few answers. Did David have any enemies? Were there problems at home? Is it possible he intentionally ran in front of the vehicle? Did they know anyone who drove a green vehicle? Perhaps an SUV or a small truck? Although the investigation was ongoing, they were allowed to go ahead with the funeral. Condolences and flowers poured in. A simple note from Brock and Leta; a lavish arrangement from Carmen and Tony. Offers to come to her side from Aaron and Patrice, from Phillip and the Savages. Phone calls from Brenda, Loren and Harold. So much compassion for the beautiful young widow, who responded graciously to each telegram, each letter, each sympathy card. The sophisticated, lovely widow who would never, ever, let her family and friends know the truth about her errant husband.

CHAPTER FIFTY-SIX

The gray skies of November engulfed the city. It was bitter cold and blustery but there was no snow. The weather matched Cydney's mood. Of course the pain of losing David was overwhelming, but what was even worse was the pain of knowing that he had been unfaithful to her and that he lied about it and the painful self-admission that she never was able to compete with his love for his music.

The phone calls and cards had waned but about once a week someone from NYPD called to say there were no leads in the case.

Max had dropped school with the promise of returning the second semester and Cydney had to admit she welcomed his constant presence. Max, who had just turned nineteen a few days after his father's death, had become her savior. He screened the phone calls, and he began handling the business and legal affairs that needed immediate attention.

Harland actually seemed to welcome Max's company. Cydney didn't know if it was because it took some of the burden off of Harland so he wouldn't have to speak to her, or if he genuinely liked having Max around again.

Tom Caprock called and suggested that they meet to discuss David's estate. Cydney didn't feel up to going out so Max asked him to come to the apartment to read the will. Cydney made tea and Max and Harland joined them in the study. Tom always liked Cydney. She was authentic. She never pretended to be anything but the caring, wonderful person she was and Tom was overjoyed that David had opted to leave everything to Cydney and Max and give Harland a lump sum of money. Harland had his own wealth and he could fend for himself but Tom also knew that Harland expected more and would be livid when he found out that he was only getting $250,000.

Harland didn't care much for Tom but they exchanged pleasantries while Cydney poured the tea. Finally, Tom cleared his throat and got down to business.

"Having to be here today deeply saddens me," he told them. "David was a dear friend, as are you," he said, nodding toward Cydney. "I value the professional relationship I had with David, and Joyce and I cherish the friendship we have with you." He cast a conservative smile at Cydney. "The reality of this matter is that David, at times, was very difficult to deal with. The advice I gave him was, in my opinion, in the best interest of you, his family. Although, it took some persuasion before he reached his final decision as to the contents of his will."

No one asked questions. The silence was almost deafening. Cydney felt a twinge in her stomach. It didn't matter to her what David did with his money, but she said a silent prayer that he had not shunned Max.

Harland looked smug. He was pretty confident from what Tom was saying that Cydney and Max would be left out. He'd finally be rid of her. She could go back to her small-town and her half-breed family.

Max was getting angry. He didn't care about himself but that son-of-a-bitch better take care, *good care*, of his mother.

Tom continued in a subtle, professional voice. "Harland, David has given you a lump sum payment of $250,000. He did this because he knows that coupled with your own wealth, you can live the rest of your life in luxury. He thanks you for the care you gave him as a child and for steering him to a career in music and helping him achieve the fame that he enjoyed."

Tom's perception had been right. Harland didn't say a word, but the color drained from his face and a blood vessel in his right temple became prominent and began throbbing. Tom ignored him and pressed on.

"Cydney, you now own this penthouse free and clear along with the condo in Cancun. You also will receive royalties from any of David's music, and a trust fund has been established to provide you with a monthly allowance. You will have no financial worries for the rest of your life. David was so happy that you chose to share his life with him. He loved you deeply, more than words could ever say." Tom looked deep into her eyes and Cydney knew that those words were his and not David's. She only nodded, too emotional to speak and continued to pray silently that David had included Max. Finally, Tom turned in his direction.

"Max," he said, looking the young man straight in the eye, "your father was an extremely wealthy man. The money he willed to Harland and the money in trust for your mother is only a small portion of his estate. You will receive the balance of it, which amounts to millions." Tom's voice softened now, "Along with that your father wanted you to know that he loved you. He always has, he just couldn't express it and he regrets that he failed you."

Cydney, relieved, closed her eyes as quiet tears washed down her face. David could have done better. He could have said he loved Max **very** much. But some was better than none. Max was speechless. He looked in Cydney's direction and she smiled through her tears. Harland still did not speak.

"Finally," Tom went on, "David has established a musical scholarship to Julliard School of Music. His last request was that his violin be donated to the archives at the New York School of Music." Tom closed the file he was using and looked around. "Any questions or comments?"

No one spoke.

"If you think of any questions later, feel free to call me. I will begin the paperwork necessary for all of these bequests to take place." He stood up and filled his briefcase with the papers lying on the desk.

Max was on his feet immediately. "I'll show you out, Tom. Thanks for coming." Tom stopped by Cydney's chair and planted a kiss on her cheek.

"Thank you," she said, weakly. Tom smiled and left the room with Max.

They sat silently, side by side. Their chairs close but not touching. Cydney controlled her tears, dabbed her eyes with a tissue and stopped the dribble from her nose. The war was over and the victory was sweet. When she spoke it was with grace and dignity.

"Harland, I would appreciate it if you would pack your things and leave my home as soon as possible. I think three days should be sufficient time for you to make other living arrangements." She got up and left the study, quietly closing the door behind her.

Harland was shocked and enraged. He tried to control his temper. His knuckles turned white as he gripped the arms of the chair. The bitch was throwing him out!

Once behind closed doors Cydney let her guard down. She sat on the edge of the bed. The tears started up again. She thanked God that David had found someway, albeit trivial, to tell Max he cared about him. But was it true? She didn't know. What she did know was that often times, during his life, David complimented or congratulated people and later told her he didn't mean a single word of it. Two-faced. That's what David was. Two-faced. Cydney wasn't being malicious. Just honest.

Max tapped lightly on her bedroom door and entered when she called out to him. She stood up and he cradled her in his arms, his lanky frame supporting her and her head resting on his shoulder. Together they cried. Her tears a conglomerate of pain, joy, relief. His of bittersweet victory. Had he really won his father over?

Later, over a glass of wine in front of a roaring fire, Cydney and Max mapped out a plan.

"Mother," Max said, "Brock called earlier. He wants us to come to the farm for Christmas."

Cydney felt a small burst of panic. She couldn't go now. It was too soon! The grief was still too fresh. She was too vulnerable! She spoke slowly, hoping her voice was calm, "You go, Max. I can't go right now. I'm just not ready. Not up to it."

"It will be good for you, Mother."

She shook her head. "Not right now. But you go, please. I want you to go."

"I'm not sure I want to go without you. Maybe I need to be here to keep an eye on Harland."

"Don't worry about him, Max. I've dealt with him all these years. Besides, I've asked him to leave. In three days he'll be gone."

Their sparring was amicable. Max insisting she go with him. Cydney, really wanting to, but knowing she couldn't bear to see Brock right now. After much discussion, they agreed. Max would go to Wisconsin for the holidays and she would stay in New York. She assured him she would not be lonely. She had many friends who would help her get through. After all, she was used to spending holidays without David. Max would return to Penn State in January. By that time business and legal matters should be finalized. If Cydney needed a respite, she would go to Cancun. The sun and warm weather would help her, both physically and mentally.

CHAPTER FIFTY-SEVEN

David's memories were everywhere, even the unpleasant ones and although he and Cydney had not been very close over the past few years, she was shrouded in loneliness. Max had, as planned, gone to Wisconsin for Christmas. Brock and Leta, Aaron and Patrice were all so disappointed that Cydney did not make the trip. But they understood. Everyone grieves in their own way.

The farmhouse was beautiful, warm and inviting. Max and Brock were inseparable during his stay and when it was time to leave, Max felt a new sense of loss. A feeling in your gut and in your heart. The feeling you get when you long for the way things used to be. Max remembered as a child being hoisted up on Brock's shoulders in the early spring and walking through the fields; or playing by the pond on hot summer days and splashing water at Brock and Cydney while they sat in the sand nearby. He remembered cold winter mornings, rosy cheeks and a runny nose, hunting or looking for the perfect Christmas tree. He recalled seeing deer running through the woods, their white tails flapping as they bounded off. But Max was an adult now and he had a lot on his plate. He would have to look after his mother and fulfill his promise to her that he would return to college. He had discussed this with Brock on one of their many walks around the farm and Brock reassured him, Cydney would always be cared for. It made going back to school a little easier.

When Max returned to New York with wonderful family stories, he was distressed to learn that Cydney had spent the holidays mostly by herself. She had accepted a few invitations to small cocktail parties or intimate dinners but for the most part, she preferred to be alone, at least for now.

However, Cydney had a story of her own to tell and it was very intriguing! It was on the Tuesday after Christmas and as usual, Cydney was home alone, curled up in front of the fire. She was so engrossed in her book that the ringing telephone actually made her jump.

"Hello, DuPreys." Cydney's voice was soft and relaxed now.

"Hello, is this Cydney Brown DuPrey?" the female caller asked.

"Yes it is. Who's calling please?" There was silence on the line and Cydney asked again, "Who's calling?"

The voice on the other end broke slightly. Cydney waited patiently, thinking it was the press or maybe some information on the investigation.

"Cydney, my name is – uhm, – my name is Sarah. Sarah Brown. I'm – um," the woman cleared her throat. "I'm your mother." Cydney was dumbstruck! Lights flashed across her brain; bells and whistles wailed. Her mind raced as she tried to absorb the words. It was difficult to think straight. Her legs were about to collapse. Seconds ticked by and neither woman spoke. Cydney searched for words. Sarah bit her lip and tired to stymie the unexpected tears that threatened to expose a soft spot in her heart.

"Well," Cydney said at last, still hunting in vain for something sensible to say, "this is very unexpected. I don't know quite what to say."

Sarah, composed now, picked up the conversation. "Just don't hang up! Please, don't hang up. It's not necessary for you to say anything right now. Just let me explain why I'm calling."

Cydney tried not to sound sarcastic or miffed and she consciously softened her voice.

"Go ahead," she said, her voice trembling ever so slightly, "I will listen."

"Well," Sarah breathed a sigh of relief, "I read in the paper that your husband died a few months ago and I wanted to extend my sympathy

317

to you and your family." Cydney was thinking more clearly now. Memories, mostly bad, rushed over her.

"Where are you and what do you know of me and my family?"

"I'm in New York, Cydney. I live here. I have for many years. I knew who you were married to and I read all the stories in the newspaper about your husband and his career." Sarah spoke easier now and tried to sound sophisticated.

"How long have you lived in New York?"

"About eight years." Sarah fudged on the numbers.

"Eight years! You've been in New York for eight years and you never contacted me until now?" Cydney felt some anger rising in her voice and tried to squelch it.

"New York is a very big city, Cydney. I know this is no excuse. But, I didn't know if you would accept me, or even talk to me. After all, I did abandon you."

"Yes, you did. You abandoned your whole family! Do you know that grandfather died?"

"I just assumed so. He was old the last time I saw him. When did he die and how?"

Cydney felt confused and a bit disoriented, "I'm not sure I want to talk with you anymore, Sarah. You hurt me and our whole family so deeply. I just need some time to digest this all."

"Of course." Sarah's voice was full or remorse and Cydney could sense it.

"Did you know you have a grandson?" Cydney asked with some pride in her tone.

"Yes. I read your husband's obituary. How old is Maxwell?" Sarah asked feigning ignorance.

"He's nineteen and a wonderful young man."

"I'm sure he is, Cydney, with you for a mother, I'm sure he is. I know this call has been a shock to you but I'm getting old and I just wanted you to know that although I did abandon you physically, I have always been concerned about your well-being and—"

Cydney interrupted, "Do you keep in touch with Aunt Patrice and Uncle Aaron?" Cydney knew the answer. She knew that no one had heard from Sarah for many years and Aaron tried, to no avail, to track her down when Caleb died in 1990.

"No Cydney, I've had no contact with anyone for years. My last visit to the farm was – oh, I don't know for sure, the late eighties I used to write to Patrice or sometimes call her. She was always so nice to me, even when things were so bad at home," she paused but Cydney didn't speak, so Sarah pressed on, "But about us, I was hoping," another long pause, "truly hoping, that we could meet sometime, have a reunion so to speak." There was a sense of pleading in her voice. The request hung in mid air. Sarah waited for an answer. Cydney rummaged for words to mirror her emotions.

"It was very thoughtful of you to phone me," she said, trying desperately to imagine what Sarah might look like and mentally calculated her age at 62, "but as I said earlier, I need some time to think about this. I've had a difficult few months and right now I'm flabbergasted. I just can't make a decision right now on this matter."

"Would it be better if I called back in a few days?" Sarah sounded hopeful now.

"Maybe a week or so. I just need some time. Thank you for calling." Cydney hung up the phone and just stood there, frozen.

Sarah let the receiver slip away from her ear and mentally assessed how the conversation went. It sounded promising. She'd know in about a week.

Cydney returned to the sofa but could no longer concentrate on her book. She sat there in front of the warm fire, trembling and with goose bumps. The conversation kept rewinding in her mind. Eight years. Sarah had been in New York for eight years! Did David's death suddenly jolt her into needing to console her daughter? She sounded so sincere. What was her objective? Did she have an ulterior motive?

When she shared the story with Max, he asked the same questions. Cydney told him as much as she could remember about Sarah leaving the farm and she told him what Leta had relayed to her about Sarah's last visit and her encounter with Brock.

"What are you going to do, Mother?" he asked. "Are you going to meet with her?"

"I don't know, Max. What do you think? Should I? Truthfully, I am curious as to what she looks like. She sounded genuinely concerned and I feel like I should maybe give her a chance."

"A chance to do what? You do realize, Mother, that you tend to be very gullible at times and you sometimes let people take advantage of you. Maybe she's looking for a handout. Did she say what she does? If she works?"

"No," Cydney exhaled deeply. "We never got that far into the conversation. But if she wanted a hand out why would she have waited eight years to contact me? If she's been living in New York that long, she must have some means to support herself. I'm just so torn. I don't know what to do."

"Well, Cydney Ellice," using his pet name for her, "it's your choice. It's totally up to you. Whatever you decide will be okay with me. You just need to promise me that you will be strong and not let her talk you into anything. Promise?"

"Promise." Cydney spent many sleepless nights searching for the answer. She called on God and Caleb, in that order, to give her some guidance. When Sarah called back, ten days later, Cydney had already made her decision.

CHAPTER FIFTY-EIGHT

They met for lunch on a pleasant January day, at the Tavern on the Green in Central Park.

"How will I know you?" Cydney had asked.

"Don't worry," Sarah replied, "I'm sure I'll recognize you. I have a picture of you in my heart and mind."

Sarah rose and walked forward as Cydney entered the restaurant. The two stood face to face. Neither reached out for the other.

"Hello, Cydney," Sarah finally managed to say, "I'm your mother." Cydney could only nod. Her eyes filled, not only with emotion but with pity as she stared at the haggard woman before her. The make-up she wore couldn't hide the gaunt look. Her hair, once soft and blond, was now coarse and streaked with gray. She looked much older than Cydney had pictured her.

Sarah actually thought she looked pretty good. She had used very little make-up that morning and opted for a shade of lipstick less harsh than the bright red she usually wore. She styled her hair so as to hide most of the gray and even splurged and bought herself a new outfit to wear.

Cydney looked lovely as usual. She was never heavy, but had thinned down considerably after David died. The stress, which showed in her face, didn't hide the underlying beauty, the bright eyes and soft, supple skin. A twinge of jealousy poked at Sarah but she beat it down, remembering that she was once as striking as the daughter who stood before her now.

Awkwardly, Sarah gestured with her hand and they sat down opposite each other at the small table in the back of the restaurant. Cydney had suggested this place hoping they would be afforded some privacy and she was right. The tables in this dinning room were mostly empty. Cydney was about to speak when the waiter came with water and menus. Cydney ordered wine and Sarah, not knowing what to order, asked for the same. When they were alone again, Sarah spoke first.

"I was overjoyed that you agreed to meet me. Thank you."

"It was a difficult decision," Cydney said, trying not to sound like a snob.

"I'm sure it was. I apologize if my phone call came as a big shock to you. It took me months to conjure up the courage to call you."

"It *was* a big shock to say the least. I never expected to hear from you. To be truthful, I hadn't thought about you in years."

"Well, if we're being truthful," Sarah went on, "I think about you almost every day."

"Then why did you wait eight years to contact me?" Cydney was troubled.

"As I said on the phone, I just didn't know how you would react. But when I read about your husband, well, I just knew you would be overcome with grief and I felt compelled to reach out to you."

Max's words of caution resounded in her mind and Carmen's words from years and years ago, regarding deep breathing suddenly leaped into her head. She heeded both their advice. Cydney asked all the right questions. Sarah had all the answers.

They spent the next two hours reliving the past. Cydney told Sarah how she met David and touched on the highlights of their life together. She told her about Caleb's passing and how the farm stayed in the family. How Brock worked so hard to renovate the house and that it was once again so comfortable and inviting. She told about the many trips she and Max had made to the farm and how it would always be her special place, her haven, her home.

Sarah was quite talkative, too. She told Cydney how the gossip in Balsam Hills was just too much to overcome. How it just drove her away. A small town is so unforgiving. She talked about her struggles, first in Chicago and then in New York. She lied about her reasons for coming to New York and of course, Sarah left out the part about Jeremiah and all the con games they played to make money. She didn't tell Cydney about the drugs and the booze and how Jerry badgered her everyday about hooking up with her "rich relative". She told Cydney how she was working as a hairdresser but having difficulty making ends meet.

"New York is a very expensive place to live," she reiterated. She said she was too embarrassed and ashamed to continue corresponding with Patrice. Patrice and Aaron were so successful, it seemed like they, too, would look down on her. Sarah admitted that she blamed her own mother for most of her problems and she was too immature to take responsibility for her actions or to raise a child. And she let her pride get in the way.

"That's why I left," Sarah said flatly. "I knew Leta would do a wonderful job of raising you. I was right. She did. Just look at you. Can you ever forgive me?"

Cydney continued to mask her emotions. "I don't know, Sarah. Right now, I can't say. But maybe you need to forgive yourself before you ask others to forgive you. Guilt and anger can be destructive. Have you considered calling Patrice and Aaron?"

"I need to work this out first," Sarah said, toying with the food on her plate. "I need to know where I stand with you before I move on."

"I'm sorry. I can't answer that question right now. This is a very emotional time for me. Maybe we need to get to know each other a little better. Let's take some time and mull over all the things we've talked about today. Then maybe we can meet again. How does that sound?"

"It's more than I hoped for, Cydney." It was obvious that lunch was over. Cydney began rummaging in her handbag.

"Are you okay? Do you need anything? Some money?"

Sarah shook her head, "No, I don't need any money, but," she paused trying to hide her embarrassment, "this is a very expensive restaurant and I don't think I have enough money to pay for my lunch."

Cydney smiled, "Don't worry. I wanted to buy lunch anyway."

Sarah felt a catch in her throat and only nodded, mouthing the words, "thank you."

Cydney stood up to leave. "Why not call me in a couple of days and maybe I'll be in better control of my emotions. Maybe we can get together again."

"I will," Sarah said. "Thank you, Cydney. Thank you very much." There was no touch, no caress, not even a handshake. But it was a start. Cydney left weighted down with a feeling of sentiment and uncertainty. She knew there would be more sleepless nights as she sorted out her feelings.

Sarah watched Cydney go and smiled slightly to herself. This was progressing quite nicely. It seemed like she was winning Cydney over. There was only one hurdle remaining. Jerry!

CHAPTER FIFTY-NINE

The dark crescents reappeared beneath Cydney's lovely eyes and it was obvious to her family and friends that she was under an enormous amount of stress.

Should she attempt to reunite with her mother? Cydney sought advice from all her friends, from Max and even from Tom Caprock; but the answer was always the same. It was her decision and no one could make it for her. Memories of David and now of Sarah haunted her. She put off taking calls from Sarah, rationalizing that she was unable to build a relationship with her right now. Time, precious time. She needed more time.

One afternoon, Sarah boldly made an unannounced visit. Cydney was annoyed but did not want to turn her away, so she buzzed her up on the condition that the meeting be brief.

"I wish you had called first," Cydney said when she met Sarah at the elevator in the foyer, "I'm not up to having guests today."

"I'm sorry, Cydney, truly I am, but you weren't taking my calls and I was so afraid that you would distance yourself from me. Now that I've seen you and talked with you, I am desperate to keep in touch with you. To get to know you better."

Cydney showed her into the main living quarters. Sarah tried frantically to keep her emotions in check as she glimpsed the opulence of the apartment. Cydney made tea and they picked up on their conversation from their meeting several days before. Sarah was in a state of nervousness and Cydney sensed it immediately. Cydney felt like she was being pressured and she remembered the promise she made to Max. She would not be gullible and she would not let Sarah talk her into doing something she didn't want to do. While Sarah prattled on, emphasizing all the reasons they should build a relationship together, Cydney sized her up. She really looked worn. She had done her best to make a good impression but Cydney was able to see through the façade. She knew Sarah had lived hard and now she was playing on Cydney's raw emotions. This was not good. She could feel herself slipping.

"Don't be naïve," she told herself, "this woman has an agenda. You need to stop her now." Cydney put up her hand.

"Sarah," she said, trying to be kind, "please stop. I've told you over and over, I not sure how I feel about establishing a friendship with you right now. These past few months have been overwhelming. I'm sure I sound like a broken record, but I need more time. I'm going away for several weeks. When I return, we will get together again. Maybe by that time, my nerves will be settled and I will be able to think more clearly."

Sarah stopped talking and looked directly at Cydney as she spoke. Sarah felt a little tightness in her throat and in her chest. By putting all this pressure on her daughter, she may have destroyed the very foundation she was trying to cement. What had she done?

"How awful of me," Sarah said rising slowly to her feet. "I truly didn't mean to add to your grief. I'll go now." She walked toward the door like a hurt child and Cydney followed, consciously not speaking for fear she would give in.

"Is there a number where I can call you?" Cydney asked, "I'm not sure when I'll return."

"No" Sarah's answer was abrupt. "I'll just keep trying to call you." She left with no further exchange of words.

Cydney had been toying with the idea of going to Cancun, but in that split second, when Sarah had pressed her so hard; she decided right then and there to go. A month or so in Cancun would be perfect. She would begin making the arrangements immediately.

She loved Mexico but she now preferred the farm. Cydney had considered selling the condo. David had bought it without consulting her during the time she was having the farmhouse remodeled. It was almost like a "get even" gesture. Yet he maintained he was happy that she was refurbishing the house. She wondered now, as she finished her tea at the kitchen counter, if he would have told her anything about the condo if Tom Caprock hadn't let the cat out of the bag. Tom called one day and Cydney happened to answer the phone. He assumed she knew about David's purchase and began talking about it. Cydney pretended she knew to save both David and herself some embarrassment. Like always, when she confronted David, he seemed put out that she brought up the matter.

"You have your farmhouse," he said sarcastically. "I felt like I needed a sanctuary, too."

Cydney was crushed and she remembered the feeling she had that David was keeping something from her.

"But, David, I consulted you every step of the way about the plans, the finances, everything. I would never have gone ahead with the project if you had disapproved of it."

"I don't disapprove. I just need my space." Cydney was furious. "I'm not doing this because I need space. I'm doing it for us!"

David was sneering at her, "I thought I made it clear a long time ago. I don't like Wisconsin, I've never liked Wisconsin, so don't tell me you're doing it for us."

She stood there staring at him in disbelief. "Sometimes I wonder why you married me. It's obvious you don't like my family, my background or the things I do." Tears were stinging her eyes but she was too proud to let them fall.

"That's absurd!" David snarled. "I married you because I love you." He turned away, indicating the conversation was over.

Cydney turned away as well, his words still stinging. "Maybe you could improve on the way you show it."

"Maybe you could improve a little, too. It looks like you could stand to lose a few pounds and your hair are starting to get gray." Again, Cydney remained silent. Too proud to let him know he had hurt her deeply once again.

She never knew for sure how many trips David made to Cancun without her but on several occasions they did travel there together.

The first time she went with David was to help decorate, the second time was to hire staff. That was how she came to know and love Juan and Hermi but none of the trips were as exciting or as blissful as their honeymoon had been.

Cydney surely didn't expect this trip to be exciting but she hoped it would be restful. She could find some solace in the warmth and the sun and hopefully, make a decision about how Sarah would fit into her future.

First she called the airline and then Hermi to let her know when she would arrive. She added an extra day to her spa schedule, had her hair highlighted and spent some time in the tanning booth so she wouldn't look so gaunt when she got to the condo. Finally, she went shopping. Nothing raises your spirits like a new outfit!

CHAPTER SIXTY

The sun was already oozing in through the vertical blinds when Cydney woke to the sound of the surf hammering the shore and the smell of fresh brewed coffee. She had slept extremely well and now was starving because the pasta salad had, for the most part, gone uneaten in favor of the sangria.

Not bothering to even wash her face, she pulled her hair back and secured it with a barrette, threw on a pair of sweats and rummaged in the closet for a pair of flip-flops, left over from a previous visit. Hermi wasn't in the kitchen but the muffins, still warm on the counter top, betrayed her absence. Cydney didn't bother to sit down, she woofed down a muffin and headed for the back stairs that led to the beach.

A few swimmers braved the chill of the early morning and shrimp scurried for cover as the turquoise waves receded, abandoning them on the white sand. Scalpers touted their wares tucked safely inside their jackets, worn more for cover than for warmth.

Cydney headed south, plotting along the beach, the frothy water gushing into her footprints as she moved forward. Her pace quickened. This was her favorite part of Cancun, early morning on the beach. Her thoughts were focused inward and she prayed in silence as she walked, asking for guidance, strength and inner peace. She understood why David loved it so much but she just couldn't comprehend why he preferred to be here alone. Cydney, well she had no choice, but the solitude would provide her time to decide if she wanted to continue to see Sarah and she was determined to take her time in choosing.

The early morning walks became her routine. She didn't expect it would be interrupted so soon.

Cydney first saw Enrique on the beach. The first morning she noticed him he was walking toward her. He was wearing Bermuda shorts and beach sandals. His t-shirt was rolled up and hung around his neck, partially obscuring a thick gold chain. A safari hat was perched atop his ebony hair and his bronzed skin glistened in the sun. But it was the heady smell of musk that caused her to look in his direction as they passed each other and for just a second, their eyes locked.

The next morning, he smiled and doffed his hat.

The third morning, he spoke to her. *"Buenos dias, Señora.* It is a beautiful day."

"Si," she replied, "Very nice." But she kept her stride.

Later that day in the open market, as Cydney examined the abundant supply of fresh fruits and vegetables she got another whiff of musk and turned her head in that direction.

There he was, looking directly at her, smiling. His teeth stark white against his dark skin.

"Ah, Señora, we meet again." He removed his misshaped, faded hat. Cydney couldn't help but smile. He wore the same shorts and sandals but his shirt was a bright tropical print. The top three buttons were opening exposing the gold necklace nestled in thick black chest hair. In one sweeping gesture, he bowed. "Allow me to introduce myself. I am Enrique Gomez – at your service. How may I assist you?"

Her smile waned. "You can't. I mean – I'm fine. I don't need assistance."

Enrique continued to smile at her. "Ah, forgive me Señora. I can tell you are an American. I thought perhaps you might need help finding your way about our beautiful island. Or, maybe you need an interpreter?"

Now Cydney smiled again. "No gracias, Señor. Hablo espanol mui bien y estoy de acuerdo que su isla es muy bontia, pero puedo encontrar mi camino solo. *No thank you, sir, I speak Spanish very well and I agree that your island is very beautiful but I can find my way alone."* Enrique tossed his head back and laughed out loud.

"You like the beach," he said in English. More a fact than a question.

"Yes, very much. It's very peaceful early in the morning."

"I agree." He was so handsome and quite a gentleman. "Do you walk every morning?"

"Usually."

"Then perhaps some morning we can walk together?"

Cydney nodded without realizing it. The next thing she knew, Enrique plopped his hat back on his head and disappeared into the crowd, whistling a tune and leaving the aroma of musk lingering in the air.

The next morning he appeared out of nowhere and fell into stride beside her.

"Good morning, Señora."

"Good morning." She was pleased that he had joined her but she tried not to let it show.

"I realized when I left you in the market place that you did not tell me your name." He fell silent, obviously waiting for her to answer. Cydney was reluctant at first and they walked a few hundred feet without speaking.

Finally she answered, "You were right yesterday. I am an American. My name is Cydney DuPrey. I'm from New York City."

"Ah, New York! Such a big, big city. I hope to visit there some day and when I do, I may need **your** assistance." He laughed again as he spoke. One thing was for sure; Enrique was a very happy-go-lucky guy. "How long will our beautiful island be graced with your presence?"

Cydney felt her face flush. She was enjoying all this attention. And from such a charming man.

"A few more weeks." She looked out across the turquoise sea.

"Will you do me the honor of dining with me some evening?" His blunt request took her by surprise.

She looked into his dancing eyes and laughed lightly. She was feeling a little giddy. "You're very bold," she said.

331

"How so?" Enrique asked.

"What if I'm not free to dine with you? What if I have a husband or a significant other?"

"Then that man is a fool," Enrique said with conviction.

"Why would you think that?"

"Because a wise man would not let such a beautiful woman wonder about alone to fall prey to the likes of a rogue like me." His laugh continued.

Cydney stopped and turned to face him. "If you're such a scoundrel why would I want to have dinner with you?"

Again he toyed with her, "Because I can also be a very charming gentleman." They walked on and Cydney was silent. Enrique didn't press her.

"This is where I turn back," Cydney said.

"I know," Enrique answered and Cydney raised a questioning eyebrow. "I have watched you many mornings, Señora. We did not meet by chance." Cydney remained silent. "You did not answer my question about dinner." Once again he fell into step beside her.

Cydney pondered all of this. She had to admit she would welcome some company. Certainly dinner would be okay. Cydney would ask Hermi if she knew of this Enrique Gomez. He certainly seemed harmless.

"I'm free tomorrow evening," Cydney said and Enrique looked pleased.

"Where are you staying, Señora?"

"I have a condo up the beach," she nodded in that direction. "It's 844 Avenue of Lagoons."

"I will count the hours until we meet again." He took her hand and kissed the back of it, bowed graciously and skipped away down the beach like a lovesick schoolboy.

Hermi was surprised. "Enrique Gomez?" she shrieked. "Oh, Señora, he is a real don juan. Married and divorced five times. He pursues all the señoritas. Very handsome, very charming – but you must be careful of him."

"I'm only having dinner with him, Hermi. I'm not going to marry him."

Hermi was still busy in the kitchen when Enrique came to the door the next evening and Cydney knew she had planned it that way.

"Ah, Señora Cydney, you look beautiful." He eyed her up and down. She did look striking. She wore a white halter top dress with small orange polka dots, large hoop earrings and a chunky bracelet, also orange, which she bought at the open market, and white sandals. She was very tan. Her hair, shiny and coppery, was pulled back and held in place at the nape of her neck with a large white barrette.

Enrique wore white trousers and the familiar beach sandals. His boldly printed shirt, open at the neck, again revealed the thick gold chain and dark curly chest hair. But what Cydney liked the most was the burly musk cologne he had used in abundance.

They dined beneath the stars, near the beach, amidst flickering tiki torches. The food was scrumptious and the liquor flowed. It was so romantic, like years ago, when she and David honeymooned and she remembered to sip her drinks slowly and nosh while she drank. The conversation, while not all that intellectual, was interesting and light hearted and Cydney was really enjoying herself.

A mariachi band started to play and Enrique reached for her hand and led her to a wooden platform in the sand that served as a dance floor, ignoring her protests. Entrapped in his grip, she had no choice but to follow his rhythmic motions. Latino dancers are very erotic and he held her so tightly she was almost breathless. He pulled her close and clung to her. He pressed his body against hers and moved his hand down her back below her waist. After several more turns around the dance floor she was able to free her hand.

"Enough!" she whispered, holding her hand up in a gesture that meant stop. He released his grip on her, twirled her around one more time and led her back to the table. Enrique, although still charming and polite, was obviously drunk and Cydney was growing uncomfortable with his lavish compliments and bold sexual innuendos.

"It's late Enrique," she said softly, "I would like to go home now."

"Oh, *Querida*, the evening is young. We should dance again, no?"

"No, Enrique, it's time to go."

"Oh my lovely señora, you have heard of my love for the ladies and you are concerned. Let me assure you, I will cause you no harm."

"I'm not concerned, Enrique. I just want to leave now."

He got up and snapped his fingers. A young and beautiful, scantily clad waitress appeared immediately. Enrique tucked some money into her hand, flashed her a huge smile and a wink, helped Cydney from her chair and led her away. It was a short walk to the condo and they didn't talk much. Cydney was prepared to ward him off at the door but he made no attempt to kiss her.

Instead, he pinched his throat with his thumb and fore finger and said in a raspy voice, "Will you give a thirsty hombre a nightcap?" They laughed together. Cydney eyed him cautiously.

"Just one," she said, unlocking the door. "Just one." Enrique filled the glasses – little ice – lots of whiskey. The talk was idle chatter. Cydney noticed he was drinking very slowly and when at last he set the empty glass on the table she jumped to her feet.

"Shall we have another?" he asked flashing her that captivating smile.

"We agreed, Enrique. Just one."

Obviously disappointed, he also got to his feet. She started for the door but in one instant his arm encircled her small waist and he pulled her close. His voice was deep and sexy.

"Señora, you are so beautiful. You have made my heart sing and dance." There faces were just inches apart. He kissed her hard. She responded slightly and then pulled away trying to stay calm. His breath was hot and mingled with the smell of musk and whiskey, made her heart pound but she wasn't ready to succumb to his advances. His or any other man, for that matter. He held her tight and again pressed his lips to hers. He tried to force her lips apart with his tongue and his hands slid down her bareback. One hand rested on her butt. He tried to slip his other hand into the side of her dress. She struggled. Luckily, the alcohol had affected his balance and with all the strength she could muster up, and with one powerful push, she freed herself from his embrace. He stepped back, no longer smiling, and shook his head.

"Ah, Señora, you do not want the affection of Enrique. We could – how you say – have much fun together."

Cydney was calm now and kept her composure. "No, Enrique. I do not want your affection. I think maybe the rumors about you are true. You are a ladies' man. I don't want your affection and I don't want to have a relationship of any kind with you."

"You are missing much, Señora. Enrique could teach you much about love. But I will not force my affection on you. Perhaps I should leave now." He headed for the door, still shaking his head, as if he could not believe that any woman in her right mind could resist him.

"Thank you for dinner," she said. He nodded and walked away like a hurt child.

The next morning, Cydney did not see Enrique on the beach. In fact, she never saw him again.

For the next few days, Cydney continued her walks and in the peace and solitude of the early morning she reached a decision regarding her future and her relationship with Sarah. She called Max and he was ecstatic to hear that she was faring so well.

"Mother, you sound fabulous!"

"Oh, Max, it's so lovely here. Sunny and warm. The beach is so tranquil. I wish you could come for a few days." Of course, she didn't mention Enrique.

"Can't Mother, but I'm very happy that you're enjoying it there and getting some rest."

"I am Max, and you'll be pleased to hear what I've decided." She hesitated for just a few seconds, "I'm not going to sell the condo, Max. Maybe someday you'll want to spend some time here and in a few years, perhaps I'll have a different perspective on things and want to come back. For now, I'm going back to New York and tie up some loose ends. I want to spend the summer at the farm and I've even decided to tell Sarah that she is welcome to visit. We could have a family reunion!" Max smiled to himself as he pictured his beautiful mother bubbling over with exuberance.

"Brock will be happy, Mother. He was hoping you would go there soon."

Cydney drew in her breath. Brock! She had been thinking so much about Sarah, that she hadn't thought much about Brock. On thing was certain, she was anxious to see him. And Leta. How she missed them both. Home! Home to the farm. The more she thought about it the better it sounded.

The next morning, after one final stroll on the peaceful beach, she packed her clothes, called a taxi and left for the airport while Hermi, once again, sobbed silently into her apron.

CHAPTER SIXTY-ONE

Sarah was surprised when Cydney answered the phone. "Cydney!" she said, "It's Sarah, you're back!"

"Hello, Sarah. Yes, I got back yesterday. I heard all of your messages but you never left a number where you could be reached."

"I know, It's just that I'm so hard to reach and I don't have an answering machine, so I thought I'd just keep trying to connect with you." It was the truth. Sarah had called almost every day for the last two weeks, not knowing for sure when Cydney would return and she left a brief message each time: "Obviously, you're still gone – just wanted you to know I called. I'll try again in a few days."

"How was your trip?" Sarah asked, "Are you well rested?"

"Yes, Sarah, I am. I had a very relaxing six weeks." Cydney had silently calculated how long she had been away. She left in mid-February and it was now the beginning of April.

"I have been hoping and praying…," Sarah was trying to impress Cydney with the praying part, "that you gave some thought to our relationship." Sarah hesitated, "I really would like to see you again, you know, pick up where we left off."

Cydney was content with the decision she had made but she didn't want to sound too eager, so she strung Sarah along a little bit, not to be cruel, just to be cautious.

"As a matter of fact," Cydney began, her voice full of emotion, "a great deal of my time was spent thinking about you."

"Really?" Sarah was very hopeful.

"Grandfather always said if there was a decision to be made, it helped to write down the pros and cons. Then you have it, in black and white right in front of you and you can weigh all the options."

"And did the pros out weigh the cons?"

"About a horse apiece, Sarah, so then I had to ask myself if I could ever really forgive you."

There was an iota of silence.

"And?"

"Well, harboring ill-will is not my nature," Cydney said, "and if I hold a grudge, it won't affect you – only me. I won't pretend that I wasn't bitter. Especially when I was younger. I was the only kid in school without a mom or a dad. Then Leta took over and became my mother, so if we do pursue a relationship, I don't think it can be mother-daughter." Sarah held her breath. Cydney went on, "and I won't – can't- make you any promises, but if for now you're satisfied just being friends, we can work on that." Sarah tried to let her breath out slowly and muffle the sob that lodged in her throat.

"I'll take what I can get, Cydney. For now, we'll work on friendship. Thank you. Thank you so much!" Sarah was sincere.

"Are you free for lunch tomorrow?" Cydney took her by surprise. "I have some other things to talk over with you."

"Absolutely," Sarah was just overwhelmed. "Where should we meet?"

"Would you like to come here? To my apartment? Then we can talk in private." Again Sarah was overwhelmed.

"What time should I arrive?"

"Oneish?" Cydney asked.

"Perfect. And Cydney, thanks again." Sarah's hand was trembling as she cradled the receiver. Interesting. Cydney wanted to discuss something in private. Very interesting. Sarah was excited as she mulled over all sorts of scenarios in her mind.

She would have to tell Jeremiah another lie, but soon the lying would be over and she would be rid of him. Sarah had a premonition.

She would be back in Cydney's good graces and everything was going to be all right.

Sarah's stomach was in knots as she pressed the intercom and Cydney buzzed her up. She was waiting in the spacious foyer when Sarah stepped off the elevator. Sarah didn't expect a hug and she didn't get one. But Cydney's radiant glow and warm smile put a lump in her throat. Cydney was indeed well rested. No dark circles, no sad eyes. She lightly touched Sarah's arm as they greeted each other and Sarah laid her hand atop Cydney's. Such a small gesture- such huge implications. Sarah sat down where Cydney indicated and refused the wine she offered. She wanted a clear head; wanted to grasp all that Cydney had to say. Sarah had worked on her appearance the last few months and it showed.

"You look good, Sarah," Cydney said.

"Thank you." Sarah waited patiently for Cydney to continue.

"I had a lot of time to relax and reflect," Cydney said, "and I must say I'm more than a little curious about what you've been doing in New York for the past eight years."

Sarah thought it prudent to tell the truth. "Well," her laugh brimmed with nervousness, "I worked as a hair dresser in several different places off and on and I spent a lot of time trying to keep track of you."

Cydney looked shocked. "How did you do that?"

Again Sarah was edgy. "Well, I spent a lot of time at the library reading the Times and I attended some of your husband's concerts and sometimes I even followed you."

Cydney looked shocked again, "That was wrong, Sarah. That's stalking."

"I know, and I'm very sorry that I did that. I just wanted so desperately to know that you and Max were well."

Cydney pressed her. "Where do you live?"

Again, Sarah opted for the truth. "In a flat on East 100th Street. It's near the river and it's pretty small."

"Do you live alone?"

"No, I live with a friend."

"Male or female?"

"Male. I met him when I was working my way east."

"Are you a couple? I mean, you know – are you in love?" They both picked at their food. Sarah was taken aback by Cydney's bluntness and Sarah avoided making eye contact with her.

"I'm not sure anymore," Sarah admitted. "Maybe we were in love once. Now we've grown apart."

"And what does he – what's his name?"

"Jerry. His name is Jerry."

"What does Jerry do?"

Now Sarah was compelled to lie. "Jerry's a salesman – a good one. He work's in advertising."

"If he's such a good salesman why has your life been such a struggle?" Sarah looked into Cydney's eyes. Oh what a tangled web we weave.......

"Jerry doesn't always work. Sometimes he drinks too much."

Cydney nodded. "I see. And is he working now?"

Sarah felt her gut wrench. Cydney was digging too deep.

"I don't know." Oh, the web was growing so intricate. "Sometimes I don't see Jerry for days at a time. He binges." She looked away and swallowed hard hoping Cydney couldn't tell she was lying. "That's what I meant when I said we had grown apart. One of these days I'm sure he won't come back at all. In fact, he's been talking about going to Georgia. That's where he's from originally." Her conscience screamed *Liar! Liar!* But she went on, "I told Jerry he needed to clean up his act or he would have to leave."

"What did he say?" Cydney was sympathetic and her voice softened.

"He always says he'll quit. But maybe he can't quit. Not if he's an alcoholic. He makes empty promises and quite frankly, I don't trust him when he's drunk. A couple of times he even hit me."

Cydney drew in her breath, "Oh, Sarah, you can't stay with him if he's violent. You need to leave!"

"But I have no place to go," Sarah looked at Cydney with pleading eyes, "And I don't have much money. Even when I was working it was difficult to make ends meet. Most hairdressers have their own clientele. I never did. Maybe because I moved around so much."

There was an awkward silence. Cydney was trying to stay focused and not let pity influence her. Grandmother always said, "*You make your bed, you must lie in it.*" No wonder Sarah looked so old and worn out. The fresh air and sunshine at the farm would surely rejuvenate her.

Cydney chose her words carefully. "This is my plan, Sarah. In a few weeks I am going to the farm. I have some lose ends to tie up here. I need to meet with my accountant about taxes and see some old friends. I am committed to a charity event and I have to give my housekeeper proper notice. I expect to stay at the farm until September. I will want some time alone there but if you would like, you could come for a few weeks in August." Sarah's eyes filled with tears.

"And if things work out, well maybe you can come back for a second visit."

"Will Max be there?"

"For awhile. And I am planning to ask Uncle Aaron and Aunt Patrice to come, too. It will be a family reunion of sorts!" The excitement showed in Cydney's voice. "And Evan and Elizabeth might be able to come too. They are both so successful. They're 27 now. Elizabeth just passed her bar exam and Evan is an orthodontist." Sarah could not keep her tears in check and they ran freely down her face.

"There's just one thing," Cydney was stern now, "Jerry is not welcome."

Sarah dabbed at her eyes and nodded. This time her conscience whispered - *Perfect. Just perfect!*

CHAPTER SIXTY-TWO

At the crest of the hill, Cydney steered to the side of the road and got out. She stretched and walked around the car a few times. From this, her favorite vantage point, she looked down at the farm. Cydney was always moved by the beauty of it, albeit in the eye of the beholder. The house, wrapped in fresh paint, gleamed in the afternoon sun and was stark against the dark green of the giant balsams. The out buildings, also newly painted stood crimson against the azure sky. The majestic oaks were just now showing a tinge of green and the lawn would soon be an emerald blanket. Canada geese, homeward bound, welcomed her with raucous honking. She breathed deeply filling her lungs with the cool spring air and held it. It made her think of Brock. That was another thing he had taught her. He said it was a Chippewa cleansing ritual, a way to get rid of the winter witches. She never knew for sure if he was teasing.

What she did know, was that she missed him terribly and was anxious to see him. When Cydney called to say she was coming, he said he would count the hours. What did that mean? Brock also said he would drive up to the Bad River Indian Reservation and pick up Leta. Together they would have everything ship shape for her stay. Cydney's heart was pounding as she turned the car around in the yard. Brock was sitting on the porch steps looking carefree and happy and he stood up as she rolled to a stop. He wore his usual, jeans and a t-shirt, which stretched over his biceps, defying his 52 years. His hair, still thick, was graying at the temples. He was handsome as ever.

They embraced and although she tried to keep her composure, Cydney wept silently on his shoulder. Brock stroked her hair and whispered assurances that everything would be all right. His voice was firm, his hands were gentle. Just like a big brother. But in the deepest recesses of his heart, Brock knew that the love he felt for Cydney was anything but brotherly.

Brock carried her bags to the master bedroom just across the dining room and Cydney followed. The French doors that led to the deck were open and the whole room smelled of fresh air and sunshine. Cydney twirled around and flopped down backwards on the bed.

"Oh Brock! It smells so fresh. I can't wait to go to bed tonight."

"Why not take a nap?" he suggested, "It will be too cool tonight to have the doors open."

Cydney stood up laughing. "A nap? I never take a nap. Besides, I want to see Leta. I have a million things to tell her. Where is she?"

Brock jammed his hands into his pockets and avoided eye contact with her. A gesture Cydney knew meant there was something he didn't want to talk about. "She's not here."

"What do you mean, she's not here?"

"She's not here."

"I thought you went to pick her up?"

"I did."

"Then where is she?"

"She was here for a couple of days. She cleaned and did a mess of cooking, packed all the stuff she cooked into the freezer and said she wanted to go back home. She said she'd come back in a couple of weeks."

That wasn't quite how it happened but it was all Brock could tell her. Cydney always said Leta had a special gift. A gift to see into people's hearts and minds and Brock knew now that Cydney was right.

After two days of house work and cooking, at supper on Tuesday evening, Leta asked him, "Will you drive me home tomorrow?"

Brock was stunned, "What! Cydney won't get here until Thursday."

"I know. That's why I want to go back to the reservation tomorrow."

"I don't get it, Leta. Aren't you anxious to see her?"

"Of course I am. I can't wait to put my arms around her and give her a big bear hug. I want to tell her how happy I am that she's here, but you need to see her first."

Brock looked confused. "What am I missing?"

"Brock," Leta said firmly, "stop kidding yourself. You love Cydney. You know it and I know it and now that David is gone you can own up to it. And don't sit there looking and acting like you don't know what I'm talking about."

Brock did know what Leta was talking about. He averted his eyes to his plate and mopped up some gravy with the last of a dinner roll. When he had cleaned his plate, he asked, "How long do you think I should wait before I tell her how I feel?"

"I think Cydney knows how you feel. But don't push it. Just let her relax and enjoy herself. And enjoy each other. When the time is right, you'll both know it."

"What if she doesn't love me in return?"

"Trust me, Brock. She loves you. She always has. Just like you have always loved her. But way back, when you were young you were both too stubborn, maybe too afraid or too proud to admit it. And you wasted all those years." Leta shook her head as in disbelief.

Brock sat cross-armed. "And what were we afraid of, Miss know-it-all?"

Leta suppressed a smile. "Rejection. Think about it. Cydney wanted a career, adventure, big city life. You wanted this." She stretched out her arms as if encompassing the whole farm. "Cydney would never have asked you to give up your life style to follow her dream. And if she had, would you have done it? Would you have been happy?"

Brock pushed back from the table, lifted one foot and rested it on his other knee, "You're right, Leta. And I would never have asked Cyd to give up her dreams for me. I just wanted her to be happy. Problem is, I don't think she ever was. Oh maybe a little, right in the beginning and of course she's happy she has Max but I think she expected more from David than she ever got. Maybe being here for a while will make her forget what an asshole he was."

Leta laughed. "Somehow, I don't think Cydney thought of him in that manner. But that's exactly why I want to go home. So you can work on making her forget. The two of you need to be alone."

So Brock protested no more. Wednesday morning he drove Leta back to the Bad River Indian Reservation and then hurried back to Oakwood to await Cydney's arrival.

They were still in her bedroom, standing a few feet apart.

"Why did she leave?" Cydney was serious now and Brock could tell she was worried and very disappointed that Leta was not there.

"I don't know, Cyd." Brock hoped she couldn't tell he wasn't being truthful. "She'll be back. She's really anxious to see you. Whatever the reason she went home, it must have been important." Brock headed for the kitchen and Cydney followed. "Want a beer?" Cydney shook her head. "Iced tea?" She nodded.

"I'm worried, Brock. What could have been so urgent that she had to leave?"

"Don't worry, Cyd. Leta's fine and she'll be back soon. Meanwhile, you're stuck with me." He popped open his beer and took a long pull, keeping an eye on her. When he saw her smile, he felt better. "Wanna go for a walk?"

"Sure, where to?"

"Well, the woods. There's a doe there with a set of twins. I can't guarantee that we'll see them but they've been out about this time for the last few days. Mama stays under cover in the trees and the fawns run around in the alfalfa field."

"Let me change. I'll just be a minute." Cydney hurried off and Brock breathed a sigh of relief knowing that Leta was outta sight, outta mind, at least for now.

They walked slowly, side by side, across the fields. Brock pointed out changes in the landscape: a downed tree, the crop rotation, a dilapidated shed that needed to come down. Cydney lavished praise on him for the great job he did keeping the farm running smoothly.

Brock said, "There's always something to do. Those trees need to be cut and split for firewood but I'll wait until Max comes to do that. He loves splitting wood." The mention of Max brought a smile to Cydney's face and Brock was once again pleased that he was able to keep Cydney busy to avoid discussing Leta.

They weren't disappointed. They sat motionless on a log and watched the spotted fawns chase each other, every now and then looking back to make sure their mother was not far away. Brock watched Cydney as closely as he watched the fawns. Her smile, her demeanor, her silent laughter and he promised himself he would never again let her go.

When the fawns retreated to the woods, Brock got up and extended his hand to her. Cydney grasped it and he helped her up, drawing her near. She stiffened slightly and he sensed that she was uncomfortable. He released his hold on her. They headed home, walking at a leisure pace, not speaking but each of them aware of the magnetism that danced between them.

"Hungry?" Brock asked as they approached the house.

"Uh-huh. Famished."

"How about some burgers on the grill?"

"Sounds great. But Brock, you don't have to entertain me. You should go about your business as usual."

"You are my business, Cyd. You've been through hell and I want you to just relax and get rested up while you're here."

"I got rested up in Cancun. I have to start doing something or I'll go stir crazy."

"Start tomorrow," Brock said, pausing by the porch steps, "Let's just spend tonight catching up. Do you realize the last time you were here was July?"

"July? That long?" She looked into his eyes. Something she had been avoiding. He looked back.

"I missed you, Cyd."

"I missed you, too."

Leta's words resounded in his head. "Don't push her, don't push."

"Let's eat!" He took her hand and led her up the steps and her laughter echoed across the silent yard.

The cool, damp evening had invaded the house and Brock built a fire in the huge fieldstone fireplace in the living room while Cydney cleaned up the supper dishes.

"Coffee?" she called from the kitchen.

"Beer," he answered back, stoking the roaring blaze.

The living room was already warm and cozy when Cydney came in carrying a coffee mug and a can of Bud Lite. Brock had pulled a pair of platform rockers close to the fireplace. He squatted before the hearth poking and moving the logs around. The first thought that popped into Cydney's head was how little Brock had changed; how well he had aged. He got up, thanked her for the beer and situated himself in one of the chairs. They rocked in silence for a short time. It was Brock who finally broke the ice.

"Talk to me, Cyd. Tell me all about it. Don't shut me out. Just talking can be very therapeutic."

"You know all about it, don't you?"

"I know bits and pieces. I want to hear the whole story, from you."

Cydney sat quietly a few more minutes then slowly began her soul-baring saga. She told Brock how she and David had grown apart over the years, how David never made an effort to build a relationship with Max, how in the beginning David had actually accused her of infidelity when in the end he had been the adulterer. Cydney only told the truth, even trying to justify why David left her alone night after lonely night and why he never took the time to meet her friends. Cydney recounted how she found solace in her friends, the city, Sophie and Gracie. How much she disliked Harland and vice versa and that Max was her salvation. Brock questioned why she never left him and Cydney's answer was simple. She had promised David for better or for worse and she kept that promise. Cydney focused on Max, the farm, her family and friends and was able to endure. For 26 long years, she endured.

"For all those years, Brock," Cydney said, "for all those years, David put his music first. I was always playing second fiddle." And through the tears that cascaded silently down her cheeks, they both laughed at the pun.

Cydney refilled her coffee and got Brock another beer. Later he reciprocated and when Cydney finished her story, which included her newly found friendship with Sarah, Brock's heart ached. How could he have been so blind? How could he not have recognized how miserable she was? All those years, she put on a happy face, but he knew her better than anyone else. He should have been able to see through the façade. Brock put another log on the fire and before he sat back down, he moved his chair closer to Cydney's. When he had settled into his chair, he reached for her hand and kissed the back of it.

"Can you ever forgive me, Cyd?"

"Forgive you? For what?" She didn't withdraw her hand from his.

"For letting you be so miserable for 26 years."

"Oh Brock, that's nonsense! What could you have done about it? I was in New York, you were here and besides, I was the one who chose to stay with him."

"Did you love him?"

"I did once."

"And now?"

"I lost David a long time before he died."

"You lost him, yes, but do you still love him?" Cydney didn't answer for what seemed like an eternity. She was deep in thought and Brock silently hoped she'd say the words he wanted to hear. She sighed heavily.

"Brock, you know me well. You know I don't lie, but honestly, I'm not sure when I stopped loving David. Maybe it happened so gradually I didn't realize that it happened at all. I was comfortable with my lifestyle, comfortable with David most of the time, so I just stayed. That was wrong. Before we got married I kept telling David that his wealth didn't matter to me. What I wanted most was his love and although David always said I was first, I know I wasn't. I knew that almost from the start. I truly believe that David thought I was first. But his career and his music came first. Before me, before Max, before anything or anyone. In spite of that, I stayed. I think David loved me at first. But what he really loved was my image. Having a woman on his arm. Way back before we got married, there were rumors that he was gay, because he was 28 and still single. I was a pawn, someone to squelch that rumor. Still, I stayed, so maybe subconsciously, the wealth and life style did matter to me. So you see, I caused my own misery. But many good things came out of our marriage: Max, my dear friends, all the social graces that I learned, the arts and literature I came to love."

"I'm sorry," Brock said kissing her hand again.

"Don't be," Cydney said, sounding chipper. "I'm fine. I'm here and I'm going to be just fine." They were silent again and continued rocking, there fingers still intertwined.

Finally, Cydney said, "It's your turn."

"For what?"

"To bring me up to date."

"Nothing to tell," Brock said, trying to sound convincing.

"Yeah, right, 26 years of nothing."

"Hey," he laughed, "really, you know almost everything there is to know about me."

"It's the *almost* I want to hear about." Cydney was in a better mood now.

"Really, Cyd. What's there to tell? You know that Ellen never came back from Mason. That was about the same time you got married. After that I just hung around here. Working hard. First for Caleb, now for you. I love it here! It's peaceful and beautiful. I know it's a simple life and that it's not for everyone, but I've never considered leaving, ever!"

"Did you and Ellen actually get divorced or did she just leave?"

"I didn't hear from her for years, then one day she just showed up with divorce papers. I signed them and she left. I don't know where she is and I really don't care where she is."

"And now?"

"Now what?"

"Stop toying with me! You know what I mean! You're a very handsome man, and eligible, surely there are, or have been, a lot of women in your life."

Now Brock got serious. "There were some. There's always someone around to have a good time with. No one I want to spend the rest of my life with. Anyway, I am getting too old." Suddenly, his mood lightened, "Maybe I better find me a girl friend so when Sarah shows up she's not all over me like the last time she was here."

"That's months away," Cydney said laughing. She was so content now. The crackling fire, the coffee, the comfort of Brock so close. He was right, telling her story had cleansed her soul and she knew she could end that chapter of her life.

"I'm exhausted," she said, freeing her hand from his. She stood up and stretched. Brock got up, too.

"I'll take care of this," he said, "you go on to bed." The room was dimly lit; they looked at each other, their faces only partially visible in the dying embers. "Sleep well," Brock whispered. He took her hands and pulled her close. When her body brushed up against his, he encircled her waist with his massive arms. He brushed his lips across hers and was overjoyed that she didn't draw back.

The second kiss was warm and sensual. He held her so tight, she was breathless. Fireworks were exploding in her head and her heart beat so loudly she was sure Brock could hear it. She kissed him back and reveled in the joy she felt entrenched in his arms.

Then, in spite of the passion and electricity that ran rampant between them, Cydney freed herself from his embrace, composed herself, told him good night and went to her room. She heard muffled sounds from the living room as Brock extinguished the fire, moved the chairs back and picked up the beer cans.

The last thing Cydney heard before she drifted off to sleep was the sound of his footsteps on the stairs and his bedroom door closing. He didn't go to town! She smiled and pulled the quilt up around her neck.

CHAPTER SIXTY-THREE

The sun seemed to shine brighter the next morning and for many days and weeks to come. Brock and Cydney were inseparable. They walked the farm fields and sunned themselves at the pond. They visited the Bad River Indian Reservation and the cemetery at the Presbyterian Church. They patronized some of the bars in Balsam Hills and Cydney met Brock's friends. They shopped and Brock taught her how to cook. They were best friends.

When Leta arrived a few weeks later she was delighted to see both Cydney and Brock so happy. She stayed just long enough not to get in the way. Cydney remembered the morning Leta asked them to drive her back. They both protested but they were secretly glad that Leta ignored them and insisted on going back to the reservation. After all, they had 26 years to make up for. They knew it and so did Leta!

The drive back from Bad River was fun. They stopped at Breezy Point and Brock told her the story about how he got drunk there on her wedding day.

She in turn, relayed to him some treasured memories she had tucked away in her heart. Some from their childhood, some from only a few years before. The most poignant one being the night in the cottage when Brock, drunk that night too, professed his love for her. She thought he would forget about it by morning. Now, when he heard her voice, trembling with emotion as she recounted the events, he had to tell her the truth.

"Cyd," he said softly, brushing a wayward curl from her face, "I know what I told you that night and I meant it." She tried to speak but Brock lightly touched his finger to her lips, "Shhh, let me finish. The next morning, I was hoping you would bring it up but you didn't so I didn't either. I know you thought I was too drunk to remember, but I remember everything about that night. I loved you then and I love you now. Not like a friend, not like a sister. I love you, the woman."

Cydney was ecstatic. He still loved her! And now she was free to profess her love for him. "I love you too, Brock." Her voice was so soft and sweet. The words hung in the air. It was like a weight lifted from both their shoulders. They were finally free to love each other.

"Let's go home," Brock said, starting the truck and steering down the steep hill. They rode home without speaking, basking in the joy of knowing their love was true.

Their neighbor called. His prize Holstein was having trouble calving so Brock went to help. Cydney started dinner. She knew Brock was a meat and potatoes man so she opted for pork chops baked with sage and apples, red russet potatoes with butter and parsley and small June peas, fresh from the garden. She set the table in the dining room, using the good china and the crystal and she chilled a bottle of pinot grigio.

Brock came in about seven. "It's a girl!" he said smiling. He looked handsome in spite of the dirt and sweat and the smell of the barn. "Smells good! I'm famished but I want to take a quick shower." Cydney just nodded, trying to suppress a smile. This was Brock. This was his element and she was so happy to be here with him.

When Cydney heard the water stop, she poured the wine and lit the candles. Brock let out a low whistle as he came into the dining room. He was wearing clean jeans and a white t-shirt and a few strands of still damp hair hung recklessly on his forehead.

"Wow, Cyd! This looks great! But why all the fancy schmancy?"

"We're celebrating." She smiled up at him.

"Celebrating what?"

"Well, let's see," she counted off on her fingers, "there's the heifer calf, flag day is coming and oh yes," she was grinning now, "we can celebrate because I just made this fabulous meal for you all by myself and finally- finally- we can celebrate because we are in love!" Their eyes locked and Cydney could feel the intensity burning there.

"I'll drink to that!" Brock raised his glass, his eyes still engaging hers. They were giddy with joy. They talked about everything and about nothing at all. He praised her culinary talent and she complimented him on his birthing skills.

Brock drained his wine glass and pushed back from the table. He patted his tummy. "Keep that up and I'll get fat." Cydney couldn't keep her eyes off him.

"Dessert?" she asked.

"Absolutely!" Brock rose from the table, blew out the candles now low in their holders and grasped her hand. He switched off the dining room light and led her to the bedroom. She did not object.

The moonlight streaming in through the French doors lit the room. They faced each other. They kissed. Again and again, their passion growing. The urgency of youth was gone. Their foreplay was slow and deliberate. Years of unrequited love dissipated as they stood naked together. Brock's gentle touch revived feelings she had buried many years before she buried David. His provocative words were an erotic zone of their own and sent a chill up and down her spine. She was limp with desire and mute from emotion. After what seemed like an eternity, Brock lowered her to the bed. He hovered just inches above her still whispering all the endearments she needed and wanted to hear. When at last their bodies melded into one, Cydney cried out in pure pleasure. Brock, likewise, rejoiced in her nearness, her sweet scent, her unabridged passion and he grit his teeth and held his breath to prolong the ecstasy he felt as they reached a crazed crescendo only true lovers can experience.

Later, as they lay together talking and caressing each other's still naked bodies, Cydney admitted that she had never been happier, never felt so fulfilled. Who would have thought, who could have ever guessed that this country bumpkin was so skilled in the art of making love! Cydney and Brock. They were best of friends and now they were lovers.

Making love became their ritual. They were so much in love and indeed, trying to fill the void that 26 years of separation had created.

Cydney looked at each new day as a bonus. She was with the man she loved. The man she now knew she had always loved and knowing that he loved her in return brought her joy beyond belief.

They made love on the big rug in front of the fireplace, on the floor in the cottage where Brock first professed his love for her, by the pond, in the haymow and on the soft green grass in the meadow. They never tired of each other.

Brock continued to work the farm and Cydney volunteered at the Balsam Hills library. She set up a food pantry for the numerous Laotian people being adopted by area churches and settling in the area. She organized a benefit for a local family, whose father was seriously injured in a tractor accident and she wrote a column for the county newspaper. Still, something was missing. They talked about it over dinner one evening.

"I have an idea," Brock said. "If you feel you have too much time on your hands why not write David's memoirs? Even if he was an asshole – he had a somewhat privileged and interesting life, didn't he?"

"Brock!" Cydney chastised him for his language but was pleasantly surprised by his suggestion. "I like that idea! I don't think I would have to do much research. It's all here, and here." She tapped her temple and covered her heart with her hand.

"Max will be here in August and so will Sarah; and Uncle Aaron and Aunt Patrice are planning on visiting for a couple of weeks. Maybe I'll start in September, when they leave. I can't wait to see them all again! Speaking of family, I wonder why Sarah hasn't called."

Brock said, "Forget about her, Cyd. Write her off! If you haven't heard from her by now, you probably won't. Now that you live here she's probably forgotten all about you. Probably a good thing, too."

Cydney wasn't about to forget about Sarah. She had anguished for weeks over her and now she was hopeful that they could become friends.

"Maybe when I start my book, I'll make a trip back to New York. Just to refresh my memory. Then I can find out if she's been trying to reach me." The color drained from Brock's face. The last thing he wanted was for her to go back to New York.

"Do you really think that's necessary?"

"What?"

"A trip back to New York. Is that necessary?" Cydney could hear the panic in Brock's voice. She saw the fear in his eyes and the pained expression on his face. She got up and walked around behind his chair. She put her arms around his neck and planted a kiss on top of his head. Cydney whispered in his ear.

"I live here now, Brock. With you. This in my home. I love it here and I love you, but I may have to go back. At least for a little while." Brock was numb. The panic and the pain persisted. He tried hard not to let it show, even as she peppered his neck and face with hot kisses.

CHAPTER SIXTY-FOUR

The room reeked of smoke and cheap whiskey. Sarah and Jeremiah sat opposite each other at a small table in the shabby two-room apartment.

August was just around the corner. Sarah decided she needed to get rid of Jeremiah now! After all, Cydney was very specific. He was not welcome at the farm.

They had started drinking right after lunch and then Sarah dropped the bomb.

"You double-crossin' bitch!" Jeremiah hissed. He was drunk. Very drunk. "Ten god damn years I wasted, waiting for you to track down your daughter. Wasted more time while you tried to kiss her ass and cash in on her money. I did your dirty work for you and now you tell me she flew the coop! God damn it!" Jeremiah slammed his fist down on the table. The glasses rattled and Sarah jumped. She was trying to pacify him. Sarah had been drinking too, but she was not drunk. She had to stay sober to carry out her plan.

"I'm sorry, Jerry, really I am. How did I know that she'd leave! I thought things were going pretty well. She was softening up. She believed my story. I thought she was ready to write me a big check."

"Well you thought wrong, god damn it!" He slammed his fist on the table again. Jeremiah was shouting. He was really angry. She needed to calm him down. Sarah got up and picked up the glasses.

She added fresh ice and filled Jeremiah's full of whiskey. She put a little whiskey in hers and filled the rest with water.

"Here, Jerry," Sarah said sweetly, "have another drink. Calm down. We'll figure something out." Jeremiah took a long pull on the glass of whiskey and slammed that on the table as well. Sarah lit a cigarette, inhaled deeply and gave it to Jeremiah. His hand shook as he took the cigarette from her. It confirmed what she was thinking. She knew Jeremiah pretty well. She knew he was just about ready to pass out. Sarah mentally calculated how many drinks he had consumed. Straight whiskey. At least five or six, in a tub. That, along with the joints they smoked and the coke that Jeremiah snorted, well he was pretty well stoned.

Sarah had researched drug overdose at the library and she knew the pills she had slipped into his last drink would take care of everything. It would only be a few more hours and she would be free of him. She just needed to be patient and keep him calm but that was difficult. She was so nervous and began talking incessantly.

"Shut up!" Jeremiah shouted. "I need to think. God damn it! Why can't I think straight!" Sarah got up and walked around behind Jeremiah's chair. She started massaging his neck and shoulders.

"This will help," she said softly, "just relax, Jerry, try to relax." Sarah continued to work her hands on his upper back and could feel the tension disappear. Sure enough. In just a few minutes, Jeremiah leaned forward and laid his head on his arm, resting on the table. He mumbled something but he was already incoherent.

Sarah sat back down opposite him, her mind racing. Had she covered all the bases? She had enough money for a taxi and bus fare. She had memorized Cydney's phone number at the farm. She had left the keys in the old panel truck parked outside. In this neighborhood someone would certainly steal it and wouldn't be concerned with the green paint chipping off the damaged front bumper.

Sarah moved around the apartment, removing all traces of her being there. There wasn't much. Every once and awhile she looked back at Jeremiah. He hadn't stirred.

Sarah set her bags by the door. She would wait just a little longer. She didn't know if Jeremiah was alive or dead. Hopefully, he was dead and no one would ever be able to link him to her. He hadn't moved a muscle. But Sarah wanted to be sure and she wanted to be stone sober when she left the apartment. She could feel some affects from the alcohol and she was very tired. She checked the bus schedule she had tucked in her purse. If she couldn't make the 4:00 p.m. Greyhound there was another leaving at 7:00. Sarah was anxious to leave but she felt so tense. Jeremiah was still motionless. Surely, she could take a little more time to calm herself down.

Sarah couldn't stand to look at Jeremiah. Her hands were trembling. How could she ever justify what she had done? She went into the other room and sat down on the edge of the bed. She fumbled in her purse for a cigarette, lit it and inhaled deeply. She immediately felt the calming effects of the deep breathing but of course she credited the cigarette. When she finished it, she lit another. She would have one more cigarette and then she would have to remember to get rid of the butts but she was so drained. She lay back on the bed. She would smoke just this one more cigarette and then she would leave. She was so exhausted.

Heavy traffic and a double parked delivery truck impeded the fire trucks as they raced up First Avenue toward East 100th Street. By the time they arrived, the small dilapidated apartment building was engulfed in flames.

"Are all the residents accounted for?" the battalion captain hollered.

"No!" The duty chief answered. "We can't locate the couple from 2B. We can't get in there yet, the fire's too intense. We need to knock it down. Chances are that's where the fire started."

CHAPTER SIXTY-FIVE

Cydney woke to the sound of honking geese. She grabbed her robe and hurried out to the deck. The flock fell out of formation and set their wings, landing silently on the pond. She drew in her breath, mesmerized by the beauty of this September morning. The sun, a red fireball, had just pierced the horizon. She stood motionless, taking in the majestic view and reflecting on the events of the last few days.

Brock was adamant. He didn't want her to return to New York. Not even for a short time. He was afraid. He admitted it. Afraid he would lose her again. She thought him foolish and she told him so. She would only be gone for a few weeks. They quarreled.

Since that glorious night in June, when they first made love, Brock had shared her bed but last night in anger and frustration he retreated upstairs to his own room. About midnight she heard him leave, slamming the door behind him and spraying gravel as he pulled out of the driveway at a high rate of speed.

She hadn't slept well, worrying about Brock. Knowing he probably was drunk someplace. She missed having him beside her in bed. Missed his strong arms around her and the tantalizing smell of his cologne. She had tossed and turned trying to see things from his perspective. He drove into the yard about 2:00 a.m. but went right upstairs. Sometime toward morning she reached her decision.

Brock heard the racket, too. He jumped out of bed, ignoring his aching head. He threw on a pair of jeans and topped it off with a flannel shirt. He stood quietly on the upper deck, watching both Cydney and the geese.

She didn't hear him, but sensed his presence. She turned and looked up at him and their eyes met. Brock came down the steps and stood beside her at the railing. He jammed his hands into the pockets of his jeans, his unbuttoned shirt flapped in the breeze. He shuffled his bare feet back and forth. When he looked up, she was still looking at him.

"Stay. Please stay," Brock said, his voice breaking with emotion. "I need you Cyd. I love you so much. Please stay. Stay with me forever."

Cydney didn't answer. She didn't have to. She thrust herself into his arms. Her head nestled against his bare neck and chest. Tears mingled with their kisses. She was naked beneath the fluffy white robe. His hands found her soft skin and caressed it.

She would stay – forever. Her life was here now with her beloved Brock and the farm that had always been home.

At last, Cydney was at peace with herself. Her simple life had grown complicated when she left the farm and married David. Through it all she learned, she grew, she persevered. She had fallen into the dark abyss of grief and depression, of loneliness and uncertainty but she survived and she came full circle, home to new-found happiness.

Yes, she would write David's story. She would tell the world the truth.

And now, standing here with Brock, watching the geese glide gracefully across the pond, breathing in the fresh morning air she realized, like Brock, she never wanted to leave again.

But for years to come she wondered, over and over again, she wondered, why Sarah never called.

LaVergne, TN USA
06 October 2010
199821LV00004B/4/P